北京市高等学校教育教学改革立项项目
大学英语四级后课程建设研究

英语名著与电影系列一

英美小说与电影
English and American Novels and Films

张桂珍 编

图书在版编目（CIP）数据

英美小说与电影／张桂珍编．—北京：北京大学出版社，2011.4
（英语名著与电影系列）
ISBN 978-7-301-16608-6

Ⅰ.①英… Ⅱ.①张… Ⅲ.①小说研究—英国②小说研究—美国③电影—鉴赏—英国④电影—鉴赏—美国 Ⅳ.① I106.4 ② J905.1

中国版本图书馆 CIP 数据核字（2011）第 056024 号

书　　　　名：	英美小说与电影
著作责任者：	张桂珍　编
责 任 编 辑：	梁　雪
标 准 书 号：	ISBN 978-7-301-16608-6 / I·2330
出 版 发 行：	北京大学出版社
地　　　　址：	北京市海淀区成府路 205 号　100871
网　　　　址：	http://www.pup.cn
电　　　　话：	邮购部 62752015　发行部 62750672　编辑部 62754382
	出版部 62754962
电 子 邮 箱：	zbing@pup.pku.edu.cn
印 刷 者：	北京虎彩文化传播有限公司
经 销 者：	新华书店
	650 毫米 ×980 毫米　A5　10.125 印张　311 千字
	2011 年 4 月第 1 版　2022 年 3 月第 5 次印刷
定　　　　价：	36.00 元

未经许可，不得以任何方式复制或抄袭本书之部分或全部内容。
版权所有，侵权必究　　举报电话：010-62752024
　　　　　　　　　　　　电子邮箱：fd@pup.pku.edu.cn

前　言

《英美小说与电影》是"英语名著与电影"系列教材中的第一部，是为以非英语专业学生为教学对象的"英美小说与电影"方面的课程编写的。编者在多年的教学实践中了解到，非英语专业的学生虽然有着十多年的英语学习经历，但他们中绝大多数人从未读过英美文学经典的原著，而且他们中有相当多的人希望在学完了大学基础英语之后，能有相关的课程指导他们读些原汁原味的文学作品，尤其是那些他们渴望了解却又望而却步的英美文学经典中的长篇作品。但是他们的专业课业较重，没有很多时间用于英语学习，因此如何为他们开设这样的课程就一度成了我反复思考的问题。后来我为他们开出的"英语名著与电影"一课，终于使这个难题在一定程度上得到了解决。这门课的基本思路就是借助电影介绍名著，结合原著讲解电影，使名著的主要内容和成就在与电影的这种双重结合中得到生动、有效的呈现。此课一直受到学生们的热情欢迎和支持。从几个学期的反馈意见看，学生们感到通过此课的学习，无论在文学素养、语言水平还是在为人处世等方面，都有了很大的收获。这里把讲义和经验整理成教材，希望能进一步推进此课的教学。

本教材由上下篇八个单元组成，可用于一个学期的教学，也可根据具体情况灵活掌握。上篇介绍四位英国作家及其代表作；下篇介绍四位美国作家及其代表作。每个单元包括作家作品介绍、小说选读以及多种练习。本教材所选的对象都是英美文学史上影响广泛、而非英语专业的许多学生却所知甚少的作家作品。当然，之所以最后选定这八位作家的八部作品，还由于它们都有着观赏性较强的相应电影。名著选读除了常见的章节选读（Chapter Reading）外，还有从小说中选出的与电影重要场景相关的段落（Excerpts），和可以在讲解电影时作为参考的重要引语（Important Quotations）和段落选读（Passages for Understanding the film）。例如，对于电影《德伯家的苔丝》中提到的"adopted name"，该单元段落选读中的第一段就能提供必要的解释。我们还可以在有些选读中看到电影与小说的同与异。不少同学曾经反映，章节选读中超过大学英语四级词汇的生词较多，非常影响阅读速度，因此本书对章节选读中的那些

1

词汇提供了解释；在征求同学意见的基础上采用了两种释义方式：对词义比较单一的词采用汉译旁注，以节省篇幅；对需要较多解释的词用尾注。在练习的设计上，本书力求难度适中，既有一般性的问题，也有启发思考的问题，希望能在帮助学生拓展知识的同时，增强英语归纳和表述的能力以及自主学习的能力。

教材中所选的名著基本上都有几个版本的电影，我在课上使用的多是较忠实于原著的早期版本。但我也会介绍不同的版本，鼓励学生课下观看其他版本，互为补充，增进对电影和原著的理解。比如，根据纳桑尼尔·霍桑的《红字》改编的电影有两个可用版本，1979年版的电影较忠实于原著，而1995年版的电影则在情节重点、人物特征、叙事方式等方面与原著有着不少的差异。不过，通过将95年版电影与79年版电影或原著进行比较，我们能够发现它们在基本氛围、主要冲突、核心主题等方面的相同，以及95年版电影中的那些再创作的原始依据，也不难理解它通过发掘亚文本、强调被有意无意地忽视的那些方面来重新解读原著的基本策略和指导思想。如果把这些异同以及相关信息告诉学生，可以进一步激发学生观赏电影、阅读原著的兴趣，提高他们对不同作品的理解和欣赏水平。

在教学和教材的编写中，很多老师、朋友和学生给予了宝贵的鼓励和支持，在此表示真挚的谢意。我想特别感谢国际关系学院杨慎生教授的不吝赐教；感谢英国米德尔塞克斯大学的图书馆、音像馆、英美文学课、英美文化课为此课选材打下的基础；感谢美国伊利诺伊大学和内布拉斯加大学的图书馆和音像馆为我确定教学内容提供的帮助；感谢内布拉斯加大学英语系主任里奇（Joy S. Ritchie）教授为我的研究所提供的方便；感谢北京大学出版社和北京大学教材建设委员会的支持；感谢汪晓丹编辑和梁雪编辑为此书所付出的辛勤劳动；感谢王丹莹同学在教材编写中给予的大力协助。我还想感谢我的丈夫和女儿的理解、鼓励和支持。由于我的精力和水平有限，书中难免有这样或那样的不足，这里真诚希望使用它的教师和学生提出宝贵意见，使它更加完善，更适合非英语专业学生使用。

张桂珍
2010年6月
于北京大学

目 录

Volume One English Novels and Films

Unit 1 Jane Austen and *Pride and Prejudice* 2

    1.1   Jane Austen: Life and Works 2

        1.1.1   About the Author 2

        1.1.2   Jane Austen's Novels 4

    1.2   *Pride and Prejudice* 4

        1.2.1   About the Novel 4

        1.2.2   Characters 5

        1.2.3   Selected Readings from the Novel 6

        1.2.4   Exercises 40

Unit 2 Charles Dickens and *Oliver Twist* 44

    2.1   Charles Dickens: Life and Works 44

        2.1.1   About the Author 44

        2.1.2   Charles Dickens' Major Novels 46

    2.2   *Oliver Twist* 46

        2.2.1   About the Novel 46

        2.2.2   Characters 47

        2.2.3   Selected Readings from the Novel 48

        2.2.4   Exercises 77

Unit 3   Charlotte Brontë and *Jane Eyre* 81

3.1   Charlotte Brontë: Life and Works 81
   3.1.1   About the Author 81
   3.1.2   Charlotte Brontë's Novels 83
3.2   *Jane Eyre* 84
   3.2.1   About the Novel 84
   3.2.2   Characters 85
   3.2.3   Selected Readings from the Novel 86
   3.2.4   Exercises 117

Unit 4   Thomas Hardy and *Tess of the d'Urbervilles* 122

4.1   Thomas Hardy: Life and Works 122
   4.1.1   About the Author 122
   4.1.2   Thomas Hardy's Major Novels 124
4.2   *Tess of the d'Urbervilles* 124
   4.2.1   About the Novel 124
   4.2.2   Characters 125
   4.2.3   Selected Readings from the Novel 126
   4.2.4   Exercises 155

Volume Two   American Novels and Films

Unit 5   Nathaniel Hawthorne and *The Scarlet Letter* 160

5.1   Nathaniel Hawthorne: Life and Works 160
   5.1.1   About the Author 160
   5.1.2   Nathaniel Hawthorne's Major Works 162
5.2   *The Scarlet Letter* 163

5.2.1 About the Novel 163
5.2.2 Characters 164
5.2.3 Selected Readings from the Novel 164
5.2.4 Exercises 197

Unit 6   Mark Twain and *Adventures of Huckleberry Finn* 200

6.1 Mark Twain: Life and Works 200
    6.1.1 About the Author 200
    6.1.2 Mark Twain's Major Works 202
6.2 *Adventures of Huckleberry Finn* 202
    6.2.1 About the Novel 202
    6.2.2 Characters 203
    6.2.3 Selected Readings from the Novel 204
    6.2.4 Exercises 227

Unit 7   Edith Wharton and *The Age of Innocence* 231

7.1 Edith Wharton: Life and Works 231
    7.1.1 About the Author 231
    7.1.2 Edith Wharton's Major Works 233
7.2 *The Age of Innocence* 234
    7.2.1 About the Novel 234
    7.2.2 Characters 235
    7.2.3 Selected Readings from the Novel 236
    7.2.4 Exercises 270

Unit 8   F. Scott Fitzgerald and *The Great Gatsby* 274

8.1 F. Scott Fitzgerald: Life and Works 274
    8.1.1 About the Author 274
    8.1.2 Scott Fitzgerald's Major Works 276

8.2 *The Great Gatsby* 276
   8.2.1 About the Novel 276
   8.2.2 Characters 277
   8.2.3 Selected Readings from the Novel 278
   8.2.4 Exercises 311

主要参考书目 315

Volume One

English Novels and Films

Unit 1

Jane Austen and *Pride and Prejudice*

1.1 Jane Austen: Life and Works

1.1.1 About the Author

Jane Austen was one of the earliest British female novelists and became extremely well-known in her time. She gave the novel its distinctly modern character through her treatment of ordinary people in everyday life and created the comedy of manners about middle-class life in the England of her time in her novels.

Jane Austen was born into a middle-class family on December 16, 1775 at Steventon in Hampshire. She was the second daughter and seventh of eight children of the Reverend George Austen and Cassandra Leigh who were cultivated people. Jane Austen received very little formal education–a year with her sister Cassandra at the Abbey School in Reading in 1785, but her father encouraged her studies from a very early age. She read widely and was very familiar with the works of William Shakespeare, John Milton, Henry Fielding, Samuel Johnson, Samuel Richardson, and many others. By 1787, she had started writing for her family's amusement and her own and in 1795 she began the first draft of *Elinor and Marianne*, which would later become *Sense and Sensibility*. In

Unit 1
Jane Austen and *Pride and Prejudice*

1796, she began the book *Pride and Prejudice* and completed it in August 1797 under the title "First Impressions". Her father submitted it to a London publisher in November, but it was returned unopened shortly thereafter.

The Reverend Austen retired in December of 1800 and in May of 1801 the family moved to Bath in the west of England, a city that frequently appears in Jane Austen's fiction. The Reverend Austen's sudden death in January of 1805 left his wife and two daughters to depend on the Austen sons for financial support in Southampton and then in Chawton. There Jane Austen resumed writing and began to revise her earlier manuscripts in the hope of publishing them. In 1811 *Sense and Sensibility* was published and on January 28, 1813 *Pride and Prejudice* was published. The relative success of the two books led Jane Austen to continue to write. *Mansfield Park* was completed in 1813 and published the following year. *Emma* was completed in 1815 and published in 1816, but *Northanger Abbey* and *Persuasion* appeared after her death. She had been working up to the time of her death on a final novel, *Sandition*, but it remained unfinished when she died on July 18, 1817. She was buried in Winchester Cathedral.

Although her novels focus on courtship and marriage, Jane Austen remained single her entire life. Most of her life was given over to her family–to her parents, to her beloved sister Cassandra who also remained unmarried, to her brothers and their many children, and to numerous distant relations. She appeared to have inspired warm affection among those who knew her best, especially among her nephews and nieces, to whom she was in turn especially devoted.

Jane Austen's six novels are all, in Austen's words, "pictures of domestic life in country village." The world they depict might seem provincial and insular. Through their heroines, readers can see, as well, how harshly the hard facts of economic life bore down on ladies during this period when a lady's security depended on her making a good marriage. The problem at the center of her novels is whether such a marriage can be compatible with the independence of mind and moral integrity that Austen, like her heroines, cherishes.

There are two museums dedicated to Jane Austen. The Jane Austen Centre in Bath is a public museum located in a Georgian House in Gay Street, just a few doors down the street from Number 25 where Austen stayed in 1805. The Jane Austen's House Museum is located in Chawton cottage, in Hampshire, where Jane Austen lived from 1809 to 1817.

1.1.2　Jane Austen's Novels

Sense and Sensibility (1811)	《理智和情感》
Pride and Prejudice (1813)	《傲慢与偏见》
Mansfield Park (1814)	《曼斯菲尔德花园》
Emma (1816)	《爱玛》
Northanger Abbey (1818)	《诺桑觉寺》
Persuasion (1818)	《劝导》

1.2　Pride and Prejudice

1.2.1　About the Novel

　　Pride and Prejudice is usually considered to be the most popular of Jane Austen's novels and in some sense one of her most mature works. While the original ideas of the novel come from a girl of 21, the final version has the literary and thematic maturity of a thirty-five-year-old woman who has spent years painstakingly drafting and revising. *Pride and Prejudice*, like Austen's other novels, has been continuously in print. It has delighted academic and general readers alike with its intricate narrative structure, sparkling prose, and witty dialogue for nearly two hundred years.

　　The novel is a portrayal of a particular segment of late 18th-century society, its conventions, and its values. Jane Austen begins by focusing on the injustice of an entail system that denies inheritance to female heirs. She exposes the desperation of women whose sole assurance of security resides in the marriage contract. In the novel Jane Austen shows contemptuous feelings towards snobbery, stupidity, worldliness and vulgarity through subtle satire and irony. The dominant theme here, as in other of Jane Austen's novels, is

Unit 1
Jane Austen and Pride and Prejudice

marriage: her art is to focus critically on a few genteel characters who are affected by the progress of two or more of their number coming together in courtship, meeting with difficulties, eventually resolving them, and marrying happily at last. In the novel three marriages are made, other than that of Elizabeth and Darcy, and each in its way sheds light on the marriage of hero and heroine. Here female characters play an active part. In their pursuit of marriage, they can be categorized into three types according to their different attitudes: those who would marry for material wealth and social position, those who would marry just for beauty and passion, and those who would marry for true love with a consideration of the partner's personal merit as well as his economical and social status. Jane Austen seems to say that it is wrong to marry just for money or for beauty, but it is also wrong to marry without it.

1.2.2 Characters

- **Mr. Bennet** The ironic and somewhat irresponsible father of five daughters.
- **Mrs. Bennet** The foolish and unrestrained mother.
- **Jane Bennet** The oldest daughter, and the most beautiful and amiable of the Bennet sisters.
- **Elizabeth Bennet** The second daughter, and the intelligent and spirited heroine of the story.
- **Mary Bennet** The third daughter, "the only plain one in the family".
- **Catherine (Kitty) Bennet** The fourth daughter in the family, "weak-spirited, irritable, and completely under Lydia's guidance."
- **Lydia Bennet** The youngest of the Bennet sisters, "A stout, well-grown girl of fifteen, with a fine complexion and good-humoured countenance; a favourite with her mother."
- **Mrs. Phillips** Mrs. Bennet's sister.
- **Mr. Gardiner** Mrs. Bennet's brother. He is a merchant, but he is one of those people whom Jane Austen portrays as a natural aristocrat. He does not appear in this version of film, but his name is mentioned several times.
- **Mrs. Gardiner** Mr. Gardiner's wife, an intelligent, caring and sensible woman. She does not appear in this version of film.

- **Mr. Collins** A clergyman and a distant cousin of the Bennets, he would some day inherit Mr. Bennet's property.
- **Sir William Lucas** Inoffensive, friendly, and obliging by nature, he was all attention to everybody.
- **Lady Lucas** Sir William Lucas's wife.
- **Charlotte Lucas** Their eldest daughter and Elizabeth's "intimate friend". She is a "sensible, intelligent young woman, about twenty-seven."
- **Charles Bingley** A rich and eligible young bachelor from the north of England.
- **Caroline Bingley** Mr. Charles Bingley's sister.
- **Fitzwilliam Darcy** Mr. Charles Bingley's friend, son of a wealthy, well-established family and the master of the great estate of Pemberley.
- **Georgiana Darcy** Darcy's sister, ten years his junior. She does not appear in this version of film.
- **Lady Catherine de Bourgh** Mr. Darcy's aunt.
- **Anne de Bourgh** Lady Catherine's daughter.
- **Colonel Fitzwilliam** Cousin of Mr. Darcy.
- **Mr. Wickham** Officer in the regiment stationed at Meryton.

1.2.3 Selected Readings from the Novel

1.2.3.1 Important Quotations

(1) It is a truth universally acknowledged that a single man in possession of a good fortune must be in want of a wife. (**Chapter 1**)

(2) I could easily forgive *his* pride, if he had not mortified *mine*. (**Chapter 5, Elizabeth Bennet**)

(3) Vanity and pride are different things, though the words are often used synonymously. A person may be proud without being vain. Pride relates more to our opinion of ourselves, vanity to what we would have others think of us. (**Chapter 5, Mary Bennet**)

(4) Happiness in marriage is entirely a matter of chance. If the dispositions of the parties are ever so well known to each other, or ever so similar beforehand,

Unit 1
Jane Austen and *Pride and Prejudice*

it does not advance their felicity in the least. They always continue to grow sufficiently unlike afterwards to have their share of vexation, and it is better to know as little as possible of the defects of the person with whom you are to pass your life. (Chapter 6,Charlotte Lucas)

(5) The more I see of the world, the more am I dissatisfied with it; and everyday confirms my belief of the inconsistency of all human characters, and of the little dependence that can be placed on the appearance of either merit or sense. (Chapter 24,Elizabeth Bennet)

(6) We must not be so ready to fancy ourselves intentionally injured. We must not expect a lively young man to be always so guarded and circumspect. It is very often nothing but our own vanity that deceives us. (Chapter 24,Jane Bennet)

(7) ...that loss of virtue in a female is irretrievable—that one false step involves her in endless ruin—that her reputation is no less brittle than it is beautiful—and that she cannot be too much guarded in her behaviour towards the undeserving of the other sex. (Chapter 47, Mary Bennet)

(8) He is a gentleman; I am a gentleman's daughter; so far we are equal. (Chapter 56,Elizabeth Bennet)

(9) For what do we live, but to make sport of our neighbours, and laugh at them in our turn? (Chapter 57,Mr. Bennet)

(10) Oh, Lizzy! do anything rather than marry without affection. (Chapter 59,Jane Bennet)

1.2.3.2　Excerpts Related to Some Scenes in the Film

❧ Excerpt 1 (from Chapter 1)

Mrs. Bennet reports to her husband with elation that Netherfield Park, one of the great houses of the neighborhood, has been let to a rich and eligible young bachelor named Bingley. But Mr. Bennet hears the news with his usual dry calmness, suggesting in his mild way that perhaps Bingley is not moving into the country for the single purpose of marrying one of the Bennet daughters.

"My dear Mr. Bennet," replied his wife, "how can you be so tiresome! You must know that I am thinking of his marrying one of them."

"Is that his design in settling here?"

"Design! nonsense, how can you talk so! But it is very likely that he *may* fall in love with one of them, and therefore you must visit him as soon as he comes."

"I see no occasion for that. You and the girls may go, or you may send them by themselves, which perhaps will be still better, for as you are as handsome as any of them, Mr. Bingley might like you the best of the party."

"My dear, you flatter me. I certainly *have* had my share of beauty, but I do not pretend to be anything extraordinary now. When a woman has five grown up daughters, she ought to give over thinking of her own beauty."

"In such cases, a woman has not often much beauty to think of."

"But, my dear, you must indeed go and see Mr. Bingley when he comes into the neighbourhood."

"It is more than I engage for, I assure you."

"But consider your daughters. Only think what an establishment it would be for one of them. Sir William and Lady Lucas are determined to go, merely on that account, for in general you know they visit no newcomers. Indeed you must go, for it will be impossible for *us* to visit him if you do not."

"You are over scrupulous surely. I dare say Mr. Bingley will be very glad to see you; and I will send a few lines by you to assure him of my hearty consent to his marrying whichever he chooses of the girls; though I must throw in a good word for my little Lizzy."

"I desire you will do no such thing. Lizzy is not a bit better than the others; and I am sure she is not half so handsome as Jane, nor half so good-humoured as Lydia. But you are always giving *her* the preference."

Unit 1

Jane Austen and *Pride and Prejudice*

"They have none of them much to recommend them," replied he; "they are all silly and ignorant like other girls; but Lizzy has something more of quickness than her sisters."

"Mr. Bennet, how can you abuse your own children in such a way? You take delight in vexing me. You have no compassion on my poor nerves."

"You mistake me, my dear. I have a high respect for your nerves. They are my old friends. I have heard you mention them with consideration these last twenty years at least."

"Ah! you do not know what I suffer."

"But I hope you will get over it, and live to see many young men of four thousand a year come into the neighbourhood."

"It will be no use to us if twenty such should come since you will not visit them."

"Depend upon it, my dear, that when there are twenty, I will visit them all."

> ## Excerpt 2 (from Chapter 11)
>
> *Miss Bingley spends the evening in her vain attempts to attract Darcy's attention: first by reading, then by criticizing the foolishness of balls, and finally by walking about the room to show her elegant figure, but Darcy, at whom it is all aimed, is still inflexibly studious. In the desperation of her feelings, Miss Bingley resolves on one effort more: turning to Elizabeth, and inviting Elizabeth to walk with her. Only this time does Darcy stop reading.*

"Miss Eliza Bennet, let me persuade you to follow my example, and take a turn about the room.–I assure you it is very refreshing after sitting so long in one attitude."

Elizabeth was surprised, but agreed to it immediately. Miss Bingley succeeded no less in the real object of her civility; Mr. Darcy looked up. He was as much awake to the novelty of attention in that quarter as Elizabeth herself could be, and unconsciously closed his book. He was directly invited to join their party, but he declined it, observing that he could imagine but two motives for their choosing to walk up and down the room together, with either of which motives his joining them would interfere. "What could he mean? She was dying to know what could be his meaning"–and asked

Elizabeth whether she could at all understand him?

"Not at all," was her answer; "but depend upon it, he means to be severe on us, and our surest way of disappointing him will be to ask nothing about it."

Miss Bingley, however, was incapable of disappointing Mr. Darcy in anything, and persevered therefore in requiring an explanation of his two motives.

"I have not the smallest objection to explaining them," said he, as soon as she allowed him to speak. "You either choose this method of passing the evening because you are in each other's confidence and have secret affairs to discuss, or because you are conscious that your figures appear to the greatest advantage in walking–if the first, I should be completely in your way; and if the second, I can admire you much better as I sit by the fire."

"Oh! shocking!" cried Miss Bingley. "I never heard anything so abominable. How shall we punish him for such a speech?"

"Nothing so easy, if you have but the inclination," said Elizabeth. "We can all plague and punish one another. Tease him–laugh at him. Intimate as you are, you must know how it is to be done."

"But upon my honour, I do *not*. I do assure you that my intimacy has not yet taught me *that*. Tease calmness of temper and presence of mind! No, no–I feel he may defy us there. And as to laughter, we will not expose ourselves, if you please, by attempting to laugh without a subject. Mr. Darcy may hug himself."

"Mr. Darcy is not to be laughed at!" cried Elizabeth. "That is an uncommon advantage, and uncommon I hope it will continue, for it would be a great loss to *me* to have many such acquaintances. I dearly love a laugh."

"Miss Bingley," said he, "has given me credit for more than can be. The wisest and the best of men, nay, the wisest and best of their actions, may be rendered ridiculous by a person whose first object in life is a joke."

"Certainly," replied Elizabeth–"there are such people, but I hope I am not one of *them*. I hope I never ridicule what is wise and good. Follies and nonsense, whims and inconsistencies *do* divert me, I own, and I laugh at them whenever I can.–But these, I suppose, are precisely what you are without."

"Perhaps that is not possible for any one. But it has been the study of my life to avoid those weaknesses which often expose a strong understanding to

Unit 1

Jane Austen and *Pride and Prejudice*

ridicule."

"Such as vanity and pride."

"Yes, vanity is a weakness indeed. But pride–where there is a real superiority of mind, pride will be always under good regulation."

Elizabeth turned away to hide a smile.

"Your examination of Mr. Darcy is over, I presume," said Miss Bingley; "and pray what is the result?"

"I am perfectly convinced by it that Mr. Darcy has no defect. He owns it himself without disguise."

"No,"–said Darcy, "I have made no such pretension. I have faults enough, but they are not, I hope, of understanding. My temper I dare not vouch for. It is, I believe, too little yielding–certainly too little for the convenience of the world. I cannot forget the follies and vices of others as soon as I ought, nor their offenses against myself. My feelings are not puffed about with every attempt to move them. My temper would perhaps be called resentful. My good opinion once lost is lost forever."

"*That* is a failing indeed!" cried Elizabeth. "Implacable resentment *is* a shade in a character. But you have chosen your fault well. I really cannot *laugh* at it. You are safe from me."

"There is, I believe, in every disposition a tendency to some particular evil–a natural defect, which not even the best education can overcome."

"And *your* defect is a propensity to hate everybody."

"And yours, "he replied with a smile, "is willfully to misunderstand them."

❧ Excerpt 3 (from Chapter 19)

Thinking to alleviate the hardship caused to the Bennet girls by the entail, Mr. Collins reveals his wish to marry one of the Bennet daughters. Mrs. Bennet is delighted, but tells him that Jane is about to be engaged. Mr. Collins transfers his marital ambition to Elizabeth. Now Mr. Collins begins his proposal by stating his reasons.

"Believe me, my dear Miss Elizabeth, that your modesty, so far from doing you any disservice, rather adds to your other perfections. You would have been less amiable in my eyes had there *not* been this little unwillingness;

but allow me to assure you that I have your respected mother's permission for this address. You can hardly doubt the purport of my discourse, however your natural delicacy may lead you to dissemble; my attentions have been too marked to be mistaken. Almost as soon as I entered the house I singled you out as the companion of my future life. But before I am run away with by my feelings on this subject, perhaps it will be advisable for me to state my reasons for marrying–and moreover for coming into Hertfordshire with the design of selecting a wife, as I certainly did."

The idea of Mr. Collins, with all his solemn composure, being run away with by his feelings, made Elizabeth so near laughing that she could not use the short pause he allowed in any attempt to stop him further, and he continued:

"My reasons for marrying are, first, that I think it a right thing for every clergyman in easy circumstances (like myself) to set the example of matrimony in his parish. Secondly, that I am convinced that it will add very greatly to my happiness; and thirdly, which perhaps I ought to have mentioned earlier, that it is the particular advice and recommendation of the very noble lady whom I have the honour of calling patroness. Twice has she condescended to give me her opinion (unasked too!) on this subject; and it was but the very Saturday night before I left Hunsford–between our pools at quadrille, while Mrs. Jenkinson was arranging Miss de Bourgh's footstool, that she said, 'Mr. Collins, you must marry. A clergyman like you must marry. Choose properly, choose a gentlewoman for *my* sake; and for your *own*, let her be an active, useful sort of person, not brought up high, but able to make a small income go a good way. This is my advice. Find such a woman as soon as you can, bring her to Hunsford, and I will visit her.' Allow me, by the way, to observe, my fair cousin, that I do not reckon the notice and kindness of Lady Catherine de Bourgh as among the least of the advantages in my power to offer. You will find her manners beyond anything I can describe; and your wit and vivacity I think must be acceptable to her, especially when tempered with the silence and respect which her rank will inevitably excite. Thus much for my general intention in favour of matrimony; it remains to be told why my views were directed towards Longbourn instead of my own neighbourhood, where I assure you there are many amiable young women. But the fact is that being, as I am, to inherit this estate after the death of your

Unit 1
Jane Austen and *Pride and Prejudice*

honoured father (who, however, may live many years longer), I could not satisfy myself without resolving to choose a wife from among his daughters, that the loss to them might be as little as possible, when the melancholy event takes place–which, however, as I have already said, may not be for several years. This has been my motive, my fair cousin, and I flatter myself it will not sink me in your esteem. And now nothing remains for me but to assure you in the most animated language of the violence of my affection. To fortune I am perfectly indifferent, and shall make no demand of that nature on your father, since I am well aware that it could not be complied with; and that one thousand pounds in the 4 per cents, which will not be yours till after your mother's decease, is all that you may ever be entitled to. On that head, therefore, I shall be uniformly silent; and you may assure yourself that no ungenerous reproach shall ever pass my lips when we are married."

It was absolutely necessary to interrupt him now.

"You are too hasty, sir," she cried. "You forget that I have made no answer. Let me do it without farther loss of time. Accept my thanks for the compliment you are paying me. I am very sensible of the honour of your proposals, but it is impossible for me to do otherwise than decline them."

"I am not now to learn," replied Mr. Collins, with a formal wave of the hand, "that it is usual with young ladies to reject the addresses of the man whom they secretly mean to accept, when he first applies for their favour; and that sometimes the refusal is repeated a second or even a third time. I am therefore by no means discouraged by what you have just said, and shall hope to lead you to the altar ere long."

"Upon my word, sir," cried Elizabeth, "your hope is a rather extraordinary one after my declaration. I do assure you that I am not one of those young ladies (if such young ladies there are) who are so daring as to risk their happiness on the chance of being asked a second time. I am perfectly serious in my refusal.–You could not make *me* happy, and I am convinced that I am the last woman in the world who would make *you* so.–Nay, were your friend Lady Catherine to know me, I am persuaded she would find me in every respect ill qualified for the situation."

"Were it certain that Lady Catherine would think so," said Mr. Collins very gravely–"but I cannot imagine that her ladyship would at all disapprove of you. And you may be certain when I have the honour of seeing her again

I shall speak in the very highest terms of your modesty, economy, and other amiable qualification."

"Indeed, Mr. Collins, all praise of me will be unnecessary. You must give me leave to judge for myself, and pay me the compliment of believing what I say. I wish you very happy and very rich, and by refusing you hand, do all in my power to prevent your being otherwise. In making me the offer, you must have satisfied the delicacy of your feelings with regard to my family, and may take possession of Longbourn estate whenever it falls, without any self-reproach. This matter may be considered, therefore, as finally settled." And rising as she thus spoke, she would have quitted the room had not Mr. Collins thus addressed her,

"When I do myself the honour of speaking to you next on the subject I shall hope to receive a more favourable answer than you have now given me; though I am far from accusing you of cruelty at present, because I know it to be the established custom of your sex to reject a man on the first application, and perhaps you have even now said as much to encourage my suit as would be consistent with the true delicacy of the female character."

"Really, Mr. Collins," cried Elizabeth with some warmth, "you puzzle me exceedingly. If what I have hitherto said can appear to you in the form of encouragement, I know not how to express my refusal in such a way as to convince you of its being one."

"You must give me leave to flatter myself, my dear cousin, that your refusal of my addresses is merely words of course. My reasons for believing it are briefly these: it does not appear to me that my hand is unworthy your acceptance, or that the establishment I can offer would be any other than highly desirable. My situation in life, my connections with the family of De Bourgh, and my relationship to your own, are circumstances highly in my favour; and you should take it into farther consideration that in spite of your manifold attractions, it is by no means certain that another offer of marriage may ever be made you. Your portion is unhappily so small that it will in all likelihood undo the effects of your loveliness and amiable qualifications. As I must therefore conclude that you are not serious in your rejection of me, I shall choose to attribute it to your wish of increasing my love by suspense, according to the usual practice of elegant females."

"I do assure you, sir, that I have no pretension whatever to that kind of

Unit 1
Jane Austen and *Pride and Prejudice*

elegance which consists in tormenting a respectable man. I would rather be paid the compliment of being believed sincere. I thank you again and again for the honour you have done me in your proposals, but to accept them is absolutely impossible. My feelings in every respect forbid it. Can I speak plainer? Do not consider me now as an elegant female intending to plague you, but as a rational creature speaking the truth from her heart."

"You are uniformly charming!" cried he, with an air of awkward gallantry; "and I am persuaded that when sanctioned by the express authority of both your excellent parents, my proposals will not fail of being acceptable."

To such perseverance in wilful self-deception Elizabeth would make no reply, and immediately and in silence withdrew; determined, that if he persisted in considering her repeated refusals as flattering encouragement, to apply to her father, whose negative might be uttered in such a manner as must be decisive, and whose behavior at least could not be mistaken for the affectation and coquetry of an elegant female.

✾ Excerpt 4 (from Chapter 56)
Having heard a rumour that Darcy intends to marry Elizabeth, Lady Catherine arrives unexpectedly at Longbourn, where she orders Elizabeth with characteristic bad manners to promise not to accept Darcy's proposal. Elizabeth is not to be intimidated and outwits Lady Catherine in her intelligent answers.

As soon as they entered the copse, Lady Catherine began in the following manner:

"You can be at no loss, Miss Bennet, to understand the reason of my journey hither. Your own heart, your own conscience, must tell you why I come."

Elizabeth looked with unaffected astonishment.

"Indeed, you are mistaken, Madam. I have not been at all able to account for the honour of seeing you here."

"Miss Bennet," replied her ladyship, in an angry tone, "you ought to know, that I am not to be trifled with. But however insincere *you* may choose to be, you shall not find *me* so. My character has ever been celebrated for its sincerity and frankness, and in a cause of such moment as this, I shall certainly not depart from it. A report of a most alarming nature reached me two days ago. I was told that not only your sister was on the point of being most advantageously married, but that *you*, that Miss Elizabeth Bennet, would, in all likelihood, be soon afterwards united to my nephew, my own nephew, Mr. Darcy. Though I *know* it must be a scandalous falsehood, though I would not injure him so much as to suppose the truth of it possible, I instantly resolved on setting off for this place that I might make my sentiments known to you."

"If you believed it impossible to be true," said Elizabeth, colouring with astonishment and disdain, "I wonder you took the trouble of coming so far. What could your ladyship propose by it?"

"At once to insist upon having such a report universally contradicted."

"Your coming to Longbourn to see me and my family," said Elizabeth coolly, "will be rather a confirmation of it, if, indeed, such a report is in existence."

"If! do you then pretend to be ignorant of it? Has it not been industriously circulated by yourselves? Do you not know that such a report is spread abroad?"

"I never heard that it was."

"And can you likewise declare that there is no *foundation* for it?"

"I do not pretend to possess equal frankness with your ladyship. *You* may ask questions which *I* shall not choose to answer."

"This is not to be borne. Miss Bennet, I insist on being satisfied. Has he, has my nephew made you an offer of marriage?"

"Your ladyship has declared it to be impossible."

"It ought to be so; it must be so, while he retains the use of his reason. But *your* arts and allurements may, in a moment of infatuation, have made him forget what he owes to himself and to all his family. You may have drawn him in."

"If I have, I shall be the last person to confess it."

"Miss Bennet, do you know who I am? I have not been accustomed to such language as this. I am almost the nearest relation he has in the world, and am entitled to know all his dearest concerns."

"But you are not entitled to know *mine*; nor will such behaviour as this ever induce me to be explicit."

"Let me be rightly understood. This match, to which you have the presumption to aspire, can never take place. No, never. Mr. Darcy is engaged to *my daughter*. Now what have you to say?"

"Only this; that if he is so, you can have no reason to suppose he will make an offer to me."

Lady Catherine hesitated for a moment, and then replied,

"The engagement between them is of a peculiar kind. From their infancy, they have been intended for each other. It was the favourite wish of *his* mother, as well as of hers. While in their cradles, we planned the union: and now, at the moment when the wishes of both sisters would be accomplished in their marriage, to be prevented by a young woman of inferior birth, of no importance in the world, and wholly unallied to the family! Do you pay no regard to the wishes of his friends? To his tacit engagement with Miss De Bourgh? Are you lost to every feeling of propriety and delicacy? Have you not heard me say that from his earliest hours he was destined for his cousin?"

"Yes, and I had heard it before. But what is that to me? If there is no other objection to my marrying your nephew, I shall certainly not be kept from it by knowing that his mother and aunt wished him to marry Miss De Bourgh. You both did as much as you could in planning the marriage. Its completion depended on others. If Mr. Darcy is neither by honour nor inclination confined to his cousin, why is not he to make another choice? And if I am that choice, why may not I accept him?"

"Because honour, decorum, prudence, nay, interest, forbid it. Yes, Miss Bennet, interest; for do not expect to be noticed by his family or friends, if you wilfully act against the inclinations of all. You will be censured, slighted, and despised, by every one connected with him. Your alliance will be a disgrace; your name will never even be mentioned by any of us."

"These are heavy misfortunes," replied Elizabeth. "But the wife of Mr. Darcy must have such extraordinary sources of happiness necessarily attached to her situation that she could, upon the whole, have no cause to repine."

"Obstinate, headstrong girl! I am ashamed of you! Is this your gratitude for my attentions to you last spring? Is nothing due to me on that score? Let us sit down. You are to understand, Miss Bennet, that I came here with the determined resolution of carrying my purpose; nor will I be dissuaded from it. I have not been used to submit to any person's whims. I have not been in the habit of brooking disappointment."

"*That* will make your ladyship's situation at present more pitiable; but it will have no effect on *me*."

"I will not be interrupted. Hear me in silence. My daughter and my nephew are formed for each other. They are descended on the maternal side from the same noble line; and on the father's, from respectable, honourable, and ancient, though untitled families. Their fortune on both sides is splendid. They are destined for each other by the voice of every member of their respective houses; and what is to divide them? The upstart pretensions of a young woman without family, connections, or fortune. Is this to be endured! But it must not, shall not be. If you were sensible of your own good, you would not wish to quit the sphere in which you have been brought up."

"In marrying your nephew, I should not consider myself as quitting that sphere. He is a gentleman; I am a gentleman's daughter; so far we are equal."

"True. You *are* a gentleman's daughter. But who was your mother? Who are your uncles and aunts? Do not imagine me ignorant of their condition."

"Whatever my connections may be," said Elizabeth, "if your nephew does not object to them, they can be nothing to *you*."

"Tell me once for all, are you engaged to him?"

Though Elizabeth would not, for the mere purpose of obliging Lady Catherine, have answered this question, she could not but say, after a moment's deliberation,

"I am not."

Lady Catherine seemed pleased.

"And will you promise me never to enter into such an engagement?"

"I will make no promise of the kind."

"Miss Bennet, I am shocked and astonished. I expected to find a more reasonable young woman. But do not deceive yourself into a belief that I will ever recede. I shall not go away till you have given me the assurance I require."

"And I certainly *never* shall give it. I am not to be intimidated into anything so wholly unreasonable. Your ladyship wants Mr. Darcy to marry your daughter; but would my giving you the wished-for promise make *their*

Unit 1
Jane Austen and *Pride and Prejudice*

marriage at all more probable? Supposing him to be attached to me, would *my* refusing to accept his hand make him wish to bestow it on his cousin? Allow me to say, Lady Catherine, that the arguments with which you have supported this extraordinary application have been as frivolous as the application was ill-judged. You have widely mistaken my character, if you think I can be worked on by such persuasions as these. How far your nephew might approve of your interference in his affairs, I cannot tell; but you have certainly no right to concern yourself in mine. I must beg, therefore, to be importuned no farther on the subject."

"Not so hasty, if you please. I have by no means done. To all the objections I have already urged, I have still another to add. I am no stranger to the particulars of your youngest sister's infamous elopement. I know it all; that the young man's marrying her was a patched-up business, at the expence of your father and uncles. And is *such* a girl to be my nephew's sister? Is *her* husband, the son of his late father's steward, to be his brother? Heaven and earth!—of what are you thinking? Are the shades of Pemberley to be thus polluted?"

"You can *now* have nothing farther to say," she resentfully answered. "You have insulted me in every possible method. I must beg to return to the house."

And she rose as she spoke. Lady Catherine rose also, and they turned back. Her ladyship was highly incensed.

"You have no regard, then, for the honour and credit of my nephew! Unfeeling, selfish girl! Do you not consider that a connection with you must disgrace him in the eyes of everybody?"

"Lady Catherine, I have nothing farther to say. You know my sentiments."

"You are then resolved to have him?"

"I have said no such thing. I am only resolved to act in that manner, which will, in my own opinion, constitute my happiness, without reference to *you*, or to any person so wholly unconnected with me."

"It is well. You refuse, then, to oblige me. You refuse to obey the claims of duty, honour, and gratitude. You are determined to ruin him in the opinion of all his friends, and make him the contempt of the world."

"Neither duty, nor honour, nor gratitude," replied Elizabeth, "have any possible claim on me in the present instance. No principle of either would be violated by my marriage with Mr. Darcy. And with regard to the resentment of his family, or the indignation of the world, if the former *were* excited by his marrying me, it would not give me one moment's concern–and the world in general would have too much sense to join in the scorn."

"And this is your real opinion! This is your final resolve! Very well. I shall now know how to act. Do not imagine, Miss Bennet, that your ambition will ever be gratified. I came to try you. I hoped to find you reasonable; but depend upon it I will carry my point."

In this manner Lady Catherine talked on, till they were at the door of the carriage, when turning hastily round, she added,

"I take no leave of you, Miss Bennet. I send no compliments to your mother. You deserve no such attention. I am most seriously displeased."

Excerpt 5 (from Chapter 58)

Lady Catherine repeats to Darcy the substance of her conversation with Elizabeth. Darcy knows Elizabeth well enough to surmise that her feelings toward him has greatly changed. So he comes with Bingley to Longbourn, and makes his second proposal to Elizabeth when she manages to express feelings of gratitude to him for his great help over Lydia. Both of them wish to apologize for their past conduct.

"Mr. Darcy, I am a very selfish creature; and, for the sake of giving relief to my own feelings, care not how much I may be wounding yours. I can no longer help thanking you for your unexampled kindness to my poor sister. Ever since I have known it, I have been most anxious to acknowledge to you how gratefully I feel it. Were it known to the rest of my family, I should not have merely my own gratitude to express."

"I am sorry, exceedingly sorry," replied Darcy, in a tone of surprise and emotion, "that you have ever been informed of what may, in a mistaken light, have given you uneasiness. I did not think Mrs. Gardiner was so little to be trusted."

"You must not blame my aunt. Lydia's thoughtlessness first betrayed to me that you had been concerned in the matter; and, of course, I could not rest till I knew the particulars. Let me thank you again and again, in the name of all my family, for that generous compassion which induced you to take so

Unit 1
Jane Austen and *Pride and Prejudice*

much trouble, and bear so many mortifications, for the sake of discovering them."

"If you *will* thank me," he replied, "let it be for yourself alone. That the wish of giving happiness to you might add force to the other inducements which led me on, I shall not attempt to deny. But your *family* owe me nothing. Much as I respect them, I believe I thought only of *you*."

Elizabeth was too much embarrassed to say a word. After a short pause, her companion added, "You are too generous to trifle with me. If your feelings are still what they were last April, tell me so at once. *My* affections and wishes are unchanged, but one word from you will silence me on this subject forever."

Elizabeth feeling all the more than common awkwardness and anxiety of his situation now forced herself to speak; and immediately, though not very fluently, gave him to understand that her sentiments had undergone so material a change, since the period to which he alluded, as to make her receive with gratitude and pleasure his present assurances. The happiness which this reply produced, was such as he had probably never felt before; and he expressed himself on the occasion as sensibly and as warmly as a man violently in love can be supposed to do. Had Elizabeth been able to encounter his eye, she might have seen how well the expression of heart-felt delight, diffused over his face, became him; but though she could not look, she could listen, and he told her of feelings, which, in proving of what importance she was to him, made his affection every moment more valuable.

They walked on, without knowing in what direction. There was too much to be thought, and felt, and said, for attention to any other objects. She soon learnt that they were indebted for their present good understanding to the efforts of his aunt, who *did* call on him in her return through London, and there relate her journey to Longbourn, its motive, and the substance of her conversation with Elizabeth; dwelling emphatically on every expression of the latter, which, in her ladyship's apprehension, peculiarly denoted her perverseness and assurance in the belief that such a relation must assist her endeavours to obtain that promise from her nephew which *she* had refused to give. But, unluckily for her ladyship, its effect had been exactly contrariwise.

"It taught me to hope," said he, "as I had scarcely ever allowed myself to hope before. I knew enough of your disposition to be certain that, had you been absolutely, irrevocably decided against me, you would have acknowledged it to Lady Catherine, frankly and openly."

Elizabeth coloured and laughed as she replied, "Yes, you know enough of my *frankness* to believe me capable of *that*. After abusing you so abominably to your face, I could have no scruple in abusing you to all your relations."

"What did you say of me that I did not deserve? For, though your accusations were ill-founded, formed on mistaken premises, my behaviour to you at the time had merited the severest reproof. It was unpardonable. I cannot think of it without abhorrence."

"We will not quarrel for the greater share of blame annexed to that evening," said Elizabeth. "The conduct of neither, if strictly examined, will be irreproachable; but since then, we have both, I hope, improved in civility."

"I cannot be so easily reconciled to myself. The recollection of what I then said, of my conduct, my manners, my expressions during the whole of it, is now, and has been many months, inexpressibly painful to me. Your reproof, so well applied, I shall never forget: 'had you behaved in a more gentleman-like manner.' Those were your words. You know not, you can scarcely conceive, how they have tortured me; though it was some time, I confess, before I was reasonable enough to allow their justice."

"I was certainly very far from expecting them to make so strong an impression. I had not the smallest idea of their being ever felt in such a way."

"I can easily believe it. You thought me then devoid of every proper feeling, I am sure you did. The turn of your countenance I shall never forget, as you said that I could not have addressed you in any possible way that would induce you to accept me."

"Oh! do not repeat what I then said. These recollections will not do at all. I assure you that I have long been most heartily ashamed of it."

Darcy mentioned his letter. "Did it," said he, "did it *soon* make you think better of me? Did you, on reading it, give any credit to its contents?"

She explained what its effect on her had been, and how gradually all her former prejudices had been removed.

"I knew," said he, "that what I wrote must give you pain, but it was necessary. I hope you have destroyed the letter. There was one part especially, the opening of it, which I should dread your having the power of reading

Unit 1
Jane Austen and *Pride and Prejudice*

again. I can remember some expressions which might justly make you hate me."

"The letter shall certainly be burnt, if you believe it essential to the preservation of my regard; but though we have both reason to think my opinions not entirely unalterable, they are not, I hope, quite so easily changed as that implies."

"When I wrote that letter," replied Darcy, "I believed myself perfectly calm and cool, but I am since convinced that it was written in a dreadful bitterness of spirit."

"The letter, perhaps, began in bitterness, but it did not end so. The adieu is charity itself. But think no more of the letter. The feelings of the person who wrote and the person who received it, are now so widely different from what they were then that every unpleasant circumstance attending it ought to be forgotten. You must learn some of my philosophy. Think only of the past as its remembrance gives your pleasure."

"I cannot give you credit for any philosophy of the kind. *Your* retrospections must be so totally void of reproach that the contentment arising from them is not of philosophy, but what is much better, of ignorance. But with *me*, it is not so. Painful recollections will intrude which cannot, which ought not to be repelled. I have been a selfish being all my life in practice, though not in principle. As a child I was taught what was *right*, but I was not taught to correct my temper. I was given good principles, but left to follow them in pride and conceit. Unfortunately an only son (for many years an only *child*), I was spoilt by my parents, who though good themselves (my father, particularly, all that was benevolent and amiable), allowed, encouraged, almost taught me to be selfish and overbearing, to care for none beyond my own family circle; to think meanly of all the rest of the world, to *wish* at least to think meanly of their sense and worth compared with my own. Such I was from eight to eight and twenty; and such I might still have been but for you, dearest, loveliest Elizabeth! What do I not owe you! You taught me a lesson, hard indeed at first, but most advantageous. By you I was properly humbled. I came to you without a doubt of my reception. You showed me how insufficient were all my pretensions to please a woman worthy of being pleased."

1.2.3.3 Passages for Understanding the Film

(1) Mr. Bennet was so odd a mixture of quick parts, sarcastic humour, reserve, and caprice, that the experience of three and twenty years had been insufficient to make his wife understand his character. *Her* mind was less difficult to develop. She was a woman of mean understanding, little information, and uncertain temper. When she was discontented she fancied herself nervous. The business of her life was to get her daughters married; its solace was visiting and news. **(Chapter 1)**

(2) They were in fact very fine ladies; not deficient in good humour when they were pleased, nor in the power of being agreeable when they chose it; but proud and conceited. They were rather handsome, had been educated in one of the first private seminaries in town, had a fortune of twenty thousand pounds, were in the habit of spending more than they ought, and of associating with people of rank and were therefore in every respect entitled to think well of themselves, and meanly of others. They were of a respectable family in the north of England, a circumstance more deeply impressed on their memories than that their brother's fortune and their own had been acquired by trade.

Mr. Bingley inherited property to the amount of nearly an hundred thousand pounds from his father, who had intended to purchase an estate, but did not live to do it. **(Chapter 4)**

(3) Occupied in observing Mr. Bingley's attentions to her sister, Elizabeth was far from suspecting that she was herself becoming an object of some interest in the eyes of his friend. Mr. Darcy had at first scarcely allowed her to be pretty; he had looked at her without admiration at the ball; and when they next met, he looked at her only to criticize. But no sooner had he made it clear to himself and his friends that she hardly had a good feature in her face, than he began to find it was rendered uncommonly intelligent by the beautiful expression of her dark eyes. To this discovery succeeded some others equally mortifying. Though he had detected with a critical eye more than one failure of perfect symmetry in her form, he was forced to acknowledge her figure to be light and pleasing; and in spite of his asserting that her manners were not those of the fashionable world, he was caught by their easy playfulness.

Unit 1
Jane Austen and *Pride and Prejudice*

Of this she was perfectly unaware; to her he was only the man who made himself agreeable nowhere, and who had not thought her handsome enough to dance with.

He began to wish to know more of her, and as a step towards conversing with her himself, attended to her conversation with others. His doing so drew her notice. **(Chapter 6)**

(4) Mr. Bennet's property consisted almost entirely in an estate of two thousand a year, which, unfortunately for his daughters, was entailed, in default of heirs male, on a distant relation; and their mother's fortune, though ample for her situation in life, could but ill supply the deficiency of his. Her father had been an attorney in Meryton, and had left her four thousand pounds.

She had a sister married to a Mr. Phillips, who had been a clerk to their father and succeeded him in the business, and a brother settled in London in a respectable line of trade. **(Chapter 7)**

(5) Mr. Collins was not a sensible man, and the deficiency of nature had been but little assisted by education or society–the greatest part of his life having been spent under the guidance of an illiterate and miserly father–and though he belonged to one of the universities, he had merely kept the necessary terms, without forming at it any useful acquaintance. The subjection in which his father had brought him up had given him originally great humility of manner, but it was now a good deal counteracted by the self-conceit of a weak head, living in retirement, and the consequential feelings of early and unexpected prosperity. A fortunate chance had recommended him to Lady Catherine de Bourgh when the living of Hunsford was vacant; and the respect which he felt for her high rank, and his veneration for her as his patroness, mingling with a very good opinion of himself, of his authority as a clergyman, and his right as a rector, made him altogether a mixture of pride and obsequiousness, self-importance and humility.

Having now a good house and a very sufficient income, he intended to marry; and in seeking a reconciliation with the Longbourn family he had a wife in view, as he meant to choose one of the daughters, if he found them as handsome and amiable as they were represented by common report. This was his plan off amends–of atonement–for inheriting their father's estate; and he thought it an excellent one, full of eligibility and suitableness, and excessively generous and disinterested on his own part. **(Chapter 15)**

(6) Her (Charlotte's) reflections were in general satisfactory. Mr. Collins to be sure was neither sensible nor agreeable; his society was irksome, and his attachment to her must be imaginary. But still he would be her husband. Without thinking highly either of men or matrimony, marriage had always been her object; it was the only honourable provision for well-educated young women of small fortune, and however uncertain of giving happiness, must be their pleasantest preservative from want. This preservative she had now obtained; and at the age of twenty-seven, without having ever been handsome, she felt all the good luck of it. **(Chapter 22)**

(7) Had Elizabeth's opinion been all drawn from her own family, she could not have formed a very pleasing opinion of conjugal felicity or domestic comfort. Her father, captivated by youth and beauty, and that appearance of good humour which youth and beauty generally give, had married a woman whose weak understanding and illiberal mind had very early in their marriage put an end to all real affection for her. Respect, esteem, and confidence had vanished for ever; and all his views of domestic happiness were overthrown. But Mr. Bennet was not of a disposition to seek comfort for the disappointment which his own imprudence had brought on in any of those pleasures which too often console the unfortunate for their folly of their vice. He was fond of the country and of books; and from these tastes had arisen his principal enjoyments. To his wife he was very little otherwise indebted, than as her ignorance and folly had contributed to his amusement. This is not the sort of happiness which a man would in general wish to owe to his wife; but where other powers of entertainment are wanting, the true philosopher will derive benefit from such as are given.

Elizabeth, however, had never been blind to the impropriety of her father's behaviour as a husband. She had always seen it with pain; but respecting his abilities, and grateful for his affectionate treatment of herself, she endeavoured to forget what she could not overlook, and to banish from her thoughts that continual breach of conjugal obligation and decorum which, in exposing his wife to the contempt of her own children, was so highly reprehensible. But she had never felt so strongly as now the disadvantages which must attend the children of so unsuitable a marriage, nor ever been so fully aware of the evils arising from so ill-judged a direction of talents, talents, which, rightly used, might at least have preserved the respectability of his

Unit 1

Jane Austen and *Pride and Prejudice*

daughters, even if incapable of enlarging the mind of his wife. **(Chapter 42)**

(8) She (Elizabeth) began now to comprehend that he (Darcy) was exactly the man who, in disposition and talents, would most suit her. His understanding and temper, though unlike her own, would have answered all her wishes. It was an union that must have been to the advantage of both-by her ease and liveliness, his mind might have been softened, his manners improved; and from his judgment, information, and knowledge of the world, she must have received benefit of greater importance. **(Chapter 50)**

(9) "Lizzy," said her father, "I have given him my consent. He is the kind of man, indeed, to whom I should never dare refuse anything which he condescended to ask. I now give it to *you*, if you are resolved on having him. But let me advise you to think better of it. I know your disposition, Lizzy. I know that you could be neither happy nor respectable, unless you truly esteemed your husband unless you looked up to him as a superior. Your lively talents would place you in the greatest danger in an unequal marriage. You could scarcely escape discredit and misery. My child, let me not have the grief of seeing *you* unable to respect your partner in life. You know not what you are about." **(Chapter 59)**

(10) His (Wickham's) affection for her (Lydia) soon sunk into indifference; hers lasted a little longer; and in spite of her youth and her manners, she retained all the claims to reputation which her marriage had given her. **(Chapter 61)**

1.2.3.4　Chapter Reading

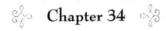

Chapter 34

When they were gone, Elizabeth, as if intending to <u>exasperate</u> herself as much as possible against Mr. Darcy, chose for her employment the examination of all the letters which Jane had written to her since her being in Kent. They contained no actual complaint, nor was there any revival of past occurrences, or any communication of present suffering. But in all, and in almost every line of each, there was a want of that cheerfulness which had been used to characterize her style, and which, proceeding from the <u>serenity</u>

(平静) of a mind at ease with itself, and kindly disposed towards everyone, had been scarcely ever clouded. Elizabeth noticed every sentence conveying the idea of uneasiness, with an attention which it had hardly received on the first perusal (细读). Mr. Darcy's shameful boast of what misery he had been able to inflict gave her a keener sense of her sister's sufferings. It was some consolation to think that his visit to Rosings was to end on the day after the next, and a still greater that in less than a fortnight she should herself be with Jane again, and enabled to contribute to the recovery of her spirits by all that affection could do.

She could not think of Darcy's leaving Kent, without remembering that his cousin was to go with him; but Colonel Fitzwilliam had made it clear that he had no intentions at all, and agreeable as he was, she did not mean to be unhappy about him.

While settling this point, she was suddenly roused by the sound of the doorbell, and her spirits were a little fluttered (波动) by the idea of its being Colonel Fitzwilliam himself, who had once before called late in the evening, and might now come to inquire particularly after her. But this idea was soon banished (消除), and her spirits were very differently affected, when, to her utter amazement, she saw Mr. Darcy walk into the room. In an hurried manner he immediately began an inquiry after her health, imputing his visit to a wish of hearing that she were better. She answered him with cold civility (礼貌). He sat down for a few moments, and then getting up walked about the room. Elizabeth was surprised, but said not a word. After a silence of several minutes he came towards her in an agitated (激动不安的) manner, and thus began,

"In vain have I struggled. It will not do. My feelings will not be repressed (抑制). You must allow me to tell you how ardently I admire and love you."

Elizabeth's astonishment was beyond expression. She stared, coloured, doubted, and was silent. This he considered sufficient encouragement, and the avowal of all that he felt and had long felt for her immediately followed. He spoke well, but there were feelings besides those of the heart to be detailed, and he was not more eloquent on the subject of tenderness than of pride. His sense of her inferiority–of its being a degradation–of the family obstacles which judgment had always opposed to inclination were dwelt on with a warmth which seemed due to the consequence he was wounding, but was very unlikely to recommend his suit.

In spite of her deeply-rooted dislike, she could not be insensible to the compliment of such a man's affection, and though her intentions did not vary for an instant, she was at first sorry for the pain he was to receive; till, roused to resentment by his subsequent language, she lost all compassion in anger. She tried, however, to compose herself to answer him with patience, when he should have done. He concluded with representing to her the strength of that attachment (爱慕) which, in spite of all his endeavours, he had found impossible to conquer; and with expressing his hope that it would now be rewarded by her acceptance of his hand. As he said this, she could easily see that he had no doubt of a favourable answer. He *spoke* of apprehension (忧惧) and anxiety, but his countenance (表情) expressed real security. Such a circumstance could only exasperate farther, and when he ceased, the colour rose into her cheeks, and she said,

"In such cases as this, it is, I believe, the established mode to express a sense of obligation for the sentiments avowed, however unequally they may be returned. It is natural that obligation should be felt, and if I could *feel* gratitude, I would now thank you. But I cannot—I have never desired your good opinion, and you have certainly bestowed (给予) it most unwillingly. I am sorry to have occasioned pain to anyone. It has been most unconsciously done, however, and I hope will be of short duration. The feelings which, you tell me, have long prevented the acknowledgment of your regard can have little difficulty in overcoming it after this explanation."

Mr. Darcy, who was leaning against the mantelpiece (壁炉台) with his eyes fixed on her face, seemed to catch her words with no less resentment than surprise. His complexion became pale with anger, and the disturbance of his mind was visible in every feature. He was struggling for the appearance of composure, and would not open his lips till he believed himself to have attained it. The pause was to Elizabeth's feelings dreadful. At length (最后), in a voice of forced calmness, he said,

"And this is all the reply which I am to have the honour of expecting! I might, perhaps, wish to be informed why, with so little *endeavour* at civility, I am thus rejected. But it is of small importance."

"I might as well inquire," replied she, "why with so evident a design of offending and insulting me, you chose to tell me that you liked me against your will, against your reason, and even against your character? Was not this some excuse for incivility, if I *was* uncivil? But I have other provocations（激怒的原因）. You know I have. Had not my own feelings decided against you, had they been indifferent, or had they even been favourable, do you think that any consideration would tempt me to accept the man who has been the means of ruining, perhaps forever, the happiness of a most beloved sister?"

As she pronounced these words, Mr. Darcy changed colour; but the emotion was short, and he listened without attempting to interrupt her while she continued.

"I have every reason in the world to think ill of you. No motive can excuse the unjust and ungenerous part you acted *there*. You dare not, you cannot deny that you have been the principal, if not the only means, of dividing them from each other, of exposing one to the censure（谴责）of the world for caprice（无定性）and instability, the other to its derision（窘迫）for disappointed hopes, and involving them both in misery of the acutest kind."

She paused, and saw with no slight indignation（义愤）that he was listening with an air which proved him wholly unmoved by any feeling of remorse（痛悔，自责）. He even looked at her with a smile of affected incredulity（怀疑）.

"Can you deny that you have done it?" she repeated.

With assumed tranquility, he then replied, "I have no wish of denying that I did everything in my power to separate my friend from your sister, or that I rejoice（欣喜）in my success. Towards *him* I have been kinder than towards myself."

Elizabeth disdained the appearance of noticing this civil reflection, but its meaning did not escape, nor was it likely to conciliate her.

"But it is not merely this affair," she continued, "on which my dislike is founded. Long before it had taken place, my opinion of you was decided. Your character was unfolded in the recital which I received many months ago from Mr. Wickham. On this subject, what can you have to say? In what imaginary act of friendship can you here defend yourself? Or under what misrepresentation can you here impose upon others?"

"You take an eager interest in that gentleman's concerns," said Darcy in a less tranquil tone, and with a heightened colour.

Unit 1
Jane Austen and *Pride and Prejudice*

"Who that knows what his misfortunes have been can help feeling an interest in him?"

"His misfortunes!" repeated Darcy contemptuously（轻蔑地）; "yes, his misfortunes have been great indeed."

"And of your infliction," cried Elizabeth with energy. "You have reduced him to his present state of poverty, comparative poverty. You have withheld the advantages, which you must know to have been designed for him. You have deprived（剥夺）the best years of his life of that independence which was no less his due than his desert. You have done all this! and yet you can treat the mention of his misfortunes with contempt and ridicule."

"And this," cried Darcy, as he walked with quick steps across the room, "is your opinion of me! This is the estimation in which you hold me! I thank you for explaining it so fully. My faults, according to this calculation, are heavy indeed! But perhaps," added he, stopping in his walk, and turning towards her, "these offenses might have been overlooked, had not your pride been hurt by my honest confession of the scruples that had long prevented my forming any serious design. These bitter accusations might have been suppressed（止住）, had I with greater policy concealed my struggles, and flattered you into the belief of my being impelled by unqualified, unalloyed（纯粹的）inclination; by reason, by reflection, by everything. But disguise of every sort is my abhorrence（憎恶）. Nor am I ashamed of the feelings I related. They were natural and just. Could you expect me to rejoice in the inferiority of your connections? To congratulate myself on the hope of relations whose condition in life is so decidedly beneath my own?"

Elizabeth felt herself growing more angry every moment; yet she tried to the utmost to speak with composure when she said,

"You are mistaken, Mr. Darcy, if you suppose that the mode of your declaration affected me in any other way than as it spared me the concern which I might have felt in refusing you, had you behaved in a more gentlemanlike manner."

She saw him start at this, but he said nothing, and she continued,

"You could not have made me the offer of your hand in any possible way that would have tempted me to accept it."

Again his astonishment was obvious; and he looked at her with an expression of mingled incredulity and mortification. She went on.

"From the very beginning, from the first moment, I may almost say, of my acquaintance with you, your manners impressing me with the fullest belief of your arrogance (自高自大), your conceit, and your selfish disdain of the feelings of others, were such as to form that groundwork (基础) of disapprobation on which succeeding events have built so immovable (无法改变的) a dislike; and I had not known you a month before I felt that you were the last man in the world whom I could ever be prevailed on (说服, 劝说) to marry."

"You have said quite enough, madam. I perfectly comprehend your feelings, and have now only to be ashamed of what my own have been. Forgive me for having taken up so much of your time, and accept my best wishes for your health and happiness."

And with these words he hastily left the room, and Elizabeth heard him the next moment open the front door and quit the house.

The tumult of her mind was now painfully great. She knew not how to support herself, and from actual weakness sat down and cried for half an hour. Her astonishment, as she reflected on what had passed, was increased by every review of it. That she should receive an offer of marriage from Mr. Darcy! that he should have been in love with her for so many months! so much in love as to wish to marry her in spite of all the objections which had made him prevent his friend's marrying her sister, and which must appear at least with equal force in his own case, was almost incredible! It was gratifying (悦人的) to have inspired unconsciously so strong an affection. But his pride, his abominable (令人生厌的) pride, his shameless avowal of what he had done with respect to (关于) Jane, his unpardonable assurance in acknowledging, though he could not justify it, and the unfeeling manner in which he had mentioned Mr. Wickham, his cruelty towards whom he had not attempted to deny, soon overcame the pity which the consideration of his attachment had for a moment excited.

She continued in very agitating reflections till the sound of Lady Catherine's carriage made her feel how unequal she was to encounter Charlotte's observation, and hurried away to her room.

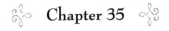
Jane Austen and *Pride and Prejudice*

Chapter 35

Elizabeth awoke the next morning to the same thoughts and <u>meditations</u> (沉思) which had at length closed her eyes. She could not yet recover from the surprise of what had happened; it was impossible to think of anything else and totally indisposed for employment, she resolved soon after breakfast to indulge herself in air and exercise. She was proceeding directly to her favourite walk, when the recollection of Mr. Darcy's sometimes coming there stopped her, and instead of entering the park, she turned up the lane, which led farther from the <u>turnpike road</u> (收费公路, 大路). The park <u>paling</u> (栅栏) was still the boundary on one side, and she soon passed one of the gates into the ground.

After walking two or three times along that part of the lane, she was tempted, by the pleasantness of the morning, to stop at the gates and look into the park. The five weeks which she had now passed in Kent had made a great difference in the country, and every day was adding to the <u>verdure</u> (青翠) of the early trees. She was <u>on the point of</u> (正要) continuing her walk, when she caught a glimpse of a gentleman within the sort of grove which edged the park; he was moving that way; and fearful of its being Mr. Darcy, she was directly retreating. But the person who advanced was now near enough to see her, and stepping forward with eagerness, pronounced her name. She had turned away; but on hearing herself called, though in a voice which proved it to be Mr. Darcy, she moved again towards the gate. He had by that time reached it also, and holding out a letter, which she instinctively took, said with a look of <u>haughty</u> composure, "I have been walking in the grove sometime in the hope of meeting you. Will you do me the honour of reading that letter?" And then, with a slight bow, turned again into the plantation, and was soon out of sight.

With no expectation of pleasure, but with the strongest curiosity, Elizabeth opened the letter, and to her still increasing wonder, perceived an envelope containing two sheets of letter paper, written quite through, in a very close hand.–The envelope itself was likewise full.–Pursuing her way along the lane, she then began it. It was dated from Rosings, at eight o'clock in the morning, and was as follows:

"Be not alarmed, madam, on receiving this letter, by the apprehension of its containing any repetition of those sentiments, or renewal of those offers, which were last night so disgusting to you. I write without any intention of paining you, or humbling myself, by dwelling on wishes, which, for the happiness of both, cannot be too soon forgotten; and the effort which the formation and the perusal of this letter must occasion should have been spared, had not my character required it to be written and read. You must, therefore, pardon the freedom with which I demand your attention; your feelings, I know, will bestow it unwillingly, but I demand it of your justice.

"Two offenses of a very different nature, and by no means of equal magnitude, you last night laid to my charge. The first mentioned was that regardless of the sentiments of either, I had detached(分开) Mr. Bingley from your sister–and the other, that I had, in defiance of (无 视) various claims, in defiance of honour and humanity, ruined the immediate prosperity, and blasted the prospects of Mr. Wickham. Wilfully (任性地) and wantonly (恣意地) to have thrown off the companion of my youth, the acknowledged favourite of my father, a young man who had scarcely any other dependence than on our patronage (资助), and who had been brought up to expect its exertion, would be a depravity, to which the separation of two young persons, whose affection could be the growth of only a few weeks, could bear no comparison. But from the severity of that blame which was last night so liberally bestowed, respecting each circumstance, I shall hope to be in future secured, when the following account of my actions and their motives has been read. If, in the explanation of them which is due to myself, I am under the necessity of relating feelings which may be offensive to yours, I can only say that I am sorry.–The necessity must be obeyed–and farther apology would be absurd.–I had not been long in Hertfordshire before I saw, in common with others, that Bingley preferred your eldest sister to any other young woman in the country.–But it was not till the evening of the dance at Netherfield that I had any apprehension of his feeling a serious attachment.–I had often seen him in love before. At that ball, while I had the honour of dancing with you, I was first made acquainted, by Sir William Lucas's accidental information, that Bingley's attentions to your sister had given rise to a general expectation of their marriage. He spoke of it as a certain event, of which the time alone could be undecided. From that moment I observed my friend's behaviour attentively; and I could then perceive (察觉) that

Unit 1
Jane Austen and *Pride and Prejudice*

his partiality for Miss Bennet was beyond what I had ever witnessed in him. Your sister I also watched.–Her look and manners were open, cheerful and engaging as ever, but without any symptom of peculiar regard, and I remained convinced from the evening's scrutiny（仔细的观察）that though she received his attentions with pleasure, she did not invite them by any participation of sentiment.–If *you* have not been mistaken here, *I* must have been in an error. Your superior knowledge of your sister must make the latter probable.–If it be so, if I have been misled by such error to inflict pain on her, your resentment has not been unreasonable. But I shall not scruple to assert that the serenity of your sister's countenance and air was such as might have given the most acute observer a conviction that, however, amiable her temper, her heart was not likely to be easily touched. That I was desirous of believing her indifferent is certain–but I will venture to say that my investigations and decisions are not usually influenced by my hopes or fears. I did not believe her to be indifferent because I wished it; I believed it on impartial（不带偏见的）conviction, as truly as I wished it in reason. My objections to the marriage were not merely those, which I last night acknowledged to have required the utmost force of passion to put aside in my own case; the want of connection could not be so great an evil to my friend as to me. But there were other causes of repugnance–causes which, though still existing, and existing to an equal degree in both instances, I had myself endeavoured to forget, because they were not immediately before me.–These causes must be stated, though briefly.–The situation of your mother's family, though objectionable, was nothing in comparison of that total want of propriety so frequently, so almost uniformly betrayed by herself, by your three younger sisters, and occasionally even by your father.–Pardon me.–It pains me to offend you. But amidst your concern for the defects of your nearest relations, and your displeasure at this representation of them, let it give you consolation to consider that to have conducted yourselves so as to avoid any share of the like censure, is praise no less generally bestowed on you and your eldest sister than it is honourable to the sense and disposition of both. I will only say farther that from what passed that evening, my opinion of all parties was confirmed, and every inducement heightened, which could have led me before to preserve my friend from what I esteemed a most unhappy connection. He left Netherfield for London on the day following, as you, I am certain, remember, with the design of soon returning. The part which I acted is now to be explained. His sisters' uneasiness had been equally excited with my own; our coincidence of feeling was soon discovered; and, alike sensible that no time was to be lost in detaching their brother, we shortly resolved on joining him directly in London. We accordingly went—and there I readily engaged in the office of pointing out to my friend the certain evils of such a choice. I described and enforced them earnestly. But, however this <u>remonstrance</u>（抗议，进谏）might have staggered or delayed his determination, I do not suppose that it would ultimately have prevented the marriage, had it not been seconded by the assurance, which I hesitated not in giving, of your sister's indifference. He had before believed her to return his affection with sincere, if not with equal regard. But Bingley has great natural modesty, with a stronger dependence on my judgment than on his own. To convince him, therefore, that he had deceived himself, was no very difficult point. To persuade him against returning into Hertfordshire, when that conviction had been given, was scarcely the work of a moment. I cannot blame myself for having done thus much. There is but one part of my conduct in the whole affair on which I do not reflect with satisfaction; it is that I <u>condescended</u> to adopt the measures of art so far as to conceal from him your sister's being in town. I knew it myself, as it was known to Miss Bingley, but her brother is even yet ignorant of it. That they might have met without ill consequence is perhaps probable; but his regard did not appear to me enough extinguished for him to see her without some danger. Perhaps this concealment, this disguise, was beneath me. It is done, however, and it was done for the best. On this subject I have nothing more to say, no other apology to offer. If I have wounded your sister's feelings, it was unknowingly done; and though the motives which governed me may to you very naturally appear insufficient, I have not yet learned to condemn them. With respect to that other, more weighty accusation, of having injured Mr. Wickham, I can only refute it by laying before you the whole of his connection with my family. Of what he has *particularly* accused me I am ignorant; but of the truth of what I shall relate, I can summon more than one witness of undoubted <u>veracity</u>（真实性）. Mr. Wickham is the son of a very respectable man, who had for many years the management of all the Pemberley estates; and whose good conduct in the discharge of his trust naturally inclined my father to be of service to him, and on George Wickham, who was his godson, his kindness was therefore liberally bestowed. My father supported him at school, and afterwards at Cambridge—

Unit 1
Jane Austen and *Pride and Prejudice*

most important assistance, as his own father, always poor from the extravagance of his wife, would have been unable to give him a gentleman's education. My father was not only fond of this young man's society, whose manner were always engaging; he had also the highest opinion of him, and hoping the church would be his profession, intended to provide for him in it. As for myself, it is many, many years since I first began to think of him in a very different manner. The vicious propensities (习性) –the want of principle which he was careful to guard from the knowledge of his best friend could not escape the observation of a young man of nearly the same age with himself, and who had opportunities of seeing him in unguarded moments, which Mr. Darcy could not have. Here again I shall give you pain–to what degree you only can tell. But whatever may be the sentiments which Mr. Wickham has created, a suspicion of their nature shall not prevent me from unfolding his real character. It adds even another motive. My excellent father died about five years ago; and his attachment to Mr. Wickham was to the last so steady that in his will he particularly recommended it to me to promote his advancement in the best manner that his profession might allow, and if he took orders, desired that a valuable family living might be his as soon as it became vacant. There was also a legacy of one thousand pounds. His own father did not long survive mine, and within half a year from these events, Mr. Wickham wrote to inform me that, having finally resolved against taking orders, he hoped I should not think it unreasonable for him to expect some more immediate pecuniary (金钱上的) advantage, in lieu of (替代) the preferment by which he could not be benefited. He had some intention, he added, of studying the law, and I must be aware that the interest of one thousand pounds would be a very insufficient support therein. I rather wished, than believed him to be sincere; but at any rate, was perfectly ready to accede (同意) to his proposal. I knew that Mr. Wickham ought not to be a clergyman. The business was therefore soon settled. He resigned all claim to assistance in the church, were it possible that he could ever be in a situation to receive it, and accepted in return three thousand pounds. All connection between us seemed now dissolved. I thought too ill of him to invite him to Pemberley, or admit his society in town. In town I believe he chiefly lived, but his studying the law was a mere pretence, and being now free from all restraint, his life was a life of idleness and dissipation (放荡) . For about three years I heard little of him; but on the decease (死亡) of the incumbent (牧师) of the living which had been designed for him, he applied to me again by letter for the presentation. His circumstances, he assured me, and I had no difficulty in believing it, were exceedingly bad. He had found the law a most unprofitable study, and was now absolutely resolved on being ordained (任命), if I would present him to the living in question–of which he trusted there could be little doubt, as he was well assured that I had no other person to provide for, and I could not have forgotten my revered (受人尊敬的) father's intentions. You will hardly blame me for refusing to comply with this entreaty, or for resisting every repetition to it. His resentment was in proportion to the distress of his circumstances–and he was doubtless as violent in his abuse of me to others as in his reproaches to myself. After this period, every appearance of acquaintance was dropped. How he lived I know not. But last summer he was again most painfully obtruded on my notice. I must now mention a circumstance which I would wish to forget myself, and which no obligation less than the present should induce (促使) me to unfold to any human being. Having said thus much, I feel no doubt of your secrecy. My sister, who is more than ten years my junior, was left to the guardianship of my mother's nephew, Colonel Fitzwilliam, and myself. About a year ago, she was taken from school, and an establishment formed for her in London; and last summer she went with the lady who presided (掌管) over it to Ramsgate; and thither (到那里) also went Mr. Wickham, undoubtedly by design; for there proved to have been a prior acquaintance between him and Mrs. Younge, in whose character we were most unhappily deceived; and by her connivance and aid, he so far recommended himself to Georgiana, whose affectionate heart retained a strong impression of his kindness to her as a child, that she was persuaded to believe herself in love, and to consent to an elopement (私奔). She was then but fifteen, which must be her excuse; and after stating her imprudence (轻率), I am happy to add that I owed the knowledge of it to herself. I joined them unexpectedly a day or two before the intended elopement, and then Georgiana, unable to support the idea of grieving and offending a brother whom she almost looked up to as a father, acknowledged the whole to me. You may imagine what I felt and how I acted. Regard for my sister's credit and feelings prevented any public exposure, but I wrote to Mr. Wickham, who left the place immediately, and Mrs. Younge was of course removed from her charge. Mr. Wickham's chief object was unquestionably my sister's fortune, which is thirty thousand pounds; but I

Unit 1
Jane Austen and *Pride and Prejudice*

cannot help supposing that the hope of revenging himself on me was a strong inducement. His revenge would have been complete indeed. This, madam, is a faithful narrative of every event in which we have been concerned together; and if you do not absolutely reject it as false, you will, I hope, acquit me henceforth (从此) of cruelty towards Mr. Wickham. I know not in what manner, under what form of falsehood he had imposed on you; but his success is not perhaps to be wondered at. Ignorant as you previously were of everything concerning either, detection could not be in your power, and suspicion certainly not in your inclination. You may possibly wonder why all this was not told you last night. But I was not then master enough of myself to know what could or ought to be revealed. For the truth of everything here related, I can appeal more particularly to the testimony (证明) of Colonel Fitzwilliam, who from our near relationship and constant intimacy, and still more as one of the executors of my father's will, has been unavoidably acquainted with every particular of these transactions. If your abhorrence of *me* should make *my* assertions valueless, you cannot be prevented by the same cause from confiding in my cousin; and that there may be the possibility of consulting him, I shall endeavour to find some opportunity of putting this letter in your hands in the course of the morning. I will only add, God bless you.

"FITZWILLIAM DARCY."

 Notes and Glossary for Chapter Reading

(1) exasperate /ig'zɑːspəreit/ *v.* to annoy or make extremely angry, esp. by testing the patience of 激怒, 使恼怒

(2) inflict /in'flikt/ *vt.* to force someone to experience (something very unpleasant) 使遭受

(3) impute /im'pjuːt/ *vt.* (to) to attribute 归咎于；归因于

(4) avow /ə'vaʊ/ *vt.* to acknowledge openly, boldly, and unashamedly 坦率承认 // avowal *n.*

(5) disdain /dis'dein/ *n. & v.* to regard or treat with haughty contempt; despise

鄙视，蔑视，鄙弃，轻视

(6) conciliate /kənˈsiːlieit/ vt. to soothe the hostility of, reconcile 抚慰，安抚，博得好感

(7) withhold /wiðˈhəuld/ vt. (withheld) to refuse to give 拒给

(8) scruple /ˈskruːpəl/ n. An uneasy feeling arising from conscience or principle that tends to hinder action 顾忌，顾虑

(9) impel /imˈpel/ vt. (-led, -ling) urge, drive forward 驱使，迫使

(10) mortification /ˌmɔːtifiˈkeiʃən/ n. a feeling of shame, humiliation, or wounded pride 羞愧感，窘迫感

(11) disapprobation /ˌdisæprəˈbeiʃən/ n. disapproval, esp. of something immoral 不以为然，不赞成

(12) tumult /ˈtjuːmʌlt/ n. state of confusion and excitement 波动，激动

Chapter 35

(13) haughty /ˈhɔːti/ a. arrogantly self-admiring and disdainful 高傲的；目中无人的

(14) depravity /diˈpræviti/ n. moral corruption, wickedness 道德败坏，堕落

(15) repugnance /riˈpʌgnəns/ n. a strong feeling of dislike for something; disgust 强烈的反感，厌恶

(16) propriety /prəˈpraiəti/ n. correctness of social or moral behaviour 适当，妥当，正当，得体

(17) condescend /ˌkɔndiˈsend/ vt. descend to the level of one considered inferior; lower oneself 屈尊，自我贬抑

(18) vicious /ˈviʃəs/ a. evil, immoral, or depraved; malicious 恶意的

(19) preferment /priˈfəːmənt/ n. appointment to a higher rank or position, esp. in the church 提升，升级

(20) obtrude /əbˈtruːd/ vt. to come without being invited or wanted 闯入

(21) connivance /kəˈnaivəns/ n. not trying to stop something wrong from happening 纵容，默许

(22) acquit /əˈkwit/ vt. free or clear from a charge or accusation 免除或洗脱指控

1.2.4 Exercises

❶ Identify the following characters

(1) _____, wonderfully handsome, gentlemanlike, lively and

Unit 1
Jane Austen and *Pride and Prejudice*

unreserved, captivates every one at the ball by his charming personality and friendly outgoing manner. He has great natural modesty with a stronger dependence on his friend's judgment than on his own.

(2) _____, lively, quick-witted, sharp-tongued, bold and intelligent, is concerned with propriety, good-manners, and virtue, but is not impressed by mere wealth or titles.

(3) _____, beautiful, good-tempered, sweet, amiable, humble and selfless, is universally well-liked. She refuses to judge anyone badly, always making excuses for people when her sister brings their faults to her attention.

(4) _____ is proud, haughty and extremely conscious of class differences at the beginning of the novel. He does, however, have a strong sense of honor and virtue.

(5) _____ is an intelligent man, and a "gentleman" by birth. But having made an unwise marriage with a woman of low intelligence, he retreats into his library. He often makes penetrating remarks, and is the source of much of Jane Austen's choicest irony.

(6) _____ worked hard for knowledge and accomplishments, and was always impatient for display. She is constantly moralizing or trying to make profound observations about human nature and life in general.

(7) _____, mix of obsequiousness and pride, is fond of making long and silly speeches and stating formalities which have absolutely no meaning in themselves.

(8) _____ is wealthy and extremely conscious of class differences, and likes to let others know of their inferiority to her. She loves to give people advice about how to conduct their lives down to the minutest details.

(9) _____ is childish, self-centered, and uncharitable in her judgment of everybody outside her family. Her rudeness and opinionated vulgarity torture her intelligent daughter with embarrassment.

(10) _____ was quickly judged to be a perfectly good and

amiable man because of his friendliness and the ease of his manners, but three months later, everybody declared that he was the wickedest young man in the world.

❷ Plot Review

Pride and Prejudice, begun in 1796 and completed the following year under the title (1)"_____", appeared in 1813. The story concerns the middle-class household of the Bennets. The empty-headed and garrulous (2)_____ has but one aim in life: to find (3) a _____ for each of her five daughters. Charles Bingley, a rich young bachelor, takes Netherfield, a house near Longbourn, bringing with him his two sisters and his friend Fitzwilliam Darcy, (4)_____ of Lady Catherine. At the ball, Bingley and Jane very soon fall in love. Darcy, though attracted to the lively and spirited Elizabeth, greatly offends her by his (5)_____ behaviour. This dislike is increased by the account given her by George Wickham, of the (6)_____ treatment he has met with at Darcy's hands. The aversion is further intensified when Darcy and Bingley's two sisters, disgusted with the (7) _____ of Mrs. Bennet and her two youngest daughters, effectively (8) _____ Bingley from Jane. Darcy (9) _____ believes that Jane is only seeking an advantageous match and that her feelings are not (10)_____.

The Bennet family is visited by William Collins, who will (11) _____Mr. Bennet's entailed property on his death. Urged to marry by Lady Catherine, and thinking to remedy the hardship caused to the Bennet girls by the (12) _____, he proposes to Elizabeth. When firmly (13) _____, he promptly transfers his affections to Charlotte Lucas, a friend of Elizabeth's, who (14)_____ him.

In spite of his (15) _____ of the Bennet family, Darcy cannot keep himself from falling in love with Elizabeth. He unexpectedly comes to the parsonage and suddenly declares his (16) _____ and asks her to marry him. The tone of the proposal and her own (17) _____cause Elizabeth coldly to (18) _____ him. His subsequent support of a renewal of Bingley's suit with Jane and his considerable assistance throughout the foolish (19) _____ of young Lydia with Wickham, show Darcy's ability to recognize and correct

Unit 1
Jane Austen and Pride and Prejudice

his own (20) _____ pride, and Elizabeth's prejudice dissolves.

❸ General Questions

(1) What does it mean that Mr. Bennet's property is "entailed"?
(2) Why does Miss Bingley dislike Elizabeth?
(3) Why is Elizabeth so anxious to distrust Mr. Darcy at the start of the novel and to trust Mr. Wickham?
(4) Why does Mr. Collins come to Longbourn?
(5) Why does Elizabeth reject Mr. Collins's proposal?
(6) Why does Charlotte Lucas agree to marry Mr. Collins?
(7) Why does Elizabeth reject Darcy's initial proposal?
(8) Why does Mr. Darcy write a long letter to Elizabeth? And what does he mainly explain in his letter?
(9) How does Lydia's elopement affect the Bennet family? How do Mr. Bennet, Mrs. Bennet and Elizabeth respond to Lydia when she comes home for a visit?
(10) Why does Lady Catherine de Bourgh stop at Longbourn? How does Elizabeth respond to Lady Catherine's questions and demands?

❹ Questions for essay or discussion

(1) Jane Austen's original title for the novel was *First Impressions*. What role do first impressions play in *Pride and Prejudice*?
(2) Explore the developing relationship between Elizabeth and Mr. Darcy. How do they misunderstand each other, and when do they reach accord?
(3) Consider the kinds of marriages that appear throughout *Pride and Prejudice*. What kinds of relationships between a man and a woman does Jane Austen idealize?
(4) Discuss the importance of social class in the novel, especially as it impacts the relationship between Elizabeth and Darcy.
(5) Discuss where Mr. Bennet's continual irony is justified, and where it is irresponsible.

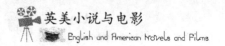

Unit 2

Charles Dickens and *Oliver Twist*

2.1   Charles Dickens: Life and Works

2.1.1   About the Author

Charles Dickens is generally considered the greatest novelist of the Victorian era. He enjoyed a wider popularity than had any previous author during his lifetime. His popularity has never ceased and his present critical standing is higher than ever before.

Charles Dickens was born in Portsmouth, England on February 7, 1812, to Elizabeth and John Dickens. His father, a clerk in the Navy Pay Office, was well paid, but his father's financial mismanagement often brought his family to financial embarrassment or disaster. In 1824 John Dickens was put into prison for debt. Charles was subsequently withdrawn from school and put to manual work in a small factory warehouse for six or seven shillings a week. These shocks deeply affected Charles. Years later he wrote:

> No words can express the secret agony of my soul as I sunk into this companionship, compared these everyday associates with those of my happier childhood; and felt my early hopes of growing up to be a learned and distinguished man, crushed in my breast.

Unit 2
Charles Dickens and *Oliver Twist*

His brush with hard times and poverty affected him so deeply that this experience of his childhood became a recurring subject in his novels although he was there only for half a year. After his father's release, he was able briefly to attend school again, but in 1827 he left school for good and became a clerk in a solicitor's office. While working there, he spent his spare time learning shorthand and later became a parliamentary and newspaper reporter. His work gave him firsthand experience of the courts of England, which would later prove to be fertile material for his works of fiction.

In 1833 Charles Dickens saw his first story published in Monthly Magazine. Not long thereafter, he wrote his first book *Sketches by Boz* and began to attract attention as a young and capable writer. *The Pickwick Papers* established him as a master of literary comedy and earned him a considerable amount of fame and wealth. The financial success of the book enabled him to give up reporting and settle down to the writing of novels. A number of novels rapidly followed one after another: *Oliver Twist, Nicholas Nickleby, The Old Curiosity Shop*, and *Barnaby Rudge*. Dickens attacked in each book one or more specific evils in the Victorian world: debtors' prisons, workhouses, legal fraud, capital punishment, envy and self-righteousness disguised as religion and justice. In 1842 he took a five-month vacation in America, where he advocated international copyright and the abolition of slavery. His unfavourable impressions of the life in the USA were reflected in *American Notes* and *Martin Chuzzlewit*. In the years 1843–1845 appeared his Christmas stories, including chiefly *A Christmas Carol, The Chimes, The Cricket on the Hearth*. In these stories Dickens showed his profound sympathy for the poor and described how the rich were converted after undergoing severe tests.

After 1844, Dickens spent most of his time on the Continent of Europe, particularly in France and Italy. The revolutionary fervor of the forties both in England and on the Continent inspired him to write his great novels of sharp social criticism, *Dombey and Son, David Copperfield, Bleak House, Hard Times*, and *Little Dorrit*. At the same time he edited newspapers and magazines and gave public readings of his novels. In 1859 he published his historical novel about the French Revolution, *A Tale of Two Cities*, which was followed by novels on contemporary themes, *Great Expectations* and *Our Mutual Friend*. In 1867–1868 Dickens made his second trip to America.

Back in England, Dickens started *The Mystery of Edwin Drood*, but on June 9, 1870, he died of a stroke, leaving his last work unfinished, and was buried in the Poet's Corner of Westminster Abbey.

2.1.2 Charles Dickens' Major Novels

The Pickwick Papers (1837)	《匹克威克外传》
Oliver Twist (1838)	《奥列佛·退斯特》(《雾都孤儿》)
Nicholas Nickleby (1839)	《尼古拉斯·尼克尔贝》
The Old Curiosity Shop (1841)	《老古玩店》
Barnaby Rudge (1841)	《巴纳比·拉奇》
Martin Chuzzlewit (1843)	《马丁·朱述尔维特》
Dombey and Son (1848)	《董贝父子》
David Copperfield (1850)	《大卫·科波菲尔》
Bleak House (1853)	《荒凉山庄》
Hard Times (1854)	《艰难时世》
Little Dorrit (1857)	《小杜丽》
A Tale of Two Cities (1859)	《双城记》
Great Expectations (1861)	《远大前程》
Our Mutual Friend (1865)	《我们共同的朋友》

2.2 *Oliver Twist*

2.2.1 About the Novel

Oliver Twist is Charles Dickens' second novel and one of his most popular works. It was originally published in *Bentley's Miscellany* as a serial in monthly installments that began appearing in the month of February 1837 and continued through April 1839. The novel depicts the world of poverty and the workhouse of the 19th-century London, concerned with crime, evil, death, deprivation, social injustice, and urban squalor, and satirical about

Unit 2
Charles Dickens and *Oliver Twist*

the New Poor Law of 1834, which dictated that all public charity must be channeled through workhouses.

"Life in London, as revealed in the pages of Boz, opens a new world to thousands born and bred in the same city," wrote the *Quarterly Review* (June 1839). In the novel Dickens mocks the hypocrisies of the time by surrounding the novel's serious themes with sarcasm and dark humour. He explores individual as much as social evil in his depiction of Fagin and Sikes and their associates. The book calls the public's attention to various contemporary social evils, including the workhouse, child labour, and the recruitment of children as criminals. It is a powerful attack on the social evils and actually helped to alleviate the sufferings of the poor, for it has been said that *Oliver Twist* was responsible to a certain extent for the bettering of conditions in the English workhouses of the author's day.

The story in *Oliver Twist* is chiefly about a workhouse orphan running away to London from intolerable miseries in the workhouse and at an undertaker's shop, his falling into a gang of thieves in the English capital, his being rescued by a kindly gentleman, and finally his being discovered as the lost son of a good family and restored to a life of happiness and wealth.

2.2.2 Characters

- **Agnes Fleming** Oliver's mother.
- **Oliver Twist** The novel's protagonist.
- **Old Sally** An elderly pauper who serves as the nurse at Oliver's birth.
- **Mr. Bumble** The parish beadle - a minor church official-for the workhouse where Oliver is born.
- **Mrs. Corney** The matron of the workhouse where Oliver is born.
- **Mrs. Mann** The superintendent of the juvenile workhouse where Oliver is raised.
- **Mr. Sowerberry** The undertaker to whom Oliver is apprenticed.
- **Mrs. Sowerberry** Sowerberry's wife. She is a mean woman who henpecks her husband.
- **Noah Claypole** A charity boy and Mr. Sowerberry's apprentice.
- **Charlotte** Servant to Mrs. Sowerberry.

- **Fagin** A thief-trainer.
- **Nancy** A young prostitute and one of Fagin's former child pickpockets.
- **Bill Sikes** A brutal professional burglar brought up in Fagin's gang.
- **The Artful Dodger** The cleverest of Fagin's pickpockets. His real name is Jack Dawkins.
- **Charley Bates** One of Fagin's pickpockets. Charley is ready to laugh at anything.
- **Monks** Son of Edwin Leeford and his legal wife; Oliver's half-brother.
- **Toby Crackit** One of Fagin and Sikes's associates. Toby participates in the attempted burglary of Mrs. Maylie's home.
- **Mr. Fang** The harsh, irrational, power-hungry magistrate who presides over Oliver's trial for pickpocketing.
- **Mr. Brownlow** A well-off, erudite gentleman who serves as Oliver's first benefactor.
- **Mrs. Bedwin** Mr. Brownlow's kindhearted housekeeper.
- **Mr. Grimwig** Brownlow's pessimistic, gruff friend.

2.2.3 Selected Readings from the Novel

2.2.3.1 Important Quotations

(1) Oliver cried lustily. If he could have known that he was an orphan, left to the tender mercies of churchwardens and overseers, perhaps he would have cried the louder. (CHAPTER I)

(2) So they established the rule that all poor people should have the alternative (for they would compel nobody, not they) of being starved by a gradual process in the house, or by a quick one out of it. (CHAPTER II)

(3) Please, sir, I want some more. (CHAPTER II, Oliver Twist)

(4) Although Oliver had been brought up by philosophers, he was not theoretically acquainted with the beautiful axiom that self-preservation is the first law of nature. (CHAPTER X)

(5) The persons on whom I have bestowed my dearest love, lie deep in their graves; but, although the happiness and delight of my life lie buried there

Unit 2
Charles Dickens and *Oliver Twist*

too, I have not made a coffin of my heart, and sealed it up, for ever, on my best affections. Deep affliction has but strengthened and refined them. (CHAPTER XIV, Mr Brownlow)

(6) That it was possible even for justice itself to confound the innocent with the guilty when they were in accidental companionship, he (Oliver) knew already; and that deeply-laid plans for the destruction of inconveniently knowing or over-communicative persons, had been really devised and carried out by the old Jew on more occasions than one... (CHAPTER XVIII)

(7) The great principle of out-of-door relief is to give the paupers exactly what they don't want, and then they get tired of coming. (CHAPTER XXIII, Mr Bumble)

(8) But tears were not the things to find their way to Mr. Bumble's soul; his heart was waterproof. (CHAPTER XXXVII)

(9) The past has been a dreary waste with you, of youthful energies mis-spent, and such priceless treasures lavished as the Creator bestows but once and never grants again, but, for the future, you may hope. (CHAPTER XLVI, Mr Brownlow speaks to Nancy.)

(10) I am chained to my old life. I loathe and hate it now, but I cannot leave it. I must have gone too far to turn back.... To such a home as I have raised for myself with the work of my whole life. (CHAPTER XLVI, Nancy)

2.2.3.2 Excerpts Related to Some Scenes in the Film

❧ Excerpt 1 (from Chapter 6)

Mr. Sowerberry, an undertaker employed by the parish, takes Oliver into his service. Later he uses Oliver as the mourner at children's funerals because of the boy's sorrowful countenance. Noah Claypole, another apprentice, is jealous of Oliver's promotion. One day, in an attempt to aggravate and tantalize young Oliver, Noah makes disparaging comment on Oliver's dead mother. Goaded beyond endurance, Oliver fiercely attacks the bigger boy although for many times Oliver meekly submits to the domination and ill-treatment of Noah.

One day, Oliver and Noah had descended into the kitchen at the usual dinner hour to banquet upon a small joint of mutton—a pound and a half of the worst end of the neck—when Charlotte being called out of the way, there ensued a brief interval of time which Noah Claypole, being hungry and vicious, considered he could not possibly devote to a worthier purpose than aggravating and tantalising young Oliver Twist.

Intent upon this innocent amusement, Noah put his feet on the table-cloth, and pulled Oliver's hair, and twitched his ears, and expressed his opinion that he was a "sneak," and furthermore announced his intention of coming to see him hanged, whenever that desirable event should take place, and entered upon various other topics of petty annoyance, like a malicious and ill-conditioned charity-boy as he was. But, none of these taunts producing the desired effect of making Oliver cry, Noah attempted to be more facetious still, and in this attempt, did what many small wits, with far greater reputations than Noah, sometimes do to this day, when they want to be funny. He got rather personal.

"Work'us," said Noah, "how's your mother?"

"She's dead," replied Oliver; "don't you say anything about her to me!"

"Oliver's colour rose as he said this; he breathed quickly, and there was a curious working of the mouth and nostrils, which Mr. Claypole thought must be the immediate precursor of a violent fit of crying. Under this impression he returned to the charge.

"What did she die of, Work'us?" said Noah.

"Of a broken heart, some of our old nurses told me," replied Oliver, more as if he were talking to himself, than answering Noah. "I think I know what it must be to die of that!"

"Tol de rol lol lol, right fol lairy, Work'us," said Noah, as a tear rolled down Oliver's cheek. "What's set you a snivelling now?"

"Not *you*, replied Oliver, hastily brushing the tear away. "Don't think it."

"Oh, not me, eh!" sneered Noah.

"No, not you," replied Oliver, sharply. "There, that's enough. Don't say anything more to me about her; you'd better not!"

"Better not!" exclaimed Noah. "Well! Better not! Work'us, don't be impudent. *Your* mother, too! She was a nice 'un, she was. Oh, Lor!" And here Noah nodded his head expressively, and curled up as much of his small red nose as muscular action could collect together for the occasion.

"Yer know, Work'us," continued Noah, emboldened by Oliver's silence, and speaking in a jeering tone of affected pity, of all tones the most annoying, "Yer know, Work'us, it can't be helped now, and of course yer couldn't help it then, and I'm very sorry for it, and I'm sure we all are, and pity yer very much. But yer must know, Work'us, yer mother was a regular right-down bad 'un."

"What did you say?" inquired Oliver, looking up very quickly.

"A regular right-down bad 'un, Work'us," replied Noah, coolly. "And it's a great deal better, Work'us, that she died when she did, or else she'd have been hard labouring in Bridewell, or transported, or hung, which is more likely than either, isn't it?"

Crimson with fury, Oliver started up, overthrew the chair and table, seized Noah by the throat, shook him, in the violence of his rage, till his teeth chattered in his head, and, collecting his whole force into one heavy blow, felled him to the ground.

A minute ago the boy had looked the quiet, mild, dejected creature that harsh treatment had made him. But his spirit was roused at last; the cruel insult to his dead mother had set his blood on fire. His breast heaved; his attitude was erect, his eye bright and vivid; his whole person changed, as he stood glaring over the cowardly tormentor who now lay crouching at his feet, and defied him with an energy he had never known before.

> ### Excerpt 2 (from Chapter 14)
> *Pitying the sickly young Oliver, Mr. Brownlow, the man whose pocket Oliver was accused of having picked, takes Oliver home and cares for him. Oliver soon recovers with the experienced nursing of the kindly housekeeper, Mrs. Bedwin. One evening, as he was talking to Mrs. Bedwin, there came a message down from Mr. Brownlow, that if Oliver Twist felt pretty well, he should like to see him in his study, and talk to him a little while.*

"There are a good many books, are there not, my boy?" said Mr. Brownlow, observing the curiosity with which Oliver surveyed the shelves that reached from the floor to the ceiling.

"A great number, sir," replied Oliver. "I never saw so many."

"You shall read them, if you behave well," said the old gentleman kindly; "and you will like that, better than looking at the outsides–that is, in some cases; because there *are* books of which the backs and covers are by far the best parts."

"I suppose they are those heavy ones, sir," said Oliver, pointing to some large quartos with a good deal of gilding about the binding.

"Not always those," said the old gentleman, patting Oliver on the head, and smiling as he did so; "there are other equally heavy ones, though of a much smaller size. How should you like to grow up a clever man, and write books, eh?"

"I think I would rather read them, sir," replied Oliver.

"What! Wouldn't you like to be a book-writer?" said the old gentleman.

Oliver considered a little while, and at last said he should think it would be a much better thing to be a book-seller, upon which the old gentleman laughed heartily, and declared he had said a very good thing. Which Oliver felt glad to have done, though he by no means knew what it was.

"Well, well," said the old gentleman, composing his features. "Don't be afraid! We won't make an author of you, while there's an honest trade to be learnt, or brick-making to turn to."

"Thank you, sir," said Oliver. At the earnest manner of his reply, the old gentleman laughed again and said something about a curious instinct, which Oliver, not understanding, paid no very great attention to.

Unit 2
Charles Dickens and *Oliver Twist*

"Now," said Mr. Brownlow, speaking if possible in a kinder, but at the same time in a much more serious manner, than Oliver had ever known him assume yet, "I want you to pay great attention, my boy, to what I am going to say. I shall talk to you without any reserve, because I am sure you are well able to understand me as many older persons would be."

"Oh, don't tell you are going to send me away, sir, pray!" exclaimed Oliver, alarmed at the serious tone of the old gentleman's commencement! "Don't turn me out of doors to wander in the streets again. Let me stay here, and be a servant. Don't send me back to the wretched place I came from. Have mercy upon a poor boy, sir!"

"My dear child," said the old gentleman, moved by the warmth of Oliver's sudden appeal; "you need not be afraid of my deserting you, unless you give me cause."

"I never, never will, sir," interposed Oliver.

"I hope not," rejoined the old gentleman. "I do not think you ever will."

⚙ Excerpt 3 (from Chapter 16)

One day when Mr. Brownlow entrusts Oliver to return and pay for some books to the bookseller for him, Oliver is intercepted by Nancy and the brutal robber Bill Sikes, so once more Oliver is in the hands of Fagin. Desperate, Oliver jumps suddenly to his feet, and tears wildly from the room, uttering shrieks for help. Sikes threatens to set his vicious dog, Bull's-eye, on him. Nancy leaps to Oliver's defense. When Fagin tries to beat Oliver for his escape attempt, Nancy flies at Fagin in a rage.

"Keep back the dog, Bill!" cried Nancy, springing before the door, and closing it, as the Jew and his two pupils darted out in pursuit. "Keep back the dog; he'll tear the boy to pieces."

"Serve him right!" cried Sikes, struggling to disengage himself from the girl's grasp. "Stand off from me, or I'll split your head against the wall."

"I don't care for that, Bill, I don't care for that," screamed the girl, struggling violently with the man: "the child shan't be torn down by the dog, unless you kill me first."

"Shan't he!" said Sikes, setting his teeth. "I'll soon do that if you don't keep off."

* * * * * * * *

"So you wanted to get away, my dear, did you?" said the Jew, taking up a jagged and knotted club which law in a corner of the fireplace; "eh?"

Oliver made no reply. But he watched the Jew's motions, and breathed quickly.

"Wanted to get assistance; called for the police, did you?" sneered the Jew, catching the boy by the arm. "We'll cure you of that, my young master."

The Jew inflicted a smart blow on Oliver's shoulders with the club, and was raising it for a second when the girl, rushing forward, wrested it from his hand. She flung it into the fire with a force that brought some of the glowing coals whirling out into the room.

"I won't stand by and see it done, Fagin," cried the girl. "You've got the boy, and what more would you have?–Let him be–let him be–or I shall put that mark on some of you, that will bring me to the gallows before my time."

The girl stamped her foot violently on the floor as she vented this threat, and with her lips compressed, and her hands clenched, looked alternately at the Jew and the other robber, her face quite colourless from the passion of rage into which she had gradually worked herself.

"Why, Nancy!" said the Jew, in a soothing tone, after a pause, during which he and Mr. Sikes had stared at one another in a disconcerted manner; "you,–you're more clever than ever tonight. Ha! ha! my dear, you are acting beautifully."

"Am I!" said the girl. "Take care I don't overdo it. You will be the worse for it, Fagin, if I do; and so I tell you in good time to keep clear of me."

* * * * * * * *

"You're a nice one," added Sikes, as he surveyed her with a contemptuous air, "to take up the humane and gen–teel side! A pretty subject for the child, as you call him, to make a friend of!"

"God Almighty help me, I am!" cried the girl passionately; "and I wish I had been struck dead in the street, or had changed places with them we passed so near tonight, before I had lent a hand in bringing him here. He's a thief, a liar, a devil, all that's bad, from this night forth. Isn't that enough for the old wretch, without blows?"

"Come, come, Sikes," said the Jew, appealing to him in a remonstratory tone, and motioning towards the boys, who were eagerly attentive to all that passed; "we must have civil words; civil words, Bill."

"Civil words!" cried the girl, whose passion was frightful to see. "Civil words, you villain! Yes, you deserve 'em from me. I thieved for you when I was a child not half as old as this!" pointing to Oliver. "I have been in the same trade, and in the same service, for twelve years since. Don't you know it? Speak out! Don't you know it?"

"Well, well," replied the Jew, with an attempt at pacification; "and, if you have, it's your living!"

"Aye, it is!" returned the girl, not speaking, but pouring out the words in one continuous and vehement scream. "It is my living; and the cold, wet, dirty streets are my home; and you're the wretch that drove me to them long ago, and that'll keep me there, day and night, day and night, till I die!"

"I shall do you a mischief!" interposed the Jew, goaded by these reproaches; "a mischief worse than that, if you say much more!"

The girl said nothing more; but, tearing her hair and dress in a transport of passion, made such a rush at the Jew as would probably have left signal marks of her revenge upon him, had not her wrists been seized by Sikes at the right moment; upon which, she made a few ineffectual struggles, and fainted.

Excerpt 4 (from Chapter 37)

Mrs. Corney's material wealth draws Mr. Bumble's eyes and heart in her direction, and then he proposes to the widow. After marriage, he soon discovers that married life with the former Mrs. Corney was not at all happiness, for she dominates him completely.

"And to-morrow two months it was done!" said Mr. Bumble, with a sigh. "It seems a age."

Mr. Bumble might have meant that he had concentrated a whole existence of happiness into the short space of eight weeks; but the sigh–there was a vast deal of meaning in the sigh.

"I sold myself," said Mr. Bumble, pursuing the same train of reflection, "for six teaspoons, a pair of sugar-tongs, and a milk-pot, with a small quantity of second-hand furniture and twenty pound in money. I went very reasonable. Cheap, dirt cheap!"

"Cheap!" cried a shrill voice in Mr. Bumble's ear: "you would have been dear at any price; and dear enough I paid for you, Lord above knows that!"

Mr. Bumble turned and encountered the face of his interesting consort, who, imperfectly comprehending the few words she had overheard of his complaint, had hazarded the foregoing remark at a venture.

"Mrs. Bumble, ma'am!" said Mr. Bumble, with sentimental sternness.

"Well!" cried the lady.

"Have the goodness to look at me," said Mr. Bumble, fixing his eyes upon her. ("If she stands such a eye as that," said Mr. Bumble to himself, "she can stand anything. It is a eye I never knew to fail with paupers. If it fails with her, my power is gone.")

Whether an exceedingly small expansion of eye be sufficient to quell paupers, who, being lightly fed, are in no very high condition, or whether the late Mrs. Corney was particularly proof against eagle glances, are matters of opinion. The matter of fact, is, that the matron was in no way overpowered by Mr. Bumble's scowl, but, on the contrary, treated it with great disdain, and even raised a laugh thereat which sounded as though it were genuine.

On hearing this most unexpected sound, Mr. Bumble looked, first incredulous, and afterwards amazed. He then relapsed into his former state, nor did he rouse himself until his attention was again awakened by the voice of his partner.

"Are you going to sit snoring there all day?" inquired Mrs. Bumble.

"I am going to sit here, as long as I think proper, ma'am," rejoined Mr. Bumble; "and although I was *not* snoring, I shall snore, gape, sneeze, laugh, or cry, as the humour strikes me, such being my prerogative."

"*Your* prerogative!" sneered Mrs. Bumble, with ineffable contempt.

"I said the word, ma'am," said Mr. Bumble. "The prerogative of a man is to command."

"And what's the prerogative of a woman, in the name of Goodness?" cried the relict of Mr. Corney deceased.

"To obey, ma'am," thundered Mr. Bumble. "Your late unfortunate husband should have taught it you; and then, perhaps, he might have been alive now. I wish he was, poor man!"

Mrs. Bumble, seeing at a glance that the decisive moment had now arrived, and that a blow struck for the mastership on one side or other must necessarily be final and conclusive, no sooner heard this allusion to the dead

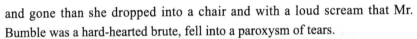

Unit 2
Charles Dickens and *Oliver Twist*

and gone than she dropped into a chair and with a loud scream that Mr. Bumble was a hard-hearted brute, fell into a paroxysm of tears.

But tears were not the things to find their way to Mr. Bumble's soul; his heart was waterproof. Like washable beaver hats that improve with rain, his nerves were rendered stouter and more vigorous by showers of tears, which, being tokens of weakness, and so far tacit admissions of his own power, pleased and exalted him. He eyed his good lady with looks of great satisfaction, and begged, in an encouraging manner, that she should cry her hardest, the exercise being looked upon by the faculty as strongly conducive to health.

"It opens the lungs, washes the countenance, exercises the eyes, and softens down the temper," said Mr. Bumble. "So cry away."

As he discharged himself of this pleasantry, Mr. Bumble took his hat from a peg, and putting it on, rather rakishly, on one side, as a man might who felt he had asserted his superiority in a becoming manner, thrust his hands into his pockets and sauntered towards the door, with much ease and waggishness depicted in his whole appearance.

Now, Mrs. Corney that was, had tried the tears because they were less troublesome than a manual assault; but she was quite prepared to make trial of the latter mode of proceeding, as Mr. Bumble was not long in discovering.

The first proof he experienced of the fact was conveyed in a hollow sound, immediately succeeded by the sudden flying off of his hat to the opposite end of the room. This preliminary proceeding laying bare his head, the expert lady, clasping him tightly round the throat with one hand, inflicted a shower of blows (dealt with singular vigour and dexterity) upon it with the other. This done, she created a little variety by scratching his face and tearing his hair; and, having, by this time, inflicted as much punishment as she deemed necessary for the offence, she pushed him over a chair which was luckily well situated for the purpose, and defied him to talk about his prerogative again if he dared.

"Get up!" said Mrs. Bumble, in a voice of command. "And take yourself away from here, unless you want me to do something desperate."

Mr. Bumble rose with a very rueful countenance, wondering much what something desperate might be. Picking up his hat, he looked towards the door.

Excerpt 5 (from Chapter 46)

A mysterious man named Monks is plotting with Fagin to destroy Oliver's reputation. Nancy overhears the two villains. Now thoroughly ashamed of her role in Oliver's kidnapping and fearful for the boy's safety, she decides to go to see Rose Maylie (in the novel) and Mr. Brownlow(in the film).

"Why, for what," said the gentleman in a kinder tone, "for what purpose can you have brought us to this strange place? Why not have let me speak to you above there, where it is light and there is something stirring, instead of bringing us to this dark and dismal hole?"

"I told you before,' replied Nancy, "that I was afraid to speak to you there. I don't know why it is," said the girl, shuddering, "but I have such a fear and dread upon me tonight that I can hardly stand."

"A fear of what?" asked the gentleman, who seemed to pity her.

"I scarcely know of what,' replied the girl. "I wish I did. Horrible thoughts of death, and shrouds with blood upon them, and a fear that has made me burn as if I was on fire, have been upon me all day. I was reading a book tonight, to while the time away, and the same things came into the print."

"Imagination," said the gentleman, soothing her.

"No imagination," replied the girl in a hoarse voice. "I'll swear I saw 'coffin' written in every page of the book in large black letters–aye, and they carried one close to me, in the streets to-night."

"There is nothing unusual in that," said the gentleman. "They have passed me often."

"*Real ones*," rejoined the girl. "This was not."

There was something so uncommon in her manner that the flesh of the concealed listener crept as he heard the girl utter these words, and the blood chilled within him. He had never experienced a greater relief than in hearing the sweet voice of the young lady as she begged her to be calm, and not allow herself to become the prey of such fearful fancies.

"Speak to her kindly," said the young lady to her companion. "Poor creature! She seems to need it."

"Your haughty religious people would have held their heads up to see

Unit 2
Charles Dickens and *Oliver Twist*

me as I am tonight, and preached of flames and vengeance," cried the girl. "Oh, dear lady, why ar'n't those who claim to be God's own folks as gentle and as kind to us poor wretches as you, who, having youth, and beauty, and all that they have lost, might be a little proud instead of so much humbler?"

"Ah!" said the gentleman. "A Turk turns his face, after washing it well, to the East, when he says his prayers; these good people, after giving their faces such a rub against the World as to take the smiles off, turn with no less regularity to the darkest side of Heaven. Between the Mussulman and the Pharisee, commend me to the first!"

These words appeared to be addressed to the young lady, and were perhaps uttered with the view of affording Nancy time to recover herself. The gentleman shortly afterwards addressed himself to her."

"You were not here last Sunday night," he said.

"I couldn't come," replied Nancy; "I was kept by force."

"By whom?"

"Him that I told the young lady of before."

"You were not suspected of holding any communication with anybody on the subject which has brought us here tonight, I hope?" asked the old gentleman.

"No," replied the girl, shaking her head. "It's not very easy for me to leave him unless he knows why; I couldn't have seen the lady when I did, but that I gave him a drink of laudanum before I came away."

"Did he awake before you returned?" inquired the gentleman.

"No; and neither he nor any of them suspect me."

"Good," said the gentleman. "Now listen to me."

"I am ready," replied the girl, as he paused for a moment.

"This young lady," the gentleman began, "has communicated to me, and to some other friends who can be safely trusted, what you told her nearly a fortnight since. I confess to you that I had doubts, at first, whether you were to be implicitly relied upon, but now I firmly believe you are."

"I am," said the girl earnestly.

"I repeat that I firmly believe it. To prove to you that I am disposed to trust you, I tell you without reserve that we propose to extort the secret, whatever it may be, from the fear of this man Monks. But if–if–" said the gentleman, "he cannot be secured, or, if secured, cannot be acted upon as we wish, you must deliver up the Jew."

"Fagin," cried the girl, recoiling.

"That man must be delivered up by you," said the gentleman.

"I will not do it! I will never do it!" replied the girl. "Devil that he is, and worse than devil as he has been to me, I will never do that."

"You will not?" said the gentleman, who seemed fully prepared for this answer.

"Never!" returned the girl.

"Tell me why?"

"For one reason," rejoined the girl firmly, "for one reason that the lady knows and will stand by me in, I know she will, for I have her promise; and for this other reason, besides, that, bad life as he has led, I have led a bad life too; there are many of us who have kept the same courses together, and I'll not turn upon them who might–any of them–have turned upon me, but didn't, bad as they are."

🎬 Excerpt 6 (from Chapter 47)

Noah Claypole in the novel(The Artful Dodger in the film) is sent by Fagin to "dodge" Nancy to discover her secret. Now Fagin angrily passes the information on to Sikes, twisting the story just enough to make it sound as if Nancy had informed on him.

"I've got that to tell you, Bill," said Fagin, drawing his chair nearer, "will make you worse than me."

"Aye?" returned the robber with an incredulous air. "Tell away! Look sharp, or Nance will think I'm lost."

"Lost!" cried Fagin. "She has pretty well settled that, in her own mind, already."

Sikes looked with an aspect of great perplexity into the Jew's face, and reading no satisfactory explanation of the riddle there clenched his coat collar in his huge hand and shook him soundly.

"Speak, will you!" he said; "or if you don't, it shall be for want of breath. Open your mouth and say wot you've got to say in plain words. Out with it, you thundering old cur, out with it!"

"Suppose that lad that's laying there–" Fagin began.

Unit 2
Charles Dickens and *Oliver Twist*

Sikes turned round to where Noah was sleeping, as if he had not previously observed him. "Well!" he said, resuming his former position.

"Suppose that lad," pursued Fagin, "was to peach–to blow upon us all–first seeking out the right folks for the purpose, and then having a meeting with 'em in the street to paint our likenesses, describe every mark that they might know us by, and the crib where we might be most easily taken. Suppose he was to do all this, and besides to blow upon a plant we've all been in, more or less–of his own fancy; not grabbed, trapped, tried, earwigged by the parson, and brought to it on bread and water–but of his own fancy, to please his own taste, stealing out at nights to find those most interested against us, and peaching to them. Do you hear me?" cried the Jew, his eyes flashing with rage. "Suppose he did all this, what then?"

"What then!" replied Sikes; with a tremendous oath. "If he was left alive till I came, I'd grind his skull under the iron heel of my boot into as many grains as there are hairs upon his head."

"What if *I* did it!" cried Fagin almost in a yell. "*I*, that know so much, and could hang so many besides myself!"

"I don't know," replied Sikes, clenching his teeth and turning white at the mere suggestion. "I'd do something in the jail that 'ud get me put in irons; and if I was tried along with you, I'd fall upon you with them in the open court, and beat your brains out afore the people. I should have such strength," muttered the robber, poising his brawny arm, "that I could smash your head as if a loaded wagon had gone over it."

"You would?"

"Would I!" said the housebreaker. "Try me."

"If it was Charley, or the Dodger, or Bet, or–"

"I don't care who," replied Sikes impatiently. "Whoever it was, I'd serve them the same."

Fagin looked hard at the robber; and, motioning him to be silent, stooped over the bed upon the floor, and shook the sleeper to rouse him. Sikes leant forward in his chair, looking on with his hands upon his knees, as if wondering much what all this questioning and preparation was to end in.

"Bolter, Bolter! Poor lad!" said Fagin, looking up with an expression of devilish anticipation, and speaking slowly and with marked emphasis. "He's tired–tired with watching for *her* so long–watching for *her*, Bill."

"Wot d'ye mean?" asked Sikes, drawing back.

Fagin made no answer, but bending over the sleeper again, hauled him into a sitting posture. When his assumed name had been repeated several times, Noah rubbed his eyes and, giving a heavy yawn, looked sleepily about him.

"Tell me that again–once again, just for him to hear," said the Jew, pointing to Sikes as he spoke.

"Tell yer what?" asked the sleepy Noah, shaking himself pettishly.

"That about–NANCY," said Fagin, clutching Sikes by the wrist, as if to prevent his leaving the house before he had heard enough. "You followed her?"

"Yes."

"To London Bridge?"

"Yes.'

"Where she met two people?"

"So she did."

"A gentleman and a lady that she had gone to of her own accord before, who asked her to give up all her pals, and Monks first, which she did–and to describe him, which she did–and to tell her what house it was that we meet at, and go to, which she did–and where it could be best watched from, which she did–and what time the people went there, which she did. She did all this. She told it all every word without a threat, without a murmur–she did–did she not?" cried Fagin, half mad with fury.

"All right," replied Noah, scratching his head. "That's just what it was!"

"What did they say, about last Sunday?"

"About last Sunday!" replied Noah, considering. "Why I told yer that before."

"Again. Tell it again!" cried Fagin, tightening his grasp on Sikes, and brandishing his other hand aloft, as the foam flew from his lips.

"They asked her," said Noah, who, as he grew more wakeful, seemed to have a dawning perception who Sikes was, "they asked her why she didn't come last Sunday as she promised. She said she couldn't."

"Why–why? Tell him that."

"Because she was forcibly kept at home by Bill, the man she had told them of before," replied Noah.

"What more of him?" cried Fagin. "What more of the man she had told them of before? Tell him that, tell him that."

Unit 2
Charles Dickens and *Oliver Twist*

"Why, that she couldn't very easily get out of doors unless he knew where she was going to," said Noah; "and so the first time she went to see the lady, she–ha! ha! ha! it made me laugh when she said it, that it did–she gave him a drink of laudanum."

"Hell's fire!" cried Sikes, breaking fiercely from the Jew. "Let me go!"

Flinging the old man from him, he rushed from the room and darted, wildly and furiously, up the stairs.

"Bill, Bill!" cried Fagin, following him hastily. "A word. Only a word."

The word would not have been exchanged, but that the housebreaker was unable to open the door, on which he was expending fruitless oaths and violence when the Jew came panting up.

"Let me out," said Sikes. "Don't speak to me; it's not safe. Let me out, I say!"

"Hear me speak a word," rejoined Fagin, laying his hand upon the lock. "You won't be–"

"Well," replied the other.

"You won't be–too–violent, Bill?"

The day was breaking, and there was light enough for the men to see each other's faces. They exchanged one brief glance; there was a fire in the eyes of both, which could not be mistaken.

"I mean," said Fagin, showing that he felt all disguise was now useless, "not too violent for safety. Be crafty, Bill, and not too bold."

2.2.3.3 Passages for Understanding the Film

(1) FOR A WEEK AFTER THE COMMISSION OF THE IMPIOUS and profane offence of asking for more, Oliver remained a close prisoner in the dark and solitary room to which he had been consigned by the wisdom and mercy of the board. It appears, at first sight, not unreasonable to suppose that, if he had entertained a becoming feeling of respect for the prediction of the gentleman in the white waistcoat, he would have established that sage individual's prophetic character, once and for ever, by tying one end of his pocket-handkerchief to a hook in the wall, and attaching himself to the other. To the performance of this feat, however, there was one obstacle:

namely, that pocket-handkerchiefs, being decided articles of luxury, had been, for all future times and ages, removed from the noses of paupers by the express order of the board in council assembled, solemnly given and pronounced under their hands and seals. There was a still greater obstacle in Oliver's youth and childishness. He only cried bitterly all day, and, when the long, dismal night came on, spread his little hands before his eyes to shut out the darkness, and crouching in the corner, tried to sleep, ever and anon waking with a start and tremble, and drawing himself closer and closer to the wall, as if to feel even its cold hard surface were a protection in the gloom and loneliness which surrounded him. **(CHAPTER III)**

(2) Noah was a charity boy, but not a workhouse orphan. No chance-child was he, for he could trace his genealogy all the way back to his parents, who lived hard by, his mother being a washerwoman and his father a drunken soldier, discharged with a wooden leg and a diurnal pension of twopence halfpenny and an unstateable fraction. The shop-boys in the neighbourhood had long been in the habit of branding Noah, in the public streets, with the ignominious epithets of "leathers," "charity," and the like; and Noah had borne them without reply. But, now that fortune had cast in his way a nameless orphan at whom even the meanest could point the finger of scorn, he retorted on him with interest. This affords charming food for contemplation. It shows us what a beautiful thing human nature may be made to be, and how impartially the same amiable qualities are developed in the finest lord and the dirtiest charity boy. (CHAPTER V)

(3) Oliver's clothes had been torn in the beating he had received; his face was bruised and scratched, and his hair scattered over his forehead. The angry flush had not disappeared, however; and when he was pulled out of his prison, he scowled boldly on Noah and looked quite undismayed.

* * * * * * * *

It was not until he was left alone in the silence and stillness of the gloomy workshop of the undertaker that Oliver gave way to the feelings which the day's treatment may be supposed likely to have awakened in a mere child. He had listened to their taunts with a look of contempt; he had borne the lash without a cry, for he felt that pride swelling in his heart which would have kept down a shriek to the last, though they had roasted him alive. But now, when there were none to see or hear him, he fell upon his knees on the floor and, hiding his face in his hands, wept such tears as–God send for the credit of our nature–few so young may ever have cause to pour out before

Him! (CHAPTER VII)

(4) "And wot," said Sikes, scowling fiercely on his agreeable friend, "wot makes you take so much pains about one chalk-faced kid, when you know there are fifty boys snoozing about Common Garden every night, as you might pick and choose from?"

"Because they're of no use to me, my dear," replied the Jew, with some confusion, "not worth the taking. Their looks convict 'em when they get into trouble, and I lose 'em all. With this boy, properly managed, my dears, I could do what I couldn't with twenty of them. Besides," said the Jew, recovering his self-possession, "he has us now if he could only give us leg-bail again; and he *must* be in the same boat with us. Never mind how he came there; it's quite enough for my power over him that he was in a robbery; that's all I want. Now, how much better this is than being obliged to put the poor leetle boy out of the way—which would be dangerous, and we should lose by it besides." (CHAPTER XIX)

(5) I know that of the wretched marriage into which family pride, and the most sordid and narrowest of all ambition, forced your unhappy father when a mere boy, you were the sole and most unnatural issue...the misery, the slow torture, the protracted anguish of that ill-assorted union. I know how listlessly and wearily each of that wretched pair dragged on their heavy chain through a world that was poisoned to them both. I know how cold formalities were succeeded by open taunts, how indifference gave place to dislike, dislike to hate, and hate to loathing, until at last they wrenched the clanking bond asunder and, retiring a wide space apart, carried each a galling fragment, of which nothing but death could break the rivets, to hide it in new society beneath the gayest looks they could assume. Your mother succeeded; she forgot it soon. But it rusted and cankered at your father's heart for years... (CHAPTER XLIX, Mr Brownlow)

(6) "The will," said Mr. Brownlow, speaking for him, "was in the same spirit as the letter. He talked of miseries which his wife had brought upon him; of the rebellious disposition, vice, malice, and premature bad passions of you his only son, who had been trained to hate him; and left you and your mother each an annuity of eight hundred pounds. The bulk of his property he divided into two equal portions—one for Agnes Fleming and the other for their child, it it should be born alive and ever come of age. If it were a girl, it

was to inherit the money unconditionally; but if a boy, only on the stipulation that in his minority he should never have stained his name with any public act of dishonour, meanness, cowardice, or wrong. He did this, he said, to mark his confidence in the mother and his conviction—only strengthened by approaching death—that the child would share her gentle heart, and noble nature. If he were disappointed in this expectation, then the money was to come to you; for then, and not till then, when both children were equal, would he recognise your prior claim upon his purse, who had none upon his heart, but had, from an infant, repulsed him with coldness and aversion."
(CHAPTER LI)

2.2.3.4 Chapter Reading

Chapter II
Treats of Oliver Twist's growth, education, and board

FOR THE NEXT EIGHT OR TEN MONTHS, OLIVER WAS the victim of a systematic course of treachery (背信) and deception (欺骗). He was brought up by hand. The hungry and destitute (穷困的) situation of the infant orphan was duly (按时地) reported by the workhouse authorities to the parish (教区) authorities. The parish authorities inquired with dignity of the workhouse authorities whether there was no female then domiciled (定居的) in "the house" who was in a situation to impart (给予) to Oliver Twist the consolation and nourishment of which he stood in need. The workhouse authorities replied with humility (谦卑) that there was not. Upon this, the parish authorities magnanimously (宽宏大量地) and humanely (仁慈地) resolved that Oliver should be "farmed (寄养)" or, in other words, that he should be despatched (派遣) to a branch workhouse some three miles off, where twenty or thirty other juvenile (青少年的) offenders against the poor-laws rolled about the floor all day, without the inconvenience of too much food or too much clothing, under the parental superintendence (监督) of an elderly female, who received the culprits (犯人) at and for the consideration of sevenpence halfpenny per small head per week. Sevenpence halfpenny's worth per week is a good round diet for a child; a great deal may be got for sevenpence

Unit 2

Charles Dickens and *Oliver Twist*

halfpenny, quite enough to overload its stomach, and make it uncomfortable. The elderly female was a woman of wisdom and experience; she knew what was good for children, and she had a very accurate perception of what was good for herself. So, she appropriated the greater part of the weekly stipend (生活津贴) to her own use, and consigned (拨出用于) the rising parochial (教区的) generation to even a shorter allowance (补贴) than was originally provided for them. Thereby (因此) finding in the lowest depth a deeper still, and proving herself a very great experimental philosopher.

    Everybody knows the story of another experimental philosopher who had a great theory about a horse being able to live without eating, and who demonstrated it so well, that he had got his own horse down to a straw a day, and would unquestionably have rendered (使成为) him a very spirited and rampacious animal on nothing at all, if he had not died four-and-twenty hours before he was to have had his first comfortable bait of air. Unfortunately for the experimental philosophy of the female to whose protecting care Oliver Twist was delivered over, a similar result usually attended the operation of *her* system; for at the very moment when a child had contrived (设法) to exist upon the smallest possible portion of the weakest possible food, it did perversely (有悖常理地) happen in eight and a half cases out of ten, either that it sickened from want and cold, or fell into the fire from neglect, or got half-smothered (闷死) by accident, in any one of which cases the miserable little being was usually summoned into another world, and there gathered to the fathers it had never known in this.

    Occasionally, when there was some more than usually interesting inquest upon a parish child who had been overlooked in turning up a bedstead, or inadvertently (因疏忽造成的) scalded (烫伤) to death when there happened to be a washing—though the latter accident was very scarce, anything approaching to a washing being of rare occurrence in the farm—the jury would take it into their heads to ask troublesome questions, or the parishioners (教区居民) would rebelliously affix (附上) their signatures to a remonstrance (谏书, 抗议). But these impertinences (无礼的举动或言语) were speedily checked by the evidence of the surgeon and the testimony of the beadle, the former of whom had always opened the body and found nothing inside (which was very probable indeed), and the latter of whom invariably (总是) swore whatever the parish wanted, which was very self-devotional. Besides, the board made periodical pilgrimages to the farm, and always sent the beadle the day before to say they were going. The children were neat and clean to behold (看), when *they* went; and what more would the people have!

It cannot be expected that this system of farming would produce any very extraordinary or luxuriant (茂盛的) crop. Oliver Twist's ninth birthday found him a pale, thin child, somewhat diminutive (小的) in stature (身材), and decidedly small in circumference (周长). But nature or inheritance had implanted a good sturdy (顽强的) spirit in Oliver's breast. It had had plenty of room to expand, thanks to the spare diet of the establishment; and perhaps to this circumstance may be attributed his having any ninth birthday at all. Be this as it may, however, it *was* his ninth birthday; and he was keeping it in the coal-cellar with a select party of two other young gentleman, who, after participating with him in a sound thrashing (痛打), had been locked up for atrociously (万恶不赦地) presuming to be hungry, when Mrs. Mann, the good lady of the house, was unexpectedly startled by the apparition (幽灵) of Mr. Bumble, the beadle (教区执事), striving to undo the wicket (小门) of the garden gate.

"Goodness gracious! Is that you, Mr. Bumble, sir?" said Mrs. Mann, thrusting her head out of the window in well-affected ecstasies (狂喜) of joy. "(Susan, take Oliver and them two brats (小子) upstairs, and wash 'em directly.) My heart alive! Mr. Bumble, how glad I am to see you, sure-ly!"

Now, Mr. Bumble was a fat man, and a choleric (易怒的); so, instead of responding to this open-hearted salutation in a kindred spirit, he gave the little wicket a tremendous shake, and then bestowed upon it a kick which could have emanated (发出) from no leg but a beadle's.

"Lor, only think," said Mrs. Mann, running out—for the three boys had been removed by this time—"only think of that! That I should have forgotten that the gate was bolted on the inside, on account of them dear children! Walk in, sir; walk in, pray, Mr. Bumble, do, sir."

Although this invitation was accompanied with a curtsey (屈膝礼) that might have softened the heart of a church-warden, it by no means mollified (安抚) the beadle.

"Do you think this respectful or proper conduct, Mrs. Mann," inquired Mr. Bumble, grasping his cane, "to keep the parish officers a waiting at your garden gate, when they come here upon porochial business with the porochial

Unit 2

Charles Dickens and *Oliver Twist*

orphans? Are you aweer, Mrs. Mann, that you are, as I may say, a porochial delegate, and a stipendiary?"

"I'm sure Mr. Bumble, that I was only a telling one or two of the dear children as is so fond of you, that it was you a-coming," replied Mrs. Mann with great humility.

Mr. Bumble had a great idea of his <u>oratorical</u>（雄辩的）powers and his importance. He had displayed the one, and <u>vindicated</u>（证实）the other. He relaxed.

"Well, well, Mrs. Mann," he replied in a calmer tone, "it may be as you say; it may be. Lead the way in, Mrs. Mann, for I come on business, and have something to say."

Mrs. Mann ushered the beadle into a small parlour with a brick floor, placed a seat for him, and <u>officiously</u>（过分殷勤地）deposited his cocked hat and cane on the table before him. Mr. Bumble wiped from his forehead the <u>perspiration</u>（汗）which his walk had <u>engendered</u>（造成）, glanced <u>complacently</u> （沾沾自喜地）at the cocked hat, and smiled. Yes, he smiled. Beadles are but men, and Mr. Bumble smiled.

"Now don't you be offended at what I'm a-going to say," observed Mrs. Mann, with captivating sweetness. "You've had a long walk, you know, or I wouldn't mention it. Now, will you take a little drop of somethink, Mr. Bumble?"

"Not a drop. Nor a drop," said Mr. Bumble, waving his right hand in a dignified, but <u>placid</u>（平和的）manner.

"I think you will," said Mrs. Mann, who had noticed the tone of the refusal, and the gesture that had accompanied it. "Just a leetle drop, with a little cold water, and a lump of sugar."

Mr. Bumble coughed.

"Now, just a leetle drop," said Mrs. Mann persuasively.

"What is it?" inquired the beadle.

"Why, it's what I'm obliged to keep a little of in the house, to put into the blessed infants' <u>Daffy</u>（达菲糖浆）, when they ain't well, Mr. Bumble," replied Mrs. Mann as she opened a corner cupboard, and took down a bottle and glass. "It's <u>gin</u>（杜松子酒）. I'll not deceive you, Mr. B. It's gin."

"Do you give the children Daffy, Mrs. Mann?" inquired Bumble, following with his eyes the interesting process of mixing.

"Ah, bless 'em, that I do, dear as it is," replied the nurse. "I couldn't see 'em suffer before my very eyes, you know, sir."

"No," said Mr. Bumble approvingly, "no, you could not. You are a humane woman, Mrs. Mann." (Here she set down the glass.) "I shall take a early opportunity of mentioning it to the board, Mrs. Mann." (He drew it towards him.) "You feel as a mother, Mrs. Mann." (He stirred the gin-and-water.) "I–I drink your health with cheerfulness, Mrs. Mann," and he swallowed half of it.

"And now about business," said the beadle, taking out a leathern pocket-book. "The child that was half-baptized Oliver Twist is nine year old to-day."

"Bless him!" interposed (插话) Mrs. Mann, inflaming (使变红) her left eye with the corner of her apron.

"And notwithstanding (虽然) a offered reward of ten pound, which was afterwards increased to twenty pound–notwithstanding the most superlative, and, I may say, supernat'ral exertions on the part of this parish," said Bumble, "we have never been able to discover who is his father, or what was his mother's settlement, name, or con–dition."

Mrs. Mann raised her hands in astonishment, but added, after a moment's reflection, "How comes he to have any name at all, then?"

The beadle drew himself up with great pride, and said, "I inwented it."

"You, Mr. Bumble!"

"I, Mrs. Mann. We name our fondlings in alphabetical order. The last was a S–Swubble, I named him. This was a T-Twist, I named *him*. The next one comes will be Unwin, and the next Vilkins. I have got names ready made to the end of the alphabet, and all the way through it again, when we come to Z."

"Why, you're quite a literary character, sir!" said Mrs. Mann.

"Well, well," said the beadle, evidently gratified (使满足) with the compliment, "perhaps I may be. Perhaps I may be, Mrs. Mann." He finished the gin-and-water, and added, "Oliver being now too old to remain here, the board have determined to have him back into the house. I have come out myself to take him there. So let me see him at once."

"I'll fetch him directly," said Mrs. Mann, leaving the room for that purpose. Oliver, having had by this time as much of the outer coat of dirt which encrusted (在…上结壳) his face and hands, removed, as could be

Unit 2
Charles Dickens and *Oliver Twist*

scrubbed (洗擦) off in one washing, was led into the room by his benevolent protectress (女保护人).

"Make a bow to the gentleman, Oliver," said Mrs. Mann.

Oliver made a bow, which was divided between the beadle on the chair and the cocked hat on the table.

"Will you go along with me, Oliver?" said Mr. Bumble, in a majestic voice.

Oliver was about to say that he would go along with anybody with great readiness, when, glancing upward, he caught sight of Mrs. Mann, who had got behind the beadle's chair, and was shaking her fist at him with a furious countenance. He took the hint at once, for the fist had been too often impressed upon his body not to be deeply impressed upon his recollection.

"Will *she* go with me?" inquired poor Oliver.

"No, she can't," replied Mr. Bumble, "But she'll come and see you sometimes."

This was no very great consolation to the child. Young as he was, however, he had sense enough to make a feint (假装) of feeling great regret at going away. It was no very difficult matter for the boy to call tears into his eyes. Hunger and recent ill-usage are great assistants if you want to cry; and Oliver cried very naturally indeed. Mrs. Mann gave him a thousand embraces, and, what Oliver wanted a great deal more, a piece of bread and butter, lest he should seem too hungry when he got to the workhouse. With the slice of bread in his hand, and the little brown-cloth parish cap on his head, Oliver was then led away by Mr. Bumble from the wretched home where one kind word or look had never lighted the gloom of his infant years. And yet he burst into an agony of childish grief as the cottage gate closed after him. Wretched as were the little companions in misery he was leaving behind, they were the only friends he had ever known; and a sense of his loneliness in the great wide world sank into the child's heart for the first time.

Mr. Bumble walked on with long strides; little Oliver, firmly grasping his gold-laced cuff, trotted beside him, inquiring at the end of every quarter of a mile whether they were "nearly there." To these interrogations Mr. Bumble returned very brief and snappish replies, for the temporary blandness which gin-and-water awakens in some bosoms had by this time evaporated (蒸发), and he was once again a beadle.

Oliver had not been within the walls of the workhouse a quarter of an hour, and had scarcely completed the demolition of a second slice of bread, when Mr. Bumble, who had handed him over to the care of an old woman, returned and, telling him it was a board night, informed him that the board had said he was to appear before it forthwith (立刻).

Not having a very clearly defined notion of what a live board was, Oliver was rather astounded by this intelligence, and was not quite certain whether he ought to laugh or cry. He had no time to think about the matter, however; for Mr. Bumble gave him a tap on the head, with his cane, to wake him up, and another on the back to make him lively, and bidding him to follow, conducted him into a large whitewashed room, where eight or ten fat gentlemen were sitting round a table. At the top of the table, seated in an armchair rather higher than the rest, was a particularly fat gentleman with a very round, red face.

"Bow to the board," said Bumble. Oliver brushed away two or three tears that were lingering in his eyes, and seeing no board but the table, fortunately bowed to that.

"What's your name, boy?" said the gentleman in the high chair.

Oliver was frightened at the sight of so many gentlemen, which made him tremble, and the beadle gave him another tap behind, which made him cry. These two causes made him answer in a very low and hesitating voice, whereupon a gentleman in a white waistcoat said he was a fool. Which was a capital way of raising his spirits, and putting him quite at his ease.

"Boy," said the gentleman in the high chair, "listen to me. You know you're an orphan, I suppose?"

"What's that, sir?" inquired poor Oliver.

"The boy *is* a fool—I thought he was," said the gentleman in the white waistcoat.

"Hush!" said the gentleman who had spoken first. "You know you've got no father or mother, and that you were brought up by the parish, don't you?"

"Yes, sir," replied Oliver, weeping bitterly.

"What are you crying for?" inquired the gentleman in the white waistcoat. And to be sure it was very extraordinary. What *could* the boy be crying for?

"I hope you say your prayers every night," said another gentleman in a

Unit 2

Charles Dickens and *Oliver Twist*

gruff（粗暴的）voice, "and pray for the people who feed you, and take care of you–like a Christian."

"Yes, sir," stammered（结结巴巴地说）the boy. The gentleman who spoke last was unconsciously right. It would have been *very* like a Christian, and a marvellously good Christian, too, if Oliver had prayed for the people who fed and took care of *him*. But he hadn't, because nobody had taught him.

"Well! You have come here to be educated, and taught a useful trade," said the red-faced gentleman in the high chair.

"So you'll begin to pick oakum（麻絮）to-morrow morning at six o'clock," added the surly one in the white waistcoat.

For the combination of both these blessings in the one simple process of picking oakum, Oliver bowed low by the direction of the beadle, and was then hurried away to a large ward, where, on a rough, hard bed, he sobbed himself to sleep. What a noble illustration of the tender laws of England! They let the paupers（穷人）go to sleep!

Poor Oliver! He little thought, as he lay sleeping in happy unconsciousness of all around him, that the board had that very day arrived at a decision which would exercise the most material influence over all his future fortunes. But they had. And this was it:

The members of this board were very sage（贤明的）, deep, philosophical men; and when they came to turn their attention to the workhouse, they found out at once what ordinary folks would never have discovered–the poor people liked it! It was a regular place of public entertainment for the poorer classes; a tavern（酒馆）where there was nothing to pay; a public breakfast, dinner, tea, and supper all the year round; a brick and mortar（灰泥）elysium, where it was all play and no work. "Oho!" said the board, looking very knowing, "we are the fellows to set this to rights; we'll stop it all, in no time." So they established the rule that all poor people should have the alternative (for they would compel nobody, not they) of being starved by a gradual process in the house, or by a quick one out of it. With this view, they contracted with the waterworks to lay on an unlimited supply of water, and with a corn-factor（谷物商）to supply periodically small quantities of oatmeal（麦片）, and issued three meals of thin gruel a day, with an onion twice a week and half a roll on Sundays. They made a great many other wise and humane regulations, having reference to the ladies, which it is not necessary to repeat; kindly undertook to divorce poor married people, in consequence of the great expense of a suit in Doctors' Commons; and, instead of compelling a man to support his family, as they had theretofore（直到那时）done, took his family away from him, and made him a bachelor! There is no saying how many applicants for relief, under these last two heads, might have started up in all classes of society, if it had not been coupled with the workhouse; but the board were long-headed men, and had provided for this difficulty. The relief was inseparable from the workhouse and the gruel, and that frightened people.

For the first six months after Oliver Twist was removed, the system was in full operation. It was rather expensive at first, in consequence of the increase in the undertaker's（丧事承办人）bill, and the necessity of taking in the clothes of all the paupers, which fluttered loosely on their wasted, shrunken forms, after a week or two's gruel. But the number of workhouse inmates got thin as well as the paupers, and the board were in ecstasies.

The room in which the boys were fed was a large stone hall, with a copper at one end, out of which the master, dressed in an apron for the purpose, and assisted by one or two women, ladled the gruel at meal-times. Of this festive composition each boy had one porringer（粥碗）, and no more—except on occasions of great public rejoicing, when he had two ounces and a quarter of bread besides. The bowls never wanted washing. The boys polished them with their spoons till they shone again; and when they had performed this operation (which never took very long, the spoons being nearly as large as the bowls), they would sit staring at the copper with such eager eyes as if they could have devoured the very bricks of which it was composed, employing themselves, meanwhile, in sucking their fingers most assiduously, with the view of catching up any stray splashes of gruel that might have been cast thereon. Boys have generally excellent appetites. Oliver Twist and his companions suffered the tortures of slow starvation for three months; at last they got so voracious（极度饥饿的）and wild with hunger that one boy, who was tall for his age, and hadn't been used to that sort of thing (for his father had kept a small cook-shop), hinted darkly to his companions that unless he had another basin of gruel *per diem*, he was afraid he might some night happen to eat the boy who slept next him, who happened to be a weakly youth of tender age. He had a wild, hungry eye, and they implicitly believed him. A council was held; lots were cast who should walk up to the

Unit 2

Charles Dickens and *Oliver Twist*

master after supper that evening and ask for more; and it fell to Oliver Twist.

The evening arrived; the boys took their places. The master, in his cook's uniform, stationed himself at the copper; his pauper assistants ranged themselves behind him; the gruel was served out, and a long grace was said over the short commons. The gruel disappeared; the boys whispered each other, and winked at Oliver, while his next neighbours nudged (用肘轻推) him. Child as he was, he was desperate with hunger, and reckless with misery. He rose from the table, and advancing to the master, basin and spoon in hand, said, somewhat alarmed at his own temerity:

"Please, sir, I want some more."

The master was a fat, healthy man, but he turned very pale. He gazed in stupefied astonishment on the small rebel for some seconds, and then clung for support to the copper. The assistants were paralysed with wonder, the boys with fear.

"What!" said the master at length, in a faint voice.

"Please, sir," replied Oliver, "I want some more."

The master aimed a blow at Oliver's head with the ladle, pinioned (绑住, 反剪) him in his arms, and shrieked aloud for the beadle.

The board were sitting in solemn conclave when Mr. Bumble rushed into the room in great excitement, and addressing the gentleman in the high chair, said:

"Mr. Limbkins, I beg your pardon, sir! Oliver Twist has asked for more!"

There was a general start. Horror was depicted on every countenance.

"For *more*!" said Mr. Limbkins. "Compose yourself, Bumble, and answer me distinctly. Do I understand that he asked for more, after he had eaten the supper allotted (分发) by the dietary (规定饮食量)?"

"He did, sir," replied Bumble.

"That boy will be hung," said the gentleman in the white waistcoat. "I know that boy will be hung."

Nobody controverted the prophetic gentleman's opinion. An animated discussion took place. Oliver was ordered into instant confinement; and a bill was next morning pasted on the outside of the gate, offering a reward of five pounds to anybody who would take Oliver Twist off the hands of the parish. In other words, five pounds and Oliver Twist were offered to any man or woman who wanted an apprentice to any trade, business, or calling.

"I never was more convinced of anything in my life," said the gentleman in the white waistcoat, as he knocked at the gate and read the bill next morning, "I never was more convinced of anything in my life, than I am that that boy will come to be hung."

As I purpose to show in the sequel whether the white waistcoated gentleman was right or not, I should perhaps <u>mar</u> the interest of this narrative (supposing it to possess any at all) if I ventured to hint just yet whether the life of Oliver Twist had this violent termination or no.

Notes and Glossary for Chapter Reading

(1) workhouse /ˈwəːkhaus/ *n.* public institution for reception of paupers in a parish or group of parishes. 贫民习艺所，救济院

(2) the poor-laws: the poor laws passed by Parliament in 1834, which established workhouses into which the needy people were driven and where they were exploited.

(3) appropriate /əˈprəuprieit/ *vt.* to take sth. for one's own use, often without permission 盗用

(4) implant /imˈplaːnt/ *vt.* to insert or fix 注入，嵌入

(5) half-baptized: privately, without full rites, because in danger of dying.

(6) elysium /iˈliziəm/ *n.* in Greek mythology, the dwelling place of virtuous people after death; by extension, any place or condition of ideal bliss or complete happiness; paradise 人间天堂

(7) Doctors' Commons: a court of Civil Law in London, dealing with suits concerning wills, marriages, licenses and divorce proceedings. 民法博士协会

(8) festive composition 丰盛宴会上吃的杂羹，指这些孩子们吃的粥 (gruel)，含讽刺意味。

(9) per diem /ˈdaiem/ [Latin] per day, every day ［拉丁文］每天

(10) conclave /ˈkɔnkleiv/ *n.* a secret or confidential meeting 秘密或机密的会议 / sit in conclave 举行秘密会议

(11) controvert /kɔntrəˈvəːt/ *vt.* to raise arguments against; voice opposition to. 反驳；就…展开争论；声称反对…

(12) mar /maː/ *vt.* to impair the soundness, perfection of 破坏

Unit 2
Charles Dickens and *Oliver Twist*

2.2.4 Exercises

❶ Identify the following characters

(1) _____ is "a motherly old lady, very neatly and precisely dressed." She takes care of Oliver in his illness and nurses him back to health. She never doubts his honesty even when he disappears with Mr. Brownlow's books and money.

(2) _____ is a dear, grateful, gentle child, who "instead of possessing too little feeling, possessed rather too much." He had not learned "that self-preservation is the first law of nature."

(3) _____ is a prostitute, untidy and free in manner, but "there was something of the woman's original nature left in her still."

(4) _____ serves as Oliver's first benefactor. Throughout the novel, he behaves with compassion and common sense and emerges as a natural leader. "A very respectable-looking personage" with a heart "large enough for any six ordinary old gentlemen of humane disposition."

(5) _____ behaves without compassion toward the paupers under his care. He had a decided propensity for bullying, derived no inconsiderable pleasure from the exercise of petty cruelty, and consequently was (it is needless to say) a coward.

(6) _____ is a tall, dark man, subject to fits of cowardice and epilepsy (癫痫) in the novel. With Fagin, he schemes to ruin Oliver's reputation.

(7) _____ is a charity boy employed by Sowerberry. He later, with Charlotte, steals from the Sowerberrys and runs away to London, where he joins Fagin's gang under the name of Morris Bolter.

(8) _____ is an elderly woman who conducts an infant farm where Oliver is raised. She physically abuses and half-starves the children in her care.

(9) _____ is shrewder and more reflective than his companions. "a very old shriveled Jew, whose villainous-looking and repulsive face was obscured by a quantity of matted red hair." He takes in homeless children and trains them to pick pockets for him.

(10) _____ is a rough, cruel man who makes his living by robbing houses, his anger likely to erupt at any moment.

❷ Plot Review

Oliver Twist is born in a workhouse about seventy-five miles north of London. His mother is found very sick in the street, exhausted by a long journey on foot. She dies just after Oliver's birth. Oliver spends the first nine years of his life in a badly-run home for young (1) _____ under the care of Mrs. Mann and then is transferred to the (2) _____ where he and other orphans are maltreated and constantly (3) _____ One day it falls to Oliver's lot to ask for (4) _____ gruel at the end of a meal on behalf of all the starving children in the workhouse, which shocks the authorities, then (5) _____ pounds is offered to anyone who will take the boy away from the workhouse. Oliver is eventually apprenticed to a local undertaker, Mr. Sowerberry. When another apprentice Noah Claypole (6) _____ Oliver's dead mother, the small and frail Oliver fiercely attacks him. However, Oliver is severely (7) _____. Desperate, Oliver runs away at dawn to London. Outside London, Oliver, starved and exhausted, meets Jack Dawkins (The Artful Dodger). Jack takes Oliver to Fagin's den in the London slums. There Oliver, who innocently does not understand that he is among (8) _____, becomes one of the old Jew Fagin's boys, and is trained as a (9) _____. On his first mission with two other boys he is caught and taken to the police station. Fortunately Oliver is rescued by the benevolent (10) _____, who takes the feverish boy to his home where the kind-hearted housekeeper Mrs. Bedwin nurses Oliver back to health. Mr. Brownlow is struck by Oliver's resemblance to a portrait of a young woman that hangs in his house. One day Oliver is given some books and five pounds to take to a bookseller. On his way Oliver is caught by (11) _____ and Bill Sikes and brought to Fagin.

Sikes plans to rob a house, but he needs a small boy for the job. Fagin sends Oliver to assist Sikes in the burglary. In the novel Oliver is shot by a servant of the house and, after Sikes escapes, is taken in by the women there, Mrs. Maylie and her beautiful adopted niece Rose. Over a period of weeks there, Oliver slowly begins to

Unit 2
Charles Dickens and *Oliver Twist*

recover. But Fagin and a mysterious man named Monks are set on recapturing Oliver. Meanwhile, it is revealed that Oliver's mother left behind a (12) _____ locket when she died. Monks obtains and destroys the locket, the token of Oliver's (13) _____. Nancy discovers that Monks is plotting against Oliver for some reason, bribing Fagin to (14) _____ his innocence. Then Nancy meets secretly with Rose and informs her of Fagin's designs, and later she meets with Rose and Mr. Brownlow at London (15) _____, but this time a member of Fagin's gang eavesdrops on the conversation. When word of Nancy's disclosure reaches Sikes, he brutally (16)_____ Nancy and flees London. On his frantic flight Sikes accidentally and dramatically hangs himself.

Monks' plot against Oliver is disclosed by Mr. Brownlow. Monks is Oliver's (17) _____ seeking all of the family (18) _____ for himself. Oliver's father's will states that he will leave money to Oliver on the condition that his (19)_____ is clean. Mr. Brownlow forces Monks to sign over Oliver's share to Oliver. Moreover, it is discovered that Oliver's dead mother and Rose were sisters. Finally, Oliver is (20) _____ by Mr. Brownlow, his father's old friend in the novel, but his grandfather in this version of film.

❸ General Questions
(1) What does the doctor mean when he says "the old story"?
(2) What kind of life does Oliver Twist have in the workhouse?
(3) Do you think Mrs. Mann (in the novel) is a humane woman? Why or why not?
(4) Why is five pounds offered to some master who will take Oliver off the workhouse?
(5) Why does Oliver fiercely attack Noah Claypole? What is Noah's social rank?
(6) What does Oliver decide to do after he is locked in the cellar as punishment? Why does he make such a decision?
(7) What happens to Oliver on his first mission with two other boys?
(8) Who comes to Oliver's defense after Fagin recaptures him? And why?
(9) Why are Fagin and Monks so interested in Oliver Twist?

(10) Why does Bill Sikes kill Nancy?

❹ Questions for essay or discussion

(1) There are two types of thievery in *Oliver Twist*. How are they different? What do they have in common?
(2) Discuss how the workhouse in *Oliver Twist* functions as a sign of moral hypocrisy, using evidence from the novel or the film.
(3) Why is Fagin unable to corrupt Oliver?
(4) Discuss the importance of Sikes's visions of Nancy's eyes after he kills her.
(5) Discuss whether the novel creates sympathy for the members of Fagin's gang at any point.

Unit 3

Charlotte Brontë and *Jane Eyre*

3.1 Charlotte Brontë: Life and Works

3.1.1 About the Author

Charlotte Brontë is an English novelist and poet. Her life story is almost as well-known as the history of her greatest heroine, Jane Eyre. For many readers, the two become inextricably entwined. In her highly-acclaimed *Jane Eyre*, Charlotte Brontë broke the traditional, nineteenth-century fictional stereotype of a woman as submissive, dependent, beautiful, but ignorant. Its heroine is a plain woman who possesses intelligence, self-confidence, a will of her own, and moral righteousness. For her originality in form and content, Charlotte Brontë is hailed as a precursor of feminist novelist and regarded as an author whose talents were highly superior to some of her female Victorian contemporaries.

Charlotte Brontë was born on March 31, 1816, in the village of Thornton in the West Riding of Yorkshire (now West Yorkshire), England. She was the third child of the Reverend Patrick Brontë and Maria Branwell Brontë. The couple had a total of six children: Maria (1813–1825), Elizabeth (1815–1825), Charlotte (1816–1855), Patrick Branwell (1817–1848, male), Emily

(1818–1848), and Anne (1820–1849). This English family, originally of Irish descent, produced three 19th-century novelists: Charlotte, Emily, and Anne.

Charlotte's mother died of cancer on September 15, 1821, leaving five daughters and a son to the care of their aunt, Elizabeth Branwell. The Reverend Patrick Brontë knew that the daughters of a poor clergyman had very few options open to them. Their marriage prospects were poor, careers in the professions were out of the question for women at the time, and working-class occupations could not be considered. All that was left was teaching. Whatever the girls did, they needed a reasonable education. Accordingly, in 1824 he sent his four eldest daughters to the Clergy Daughters School at Cowan Bridge; conditions at the school were dreadful, worsened by the administration's belief that physical discomfort was spiritually edifying. When fever broke out at the school, the two eldest Brontë sisters Maria and Elizabeth contracted tuberculousis and died in 1825 like Helen Burns in *Jane Eyre*. More than twenty years later, Charlotte's experiences at the school would form the basis of several characters, incidents, and settings in *Jane Eyre*.

The surviving children pursued their education at home from 1825 to 1830; they read widely, wrote stories, and created their own literary community in the Reverend Brontë's parsonage. In January 1831 Charlotte was sent to Miss Wooler's school at Roe Head. Charlotte's appearance coupled with her Irish accent and uneven education set her apart from the other girls who were more demure and well-dressed. But after just six months she easily became top of the class and won the medal for achievement. In 1832 she declined an offer to become a teacher at the school, and chose to return home to instruct her sisters over whom she had educational advantages. In 1839 Charlotte took her first job as a governess; she also received and turned down proposals of marriage from two clergymen. In 1842 she went with Emily to study languages at the Pensionnat run by M. Constantin Héger, and his wife in Brussels; they were called back at the end of the year by their aunt's death and in 1843 Charlotte, whose thirst for wider experience was much greater than her sister's, returned alone for a further year. She evidently formed a passionate attachment to Mr. Héger, who failed to respond to the letters she wrote to him after her return to Haworth. In 1846 the three sisters published a joint volume of their poems, using the pseudonyms Currer, Ellis, and Acton Bell. The collection, produced at their own expense, sold only two copies. It was Charlotte who again urged publication of the novels which each of them had by then finished. Her own work, *The Professor*, which drew heavily on her experiences in Brussels, was rejected and did not appear until its posthumous publication in 1857. But the encouragement Charlotte received from the publishing house of Smith, Elder and Co. emboldened her to complete and submit *Jane Eyre*, which was published just three months later in October 1847, two months before Emily's *Wuthering Heights* and Anne's *Agnes Grey*.

In the midst of their literary success, tragedies struck the Brontë family. Branwell, who had become a hopeless alcoholic, died of tuberculosis in 1848, followed in December of that year by Emily. Anne died of the same disease the following year, leaving Charlotte the sole survivor among the original six Brontë children. Charlotte later wrote two novels: *Shirley* (1849), and *Villette* (1853), founded on her memories of Brussels. In June 1854 she overcame her father's entrenched opposition and married her father's curate Arthur Bell Nichols; the couple lived together with Mr. Brontë at the parsonage. Charlotte died the following March, apparently from complications during pregnancy.

In her lifetime, Charlotte was the most admired of the Brontë sisters, although she came in for some criticism (which deeply wounded her) on the grounds of alleged "grossness" and emotionalism, considered particularly unbecoming in a clergyman's daughter. More widespread, however, was praise for her depth of feeling and her courageous realism and her works continue to hold high popular and critical esteem.

3.1.2 Charlotte Brontë's Novels

Jane Eyre (1847) 《简爱》
Shirley (1849) 《雪莉》
Villette (1853) 《维莱特》
The Professor (1857) 《教师》

3.2 Jane Eyre

3.2.1 About the Novel

Jane Eyre is considered Charlotte Brontë's masterpiece and one of the most memorable novels in nineteenth-century literature. When it was published in October 1847, *Jane Eyre* attracted much attention and became an almost instant commercial success. So high was the demand for the book that the publisher issued a second edition within three months, followed by a third edition in April 1848.

Jane Eyre is subtitled *An Autobiography* and is narrated in the first person. The book is divided into thirty-eight chapters. Chapters 1 through 10 cover Jane's childhood and schooling. These chapters are set at Gateshead Hall and at Lowood Institution. The main conflicts and incidents include Jane's rebellion against Mrs. Reed and her friendship with Helen Burns. Chapters 11 through 27 tell of Jane's life as a governess at Thornfield Hall, where she falls in love with Edward Rochester. The dramatic action in this part centers on Jane's growing love for Mr. Rochester (and vice versa), Jane's fear that Rochester will marry Blanche Ingram, and a series of strange incidents that occur at Thornfield. Chapters 28 through the end of the novel center on Jane's life after she has fled Thornfield. Dramatic highlights in this part of the novel include Jane's attempt to find shelter, her uneasy relationship with the Reverend St. John Rivers, and her ultimate return to Mr. Rochester. Many readers and critics have found this to be the weakest, most contrived part of the book. However, the events of this part serve to test Jane's devotion to Rochester. When she returns to marry him at the end of the book, both characters (and their circumstances) have evolved and matured from what they were at the time of their planned wedding in the second part.

3.2.2 Characters

1) At Gateshead and Lowood
- **Jane Eyre** The protagonist and narrator of *Jane Eyre*.
- **Mrs. Reed** Jane's uncle Mr. Reed's wife.
- **Bessie Lee** The nurse at Gateshead Hall, she helps take care of the Reed children and young Jane Eyre.
- **John Reed** Jane's bullying cousin, brother to Eliza and Georgiana.
- **Georgiana Reed** The prettier of the two Reed girls, she ends up marrying a wealthy man.
- **Eliza Reed** Described by Jane as headstrong and selfish, Eliza later becomes a nun in France.
- **Mr. Brocklehurst** The "treasurer and manager" of Lowood Institution.
- **Helen Burns** Jane's best friend at Lowood Institution, four years older than Jane.
- **Miss Temple** The beautiful, kindly superintendent of Lowood, she serves as one of the novel's surrogate maternal figures for Jane, but she is not present in this version of film.
- **Miss Scatcherd** A nasty teacher at Lowood who is cruel to Helen in the novel.

2) At Thornfield
- **Edward Rochester** A wealthy landowner, he is the master of Thornfield Hall.
- **Mrs. Fairfax** The elderly housekeeper at Thornfield Hall.
- **Adèle Varens** The French-speaking ward of Mr. Rochester that Jane tutors.
- **Bertha Mason** Rochester's insane wife.
- **Grace Poole** A mysterious servant at Thornfield Hall.
- **Richard Mason** The brother of Bertha Mason from West Indies.
- **Blanche Ingram** A young woman, the daughter of a local aristocrat who tries to woo Rochester and nearly succeeds in marrying him for his money.
- **Mr. Briggs** The attorney of Jane's uncle, he helps Mr. Mason prevent Jane's wedding to Rochester and ultimately informs her of her inheritance.

3) At Moor House
- **St. John Rivers** The evangelist who takes Jane in at Moor House, brother to Diana and Mary and, it turns out, cousin to Jane. In this version of film,

there is no St. John Rivers, but Doctor Rivers.

- **Diana Rivers & Mary Rivers** The sisters of St. John Rivers; When Jane arrives at Moor House, hungry and penniless, seeking shelter after she has fled Thornfield Hall, Diana and Mary help restore her to health. Skilled, talented, and well-read, the Rivers sisters develop a close friendship with Jane. Like her, they are both governesses. They are not present in this version of film.

3.2.3 Selected Readings from the Novel

3.2.3.1 Important Quotations

(1) ... you are good to those who are good to you. It is all I ever desire to be. If people were always kind and obedient to those who are cruel and unjust, the wicked people would have it all their own way: they would never feel afraid, and so they would never alter, but would grow worse and worse. When we are struck at without a reason, we should strike back again very hard; I am sure we should–so hard as to teach the person who struck us never to do it again. (Chapter 6, Jane Eyre)

(2) It is not violence that best overcomes hate - nor vengeance that most certainly heals injury... Life appears to me too short to be spent in nursing animosity, or registering wrongs. (Chapter 6, Helen Burns)

(3) If all the world hated you, and believed you wicked, while your own conscience approved you, and absolved you from guilt, you would not be without friends. (Chapter 8, Helen Burns)

(4) a memory without blot or contamination must be an exquisite treasure,–an inexhaustible source of pure refreshment: (Chapter 14, Edward Rochester)

(5) Dread remorse when you are tempted to err, Miss Eyre: remorse is the poison of life. (Chapter 14, Edward Rochester)

(6) The eagerness of a listener quickens the tongue of a narrator. (Chapter 19, Jane Eyre)

(7) I am no bird; and no net ensnares me: I am a free human being with an independent will; which I now exert to leave you. (Chapter 23, Jane Eyre)

(8) Equality of position and fortune is often advisable in such cases;...I wished

to put you on your guard.... Gentlemen in his station are not accustomed to marry their governesses. (**Chapter 24, Mrs. Fairfax**)

(9) Laws and principles are not for the times when there is no temptation: they are for such moments as this, when body and soul rise in mutiny against their rigour; stringent are they; inviolate they shall be. (**Chapter 27, Jane Eyre**)

(10) Reader, I married him. (**Chapter 38, Jane Eyre**)

3.2.3.2 Excerpts Related to Some Scenes in the Film

✣ Excerpt 1 (from Chapter 4)

Orphaned at an early age, ten-year-old Jane Eyre leads a lonely life at Gateshead Hall. John Reed bullies and torments her behind his mother's back and Mrs. Reed belittles Jane and punishes her for what she regards as Jane's rebellious nature while overlooking the faults of her own children. On one occasion when John strikes her, Jane tries to defend herself. As a result, Jane is punished by being locked in the frightening "Red Room." Then Mrs. Reed arranges for Jane to be sent away to Lowood Institution. Now Mr. Brocklehurst comes to Mrs. Reed's home to examine Jane before admitting her to Lowood.

"Her size is small: what is her age?"

"Ten years."

"So much?" was the doubtful answer; and he prolonged his scrutiny for some minutes. Presently he addressed me:–

"Your name, little girl?"

"Jane Eyre, sir." In uttering these words, I looked up: he seemed to me a tall gentleman; but then I was very little; his features were large, and they and all the lines of his frame were equally harsh and prim.

"Well, Jane Eyre, and are you a good child?"

Impossible to reply to this in the affirmative: my little world held a contrary opinion: I was silent. Mrs Reed answered for me by an expressive shake of the head, adding soon, 'Perhaps the less said on that subject the better, Mr Brocklehurst."

"Sorry indeed to hear it! she and I must have some talk;" and bending from the perpendicular, he installed his person in the armchair opposite Mrs Reed's. "Come here," he said.

I stepped across the rug; he placed me square and straight before him. What a face he had, now that it was almost on a level with mine! what a great nose! and what a mouth! and what large prominent teeth!

"No sight so sad as that of a naughty child," he began, "especially a naughty little girl. Do you know where the wicked go after death?"

"They go to hell," was my ready and orthodox answer.

"And what is hell? Can you tell me that?"

"A pit full of fire."

"And should you like to fall into that pit, and to be burning there for ever?"

"No, sir."

"What must you do to avoid it?"

I deliberated a moment; my answer, when it did come, was objectionable: "I must keep in good health, and not die."

"How can you keep in good health? Children younger than you die daily. I buried a little child of five years old only a day or two since,–a good little child, whose soul is now in heaven. It is to be feared the same could not be said of you, were you to be called hence."

Not being in a condition to remove his doubt, I only cast my eyes down on the two large feet planted on the rug, and sighed; wishing myself far enough away.

Unit 3
Charlotte Brontë and *Jane Eyre*

Excerpt 2 (from Chapter 13)

In the novel Jane remains as a pupil at Lowood for six years, and then becomes a teacher for two more. When her beloved Miss Temple leaves to get married, Jane decides to advertise for a job as governess. Mrs. Fairfax replies to her advertisement, so Jane comes to Thornfield. After much waiting, Jane finally meets her employer, Edward Rochester, a brooding, detached man who seems to have a dark past.

"You have been resident in my house three months?"

"Yes, sir."

"And you came from–?"

"From Lowood school in–shire."

"Ah! a charitable concern.–How long were you there?"

"Eight years."

"Eight years! you must be tenacious of life. I thought half the time in such a place would have done up any constitution! No wonder you have rather the look of another world. I marvelled where you had got that sort of face. When you came on me in Hay Lane last night, I thought unaccountably of fairy tales, and had half a mind to demand whether you had bewitched my horse: I am not sure yet. Who are your parents?"

"I have none."

"Nor ever had, I suppose: do you remember them?"

"No."

"I thought not. And so you were waiting for your people when you sat on that stile?"

"For whom, sir?"

"For the men in green: it was a proper moonlight evening for them. Did I break through one of your rings, that you spread that damned ice on the causeway?"

I shook my head."The men in green all forsook England a hundred years ago," said I, speaking as seriously as he had done. "And not even in Hay Lane or the fields about it could you find a trace of them. I don't think either summer or harvest, or winter moon, will ever shine on their revels more."

Mrs Fairfax had dropped her knitting, and with raised eyebrows, seemed wondering what sort of talk this was.

"Well," resumed Mr Rochester, "if you disown parents, you must have some sort of kinsfolk: uncles and aunts?"

"No; none that I ever saw."

"And your home?"

"I have none."

"Where do your brothers and sisters live?"

"I have no brothers or sisters."

"Who recommended you to come here?"

"I advertised, and Mrs Fairfax answered my advertisement."

* * * * * * *

And now, what did you learn at Lowood? Can you play?"

"A little."

"Of course: that is the established answer. Go into the library–I mean, if you please. –(Excuse my tone of command; I am used to say, "Do this," and it is done: I cannot alter my customary habits for one new inmate.) –Go, then, into the library; take a candle with you; leave the door open; sit down to the piano, and play a tune."

I departed, obeying his directions.

"Enough!" he called out in a few minutes. "You play a *little*, I see; like any other English school-girl: perhaps rather better than some, but not well."

I closed the piano and returned.

* * * * * * *

"You said Mr Rochester was not strikingly peculiar, Mrs Fairfax," I observed, when I rejoined her in her room, after putting Adèle to bed.

"Well, is he?"

"I think so: he is very changeful and abrupt."

"True: no doubt he may appear so to a stranger, but I am so accustomed to his manner, I never think of it; and then, if he has peculiarities of temper, allowance should be made."

"Why?"

"Partly because it is his nature–and we can none of us help our nature; and partly, he has painful thoughts, no doubt, to harass him, and make his spirits unequal."

"What about?"

"Family troubles, for one thing."

"But he has no family."

"Not now, but he has had–or, at least, relatives. He lost his elder brother a few years since."

"His *elder* brother?"

"Yes. The present Mr Rochester has not been very long in possession of the property: only about nine years."

"Nine years is a tolerable time. Was he so very fond of his brother as to be still inconsolable for his loss?"

"Why, no–perhaps not. I believe there were some misunderstandings between them. Mr Rowland Rochester was not quite just to Mr Edward; and perhaps he prejudiced his father against him. The old gentleman was fond of money, and anxious to keep the family estate together. He did not like to diminish the property by division, and yet he was anxious that Mr Edward should have wealth, too, to keep up the consequence of the name; and, soon after he was of age, some steps were taken that were not quite fair, and made a great deal of mischief. Old Mr Rochester and Mr Rowland combined to bring Mr Edward into what he considered a painful position, for the sake of making his fortune: what the precise nature of that position was I never clearly knew, but his spirit could not brook what he had to suffer in it. He is not very forgiving: he broke with his family, and now for many years he has led an unsettled kind of life. I don't think he has ever been resident at Thornfield for a fortnight together, since the death of his brother without a will, left him master of the estate: and, indeed, no wonder he shuns the old place."

"Why should he shun it?"

"Perhaps he thinks it gloomy."

The answer was evasive–I should have liked something clearer; but Mrs Fairfax either could not, or would not, give me more explicit information of the origin and nature of Mr Rochester's trials. She averred they were a mystery to herself, and that what she knew was chiefly from conjecture. It was evident, indeed, that she wished me to drop the subject; which I did accordingly.

> ### ✥ Excerpt 3 (from Chapter 14)
> *Several days later Jane is again invited by Rochester. In their long conversation Rochester, being both older and the master, assumes the dominant role, but Jane's courage, good sense and independence save her from submitting tamely to his will or opinion. Clearly, Rochester is favorably impressed by her intelligence and personality.*

"Is Miss Eyre there?" now demanded the master, half rising from his seat to look round to the door, near which I still stood.

"Ah! well; come forward: be seated here." He drew a chair near his own. "I am not fond of the prattle of children,' he continued; 'for, old bachelor as I am, I have no pleasant associations connected with their lisp. It would be intolerable to me to pass a whole evening *tête-à-tête* with a brat. Don't draw that chair farther off, Miss Eyre; sit down exactly where I placed it–if you please, that is."

* * * * * * *

"Miss Eyre, draw your chair still a little farther forward: you are yet too far back; I cannot see you without disturbing my position in this comfortable chair, which I have no mind to do."

I did as I was bid; though I would much rather have remained somewhat in the shade: but Mr Rochester had such a direct way of giving orders, it seemed a matter of course to obey him promptly.

* * * * * * *

"You examine me, Miss Eyre," said he: "do you think me handsome?"

I should, if I had deliberated, have replied to this question by something conventionally vague and polite; but the answer somehow slipped from my tongue before I was aware: –"No, sir."

"Ah! By my word! there is something singular about you," said he: "you have the air of a little nonnette; quaint, quiet, grave, and simple, as you sit with your hands before you, and your eyes generally bent on the carpet (except, by-the-by, when they are directed piercingly to my face; as just now, for instance); and when one asks you a question, or makes a remark to which you are obliged to reply, you rap out a round rejoinder, which, if not blunt, is at least brusque. What do you mean by it?"

"Sir, I was too plain: I beg your pardon. I ought to have replied that it

Unit 3

Charlotte Brontë and *Jane Eyre*

was not easy to give an impromptu answer to a question about appearances; that tastes mostly differ; and that beauty is of little consequence, or something of that sort."

"You ought to have replied no such thing. Beauty of little consequence, indeed! And so, under pretence of softening the previous outrage, of stroking and soothing me into placidity, you stick a sly penknife under my ear! Go on: what fault do you find with me, pray? I suppose I have all my limbs and all my features like any other man?"

"Mr Rochester, allow me to disown my first answer: I intended no pointed repartee: it was only a blunder."

"Just so: I think so: and you shall be answerable for it. Criticize me: does my forehead not please you?"

He lifted up the sable waves of hair which lay horizontally over his brow, and showed a solid enough mass of intellectual organs; but an abrupt deficiency where the suave sign of benevolence should have risen.

"Now, ma'am, am I a fool?"

"Far from it, sir. You would, perhaps, think me rude if I inquired in return whether you are a philanthropist?"

"There again! Another stick of the penknife, when she pretended to pat my head: and that is because I said I did not like the society of children and old women (low be it spoken!). No, young lady, I am not a general philanthropist; but I bear a conscience;" and he pointed to the prominences which are said to indicate that faculty–and which, fortunately for him, were sufficiently conspicuous; giving, indeed, a marked breadth to the upper part of his head: 'and, besides, I once had a kind of rude tenderness of heart. When I was as old as you, I was a feeling fellow enough; partial to the unfledged, unfostered, and unlucky; but fortune has knocked me about since: she has even kneaded me with her knuckles, and now I flatter myself I am hard and tough as an India–rubber ball; pervious, though, through a chink or two still, and with one sentient point in the middle of the lump. Yes: does that leave hope for me?"

"Hope of what, sir?"

"Of my final re-transformation from Indian-rubber back to flesh?"

"Decidedly he has had too much wine," I thought; and I did not know what answer to make to his queer question: how could I tell whether he was capable of being re-transformed?

"You looked very much puzzled, Miss Eyre; and though you are not pretty any more than I am handsome, yet a puzzled air becomes you; besides, it is convenient, for it keeps those searching eyes of yours away from my physiognomy, and busies them with the worsted flowers of the rug; so puzzle on. Young lady, I am disposed to be gregarious and communicative to-night."

With this announcement he rose from his chair, and stood, leaning his arm on the marble mantel-piece: in that attitude his shape was seen plainly as well as his face; his unusual breadth of chest, disproportionate almost to his length of limb. I am sure most people would have thought him an ugly man; yet there was so much unconscious pride in his port; so much case in his demeanour; such a look of complete indifference to his own external appearance; so haughty a reliance on the power of other qualities, intrinsic or adventitious, to atone for the lack of mere personal attractiveness, that, in looking at him, one inevitably shared the indifference, and, even in a blind, imperfect sense, put faith in the confidence.

"I am disposed to be gregarious and communicative to-night," he repeated; 'and that is why I sent for you: the fire and the chandelier were not sufficient company for me; nor would Pilot have been, for none of these can talk. Adèle is a degree better, but still far below the mark; Mrs Fairfax ditto; you, I am persuaded, can suit me if you will: you puzzled me the first evening I invited you down here. I have almost forgotten you since: other ideas have driven yours from my head; but tonight I am resolved to be at ease; to dismiss what importunes, and recall what pleases. It would please me now to draw you out: to learn more of you–therefore speak."

Instead of speaking, I smiled: and not a very complacent or submissive smile either.

"Speak," he urged.

"What about, sir?"

"Whatever you like. I leave both the choice of subject and the manner of treating it, entirely to yourself."

Accordingly I sat and said nothing: "If he expects me to talk for the mere sake of talking and showing off, he will find he has addressed himself to the wrong person,' I thought.

"You are dumb, Miss Eyre."

Unit 3
Charlotte Brontë and *Jane Eyre*

I was dumb still. He bent his head a little towards me and with a single hasty glance seemed to dive into my eyes.

"Stubborn?" he said, "and annoyed. Ah, it is consistent. I put my request in an absurd, almost insolent form. Miss Eyre, I beg your pardon. The fact is, once for all, I don't wish to treat you like an inferior: that is (correcting himself), I claim only such superiority as must result from twenty years" difference in age and a century's advance in experience. This is legitimate, et j'y tiens, as Adèle would say; and it is by virtue of this superiority and this alone that I desire you to have the goodness to talk to me a little now, and divert my thoughts, which are galled with dwelling on one point: cankering as a rusty nail."

He had deigned an explanation; almost an apology: I did not feel insensible to his condescension, and would not seem so.

"I am willing to amuse you, if I can, sir: quite willing; but I cannot introduce a topic, because how do I know what will interest you? Ask me questions, and I will do my best to answer them."

"Then, in the first place, do you agree with me that I have a right to be a little masterful, abrupt; perhaps exacting, sometimes, on the grounds I stated; namely, that I am old enough to be your father, and that I have battled through a varied experience with many men of many nations, and roamed over half the globe, while you have lived quietly with one set of people in one house?"

"Do as you please, sir."

"That is no answer; or rather it is a very irritating, because a very evasive one–reply clearly."

"I don't think, sir, you have a right to command me, merely because you are older than I, or because you have seen more of the world than I have–your claim to superiority depends on the use you have made of your time and experience."

"Humph! Promptly spoken. But I won't allow that, seeing that it would never suit my case; as I have made an indifferent, not to say a bad use of both advantages. Leaving superiority out of the question then, you must still agree to receive my orders now and then, without being piqued or hurt by the tone of command–will you?"

I smiled: I thought to myself Mr Rochester *is* peculiar–he seems to forget that he pays me 30*l.* per annum for receiving his orders.

"The smile is very well," said he, catching instantly the passing expression; "but speak too."

"I was thinking, sir, that very few masters would trouble themselves to inquire whether or not their paid subordinates were piqued and hurt by their orders."

"Paid subordinates! What, you are my paid subordinate, are you? Oh yes, I had forgotten the salary! Well then, on that mercenary ground, will you agree to let me hector a little?"

"No, sir, not on that ground: but, on the ground that you did forget it, and that you care whether or not a dependent is comfortable in his dependency, I agree heartily."

"And will you consent to dispense with a great many conventional forms and phrases, without thinking that the omission arises from insolence?"

"I am sure, sir, I should never mistake informality for insolence: one I rather like, the other nothing free-born would submit to, even for a salary."

"Humbug! Most things free-born will submit to anything for a salary; therefore, keep to yourself, and don't venture on generalities of which you are intensely ignorant.

Excerpt 4 (from Chapter 15)

One night Jane Eyre is alarmed by a suspicious noise at her bedroom door. She hurries out of her room and finds Mr. Rochester's room on fire. Immediately she rushes to wake him and puts out the fire. When Jane attempts to rouse the household, Rochester cautions her to tell no one about the details of the night's incident. He thanks her for her courage and presence of mind in saving his life. In the stress of emotion he seems to be about to express a strong feeling for Jane.

"Wake! wake!" I cried–I shook him, but he only murmured and turned: the smoke had stupefied him. Not a moment could be lost: the very sheets were kindling. I rushed to his basin and ewer; fortunately, one was wide and the other deep, and both were filled with water. I heaved them up, deluged the bed and its occupant, flew back to my own room, brought my own water-jug, baptized the couch afresh, and, by God's aid, succeeded in extinguishing the flames which were devouring it.

* * * * * * * *

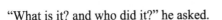

"What is it? and who did it?" he asked.

I briefly related to him what had transpired: the strange laugh I had heard in the gallery: the step ascending to the third story; the smoke–the smell of fire which had conducted me to his room; in what state I had found matters there, and how I had deluged him with all the water I could lay hands on.

He listened very gravely; his face, as I went on, expressed more concern than astonishment: he did not immediately speak when I had concluded.

"Shall I call Mrs Fairfax?" I asked.

"Mrs Fairfax? No:–what the deuce would you call her for? What can she do? Let her sleep unmolested."

"Then I will fetch Leah, and wake John and his wife."

"Not at all: just be still. You have a shawl on? If you are not warm enough, you may take my cloak yonder; wrap it about you, and sit down in the arm-chair: there,–I will put it on. Now place your feet on the stool, to keep them out of the wet. I am going to leave you a few minutes. I shall take the candle. Remain where you are till I return; be as still as a mouse. I must pay a visit to the second story. Don't move, remember, or call any one."

He went: I watched the light withdraw. He passed up the gallery very softly, unclosed the staircase door with as little noise as possible, shut it after him, and the last ray vanished. I was left in total darkness. I listened for some noise, but heard nothing. A very long time elapsed. I grew weary: it was cold, in spite of the cloak; and then I did not see the use of staying, as I was not to rouse the house. I was on the point of risking Mr Rochester's displeasure by disobeying his orders, when the light once more gleamed dimly on the gallery-wall, and I heard his unshod feet tread the matting. "I hope it is he," thought I, 'and not something worse."

He re-entered, pale and very gloomy. "I have found it all out," said he, setting his candle down on the wash-stand; "it is as I thought."

"How, sir?"

He made no reply, but stood with his arms folded, looking on the ground. At the end of a few minutes, he inquired in rather a peculiar tone:–

"I forget whether you said you saw anything when you opened your chamber door."

"No, sir, only the candlestick on the ground."

"But you heard an odd laugh? You have heard that laugh before, I should think, or something like it?"

"Yes, sir: there is a woman who sews here, called Grace Poole,–she laughs in that way. She is a singular person."

"Just so. Grace Poole–you have guessed it. She is, as you say, singular, –very. Well, I shall reflect on the subject. Meantime, I am glad that you are the only person, besides myself, acquainted with the precise details of to-night's incident. You are no talking fool: say nothing about it. I will account for this state of affairs (pointing to the bed): and now return to your own room. I shall do very well on the sofa in the library for the rest of the night. It is near four: - in two hours the servants will be up."

"Good-night, then, sir," said I, departing.

He seemed surprised–very inconsistently so, as he had just told me to go.

"What!' he exclaimed, "are you quitting me already: and in that way?"

"You said I might go, sir."

"But not without taking leave; not without a word or two of acknowledgment and good will: not, in short, in that brief, dry fashion. Why, you have saved my life!–snatched me from a horrible and excruciating death! –and you walk past me as if we were mutual strangers! At least shake hands."

He held out his hand; I gave him mine: he took it first in one, them in both his own.

"You have saved my life: I have a pleasure in owing you so immense a debt. I cannot say more. Nothing else that has being would have been tolerable to me in the character of creditor for such an obligation: but you; it is different; –I feel your benefits no burden, Jane."

He paused; gazed at me: words almost visible trembled on his lips, –but his voice was checked.

"Good-night again, sir. There is no debt, benefit, burden, obligation, in the case."

"I knew," he continued, "you would do me good in some way, at some time;–I saw it in your eyes when I first beheld you: their expression and smile did not"–(again he stopped)–did not (he proceeded hastily) strike delight to my very inmost heart so for nothing. People talk of natural sympathies: I have heard of good genii: –there are grains of truth in the wildest fable. My cherished preserver, good-night!"

Strange energy was in his voice; strange fire in his look.

Unit 3

Charlotte Brontë and *Jane Eyre*

⚔ Excerpt 5 (from Chapter 26*)*

Edward Rochester tries to rush the wedding ceremony along, but as the vows are being said, it is interrupted by a solicitor named Briggs, and Mr. Mason, who reveal that Rochester is already married and his wife is still living in Thornfield Hall.

The service began. The explanation of the intent of matrimony was gone through; and then the clergyman came a step further forward, and, bending slightly towards Mr Rochester, went on.

"I require and charge you both (as ye will answer at the dreadful day of judgment, when the secrets of all hearts shall be disclosed), that if either of you know any impediment why ye may not lawfully be joined together in matrimony, ye do now confess it; for be ye well assured that so many as are coupled together otherwise than God's Word doth allow, are not joined together by God, neither is their matrimony lawful."

He paused, as the custom is. When is the pause after that sentence ever broken by reply? Not, perhaps, once in a hundred years. And the clergyman, who had not lifted his eyes from his book, and had held his breath but for a moment, was proceeding: his hand was already stretched towards Mr Rochester, as his lips unclosed to ask, "Wilt thou have this woman for thy wedded wife?"–when a distinct and near voice said:–

"The marriage cannot go on: I declare the existence of an impediment."

The clergyman looked up at the speaker, and stood mute; the clerk did the same; Mr Rochester moved slightly, as if an earthquake had rolled under his feet: taking a firmer footing, and not turning his head or eyes, he said, "Proceed."

Profound silence fell when he had uttered that word, with deep but low intonation. Presently Mr Wood said:–

"I cannot proceed without some investigation into what has been asserted, and evidence of its truth or falsehood."

"The ceremony is quite broken off," subjoined the voice behind us. "I am in a condition to prove my allegation: an insuperable impediment to this marriage exists."

Mr Rochester heard, but heeded not: he stood stubborn and rigid: making no movement, but to possess himself of my hand. What a hot and strong grasp he had!–and how like quarried marble was his pale, firm, massive front at this moment! How his eye shone, still, watchful, and yet wild beneath!

Mr Wood seemed at a loss. "What is the nature of the impediment?" he asked. "Perhaps it may be got over–explained away?"

"Hardly," was the answer: "I have called it insuperable, and I speak advisedly."

The speaker came forward, and leaned on the rails. He continued, uttering each word distinctly, calmly, steadily, but not loudly.

"It simply consists in the existence of a previous marriage: Mr Rochester has a wife now living."

My nerves vibrated to those low-spoken words as they had never vibrated to thunder–my blood felt their subtle violence as it had never felt frost or fire: but I was collected, and in no danger of swooning. I looked at Mr Rochester: I made him look at me. His whole face was colourless rock: his eye was both spark and flint. He disavowed nothing: he seemed as if he would defy all things. Without speaking, without smiling; without seeming to recognize in me a human being, he only twined my waist with his arm, and riveted me to his side.

"Who are you?' he asked of the intruder.

"My name is Briggs–a solicitor of –street, London."

"And you would thrust on me a wife?"

"I would remind you of your lady's existence, sir; which the law recognizes, if you do not."

"Favour me with an account of her–with her name, her parentage, her place of abode."

"Certainly." Mr Briggs calmly took a paper from his pocket, and read out in a sort of official, nasal voice:–

"I affirm and can prove that on the 20th of October, AD–, (a date of fifteen years back), Edward Fairfax Rochester of Thornfield Hall, in the county of–, and of Ferndean Manor, in–shire, England, was married to my sister, Bertha Antoinetta Mason, daughter of Jonas Mason, merchant, and of Antoinetta his wife, a Creole–at–church, Spanish-Town, Jamaica. The record of the marriage will be found in the register of that church–a copy of it is now in my possession. Signed, Richard Mason."

"That–if a genuine document–may prove I have been married, but it does not prove that the woman mentioned therein as my wife is still living."

"She was living three months ago," returned the lawyer.

Unit 3

Charlotte Brontë and *Jane Eyre*

"How do you know?"

"I have a witness to the fact; whose testimony even you, sir, will scarcely controvert."

"Produce him–or go to hell."

"I will produce him first–he is on the spot: Mr Mason, have the goodness to step forward."

Mr Rochester, on hearing the name, set his teeth; he experienced, too, a sort of strong convulsive quiver; near to him as I was, I felt the spasmodic movement of fury or despair run through his frame.

3.2.3.3 Passages for Understanding the Film

(1) I am glad you are no relation of mine: I will never call you aunt again as long as I live. I will never come to see you when I am grown up; and if any one asks me how I liked you, and how you treated me, I will say the very thought of you makes me sick, and that you treated me with miserable cruelty... You think I have no feelings, and that I can do without one bit of love or kindness; but I cannot live so: and you have no pity. I shall remember how you thrust me back–roughly and violently thrust me back–into the red-room, and locked me up there, to my dying day; though I was in agony; though I cried out, while suffocating with distress, "Have mercy! Have mercy, aunt Reed!" And that punishment you made me suffer because your wicked boy struck me–knocked me down for nothing. I will tell anybody who asks me questions, this exact tale. People think you a good woman, but you are bad; hard-hearted. You are deceitful!

Ere I had finished this reply, my soul began to expand, to exult, with the strangest sense of freedom, of triumph, I ever felt. It seemed as if an invisible bond had burst, and that I had struggled out into unhoped-for liberty. Not without cause was this sentiment: Mrs Reed looked frightened; her work had slipped from her knee; she was lifting up her hands, rocking herself to and fro, and even twisting her face as if she would cry. **(Chapter 4 ,Jane Eyre)**

(2) "Helen, why do you stay with a girl whom everybody believes to be a liar?"

"Everybody, Jane? Why, there are only eighty people who have heard you called so and the world contains hundreds of millions."

"But what have I to do with millions? The eighty I know despise me."

"Jane, you are mistaken: probably not one in the school either despises or dislikes you: many, I am sure, pity you much."

"How can they pity me after what Mr Brocklehurst has said?"

"Mr Brocklehurst is not a god; nor is he even a great and admired man: he is little liked here; he never took steps to make himself liked. Had he treated you as an especial favourite, you would have found enemies, declared or covert, all around you; as it is, the greater number would offer you sympathy if they dared. Teachers and pupils may look coldly on you for a day or two, but friendly feelings are concealed in their hearts; and if you persevere in doing well, these feelings will ere long appear so much the more evidently for their temporary suppression. **(Chapter 8)**

(3) He (Rochester) then said that she (Adèle) was the daughter of a French opera-dancer, Céline Varens; towards whom he had once cherished what he called a "grande passion". This passion Céline had professed to return with even superior ardour. He thought himself her idol, ugly as he was: he believed, as he said, that she preferred his 'taille d'athlète' to the elegance of the Apollo Belvidere.

"And, Miss Eyre, so much was I flattered by this preference of the Gallic sylph for her British gnome, that I installed her in an hotel; gave her a complete establishment of servants, a carriage, cashmeres, diamonds, dentelles, &c. In short, I began the process of ruining myself in the received style; like any other spoonie. I had not, it seems, the originality to chalk out a new road to shame and destruction, but trode the old track with stupid exactness not to deviate an inch from the beaten centre. I had–as I deserved to have–the fate of all other spoonies. Happening to call one evening, when Céline did not expect me, ... It was moonlight, and gas-light besides, and very still and serene. The balcony was furnished with a chair or two; I sat down, and took out a cigar... when in an elegant close carriage drawn by a beautiful pair of English horses, and distinctly seen in the brilliant city-night, I recognized the "voiture" I had given Céline. She was returning: of course my heart thumped with impatience against the iron rails I leant upon. The carriage stopped, as I had expected, at the hotel door; my flame (that is the very word for an opera inamorata) alighted: ... Bending over the balcony I was about to murmur "Mon ange."–in a tone, of course, which should be

Unit 3
Charlotte Brontë and *Jane Eyre*

audible to the ear of love alone–when a figure jumped from the carriage after her, cloaked also; ...

When I saw my charmer thus come in accompanied by a cavalier, I seemed to hear a hiss, and the green snake of jealousy, rising on undulating coils from the moonlit balcony, glided within my waistcoat and ate its way in two minutes to my heart's core...

"I remained in the balcony. "They will come to her boudoir no doubt," thought I: "let me prepare an ambush." So putting my hand in through the open window, I drew the curtain over it, leaving only an opening through which I could take observations; then I closed the casement, all but a chink just wide enough to furnish an outlet to lovers' whispered vows: then I stole back to my chair; and as I resumed it the pair came in...

"They began to talk; their conversation eased me completely: frivolous, mercenary, heartless, and senseless, it was rather calculated to weary than enrage a listener. A card of mine lay on the table; this being perceived brought my name under discussion. Neither of them possessed energy or wit to belabour me soundly; but they insulted me as coarsely as they could in their little way: especially Céline; who even waxed rather brilliant on my personal defects–deformities she termed them. Now it had been her custom to launch out into fervent admiration of what she called my "beauté mâle": wherein she differed diametrically from you, who told me point blank at the second interview, that you did not think me handsome...

Opening the window, I walked in upon them; liberated Céline from my protection; gave her notice to vacate her hotel; offered her a purse for immediate exigencies; disregarded screams, hysterics, prayers, protestations, convulsions; made an appointment with the vicomte for a meeting at the bois de Boulogne. Next morning I had the pleasure of encountering him; left a bullet in one of his poor, etiolated arms, feeble as the wing of a chicken in the pip, and then thought I had done with the whole crew. But unluckily the Varens, six months before, had given me this *filette* Adèle; who, she affirmed, was my daughter; and perhaps she may be; though I see no proofs of such grim paternity written in her countenance: Pilot is more like me than she. Some years after I had broken with the mother, she abandoned her child and ran away to Italy with a musician, or singer. I acknowledged no natural claim on Adèle's part to be supported by me; nor do I now acknowledge any, for I am not her father, but hearing that she was quite destitute, I e'en took the poor thing out of the slime and mud of Paris, and transplanted it here, to grow up clean in the wholesome soil of an English country garden. (Chapter 15)

(4) The ease of his manner freed me from painful restraint: the friendly frankness, as correct as cordial, with which he treated me, drew me to him. I felt at times, as if he were my relation, rather than my master: yet he was imperious sometimes still; but I did not mind that; I saw it was his way. So happy, so gratified did I become with this new interest added to life, that I ceased to pine after kindred: my thin crescent-destiny seemed to enlarge; the blanks of existence were filled up; my bodily health improved; I gathered flesh and strength.

And was Mr Rochester now ugly in my eyes? No, reader: gratitude, and many associations, all pleasurable and genial, made his face the object I best liked to see; his presence in a room was more cheering than the brightest fire. Yet I had not forgotten his faults: indeed, I could not, for he brought them frequently before me. He was proud, sardonic, harsh to inferiority of every description: in my secret soul I knew that his great kindness to me was balanced by unjust severity to many others. He was moody, too; unaccountably so: I more than once, when sent for to read to him, found him sitting in his library alone, with his head bent on his folded arms; and, when he looked up, a morose, almost a malignant scowl, blackened his features. But I believed that his moodiness, his harshness, and his former faults of morality (I say *former*, for now he seemed corrected of them) had their source in some cruel cross of fate. I believed he was naturally a man of better tendencies, higher principles, and purer tastes than such as circumstances had developed, education instilled, or destiny encouraged. I thought there were excellent materials in him; though for the present they hung together somewhat spoiled and tangled. I cannot deny that I grieved for his grief, whatever that was, and would have given much to assuage it. (Chapter 15)

(5) To women who please me only by their faces, I am the very devil when I find out they have neither souls nor hearts—when they open to me a perspective of flatness, triviality, and perhaps imbecility, coarseness, and ill-temper: but to the clear eye and eloquent tongue, to the soul made of fire, and the character that bends but does not break–at once supple and stable,

tractable and consistent–I am ever tender and true. **(Chapter 24, Edward Rochester)**

(6) "I only want an easy mind, sir; not crushed by crowded obligations. Do you remember what you said of Céline Varens? –of the diamonds, the cashmeres you gave her? I will not be your English Céline Varens. I shall continue to act as Adèle's governess: by that I shall earn my board and lodging, and thirty pounds a year besides. I'll furnish my own wardrobe out of that money, and you shall give me nothing but–"

"Well, but what?"

"Your regard: and if I give you mine in return, that debt will be quit."

"Well, for cool native impudence and pure innate pride, you haven't your equal," said he. **(Chapter 24, Jane Eyre and Edward Rochester)**

(7) We all withdrew. Mr Rochester stayed a moment behind us, to give some further order to Grace Poole. The solicitor addressed me as he descended the stair.

"You, madam," said he, "are cleared from all blame: your uncle will be glad to hear it–if, indeed, he should be still living–when Mr Mason returns to Madeira."

"My uncle! What of him? Do you know him?"

"Mr Mason does: Mr Eyre has been the Funchal correspondent of his house for some years. When your uncle received your letter intimating the contemplated union between yourself and Mr Rochester, Mr Mason, who was staying at Madeira to recruit his health, on his way back to Jamaica, happened to be with him. Mr Eyre mentioned the intelligence; for he knew that my client here was acquainted with a gentleman of the name of Rochester. Mr Mason, astonished and distressed as you may suppose, revealed the real state of matters. Your uncle, I am sorry to say, is now on a sickbed; from which, considering the nature of his disease–decline–and the stage it has reached, it is unlikely he will ever rise. He could not then hasten to England himself, to extricate you from the snare into which you had fallen, but he implored Mr Mason to lose no time in taking steps to prevent the false marriage. He referred him to me for assistance. I used all despatch, and am thankful I was not too late: as you, doubtless, must be also. Were I not morally certain that your uncle will be dead ere you reach Madeira, I would advise you to accompany Mr Mason back: but as it is, I think you had better remain in England till you can hear further, either from or of Mr Eyre. (Chapter 26)

(8) "And did you ever hear that my father was an avaricious, grasping man?"

"I have understood something to that effect."

"Well, Jane, being so, it was his resolution to keep the property together; he could not bear the idea of dividing his estate and leaving me a fair portion: all, he resolved, should go to my brother, Rowland. Yet as little could he endure that a son of his should be a poor man. I must be provided for by a wealthy marriage. He sought me a partner betimes. Mr Mason, a West India planter and merchant, was his old acquaintance. He was certain his possessions were real and vast: he made inquiries. Mr Mason, he found, had a son and daughter; and he learned from him that he could and would give the latter a fortune of thirty thousand pounds: that sufficed. When I left college, I was sent out to Jamaica, to espouse a bride already courted for me. My father said nothing about her money; but he told me Miss Mason was the boast of Spanish Town for her beauty: and this was no lie. I found her a fine woman, in the style of Blanche Ingram; tall, dark, and majestic. Her family wished to secure me, because I was of a good race; and so did she…

"My bride's mother I had never seen: I understood she was dead. The honey-moon over, I learned my mistake; she was only mad, and shut up in a lunatic asylum. There was a younger brother, too; a complete dumb idiot. The elder one, whom you have seen (and whom I cannot hate, whilst I abhor all his kindred, because he has some grains of affection in his feeble mind; shown in the continued interest he takes in his wretched sister, and also in a dog-like attachment he once bore me), will probably be in the same state one day. My father, and my brother Rowland, knew all this; but they thought only of the thirty thousand pounds, and joined in the plot against me. (Chapter 27)

3.2.3.4 Chapter Reading

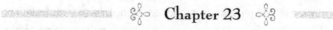

Chapter 23

A splendid Midsummer shone over England: skies so pure, suns so radiant as were then seen in long succession, seldom favour, even singly, our

Unit 3
Charlotte Brontë and *Jane Eyre*

wave-girt（波浪环绕）land. It was as if a band of Italian days had come from the South, like a flock of glorious passenger birds, and lighted to rest them on the cliffs of Albion. The hay was all got in; the fields round Thornfield were green and shorn（修剪）; the roads white and baked; the trees were in their dark prime: hedge and wood, full-leaved and deeply tinted（着色）, contrasted well with the sunny hue of the cleared meadows between.

  On Midsummer-eve, Adèle, weary with gathering wild strawberries in Hay Lane half the day, had gone to bed with the sun. I watched her drop asleep, and when I left her I sought the garden.

  It was now the sweetest hour of the twenty-four: –"Day its fervid（炽热的）fires had wasted," and dew fell cool on panting（喘息的）plain and scorched summit. Where the sun had gone down in simple state–pure of the pomp（壮丽）of clouds–spread a solemn purple, burning with the light of red jewel and furnace flame at one point, on one hill-peak, and extending high and wide, soft and still softer, over half heaven. The east had its own charm or fine, deep blue, and its own modest gem（宝石）, a rising and solitary star: soon it would boast the moon; but she was yet beneath the horizon.

  I walked a while on the pavement; but a subtle, well-known scent–that of a cigar–stole from some window; I saw the library casement（门式窗）open a handbreadth; I knew I might be watched thence; so I went apart into the orchard. No nook（隐蔽处）in the grounds more sheltered and more Eden-like; it was full of trees, it bloomed with flowers: a very high wall shut it out from the court, on one side; on the other, a beech（山毛榉）avenue screened（掩蔽）it from the lawn. At the bottom was a sunk fence; its sole separation from lonely fields: a winding walk, bordered with laurels（月桂树）and terminating in a giant horse-chestnut（七叶树）, circled at the base by a seat, led down to the fence. Here one could wander unseen. While such honey-dew fell, such silence reigned（占优势）, such gloaming（日暮）gathered, I felt as if I could haunt such shade for ever: but in threading the flower and fruit-parterres（花圃）at the upper part of the enclosure, enticed（诱使）there by the light the now-rising moon casts on this more open quarter, my step is stayed - not by sound, not by sight, but once more by a warning fragrance.

  Sweet-briar（多花蔷薇）and southernwood（青蒿）, jasmine（茉莉）, pink（石竹花）, and rose（玫瑰花）have long been yielding their evening sacrifice of incense: this new scent is neither of shrub nor flower; it is–I know it

107

well–it is Mr Rochester's cigar. I look round and I listen. I see trees laden with ripening fruit. I hear a nightingale warbling（啭鸣）in a wood half a mile off; no moving form is visible, no coming step audible（听得见的）; but that perfume increases: I must flee. I make for the wicket leading to the shrubbery, and I see Mr Rochester entering. I step aside into the ivy（常春藤）recess（幽深处）; he will not stay long: he will soon return whence he came, and if I sit still he will never see me.

But no–eventide（黄昏）is as pleasant to him as to me, and this antique（古老的）garden as attractive; and he strolls（漫步）on, now lifting the gooseberry-tree（醋栗树）branches to look at the fruit, large as plums（李子）, with which they are laden; now taking a ripe cherry（樱桃）from the wall; now stooping towards a knot of flowers, either to inhale（吸入）their fragrance（芳香）or to admire the dew-beads on their petals（花瓣）. A great moth（蛾）goes humming（嗡嗡叫）by me; it alights（飞落）on a plant at Mr Rochester's foot: he sees it, and bends to examine it.

"Now, he has his back towards me," thought I, "and he is occupied too; perhaps, if I walk softly, I can slip away unnoticed."

I trode on an edging of turf（草皮）that the crackle（劈啪声）of the pebbly gravel（卵石砂砾）might not betray me: he was standing among the beds at a yard or two distant from where I had to pass; the moth apparently engaged him. 'I shall get by very well,' I meditated（暗自思忖）. As I crossed his shadow, thrown long over the garden by the moon, not yet risen high, he said quietly, without turning:–

"Jane, come and look at this fellow."

I had made no noise: he had not eyes behind–could his shadow feel? I started at first, and then I approached him.

"Look at his wings," said he, 'he reminds me rather of a West Indian insect; one does not often see so large and gay a night-rover（夜游神）in England: there! he is flown."

The moth roamed away. I was sheepishly（羞怯地）retreating also: but Mr Rochester followed me, and when we reached the wicket, he said:–

"Turn back: on so lovely a night it is a shame to sit in the house; and surely no one can wish to go to bed while sunset is thus at meeting with moonrise（月出时分）."

It is one of my faults, that though my tongue is sometimes prompt（敏捷

Unit 3

Charlotte Brontë and *Jane Eyre*

的) enough at an answer, there are times when it sadly fails me in framing (编造) an excuse; and always the lapse (失误) occurs at some crisis, when a facile (易得到的) word or plausible pretext (看似有理的托辞) is specially wanted to get me out of painful embarrassment. I did not like to walk at this hour alone with Mr Rochester in the shadowy orchard; but I could not find a reason to allege (宣称) for leaving him. I followed with lagging (缓缓而行的) step, and thoughts busily bent on discovering a means of extrication (脱身); but he himself looked so composed and so grave also, I became ashamed of feeling any confusion: the evil–if evil existent or prospective there was–seemed to lie with me only; his mind was unconscious and quiet.

"Jane," he recommenced, as we entered the laurel-walk, and slowly strayed down in the direction of the sunk fence and the horse-chestnut, 'Thornfield is a pleasant place in summer, is it not?"

"Yes, sir."

"You must have become in some degree attached to the house,–you, who have an eye for natural beauties, and a good deal of the organ of Adhesiveness?"

"I am attached to it, indeed."

"And though I don't comprehend how it is, I perceive you have acquired a degree of regard for that foolish little child Adèle, too; and even for simple dame Fairfax?"

"Yes, sir; in different ways, I have an affection for both."

"And would be sorry to part with them?"

"Yes."

"Pity!" he said, and sighed and paused. 'It is always the way of events in this life,' he continued presently: 'no sooner have you got settled in a pleasant resting-place, than a voice calls out to you to rise and move on, for the hour of repose is expired (期满)."

"Must I move on, sir?" I asked. "Must I leave Thornfield?"

"I believe you must, Jane. I am sorry, Janet, but I believe indeed you must."

This was a blow: but I did not let it prostrate me.

"Well, sir, I shall be ready when the order to march comes."

"It is come now–I must give it to-night."

"Then you are going to be married, sir?"

"Ex-act-ly–pre-cise-ly: with your usual acuteness, you have hit the nail straight on the head."

"Soon, sir?"

"Very soon, my–that is, Miss Eyre: and you'll remember, Jane, the first time I, or Rumour, plainly intimated to you that it was my intention to put my old bachelor's neck into the sacred noose（套索）, to enter into the holy estate of matrimony（结婚）–to take Miss Ingram to my bosom, in short (she's an extensive armful: but that's not to the point–one can't have too much of such a very excellent thing as my beautiful Blanche): well, as I was saying - listen to me, Jane! You're not turning your head to look after more moths, are you? That was only a lady-clock（瓢虫）, child, "flying away home". I wish to remind you that it was you who first said to me, with that discretion（谨慎）I respect in you—with that foresight（远见）, prudence（审慎）, and humility which befit your responsible and dependent position–that in case I married Miss Ingram, both you and little Adèle had better trot（快步走）forthwith（立刻）. I pass over（忽略）the sort of slur（诋毁）conveyed in this suggestion on the character of my beloved; indeed, when you are far away, Janet, I'll try to forget it: I shall notice only its wisdom; which is such that I have made it my law of action. Adèle must go to school; and you, Miss Eyre, must get a new situation."

"Yes, sir, I will advertise immediately: and meantime, I suppose–" I was going to say, "I suppose I may stay here, till I find another shelter to betake myself to:" but I stopped, feeling it would not do to risk a long sentence, for my voice was not quite under command.

"In about a month I hope to be a bride-groom," continued Mr Rochester; "and in the interim（过渡时期）, I shall myself look out for employment and an asylum for you."

"Thank you, sir; I am sorry to give–"

"Oh, no need to apologise! I consider that when a dependent does her duty as well as you have done yours, she has a sort of claim upon her employer for any little assistance he can conveniently render her; indeed I have already, through my future mother-in-law, heard of a place that I think will suit: it is to undertake the education of the five daughters of Mrs Dionysius O'Gall of Bitternutt Lodge, Connaught, Ireland. You'll like Ireland, I think: they're such warm-hearted people there, they say."

Unit 3
Charlotte Brontë and *Jane Eyre*

"It is a long way off, sir."

"No matter–a girl of your sense will not object to the voyage or the distance."

"Not the voyage, but the distance: and then the sea is a barrier–"

"From what, Jane?'

"From England and from Thornfield: and–"

"Well?"

"From *you*, sir."

I said this almost involuntarily (不知不觉地); and, with as little sanction of free will, my tears gushed out. I did not cry so as to be heard, however; I avoided sobbing. The thought of Mrs O'Gall and Bitternutt Lodge struck cold to my heart; and colder the thought of all the brine (盐水) and foam, destined, as it seemed, to rush between me and the master at whose side I now walked; and coldest the remembrance of the wider ocean–wealth, caste (社会地位), custom intervened (介入) between me and what I naturally and inevitably loved.

"It is a long way," I again said.

"It is, to be sure; and when you get to Bitternutt Lodge, Connaught, Ireland, I shall never see you again, Jane: that's morally certain. I never go over to Ireland, not having myself much of a fancy for the country. We have been good friends, Jane; have we not?"

"Yes, sir."

"And when friends are on the eve of separation, they like to spend the little time that remains to them close to each other. Come–we'll talk over the voyage and the parting quietly, half an hour or so, while the stars enter into their shining life up in heaven yonder: here is the chestnut tree; here is the bench at its old roots. Come, we will sit there in peace to–night, though we should never more be destined to sit there together." He seated me and himself.

"It is a long way to Ireland, Janet, and I am sorry to send my little friend on such weary travels: but if I can't do better, how is it to be helped? Are you anything akin (类似的) to me, do you think, Jane?"

I could risk no sort of answer by this time: my heart was full.

"Because," he said, "I sometimes have a queer feeling with regard to you –especially when you are near me, as now: it is as if I had a string somewhere under my left ribs, tightly and inextricably （解不开地）knotted to a similar string situated in the corresponding quarter of your little frame. And if that boisterous （狂暴的）channel, and two hundred miles or so of land come broad between us, I am afraid that cord of communion will be snapt （突然折断）; and then I've a nervous notion I should take to bleeding inwardly. As for you, –you'd forget me."

"That I *never* should, sir: you know"–impossible to proceed.

"Jane, do you hear that nightingale singing in the wood? Listen!"

In listening, I sobbed convulsively （痉挛性地）; for I could repress what I endured no longer; I was obliged to yield, and I was shaken from head to foot with acute distress. When I did speak, it was only to express an impetuous （冲动的）wish that I had never been born, or never come to Thornfield.

"Because you are sorry to leave it?"

The vehemence （强烈）of emotion, stirred by grief and love within me, was claiming mastery, and struggling for full sway; and asserting a right to predominate: to overcome, to live, rise, and reign at last; yes, –and to speak.

"I grieve （伤心）to leave Thornfield: I love Thornfield: –I love it, because I have lived in it a full and delightful life, –momentarily at least. I have not been trampled （践踏）on. I have not been petrified （僵化）. I have not been buried with inferior minds, and excluded （排斥）from every glimpse of communion with what is bright and energetic, and high. I have talked, face to face, with what I reverence （敬重）; with what I delight in, –with an original, a vigorous, an expanded mind. I have known you, Mr Rochester; and it strikes me with terror and anguish （极度痛苦）to feel I absolutely must be torn from you for ever. I see the necessity of departure; and it is like looking on the necessity of death."

"Where do you see the necessity?" he asked, suddenly.

"Where? You, sir, have placed it before me."

"In what shape?"

"In the shape of Miss Ingram; a noble and beautiful woman,–your bride."

"My bride! What bride? I have no bride!"

"But you will have."

"Yes; –I will! I will!" He set his teeth.

"Then I must go: –you have said it yourself."

Unit 3

Charlotte Brontë and *Jane Eyre*

"No: you must stay! I swear it–and the oath shall be kept."

"I tell you I must go!" I <u>retorted</u>, roused to something like passion. 'Do you think I can stay to become nothing to you? Do you think I am an <u>automaton</u>（机器人）? –a machine without feelings? and can bear to have my <u>morsel</u>（一口）of bread snatched from my lips, and my drop of living water dashed from my cup? Do you think, because I am poor, <u>obscure</u>（身份卑微的）, plain, and little, I am soulless and heartless? You think wrong! –I have as much soul as you,–and full as much heart! And if God had gifted me with some beauty, and much wealth, I should have made it as hard for you to leave me, as it is now for me to leave you. I am not talking to you now through the medium of custom, <u>conventionalities</u>（常规）, nor even of mortal flesh: –it is my spirit that addresses your spirit; just as if both had passed through the grave, and we stood at God's feet, equal, –as we are!"

"As we are!" repeated Mr Rochester –"so," he added, enclosing me in his arms, gathering me to his breast, pressing his lips on my lips: "so, Jane!"

"Yes, so, sir," I <u>rejoined</u>（回答）: "and yet not so; for you are a married man - or as good as a married man, and wed to one inferior to you–to one with whom you have no sympathy–whom I do not believe you truly love; for I have seen and heard you sneer at her. I would scorn such a union: therefore I am better than you–let me go!"

"Where, Jane? To Ireland?"

"Yes–to Ireland. I have spoken my mind, and can go anywhere now."

"Jane, be still; don't struggle so, like a wild, frantic bird that is rending its own plumage in its desperation."

"I am no bird; and no net <u>ensnares</u>（捕获，诱捕）me: I am a free human being with an independent will; which I now exert to leave you."

Another effort set me at liberty, and I stood erect before him.

"And your will shall decide your destiny," he said: "I offer you my hand, my heart, and a share of all my possessions."

"You play a <u>farce</u>（闹剧）, which I merely laugh at."

"I ask you to pass through life at my side–to be my second self, and best earthly companion."

"For that fate you have already made your choice, and must <u>abide by</u>（遵守）it."

"Jane, be still a few moments; you are over-excited: I will be still too."

A waft（一阵）of wind came sweeping down the laurel-walk, and trembled through the boughs of the chestnut: it wandered away–away–to an indefinite distance–it died. The nightingale's song was then the only voice of the hour: in listening to it, I again wept. Mr Rochester sat quiet, looking at me gently and seriously. Some time passed before he spoke; he at last said: –

"Come to my side, Jane, and let us explain and understand one another."

"I will never again come to your side: I am torn away now, and cannot return."

"But, Jane, I summon you as my wife: it is you only I intend to marry."

I was silent: I thought he mocked me.

"Come, Jane–come hither（过来）."

"Your bride stands between us."

He rose, and with a stride reached me.

"My bride is here,' he said, again drawing me to him, "because my equal is here, and my likeness. Jane, will you marry me?"

Still I did not answer, and still I writhed（挣扎）myself from his grasp: for I was still incredulous（不相信的）.

"Do you doubt me, Jane?"

"Entirely."

"You have no faith in me?"

"Not a whit（一点点）."

"Am I a liar in your eyes?" he asked passionately. "Little sceptic（怀疑论者）, you *shall* be convinced. What love have I for Miss Ingram? None: and that you know. What love has she for me? None: as I have taken pains to prove: I caused a rumour to reach her that my fortune was not a third of what was supposed, and after that I presented myself to see the result; it was coldness both from her and her mother. I would not–I could not–marry Miss Ingram. You–you strange–you almost unearthly（非尘世的）thing!–I love as my own flesh. You–poor and obscure, and small and plain as you are–I entreat to accept me as a husband."

"What, me!" I ejaculated（突然说出）: beginning in his earnestness–and especially in his incivility–to credit his sincerity: "me who have not a friend in the world but you–if you are my friend: not a shilling but what you have given me?"

"You, Jane, I must have you for my own–entirely my own. Will you be mine? Say yes, quickly."

"Mr Rochester, let me look at your face: turn to the moonlight."

"Why?"

"Because I want to read your countenance; turn!"

"There: you will find it scarcely more legible (清楚的) than a crumpled (摺皱的), scratched (乱涂的) page. Read on: only make haste, for I suffer."

His face was very much agitated and very much flushed, and there were strong workings in the features, and strange gleams in the eyes

"Oh, Jane, you torture (折磨) me!" he exclaimed. "With that searching and yet faithful and generous look, you torture me!"

"How can I do that? If you are true, and your offer real, my only feelings to you must be gratitude and devotion–they cannot torture."

"Gratitude!" he ejaculated; and added wildly– "Jane accept me quickly. Say, Edward–give me my name–Edward–I will marry you."

"Are you in earnest? –Do you truly love me? –Do you sincerely wish me to be your wife?"

"I do; and if an oath is necessary to satisfy you, I swear it."

"Then, sir, I will marry you."

"Edward –my little wife!"

"Dear Edward!"

"Come to me–come to me entirely now," said he: and added, in his deepest tone, speaking in my ear as his cheek was laid on mine, "Make my happiness–I will make yours."

"God pardon me!" he subjoined (又说道) ere long; 'and man meddle (干涉) not with me: I have her, and will hold her."

"There is no one to meddle, sir. I have no kindred to interfere."

"No–that is the best of it," he said. And if I had loved him less I should have thought his accent and look of exultation (狂喜) savage: but, sitting by him, roused from the nightmare of parting–called to the paradise of union– I thought only of the bliss given me to drink in so abundant a flow. Again and again he said, "Are you happy, Jane?" And again and again I answered, "Yes." After which he murmured, "It will atone–it will atone. Have I not found her friendless, and cold, and comfortless? Will I not guard, and cherish, and solace (安慰) her? Is there not love in my heart, and constancy in my resolves? It will expiate (赎罪) at God's tribunal (法庭). I know my Maker (造物主)

sanctions what I do. For the world's judgment–I wash my hands thereof. For man's opinion–I defy (藐视) it."

But what had befallen (发生，降临) the night? The moon was not yet set, and we were all in shadow: I could scarcely see my master's face, near as I was. And what ailed (折磨) the chestnut tree? it writhed and groaned; while wind roared in the laurel walk, and came sweeping over us.

"We must go in," said Mr Rochester: "the weather changes. I could have sat with thee till morning, Jane."

"And so," thought I, "could I with you." I should have said so, perhaps, but a livid (铅色的), vivid spark leapt out of a cloud at which I was looking, and there was a crack, a crash, and a close rattling peal (隆隆声) ; and I thought only of hiding my dazzled eyes against Mr Rochester's shoulder.

The rain rushed down. He hurried me up the walk, through the grounds, and into the house; but we were quite wet before we could pass the threshold. He was taking off my shawl (披肩) in the hall, and shaking the water out of my loosened hair, when Mrs Fairfax emerged from her room. I did not observe her at first, nor did Mr Rochester. The lamp was lit. The clock was on the stroke of twelve.

"Hasten to take off your wet things," said he; 'and before you go, good-night–good-night, my darling!"

He kissed me repeatedly. When I looked up, on leaving his arms, there stood the widow, pale, grave, and amazed. I only smiled at her, and ran upstairs. 'Explanation will do for another time,' thought I. Still, when I reached my chamber, I felt a pang at the idea she should even temporarily misconstrue what she had seen. But joy soon effaced every other feeling; and loud as the wind blew, near and deep as the thunder crashed, fierce and frequent as the lightning gleamed, cataract-like (大瀑布似的) as the rain fell during a storm of two hours' duration, I experienced no fear, and little awe (敬畏) . Mr Rochester came thrice (三次) to my door in the course of it, to ask if I was safe and tranquil: and that was comfort, that was strength for anything.

Before I left my bed in the morning, little Adèle came running in to tell me that the great horse-chestnut at the bottom of the orchard had been struck by lightning in the night, and half of it split (劈开) away.

Unit 3
Charlotte Brontë and *Jane Eyre*

Notes and Glossary for Chapter Reading

(1) Albion /'ælbiən/ *n.* a literary name for England or Great Britain 英格兰或不列颠的雅称

(2) Eden /'iːdən/ *n.* [Bible] the garden that was the first home of Adam and Eve [圣经] 伊甸园，乐园

(3) trode /trəud/ <古> tread 的过去式

(4) Adhesiveness /əd'hiːsivnis/ *n.* the ability to quickly attach to sth. or sb. 依恋

(5) prostrate /'prɔstreit/ *v.* to make (oneself) bow or kneel down in humility or adoration 使（自己）拜倒

(6) betake /bi'teik/ *vt.* to cause (oneself) to go or move 使（自己）去或离开

(7) asylum /ə'sailəm/ *n.* a place offering protection and safety; a shelter 庇护所

(8) communion /kə'mjuːnjən/ *n.* the sharing or exchange of deep thoughts, ideas, and feelings, esp. of a religious kind（思想、观点、感情等的）交流

(9) predominate /pri'dɔmineit/ *vt.* to control, govern, or rule by superior authority or power 支配，统治

(10) vigorous /'vigərəs/ *a.* strong, energetic, and active in mind or body; robust. 精力充沛的，有活力的

(11) retort /ri'tɔːt/ *vi.* to reply, especially to answer in a quick, caustic, or witty manner 回答，反驳

(12) atone /ə'təun/ *vt.* to make amends, as for a sin or fault 弥补，补偿，赎罪

(13) sanction /'sæŋkʃən/ *vt.* to give official authorization or approval to; to encourage or tolerate by indicating approval 批准，许可；鼓励，容忍

(14) misconstrue /ˌmiskən'struː/ *vt.* to mistake the meaning of; misinterpret 误解，曲解

(15) efface /i'feis/ *vt.* to rub or wide out 消除，抹去

3.2.4 Exercises

❶ Identify the following characters

(1) _____ hypocritically preaches Christian beliefs while providing poor living conditions for the students.

(2) _____ regularly "bullied and punished" Jane Eyre. He grew up to become a drunken gambler, and eventually commits

suicide to escape from his massive gambling debts.
(3) _____ favors her own spoiled children and harshly punishes Jane for her impudence, even locking her up in the "red-room." On her deathbed, she reveals that she hated Jane ever since her husband took her in as an orphan and loved Jane more than the Reed children.
(4) _____ is regarded by Jane Eyre as the most sympathetic figure in Gateshead Hall. She helps Jane prepare for her departure to Lowood Institution. Jane meets her again when Jane returns to Gateshead to visit the dying Mrs. Reed.
(5) _____ is a little girl and for whom Jane is hired to be a governess. She is described as a "lively child, who had been spoilt and indulged," but she becomes a good student who is "obedient and teachable."
(6) _____, upholding the extreme Christian doctrine of tolerance and forgiveness, submits to all the cruel punishments from her teacher at Lowood. She is at peace with the thought of going to heaven, and she dies of consumption.
(7) _____ is described as having "a dark face, with stern features and a heavy brow" and not considered handsome. He is haunted by his guilty knowledge and by a past of which he is ashamed.
(8) _____ offers Jane the position of governess at Thornfield. She is a widow, and is a distant relation of Mr. Rochester by marriage. Jane finds her "a placid-tempered, kind-natured woman, of competent education and average intelligence." She warns Jane against marrying Rochester.
(9) _____ is very tall but has a proud, haughty manner, a "mocking air," and a "satirical laugh." Her speech is affected, especially when she speaks to her snobbish mother. She hopes to marry Rochester to secure her position in society.
(10) _____ was formerly a beautiful Creole woman from a prominent West Indies family. After growing insane over the course of their union, Rochester imprisoned her in the attic at Thornfield under the watch of Grace Poole, but she occasionally

Unit 3
Charlotte Brontë and *Jane Eyre*

escapes and wreaks havoc. Her last outburst (setting fire to Thornfield) leads to her own death.

❷ **Plot Review**

Jane Eyre, a penniless (1) _____ has been left to the (2) _____ of Mrs. Reed, the widow of Jane's uncle Mr. Reed. Harsh and unsympathetic (3) _____ rouses her defiant spirit, and a passionate (4) _____ leads to her consignment to Lowood Institution, a (5) _____ school where appalling physical conditions are somewhat palliated by the friendship of the gentle, long-suffering (6) _____ and Maria Temple, the kindly superintendent.

An outbreak of typhus fever leads to public interest and an improvement in conditions. Helen dies of consumption, but not (7) _____ Jane has learned from her that self-control is the surest means of retaining self-respect in (8) _____ After six years as pupil and two years as teacher, Jane leaves Lowood to take up the position of (9) _____ at Thornfield Hall to Adéle. Soon she finds herself drawn to the strange owner Edward Rochester, while he, (10) _____ by her sharp wit, self-possession and independence, after various misunderstandings, asks her to become his (11) _____ She consents gladly, but their wedding is (12) _____ by the unexpected arrival of Richard Mason, who reveals that Rochester is already (13) _____ to his sister (14) _____ a raving lunatic, even then confined at (15) _____ Jane's strong sense of self-reliance and self-respect forces her, despite her yearning to (16) _____ her lover, to flee. In the novel after nearly perishing on the moors, Jane Eyre is taken in and cared for by the Reverend St. John Rivers and his sisters Mary and Diana. It emerges that they are her cousins, and that Jane has inherited money from her uncle, John Eyre. Jane makes the decision to divide the legacy equally among the four. Under pressure from the earnest appeals and strong personality of the dedicated John Rivers, she nearly consents to marry him and share his missionary vocation in India, but is prevented by a telepathic appeal from (17) _____ She returns to Thornfield Hall to find the building (18) _____ and Rochester (19) _____ and maimed from his attempt to save his wife from the flames. Jane Eyre marries

Edward Rochester. Their marriage is the meeting of true minds, a marriage without secrets or locked doors. In the last chapter we learn that Rochester's sight is partially (20) _____.

❸ General Questions

(1) What is Jane Eyre's status, and how is she treated at Gateshead Hall?

(2) What are the conditions at Lowood School? How does Mr. Brocklehurst humiliate Jane?

(3) Why does Jane Eyre decide to leave Lowood in the novel and in the film?

(4) How does Jane first meet Mr. Rochester? What is her first impression of him after the first talk?

(5) What do Jane and Mr. Rochester think about each other's appearance?

(6) Why is Jane so drawn to Mr. Rochester? How do Jane's feelings towards Rochester change and develop?

(7) How does Rochester try to keep Jane involved in the party? And why?

(8) What does Jane Eyre blurt out to Rochester in Chapter Reading? What prompts him to propose? How does Jane react at first?

(9) Why do Richard Mason and the lawyer appear at the marriage ceremony? How did Rochester come to marry Bertha? What secret was kept from Rochester about the Mason family?

(10) What is the solution Rochester offers to Jane? What hastens Jane's retreat from Thornfield Hall?

❹ Questions for essay or discussion

(1) How do the following two philosophies of life match the characters of Jane Eyre and Helen Burns?
   (a) "An eye for an eye and a tooth for a tooth."
   (b) "Turn the other cheek and do good to them that hate you."

(2) Describe Gateshead and Lowood, particularly as the two settings reflect Jane's developing personality and world view.

(3) Does Rochester ever actually intend to marry Blanche Ingram? If so, when does he change his mind? If not, why does he go to such lengths to make Jane believe he does?

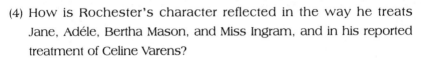

(4) How is Rochester's character reflected in the way he treats Jane, Adéle, Bertha Mason, and Miss Ingram, and in his reported treatment of Celine Varens?

(5) Do you feel sorry for Bertha Mason? Does Rochester treat her fairly? Why or why not?

Unit 4

Thomas Hardy and *Tess of the d'Urbervilles*

4.1 Thomas Hardy: Life and Works

4.1.1 About the Author

Thomas Hardy, the last important novelist of the Victorian age, is the first English novelist to write about the countryside and its inhabitants in a serious fashion. In his Wessex novels, he vividly and truthfully describes the tragic lives of the tenants in the last decade of the 19th century.

He was born on June 2, 1840 in a small thatched cottage near Dorchester, in that area of southwest England that he was to make the "Wessex" of his novels. He was the eldest of the four children of Thomas Hardy, a stonemason and a violinist, and Jemima, who enjoyed reading and relating folk tales and legends of the region. From his father Hardy gained a love of music; from his mother he learnt many of the country legends which coloured all his works.

Little Thomas was a sickly child; for the first few years his parents did not expect him to live and apparently he heard them say so. He was precocious, "being able to read almost before he could walk, and to tune the violin when of quite tender years." He attended local schools until the age

Unit 4
Thomas Hardy and *Tess of the d'Urbervilles*

of fifteen, when he was apprenticed to a Dorchester architect with whom he worked for six years. In 1861 he went to London to continue his studies and to practice as an architect. Hardy loved knowledge and during his spare time he read voraciously: language, literature, history, philosophy, and art. He won two prizes for essays on architectural subjects. And he became more and more interested in both fiction and poetry. After some early attempts at writing both short stories and poems, he decided to concentrate on fiction. His first novel was rejected by the publishers in 1868, but the encouraging advice from George Meredith, a poet whom Hardy admired, convinced the aspiring novelist to try again. The result was *Desperate Remedies*, published anonymously in 1871, followed the next year by his first real success (also published anonymously) *Under the Greenwood Tree*. The next great novel *Far from the Madding Crowd* was so popular that with the profits Hardy was able to give up architecture and marry Emma Gifford. Other popular novels followed in quick succession: *The Return of the Native*, *The Trumpet Major*, *The Mayor of Casterbridge*, *The Woodlanders*, *Tess of the D'Urbervilles*, and *Jude the Obscure*. In addition to these larger works, Hardy published three collections of short stories and five smaller novels, all moderately successful. Despite the praise Hardy's fiction received, many critics also found his works to be too shocking, especially *Tess of the d'Urbervilles* and *Jude the Obscure*. The outcry against *Jude the Obscure* was so great that Hardy decided to stop writing novels and return to his first great love, poetry. Straddling the Victorian and modern periods, Hardy published all his novels in the nineteenth century, all but the first of his poetry collections, *Wessex and Other Verses* (1898), in the twentieth. His remarkable epic-drama of the Napoleonic Wars *The Dynasts* came out in three parts between 1903 and 1908; after this he wrote mostly lyric poetry. On January 11, 1928 Hardy died and was buried with impressive ceremonies in the Poet's Corner in Westminster Abbey.

Hardy's novels show the forces of nature outside and inside individuals combining to shape human destiny. Men and women in his fiction are not masters of their fates; they are at the mercy of the indifferent forces that manipulate their behavior and their relations with others, but they can achieve dignity through endurance, heroism, or simple strength of character. Most of Hardy's novels are tragic, exploring the bitter ironies of life with an almost malevolent staging of coincidence to emphasize the disparity between human desire and ambition on the one hand and what fate has in store for the characters on the other. But fate is not a wholly external force. Men and women are driven by the demands of their own nature as much as by anything outside them.

The continuing popularity of Hardy's novels owes much to their richly varied yet always accessible style and their combination of romantic plots with convincingly presented characters. Equally important, particularly in terms of their suitability to film and television adaptation, is their nostalgic evocation of a vanished rural world through the creation of highly particularized regional settings. Hardy's verse has been slower to win full acceptance, but his unique status as a major 20th-century poet as well as a major 19th-century novelist is now universally recognized.

4.1.2 Thomas Hardy's Major Novels

Desperate Remedies (1871)	《计出无奈》
Under the Greenwood Tree (1872)	《格林伍德的绿林荫下》
Far from the Madding Crowd (1874)	《远离尘嚣》
The Return of the Native (1878)	《还乡》
The Trumpet Major (1880)	《号兵长》
The Mayor of Casterbridge (1886)	《卡斯特桥市长》
The Woodlanders (1887)	《林地居民》
Tess of the d'Urbervilles (1891)	《德伯家的苔丝》
Jude the Obscure (1895)	《无名的裘德》

4.2 *Tess of the d'Urbervilles*

4.2.1 About the Novel

Tess of the d'Urbervilles is considered by many to be Hardy's finest work, but when it appeared in 1891, it created a violent sensation. Early

Unit 4
Thomas Hardy and *Tess of the d'Urbervilles*

critics attacked Hardy for the novel's subtitle, "A Pure Woman," arguing that Tess could not possibly be considered pure. The subject matter–a milkmaid who is seduced by one man, married and rejected by another, and who eventually murders the first one–was considered unfit for publications which young people might read. They also denounced his frank–for the time–depiction of sex, criticism of organized religion, and dark pessimism. Hardy was deeply wounded by some of the particularly personal attacks he received from reviewers of the book. In 1892, he wrote in one of his notebooks, "Well, if this sort of thing continues no more novel-writing for me. A man must be a fool to deliberately stand up to be shot at." But today, the novel is praised as a courageous call for righting many of the ills Hardy found in Victorian society and as a link between the late–Victorian literature of the end of the nineteenth century and that of modern era.

The novel is divided into seven phases, all but one of which have titles directly to do with the various stages of Tess's life. An innocent and exceptionally gifted peasant girl of decayed aristocratic stock is betrayed by two men. One is rich and sensuous, the seducer of her body and, for a while, of her emotions; by him she has a child which dies in infancy. The other is the intellectual, free-thinking son of a clergyman, whom she loves with her whole being, and who abandons her when he hears, on their wedding night, of her earlier violation. Subsequently the husband comes to understand his moral and intellectual arrogance and searches for the girl, only to find that the extreme poverty of her family has driven her back to the other man. So strong is the girl's love for her husband, and so powerful her disgust at what the other man has forced her to become, that she kills the other man. Husband and wife, united but on the run from the police, spend a few days of loving reconciliation together before the girl is arrested, tried, sentenced to death for murder, and executed. Hardy's closing summary reads: "'Justice' was done, and the President of the Immortals, in Aeschylean phrase, had ended his sport with Tess."

4.2.2 Characters

- **Parson Tringham**　This clergyman in Marlott tells John Durbeyfield that his family is descended from the noted d'Urberville family.

- **Tess Durbeyfield** The novel's protagonist. She is the eldest daughter of a rural working class family.
- **John Durbeyfield** Tess's father. He "was not very industrious, and he drank a little."
- **Joan Durbeyfield** Tess's mother.
- **Liza-Lu Durbeyfield** Tess's younger sister. Before Tess is caught, she asks Angel to marry Liza-Lu after she has died.
- **Abraham Durbeyfield** Tess's younger brother.
- **Alec d'Urberville** The son of the late Mr. Simon Stoke, who added "d'Urberville" to his name.
- **Mrs. Stoke-d'Urberville** Alec's blind mother.
- **Angel Clare** The son of Reverend James Clare and the youngest of three brothers.
- **Cuthbert Clare** Angel's eldest brother, an academician.
- **Felix Clare** Angel's elder brother, and Cuthbert's younger brother. A curate at a nearby town.
- **Car Darch** Described as "a dark virago," and nicknamed the Queen of Spades.
- **Nancy Darch** Nicknamed the Queen of Diamonds, the sister of Car.
- **Richard Crick** The dairyman and owner of Talbothays Dairy.
- **Izz Huett, Marian, Retty Priddle** The dairymaids at Talbothays with whom Tess stays.
- **Mrs. Brooks** The householder at The Herons, the boarding establishment at Sandbourne where Alec and Tess stay together. She discovers Alec after Tess stabs him in the heart.

4.2.3 Selected Readings from the Novel

4.2.3.1 Important Quotations

(1) Out of the frying pan into the fire! (Chapter X, Car's mother)
(2) Was once lost always lost really true of chastity? she would ask herself. (Chapter XV)

Unit 4

Thomas Hardy and *Tess of the d'Urbervilles*

(3) My life looks as if it had been wasted for want of chances! When I see what you know, what you have read, and seen, and thought, I feel what a nothing I am! **(Chapter XIX, Tess)**

(4) I shouldn't mind learning why—why the sun do shine on the just and the unjust alike... But that's what books will not tell me. **(Chapter XIX, Tess)**

(5) Well, it is true, in one sense. I do hate the aristocratic principle of blood before everything, and do think that as reasoners the only pedigrees we ought to respect are those spiritual ones of the wise and virtuous, without regard to corporal paternity. **(Chapter XXX, Angel)**

(6) Distinction does not consist in the facile use of a contemptible set of conventions, but in being numbered among those who are true, and honest, and just, and pure, and lovely, and of good report—as you are, my Tess. **(Chapter XXXI, Angel)**

(7) I admired spotlessness, even though I could lay no claim to it, and hated impurity, as I hope I do now. **(Chapter XXXIV, Angel)**

(8) I say in all earnestness that it is a shame for parents to bring up their girls in such dangerous ignorance of the gins and nets that the wicked may set for them, whether their motive be a good one or the result of simple indifference. **(Chapter XLVI, Alec)**

(9) Once victim, always victim—that's the law! **(Chapter XLVII, Tess)**

(10) So do flux and reflux—the rhythm of change—alternate and persist in everything under the sky. **(Chapter L)**

4.2.3.2 Excerpts Related to Some Scenes in the Film

⚜ Excerpt 1 (from Chapter 8)

Feeling responsible for the family's hard times after the horse was killed, Tess agrees to go to the wealthy Mrs. d'Urberville for help. Alec is attracted to Tess's good looks and soon arranges for her to tend fowls on the d'Urberville estate. Now he comes to fetch Tess, and on the ride back makes it clear that his actions are not motivated by charity.

Ever since the accident with her father's horse Tess Durbeyfield, courageous as she naturally was, had been exceedingly timid on wheels; the least irregularity of motion startled her. She began to get uneasy at a certain recklessness in her conductor's driving.

"You will go down slow, sir, I suppose?" she said with attempted unconcern.

D'Urberville looked round upon her, nipped his cigar with the tips of his large white centre-teeth, and allowed his lips to smile slowly of themselves.

"Why, Tess," he answered, after another whiff or two, "it isn't a brave bouncing girl like you who asks that? Why, I always go down at full gallop. There's nothing like it for raising your spirits."

* * * * * * *

"Don't touch my arm! We shall be thrown out if you do! Hold on round my waist!"

She grasped his waist, and so they reached the bottom.

"Safe, thank God, in spite of your fooling!" said she, her face on fire.

"Tess—fie! that's temper!" said d'Urberville.

"Tis truth."

"Well, you need not let go your hold of me so thanklessly the moment you feel yourself our of danger."

She had not considered what she had been doing; whether he were man or woman, stick or stone, in her involuntary hold on him. Recovering her reserve she sat without replying, and thus they reached the summit of another declivity.

"Now then, again!" said d'Urberville.

"No, no!" said Tess. "Show more sense, do, please."

"But when people find themselves on one of the highest points in the county, they must get down again," he retorted.

He loosened rein, and away they went a second time. D'Urberville

Unit 4
Thomas Hardy and *Tess of the d'Urbervilles*

turned his face to her as they rocked, and said, in playful raillery: "Now then, put your arms round my waist again, as you did before, my Beauty."

"Never!" said Tess independently, holding on as well as she could without touching him.

"Let me put one little kiss on those holmberry lips, Tess, or even on that warmed cheek, and I'll stop–on my honour, I will!"

Tess, surprised beyond measure, slid farther back still on her seat, at which he urged the horse anew, and rocked her the more.

"Will nothing else do?" she cried at length, in desperation, her large eyes staring at him like those of a wild animal. This dressing her up so prettily by her mother had apparently been to lamentable purpose.

"Nothing, dear Tess," he replied.

"Oh, I don't know–very well; I don't mind!" she panted miserably.

He drew rein, and as they slowed he was on the point of imprinting the desired salute, when, as if hardly yet aware of her own modesty, she dodged aside. His arms being occupied with the reins there was left him no power to prevent her manœuvre.

"Now, damn it–I'll break both our necks!" swore her capriciously passionate companion. 'So you can go from your word like that, you young witch, can you?"

"Very well," said Tess, "I'll not move since you be so determined! But I–thought you would be kind to me, and protect me, as my kinsman!"

"Kinsman be hanged! Now!"

"But I don't want anybody to kiss me, sir!" she implored, a big tear beginning to roll down her face, and the corners of her mouth trembling in her attempts not to cry. "And I wouldn't ha' come if I had known!"

He was inexorable, and she sat still, and d'Urberville gave her the kiss of mastery. No sooner had he done so than she flushed with shame, took out her handkerchief, and wiped the spot on her cheek that had been touched by his lips. His ardour was nettled at the sight, for the act on her part had been unconsciously done.

"You are mighty sensitive for a cottage girl!" said the young man.

Tess made no reply to this remark, of which, indeed, she did not quite comprehend the drift, unheeding the snub she had administered by her instinctive rub upon her cheek. She had, in fact, undone the kiss, as far as such a thing was physically possible. With a dim sense that he was vexed she looked steadily ahead as they trotted on near Melbury Down and Wingreen, till she saw, to her consternation, that there was yet another descent to be undergone.

"You shall be made sorry for that!" he resumed, his injured tone still remaining, as he flourished the whip anew. "Unless, that is, you agree willingly to let me do it again, and no handkerchief."

She sighed. "Very well, sir!" she said. "Oh–let me get my hat!"

At the moment of speaking her hat had blown off into the road, their present speed on the upland being by no means slow. D'Urberville pulled up, and said he would get it for her, but Tess was down on the other side.

She turned back and picked up the article.

"You look prettier with it off, upon my soul, if that's possible," he said, contemplating her over the back of the vehicle. "Now then, up again! What's the matter?"

The hat was in place and tied, but Tess had not stepped forward.

"No, sir," she said, revealing the red and ivory of her mouth as her eye lit in defiant triumph; "not again, if I know it!"

"What–you won't get up beside me?"

"No; I shall walk."

"Tis five or six miles yet to Trantridge."

"I don't care if "tis dozens. Besides, the cart is behind."

"You artful hussy! Now, tell me–didn't you make that hat blow off on purpose? I'll swear you did!"

Her strategic silence confirmed his suspicion.

Then d'Urberville cursed and swore at her, and called her everything he could think of for the trick.

❦ Excerpt 2 (from Chapter 12)

It is a Sunday morning in late October, about four months after Tess Durbeyfield's arrival at Trantridge, and some few weeks subsequent to the night ride in The Chase. Tess is going on the way home. Alec is driving to overtake her. Tess has no fear of him now, and in the cause of her confidence her sorrow lies.

"Why did you slip away by stealth like this?" said d'Urberville, with upbraiding breathlessness; "on a Sunday morning, too, when people were

Unit 4
Thomas Hardy and *Tess of the d'Urbervilles*

all in bed! I only discovered it by accident, and I have been driving like the deuce to overtake you. Just look at the mare. Why go off like this? You know that nobody wished to hinder your going. And how unnecessary it has been for you to toil along on foot, and encumber yourself with this heavy load! I have followed like a madman, simply to drive you the rest of the distance, if you won't come back."

"I shan't come back," said she.

"I thought you wouldn't–I said so! Well, then, put up your basket, and let me help you on."

She listlessly placed her basket and bundle within the dog-cart, and stepped up, and they sat side by side. She had no fear of him now, and in the cause of her confidence her sorrow lay.

D'Urberville mechanically lit a cigar, and the journey was continued with broken unemotional conversation on the commonplace objects by the wayside. He had quite forgotten his struggle to kiss her when, in the early summer, they had driven in the opposite direction along the same road. But she had not, and she sat now, like a puppet, replying to his remarks in monosyllables. After some miles they came in view of the clump of trees beyond which the village of Marlott stood. It was only then that her still face showed the least emotion, a tear or two beginning to trickle down.

"What are you crying for?' he coldly asked.

"I was only thinking that I was born over there," murmured Tess.

"Well–we must all be born somewhere."

"I wish I had never been born–there or anywhere else!"

"Pooh! Well, if you didn't wish to come to Trantridge why did you come?"

She did not reply.

"You didn't come for love of me, that I'll swear."

"Tis quite true. If I had gone for love o" you, if I had ever sincerely loved you, if I loved you still, I should not so loathe and hate myself for my weakness as I do now! ... My eyes were dazed by you for a little, and that was all."

He shrugged his shoulders. She resumed–

"I didn't understand your meaning till it was too late."

"That's what every woman says."

"How can you dare to use such words!" she cried, turning impetuously upon him, her eyes flashing as the latent spirit (of which he was to see more some day) awoke in her. "My God! I could knock you out of the gig! Did it never strike your mind that what every woman says some women may feel?"

"Very well," he said, laughing; "I am sorry to wound you. I did wrong–I admit it." He dropped into some little bitterness as he continued: "Only you needn"t be so everlastingly flinging it in my face. I am ready to pay to the uttermost farthing. You know you need not work in the fields or the dairies again. You know you may clothe yourself with the best, instead of in the bald plain way you have lately affected, as if you couldn't get a ribbon more than you earn."

Her lip lifted slightly, though there was little scorn, as a rule, in her large and impulsive nature.

"I have said I will not take anything more from you, and I will not–I cannot! I *should* be your creature to go on doing that, and I won't!"

"One would think you were a princess from your manner, in addition to a true and original d'Urberville–ha! ha! Well, Tess, dear, I can say no more. I suppose I am a bad fellow–a damn bad fellow. I was born bad, and I have lived bad, and I shall die bad in all probability. But, upon my lost soul, I won't be bad towards you again, Tess. And if certain circumstances should arise–you understand–in which you are in the least need, the least difficulty, send me one line, and you shall have by return whatever you require. I may not be at Trantridge–I am going to London for a time–I can't stand the old woman. But all letters will be forwarded."

She said that she did not wish him to drive her further, and they stopped just under the clump of trees. D'Urberville alighted, and lifted her down bodily in his arms, afterwards placing her articles on the ground beside her. She bowed to him slightly, her eye just lingering in his; and then she turned to take the parcels for departure.

Alec d'Urberville removed his cigar, bent towards her, and said–

"You are not going to turn away like that, dear? Come!"

"If you wish," she answered indifferently. "See how you've mastered me!"

She thereupon turned round and lifted her face to his, and remained like a marble term while he imprinted a kiss upon her cheek–half perfunctorily, half as if zest had not yet quite died out. Her eyes vaguely rested upon the

Unit 4
Thomas Hardy and *Tess of the d'Urbervilles*

remotest trees in the lane while the kiss was given, as though she were nearly unconscious of what he did.

"Now the other side, for old acquaintance" sake."

She turned her head in the same passive way, as one might turn at the request of a sketcher or hairdresser, and he kissed the other side, his lips touching cheeks that were damp and smoothly chill as the skin of the mushrooms in the fields around.

"You don't give me your mouth and kiss me back. You never willingly do that–you'll never love me, I fear."

"I have said so, often. It is true. I have never really and truly loved you, and I think I never can." She added mournfully, "Perhaps, of all things, a lie on this thing would do the most good to me now; but I have honour enough left, little as'tis, not to tell that lie. If I did love you I may have the best o'causes for letting you know it. But I don't."

He emitted a laboured breath, as if the scene were getting rather oppressive to his heart, or to his conscience, or to his gentility.

"Well, you are absurdly melancholy, Tess. I have no reason for flattering you now, and I can say plainly that you need not be so sad. You can hold your own for beauty against any woman of these parts, gentle or simple; I say it to you as a practical man and well–wisher. If you are wise you will show it to the world more than you do before it fades.... And yet, Tess, will you come back to me? Upon my soul I don't like to let you go like this!"

"Never, never! I made up my mind as soon as I saw–what I ought to have seen sooner; and I won't come."

"Then good morning, my four months" cousin–good–bye!"

> ### ❧ Excerpt 3 (from Chapter 30)
> *Tess and Angel meet again at Talbothays Dairy where Angel is in apprenticeship for being a gentleman-farmer. Over the course of the summer the two are drawn to each other, but Angel's proposal puts Tess in a painful dilemma. Although Tess is in deep love with him by the time and does not want to deceive him, she shrinks from confessing for fear that she lose his love and admiration. The memory of her night with Alec causes her to refuse Angel again and again. At last his insistence and intensity of his love for her wins her over.*

"Now, permit me to put it in this way. You belong to me already, you know; your heart, I mean. Does it not?"

"You know as well as I. O yes–yes!"

"Then, if your heart does, why not your hand?"

"My only reason was on account of you–on account of a question. I have something to tell you–"

"But suppose it to be entirely for my happiness, and my worldly convenience also?"

"O yes; if it is for your happiness and worldly convenience. But my life before I came here–I want–"

"Well, it is for my convenience as well as my happiness. If I have a very large farm, either English or colonial, you will be invaluable as a wife to me; better than a woman out of the largest mansion in the country. So please–please, dear Tessy, disabuse your mind of the feeling that you will stand in my way."

"But my history. I want you to know it–you must let me tell you–you will not like me so well!"

"Tell it if you wish to, dearest. This precious history then. Yes, I was born at so and so, Anno Domini– "

"I was born at Marlott," she said, catching at his words as a help, lightly as they were spoken. 'And I grew up there. And I was in the Sixth Standard when I left school, and they said I had great aptness, and should make a good teacher, so it was settled that I should be one. But there was trouble in my family; father was not very industrious, and he drank a little."

"Yes, yes. Poor child! Nothing new." He pressed her more closely to his side.

"And then–there is something very unusual about it–about me. I–I was–"

Tess's breath quickened.

"Yes, dearest. Never mind."

"I–I–am not a Durbeyfield, but a d'Urberville–a descendant of the same family as those that owned the old house we passed. And–we are all gone to nothing!"

"A d'Urberville! –Indeed! And is that all the trouble, dear Tess?"

"Yes," she answered faintly.

Unit 4
Thomas Hardy and *Tess of the d'Urbervilles*

"Well—why should I love you less after knowing this?"

"I was told by the dairyman that you hated old families."

He laughed.

"Well, it is true, in one sense. I do hate the aristocratic principle of blood before everything, and do think that as reasoners the only pedigrees we ought to respect are those spiritual ones of the wise and virtuous, without regard to corporal paternity. But I am extremely interested in this news—you can have no idea how interested I am! Are you not interested yourself in being one of that well-known line?"

"No. I have thought it sad—especially since coming here, and knowing that many of the hills and fields I see once belonged to my father's people. But other hills and fields belonged to Retty's people, and perhaps others to Marian's, so that I don't value it particularly."

"Yes—it is surprising how many of the present tillers of the soil were once owners of it, and I sometimes wonder that a certain school of politicians don't make capital of the circumstance; but they don't seem to know it.... I wonder that I did not see the resemblance of your name of d'Urberville, and trace the manifest corruption. And this was the carking secret!"

She had not told. At the last moment her courage had failed her, she feared his blame for not telling him sooner; and her instinct of self-preservation was stronger than her candour.

"Of course," continued the unwitting Clare, "I should have been glad to know you to be descended exclusively from the long-suffering, dumb, unrecorded rank and file of the English nation, and not from the self-seeking few who made themselves powerful at the expense of the rest. But I am corrupted away from that by my affection for you, Tess [he laughed as he spoke], and made selfish likewise. For your own sake I rejoice in your descent. Society is hopelessly snobbish, and this fact of your extraction may make an appreciable difference to its acceptance of you as my wife, after I have made you the well-read woman that I mean to make you. My mother too, poor soul, will think so much better of you on account of it. Tess, you must spell your name correctly—d'Urberville—from this very day."

"I like the other way rather best."

"But you *must*, dearest! Good heavens, why dozens of mushroom millionaires would jump at such a possession! By the bye, there's one of that kidney who has taken the name–where have I heard of him? –Up in the neighbourhood of The Chase, I think. Why, he is the very man who had that rumpus with my father I told you of. What an odd coincidence!"

"Angel, I think I would rather not take the name! It is unlucky, perhaps!" She was agitated.

"Now then, Mistress Teresa d'Urberville, I have you. Take my name, and so you will escape yours! The secret is out, so why should you any longer refuse me?"

"If it is *sure* to make you happy to have me as your wife, and you feel that you do wish to marry me, *very*, *very* much–"

"I do, dearest, of course!"

"I mean, that it is only your wanting me very much, and being hardly able to keep alive without me, whatever my offences, that would make me feel I ought to say I will."

"You will–you do say it, I know! You will be mine for ever and ever."

He clasped her close and kissed her.

"Yes!"

She had no sooner said it than she burst into a dry hard sobbing, so violent that it seemed to rend her. Tess was not a hysterical girl by any means, and he was surprised.

"Why do you cry, dearest?"

"I can't tell–quite! –I am so glad to think–of being yours, and making you happy!"

"But this does not seem very much like gladness, my Tessy!"

"I mean–I cry because I have broken down in my vow! I said I would die unmarried!"

"But, if you love me you would like me to be your husband?"

"Yes, yes, yes! But O, I sometimes wish I had never been born!"

"Now, my dear Tess, if I did not know that you are very much excited, and very inexperienced, I should say that remark was not very complimentary. How came you to wish that if you care for me? Do you care for me? I wish you would prove it in some way."

"How can I prove it more than I have done?" she cried, in a distraction of tenderness. 'Will this prove it more?"

She clasped his neck, and for the first time Clare learnt what an

Unit 4
Thomas Hardy and *Tess of the d'Urbervilles*

impassioned woman's kisses were like upon the lips of one whom she loved with all her heart and soul, as Tess loved him.

"There–now do you believe?" she asked, flushed, and wiping her eyes.

"Yes. I never really doubted–never, never!"

> ### Excerpt 4 (from Chapter 34)
> On their wedding night, Angel confessed to his past indiscretion, an "eight-and-forty hours' dissipation with a stranger." Tess forgave him, and thinking that he would forgive her as she had him, she told him her story, speaking the words without flinching, and sparing herself nothing.

"Do you remember what we said to each other this morning about telling our faults?' he asked abruptly, finding that she still remained immovable. 'We spoke lightly perhaps, and you may well have done so. But for me it was no light promise. I want to make a confession to you, Love."

This, from him, so unexpectedly apposite, had the effect upon her of a Providential interposition.

"You have to confess something?" she said quickly, and even with gladness and relief.

"You did not expect it? Ah–you thought too highly of me. Now listen. Put your head there, because I want you to forgive me, and not to be indignant with me for not telling you before, as perhaps I ought to have done."

How strange it was! He seemed to be her double. She did not speak, and Clare went on–

"I did not mention it because I was afraid of endangering my chance of you, darling, the great prize of my life–my Fellowship I call you. My brother's Fellowship was won at his college, mine at Talbothays Dairy. Well, I would not risk it. I was going to tell you a month ago–at the time you agreed to be mine, but I could not; I thought it might frighten you away from me. I put it off; then I thought I would tell you yesterday, to give you a chance at least of escaping me. But I did not. And I did not this morning, when you proposed our confessing our faults on the landing–the sinner that I was! But I must, now I see you sitting there so solemnly. I wonder if you will forgive me?"

"O yes! I am sure that–"

"Well, I hope so. But wait a minute. You don't know. To begin at the beginning. Though I imagine my poor father fears that I am one of the eternally lost for my doctrines, I am of course, a believer in good morals, Tess, as much as you. I used to wish to be a teacher of men, and it was a great disappointment to me when I found I could not enter the Church. I admired spotlessness, even though I could lay no claim to it, and hated impurity, as I hope I do now. Whatever one may think of plenary inspiration, one must heartily subscribe to these words of Paul: "Be thou an example–in word, in conversation, in charity, in spirit, in faith, in purity." It is the only safeguard for us poor human beings. "Integer vitae," says a Roman poet, who is strange company for St. Paul–

The man of upright life, from frailties free,

Stands not in need of Moorish spear or bow.

Well, a certain place is paved with good intentions, and having felt all that so strongly, you will see what a terrible remorse it bred in me when, in the midst of my fine aims for other people, I myself fell."

He then told her of that time of his life to which allusion has been made when, tossed about by doubts and difficulties in London, like a cork on the waves, he plunged into eight-and-forty hours' dissipation with a stranger.

"Happily I awoke almost immediately to a sense of my folly," he continued. "I would have no more to say to her, and I came home. I have never repeated the offence. But I felt I should like to treat you with perfect frankness and honour, and I could not do so without telling this. Do you forgive me?"

She pressed his hand tightly for an answer.

"Then we will dismiss it at once and for ever! –too painful as it is for the occasion–and talk of something lighter."

"O, Angel–I am almost glad–because now *you* can forgive *me*! I have not made my confession. I have a confession, too–remember, I said so."

"Ah, to be sure! Now then for it, wicked little one."

"Perhaps, although you smile, it is as serious as yours, or more so."

"It can hardly be more serious, dearest."

"It cannot–O no, it cannot!" She jumped up joyfully at the hope. "No, it cannot be more serious, certainly," she cried, "because" tis just the same! I will tell you now."

Unit 4

Thomas Hardy and *Tess of the d'Urbervilles*

❧ Excerpt 5 (from Chapter 46)

After Tess encounters Alec, he begins to visit her frequently despite her dislike for him, and even asks her to marry him. Tess refuses and tells him that she is already married, but Alec derides the idea that her marriage is secure.

However, what I want to ask you is, will you put it in my power to do my duty–to make the only reparation I can make for the trick played you: that is, will you be my wife, and go with me? ... I have already obtained this precious document. It was my old mother's dying wish."

He drew a piece of parchment from his pocket, with a slight fumbling of embarrassment.

"What is it?' said she.

"A marriage licence."

"O no, sir–no!" she said quickly, starting back.

"You will not? Why is that?"

And as he asked the question a disappointment which was not entirely the disappointment of thwarted duty crossed d"Urbervilles face. It was unmistakably a symptom that something of his old passion for her had been revived; duty and desire ran hand-in-hand. ...

"You will not marry me, Tess, and make me a self-respecting man?" he repeated, as soon as they were over the furrows.

"I cannot."

"But why?"

"You know I have no affection for you."

"But you would get to feel that in time, perhaps–as soon as you really could forgive me?"

"Never!"

"Why so positive?"

"I love somebody else."

The words seemed to astonish him.

"You do?" he cried. "Somebody else? But has not a sense of what is morally right and proper any weight with you?"

"No, no, no–don't say that!"

"Anyhow, then, your love for this other man may be only a passing

139

feeling which you will overcome–"

"No–no."

"Yes, yes! Why not?"

"I cannot tell you."

"You must in honour!"

"Well then ... I have married him."

"Ah!' he exclaimed; and he stopped dead and gazed at her.

"I did not wish to tell–I did not mean to!" she pleaded. "It is a secret here, or at any rate but dimly known. So will you, *please* will you, keep from questioning me? You must remember that we are now strangers."

"Strangers–are we? Strangers!"

For a moment a flash of his old irony marked his face; but he determinedly chastened it down.

"Is that man your husband?" he asked mechanically, denoting by a sign the labourer who turned the machine.

"That man!" she said proudly. "I should think not!"

"Who, then?"

"Do not ask what I do not wish to tell!" she begged, and flashed her appeal to him from her upturned face and lash-shadowed eyes.

D'Urberville was disturbed.

"But I only asked for your sake!" he retorted hotly. "Angels of heaven! – God forgive me for such an expression–I came here, I swear, as I thought for your good. Tess–don't look at me so–I cannot stand your looks! There never were such eyes, surely, before Christianity or since! There–I won't lose my head; I dare not. I own that the sight of you had waked up my love for you, which, I believed, was extinguished with all such feelings. But I thought that our marriage might be a sanctification for us both. "The unbelieving husband is sanctified by the wife, and the unbelieving wife is sanctified by the husband," I said to myself. But my plan is dashed from me; and I must bear the disappointment!"

He moodily reflected with his eyes on the ground.

"Married. Married! ... Well, that being so," he added, quite calmly, tearing the licence slowly into halves and putting them in his pocket; 'that being prevented, I should like to do some good to you and your husband, whoever he may be. There are many questions that I am tempted to ask, but

Unit 4

Thomas Hardy and *Tess of the d'Urbervilles*

I will not do so, of course, in opposition to your wishes. Though, if I could know your husband, I might more easily benefit him and you. Is he on this farm?'

"No," she murmured. "He is far away."

"Far away? From *you*? What sort of husband can he be?"

"O, do not speak against him! It was through you! He found out–"

"Ah, is it so! ... That's sad, Tess!"

"Yes."

"But to stay away from you–to leave you to work like this!"

"He does not leave me to work!" she cried, springing to the defence of the absent one with all her fervour. 'He don't know it! It is by my own arrangement."

"Then, does he write?"

"I–I cannot tell you. There are things which are private to ourselves."

"Of course that means that he does not. You are a deserted wife, my fair Tess!"

> ### ⚑ Excerpt 6 (from Chapter 55)
> *Angel Clare returns home from Brazil, much altered by his ordeals. He wishes to rejoin Tess. He looks for her first at Flintcomb-Ash, then at her home village of Marlott, and finally at Kingsbere. There Tess's mother tells him reluctantly that Tess is at Sandbourne.*

Tess appeared on the threshold–not at all as he had expected to see her–bewilderingly otherwise, indeed. Her great natural beauty was, if not heightened, rendered more obvious by her attire. She was loosely wrapped in a cashmere dressing–gown of gray–white, embroidered in half-mourning tints, and she wore slippers of the same hue. Her neck rose out of a frill of down, and her well-remembered cable of dark-brown hair was partially coiled up in a mass at the back of her head and partly hanging on her shoulder–the evident result of haste.

He had held out his arms, but they had fallen again to his side; for she had not come forward, remaining still in the opening of the doorway. Mere yellow skeleton that he was now he felt the contrast between them, and thought his appearance distasteful to her.

"Tess!" he said huskily, "can you forgive me for going away? Can't you—come to me? How do you get to be–like this?"

"It is too late," said she, her voice sounding hard through the room, her eyes shining unnaturally.

"I did not think rightly of you–I did not see you as you were!" he continued to plead. 'I have learnt to since, dearest Tessy mine!"

"Too late, too late!' she said, waving her hand in the impatience of a person whose tortures cause every instant to seem an hour. 'Don't come close to me, Angel! No–you must not. Keep away."

"But don"t you love me, my dear wife, because I have been so pulled down by illness? You are not so fickle–I am come on purpose for you–my mother and father will welcome you now!"

"Yes–O, yes, yes! But I say, I say it is too late."

She seemed to feel like a fugitive in a dream, who tries to move away, but cannot. "Don't you know all–don't you know it? Yet how do you come here if you do not know?"

"I inquired here and there, and I found the way."

"I waited and waited for you,' she went on, her tones suddenly resuming their old fluty pathos. 'But you did not come! And I wrote to you, and you did not come! He kept on saying you would never come any more, and that I was a foolish woman. He was very kind to me, and to mother, and to all of us after father's death. He–"

"I don't understand."

"He has won me back to him."

Clare looked at her keenly, then, gathering her meaning, flagged like one plague-stricken, and his glance sank; it fell on her hands, which, once rosy, were now white and more delicate.

She continued–

"He is upstairs. I hate him now, because he told me a lie–that you would not come again; and you *have* come! These clothes are what he's put upon me: I didn't care what he did wi' me! But–will you go away, Angel, please, and never come any more?"

They stood fixed, their baffled hearts looking out of their eyes with a joylessness pitiful to see. Both seemed to implore something to shelter them

Unit 4

Thomas Hardy and *Tess of the d'Urbervilles*

from reality.

"Ah–it is my fault!" said Clare.

4.2.3.3 Passages for Understanding the Film

(1) When old Mr Simon Stoke, latterly deceased, had made his fortune as an honest merchant (some said money-lender) in the North, he decided to settle as a county man in the South of England, out of hail of his business district; and in doing this he felt the necessity of recommencing with a name that would not too readily identify him with the smart tradesman of the past, and that would be less commonplace than the original bald stark words. Conning for an hour in the British Museum the pages of works devoted to extinct, half-extinct, obscured, and ruined families appertaining to the quarter of England in which he proposed to settle, he considered that d'Urberville looked and sounded as well as any of them: and d'Urberville accordingly was annexed to his own name for himself and his heirs eternally. **(Chapter V)**

(2) Get Alec d'Urberville in the mind to marry her! He marry *her*! On matrimony he had never once said a word. And what if he had? How a convulsive snatching at social salvation might have impelled her to answer him she could not say. But her poor foolish mother little knew her present feeling towards this man. Perhaps it was unusual in the circumstances, unlucky, unaccountable; but there it was; and this, as she had said, was what made her detest herself. She had never wholly cared for him, she did not at all care for him now. She had dreaded him, winced before him, succumbed to adroit advantages he took of her helplessness; then, temporarily blinded by his ardent manners, had been stirred to confused surrender awhile: had suddenly despised and disliked him, and had run away. That was all. Hate him she did not quite; but he was dust and ashes to her, and even for her name's sake she scarcely wished to marry him. **(Chapter XII)**

(3) Tess was woman enough to realize from their avowals to herself that Angel Clare had the honour of all the dairymaids in his keeping, and her perception of his care to avoid compromising the happiness of either in the least degree bred a tender respect in Tess for what she deemed, rightly or

wrongly, the self-controlling sense of duty shown by him, a quality which she had never expected to find in one of the opposite sex, and in the absence of which more than one of the simple hearts who were his house-mates might have gone weeping on her pilgrimage. **(Chapter XXII)**

(4) There was hardly a touch of earth in her love for Clare. To her sublime trustfulness he was all that goodness could be—knew all that a guide, philosopher, and friend should know. She thought every line in the contour of his person the perfection of masculine beauty, his soul the soul of a saint, his intellect that of a seer. The wisdom of her love for him, as love, sustained her dignity; she seemed to be wearing a crown. The compassion of his love for her, as she saw it, made her lift up her heart to him in devotion. He would sometimes catch her large, worshipful eyes, that had no bottom to them, looking at him from their depths, as if she saw something immortal before her...

She had not known that men could be so disinterested, chivalrous, protective, in their love for women as he. Angel Clare was far from all that she thought him in this respect; absurdly far, indeed; but he was, in truth, more spiritual than animal; he had himself well in hand, and was singularly free from grossness. Though not cold-natured, he was rather bright than hot—less Byronic than Shelleyan; could love desperately, but with a love more especially inclined to the imaginative and ethereal; it was a fastidious emotion which could jealously guard the loved one against his very self. This amazed and enraptured Tess, whose slight experiences had been so infelicitous till now; and in her reaction from indignation against the male sex she swerved to excess of honour for Clare. **(Chapter XXXI)**

(5) Within the remote depths of his constitution, so gentle and affectionate as he was in general, there lay hidden a hard logical deposit, like a vein of metal in a soft loam, which turned the edge of everything that attempted to traverse it. It had blocked his acceptance of the Church; it blocked his acceptance of Tess. Moreover, his affection itself was less fire than radiance, and, with regard to the other sex, when he ceased to believe he ceased to follow: contrasting in this with many impressionable natures, who remain sensuously infatuated with what they intellectually despise. **(Chapter XXXVI)**

(6) This night the woman of his belittling deprecations was thinking how great and good her husband was. But over them both there hung a deeper shade

Unit 4

Thomas Hardy and *Tess of the d'Urbervilles*

than the shade which Angel Clare perceived, namely, the shade of his own limitations. With all his attempted independence of judgement this advanced and well-meaning young man, a sample product of the last five-and-twenty years, was yet the slave to custom and conventionality when surprised back into her early teachings. **(Chapter XXXIX)**

(7) During this time of absence he had mentally aged a dozen years. What arrested him now as of value in life was less its beauty than its pathos. Having long discredited the old systems of mysticism, he now began to discredit the old appraisements of morality. He thought they wanted readjusting. Who was the moral man? Still more pertinently, who was the moral woman? The beauty or ugliness of a character lay not only in its achievements, but in its aims and impulses; its true history lay, not among things done, but among things willed. **(Chapter XLIX)**

(8) Her father's life had a value apart from his personal achievements, or perhaps it would not have had much. It was the last of the three lives for whose duration the house and premises were held under a lease; and it had long been coveted by the tenant-farmer for his regular labourers, who were stinted in cottage accommodation. Moreover, 'liviers' were disapproved of in villages almost as much as little freeholders, because of their independence of manner, and when a lease determined it was never renewed. **(Chapter L)**

4.2.3.4 Chapter Reading

Phase the Fifth: The Woman Pays

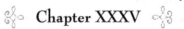

Chapter XXXV

HER narrative ended; even its re-assertions and secondary explanations were done. Tess's voice throughout had hardly risen higher than its opening tone; there had been no <u>exculpatory</u> phrase of any kind, and she had not wept.

But the complexion even of external things seemed to suffer <u>transmutation</u>（变形，变化）as her announcement progressed. The fire in the <u>grate</u>（壁炉）looked impish–demoniacally funny, as if it did not care in the least about her <u>strait</u>（困境）. The <u>fender</u>（炉栏）grinned idly, as if it too did not care. The light from the water-bottle was merely engaged in a <u>chromatic</u>（色

彩的) problem. All material objects around announced their irresponsibility with terrible iteration (重复). And yet nothing had changed since the moments when he had been kissing her; or rather, nothing in the substance of things. But the essence of things had changed.

When she ceased the auricular (听觉的) impressions from their previous endearments (爱慕) seemed to hustle away into the corner of their brains, repeating themselves as echoes from a time of supremely purblind foolishness.

Clare performed the irrelevant act of stirring the fire; the intelligence had not even yet got to the bottom of him. After stirring the embers (余烬) he rose to his feet; all the force of her disclosure had imparted itself now. His face had withered (枯萎). In the strenuousness (极力) of his concentration he treadled (踩踏) fitfully on the floor. He could not, by any contrivance (想出的办法), think closely enough; that was the meaning of his vague movement. When he spoke it was in the most inadequate, commonplace voice of the many varied tones she had heard from him.

"Tess!"

"Yes, dearest."

"Am I to believe this? From your manner I am to take it as true. O you cannot be out of your mind! You ought to be! Yet you are not ... My wife, my Tess–nothing in you warrants (保证) such a supposition (想象, 假定) as that?"

"I am not out of my mind," she said.

"And yet–" He looked vacantly at her, to resume with dazed senses: "Why didnt you tell me before? Ah, yes, you would have told me, in a way – but I hindered you, I remember!"

These and other of his words were nothing but the perfunctory babble of the surface while the depths remained paralyzed. He turned away, and bent over a chair. Tess followed him to the middle of the room where he was, and stood there staring at him with eyes that did not weep. Presently she slid down upon her knees beside his foot, and from this position she crouched (蜷缩) in a heap.

"In the name of our love, forgive me!" she whispered with a dry mouth. "I have forgiven you for the same!"

And, as he did not answer, she said again–

"Forgive me as you are forgiven! *I* forgive *you*, Angel."

Unit 4

Thomas Hardy and *Tess of the d'Urbervilles*

"You–yes, you do."

"But you do not forgive me?"

"O Tess, forgiveness does not apply to the case! You were one person; now you are another. My God–how can forgiveness meet such a grotesque–prestidigitation (变戏法) as that!"

He paused, contemplating this definition; then suddenly broke into horrible laughter–as unnatural and ghastly (可怕的) as a laugh in hell.

"Don't–don't! It kills me quite, that!" she shrieked. "O have mercy upon me–have mercy!"

He did not answer; and, sickly white, she jumped up.

"Angel, Angel! what do you mean by that laugh?" she cried out. "Do you know what this is to me?"

He shook his head.

"I have been hoping, longing, praying, to make you happy! I have thought what joy it will be to do it, what an unworthy wife I shall be if I do not! That's what I have felt, Angel!"

"I know that."

"I thought, Angel, that you loved me–me, my very self! If it is I you do love, O how can it be that you look and speak so? It frightens me! Having begun to love you, I love you for ever–in all changes, in all disgraces, because you are yourself. I ask no more. Then how can you, O my own husband, stop loving me?"

"I repeat, the woman I have been loving is not you."

"But who?"

"Another woman in your shape."

She perceived in his words the realization of her own apprehensive (提心吊胆的) foreboding (预感) in former times. He looked upon her as a species of impostor (骗子); a guilty woman in the guise (伪装) of an innocent one. Terror was upon her white face as she saw it; her cheek was flaccid (松垂的), and her mouth had almost the aspect of a round little hole. The horrible sense of his view of her so deadened her that she staggered; and he stepped forward, thinking she was going to fall.

"Sit down, sit down," he said gently. "You are ill; and it is natural that you should be."

She did sit down, without knowing where she was, that strained look still upon her face, and her eyes such as to make his flesh creep.

"I don't belong to you any more, then; do I, Angel?" she asked helplessly. "It is not me, but another woman like me that he loved, he says."

The image raised caused her to take pity upon herself as one who was ill-used. Her eyes filled as she regarded her position further; she turned round and burst into a flood of self-sympathetic tears.

Clare was relieved at this change, for the effect on her of what had happened was beginning to be a trouble to him only less than the woe（悲哀）of the disclosure itself. He waited patiently, apathetically（无动于衷地）, till the violence of her grief had worn itself out, and her rush of weeping had lessened to a catching gasp at intervals.

"Angel," she said suddenly, in her natural tones, the insane, dry voice of terror having left her now. "Angel, am I too wicked for you and me to live together?"

"I have not been able to think what we can do."

"I shan't ask you to let me live with you, Angel, because I have no right to! I shall not write to mother and sisters to say we be married, as I said I would do; and I shan't finish the good-hussif " I cut out and meant to make while we were in lodgings（租住的房间）."

"Shan't you?"

"No, I shan't do anything, unless you order me to; and if you go away from me I shall not follow'ee; and if you never speak to me any more I shall not ask why, unless you tell me I may."

"And if I order you to do anything?"

"I will obey you like your wretched slave, even if it is to lie down and die."

"You are very good. But it strikes me that there is a want of harmony between your present mood of self-sacrifice and your past mood of self-preservation."

These were the first words of antagonism（敌意）. To fling elaborate sarcasms（讽刺，挖苦）at Tess, however, was much like flinging them at a dog or cat. The charms of their subtlety passed by her unappreciated, and she only received them as inimical（敌意的）sounds which meant that anger ruled. She remained mute（缄默的）, not knowing that he was smothering his affection for her. She hardly observed that a tear descended slowly upon his cheek, a

Unit 4

Thomas Hardy and *Tess of the d'Urbervilles*

tear so large that it magnified (放大) the pores (毛孔) of the skin over which it rolled, like the object lens of a microscope. Meanwhile reillumination (再次阐明) as to the terrible and total change that her confession had wrought in his life, in his universe, returned to him, and he tried desperately to advance among the new conditions in which he stood. Some consequent action was necessary; yet what?

"Tess," he said, as gently as he could speak, "I cannot stay–in this room–just now. I will walk out a little way."

He quietly left the room, and the two glasses of wine that he had poured out for their supper–one for her, one for him–remained on the table untasted. This was what their *Agape* had come to. At tea, two or three hours earlier, they had, in the freakishness (奇特) of affection, drunk from one cup.

The closing of the door behind him, gently as it had been pulled to, roused Tess from her stupor (恍惚). He was gone; she could not stay. Hastily flinging her cloak around her she opened the door and followed, putting out the candles as if she were never coming back. The rain was over and the night was now clear.

She was soon close at his heels, for Clare walked slowly and without purpose. His form beside her light gray figure looked black, sinister, and forbidding, and she felt as sarcasm the touch of the jewels of which she had been momentarily so proud. Clare turned at hearing her footsteps, but his recognition of her presence seemed to make no difference to him, and he went on over the five yawning arches of the great bridge in front of the house.

The cow and horse tracks (足迹) in the road were full of water, and rain having been enough to charge them, but not enough to wash them away. Across these minute pools the reflected stars flitted (飞掠) in a quick transit as she passed; she would not have known they were shining overhead if she had not seen them there–the vastest things of the universe imaged in objects so mean.

The place to which they had travelled today was in the same valley as Talbothays, but some miles lower down the river; and the surroundings being open she kept easily in sight of him. Away from the house the road wound through the meads, and along these she followed Clare without any attempt to come up with him or to attract him, but with dumb and vacant fidelity (忠诚).

At last, however, her listless (无精打采的) walk brought her up alongside him, and still he said nothing. The cruelty of fooled honesty is often great after enlightenment, and it was mighty in Clare now. The outdoor air had apparently taken away from him all tendency to act on impulse; she knew that he saw her without irradiation (光彩) –in all her bareness; that Time was chanting his satiric psalm (赞美诗) at her then–

> Behold, when thy face is made bare, he that loved thee shall hate;
> Thy face shall be no more fair at the fall of thy fate.
> For thy life shall fall as a leaf and be shed as the rain;
> And the veil of thine head shall be grief, and the crown shall be pain.

He was still intently thinking, and her companionship had now insufficient power to break or divert the strain of thought. What a weak thing her presence must have become to him! She could not help addressing Clare.

"What have I done–what *have* I done! I have not told of anything that interferes with or belies (掩饰) my love for you. You don't think I planned it, do you? It is in your own mind what you are angry at, Angel; it is not in me. O, it is not in me, and I am not that deceitful woman you think me!"

"H'm–well. Not deceitful, my wife; but not the same. No, not the same. But do not make me reproach you. I have sworn that I will not; and I will do everything to avoid it."

But she went on pleading in her distraction; and perhaps said things that would have been better left to silence.

"Angel! –Angel! I was a child–a child when it happened! I knew nothing of men."

"You were more sinned against than sinning, that I admit."

"Then will you not forgive me?"

"I do forgive you, but forgiveness is not all."

"And love me?"

To this question he did not answer.

"O Angel–my mother says that it sometimes happens so! –she knows several cases where they were worse than I, and the husband has not minded it much–has got over it at least. And yet the woman had not loved him as I do you!"

"Don't, Tess; don't argue. Different societies, different manners. You

Unit 4

Thomas Hardy and *Tess of the d'Urbervilles*

almost make me say you are an unapprehending peasant woman, who have never been initiated into the proportions of social things. You don't know what you say."

"I am only a peasant by position, not by nature!"

She spoke with an impulse to anger, but it went as it came.

"So much the worse for you. I think that parson (教区牧师) who unearthed your pedigree (家谱) would have done better if he had held his tongue. I cannot help associating your decline as a family with this other fact–of your want of firmness. Decrepit families imply decrepit wills, decrepit conduct. Heaven, why did you give me a handle for despising you more by informing me of your descent! Here was I thinking you a new-sprung child of nature; there were you, the belated seedling of an effete aristocracy (衰败贵族中生不逢时的秧苗)!"

"Lots of families are as bad as mine in that! Retty's family were once large landowners, and so were Dairyman Billett's. And the Debbyhouses, who now are carters, were once the De Bayeux family. You find such as I everywhere; 'tis a feature of our county, and I can't help it."

"So much the worse for the county."

She took these reproaches in their bulk simply, not in their particulars; he did not love her as he had loved her hitherto (迄今), and to all else she was indifferent.

They wandered on again in silence. It was said afterwards that a cottager of Wellbridge, who went out late that night for a doctor, met two lovers in the pastures, walking very slowly, without converse, one behind the other, as in a funeral procession, and the glimpse that he obtained of their faces seemed to denote (表示) that they were anxious and sad. Returning later, he passed them again in the same field, progressing just as slowly, and as regardless of the hour and of the cheerless night as before. It was only on account of his preoccupation with his own affairs, and the illness in his house, that he did not bear in mind the curious incident, which, however, he recalled a long while after.

During the interval of the cottager's going and coming, she had said to her husband–

"I don't see how I can help being the cause of much misery to you all your life. The river is down there. I can put an end to myself in it. I am not afraid."

151

"I don't wish to add murder to my other follies," he said.

"I will leave something to show that I did it myself–on account of my shame. They will not blame you then."

"Don't speak so absurdly–I wish not to hear it. It is nonsense to have such thoughts in this kind of case, which is rather one for satirical laughter than for tragedy. You don't in the least understand the quality of the mishap. It would be viewed in the light of a joke by nine–tenths of the world if it were known. Please oblige me by returning to the house, and going to bed."

"I will," said she dutifully.

They had rambled round by a road which led to the well–known ruins of the Cistercian abbey behind the mill, the latter having, in centuries past, been attached to the monastic(寺院的)establishment. The mill still worked on, food being a perennial(长期的)necessity; the abbey had perished(毁灭), creeds being transient(短暂的). One continually sees the ministration of the temporary outlasting the ministration of the eternal. Their walk having been circuitous(迂回的;绕行的)they were still not far from the house, and in obeying his direction she only had to reach the large stone bridge across the main river, and follow the road for a few yards. When she got back everything remained as she had left it, the fire being still burning. She did not stay downstairs for more than a minute, but proceeded to her chamber, whither the luggage had been taken. Here she sat down on the edge of the bed, looking blankly around, and presently began to undress. In removing the light towards the bedstead its rays fell upon the tester of white dimity(白提花布帐顶); something was hanging beneath it, and she lifted the candle to see what it was. A bough of mistletoe(槲寄生). Angel had put it there; she knew that in an instant. This was the explanation of that mysterious parcel which it had been so difficult to pack and bring; whose contents he would not explain to her, saying that time would soon show her the purpose thereof. In his zest(热情)and his gaiety(兴奋)he had hung it there. How foolish and inopportune(不合时宜的)that mistletoe looked now.

Having nothing more to fear, having scarce anything to hope, for that he would relent there seemed no promise whatever, she lay down dully. When sorrow ceases to be speculative sleep sees her opportunity. Among so many happier moods which forbid repose(休息,睡眠)this was a mood which welcomed it, and in a few minutes the lonely Tess forgot existence,

Unit 4
Thomas Hardy and *Tess of the d'Urbervilles*

surrounded by the aromatic（芳香的）stillness of the chamber that had once, possibly, been the bride-chamber of her own ancestry.

Later on that night Clare also retraced（折回）his steps to the house. Entering softly to the sitting-room he obtained a light, and with the manner of one who had considered his course he spread his rugs upon the old horse-hair sofa which stood there, and roughly shaped it to a sleeping-couch. Before lying down he crept shoeless upstairs, and listened at the door of her apartment. Her measured breathing told that she was sleeping profoundly.

"Thank God!" murmured Clare; and yet he was conscious of a pang of bitterness at the thought–approximately true, though not wholly so–that having shifted the burden of her life to his shoulders she was now reposing without care.

He turned away to descend; then, irresolute（犹豫不决的）, faced round to her door again. In the act he caught sight of one of the d'Urberville dames, whose portrait was immediately over the entrance to Tess's bedchamber. In the candlelight the painting was more than unpleasant. Sinister design（阴险狡诈的用心）lurked（潜藏）in the woman's features, a concentrated purpose of revenge on the other sex–so it seemed to him then. The Caroline bodice of the portrait was low–precisely as Tess's had been when he tucked it in to show the necklace; and again he experienced the distressing sensation of a resemblance between them.

The check was sufficient. He resumed his retreat and descended.

His air remained calm and cold, his small compressed mouth indexing（表明）his powers of self-control; his face wearing still that terrible sterile expression which had spread thereon since her disclosure. It was the face of a man who was no longer passion's slave, yet who found no advantage in his enfranchisement. He was simply regarding the harrowing（痛心的）contingencies（不测事件）of human experience, the unexpectedness of things. Nothing so pure, so sweet, so virginal as Tess had seemed possible all the long while that he had adored her, up to an hour ago; but

The little less, and what worlds away!

He argued erroneously（错误地）when he said to himself that her heart was not indexed in the honest freshness of her face; but Tess had no advocate to set him right. Could it be possible, he continued, that eyes which as they gazed never expressed any divergence（差异）from what the tongue was telling, were yet ever seeing another world behind her ostensible（表面上的）one, discordant（不一致的）and contrasting?

He reclined（斜倚；躺）on his couch in the sitting-room, and extinguished the light. The night came in, and took up its place there, unconcerned and indifferent; the night which had already swallowed up his happiness, and was now digesting it listlessly; and was ready to swallow up the happiness of a thousand other people with as little disturbance or change of mien（样子，外表）.

Notes and Glossary for Chapter Reading

(1) exculpatory /iks'kʌlpətəri/ *a.* attempting to free from blame 辩解的，辩明无罪的

(2) hustle /'hʌsl/ *v.* to move energetically and rapidly; hurry, force 赶忙，挤，硬逼

(3) purblind /'pəːblaind/ *a.* partly blind; dim-sighted 半盲的；slow in understanding or discernment 迟钝的

(4) perfunctory /pə'fʌŋktəri/ *a.* acting with indifference; showing little interest or care 冷漠的，敷衍的

(5) deaden /'dedn/ *v.* to lose vigor, brilliance, or liveliness

(6) good-hussif: bag holding needle and thread 针线包

(7) Agape: (Greek) love-feast, as held by the early Christians 爱筵，早期基督徒举行的一种会餐。

(8) Behold when thy face ... pain: From a chorus in Swinburne's *Atalanta in Calydon*

你的真面目一旦显露，从前的恩爱反成冤仇，
时衰远败的时候，原先的姣好也要变得丑陋。
你的生命要像秋雨一样淋沥，秋叶一般飘零，
你的面纱是痛苦的源泉，花冠是悔恨的象征。

（引自张谷若译本）

(9) 'You were more sinned against than sinning,' 与其说是你把别人害了，不如说是别人把你害了。

Cf. Shakespeare's *King Lear*, Act III, scene II: "A man more sinned against

Unit 4

Thomas Hardy and *Tess of the d'Urbervilles*

than sinning."

(10) decrepit /di'krepit/ a. weakened, worn out, impaired, or broken down by old age, illness, or hard use 衰老的，老朽的

(11) mishap /'mishæp/ n. an unfortunate accident; misfortune 倒霉事：不幸的事件

(12) in the light of: in consideration of; in relationship to 鉴于；基于对…的考虑

(13) ramble /'ræmbl/ v. to move about aimlessly 漫无目的地走，闲逛

(14) the Cistercian abbey: 西多会寺院。西多会 (Cistercians)，天主教修会，1908年建立。最初建于法国境内勃艮第地区戎 (Dijon) 附近的西多 (Citeaux)，故名。

(15) ministration /ˌminis'treiʃən/ n. the act or process of serving or aiding 帮助，服务

(16) A bough of mistletoe: Mistletoe was traditionally believed to bring good luck and fertility.

(17) relent /ri'lent/ v. to become more lenient, compassionate, or forgiving 发慈悲：变得更加温和，宽容

(18) passion's slave: Cf. Shakespeare's *Hamlet*, Act III, scene II
Give me that man
That is not passion's slave, and I will wear him
In my heart's core, ay, in my heart of heart.

(19) a man who... in his enfranchisement: 一个摆脱了情欲却从中得不到好处的人。enfranchisement /in'fræntʃaizmənt/ 原意为"得到自由"，与上文的 slave 相呼应。

(20) The little less...away: 只少了一点儿，就有无穷的不同。From Browning's "*By the Fireside*". (引自勃朗宁诗句)

4.2.4 Exercises

❶ Identify the following characters

(1) _____ is an innocent and pretty country girl tossed into dangerous situations brought about by fate. She is dutiful and obedient as the novel begins; she gains great strength and fortitude through her suffering.

(2) _____ shows a childish pride in the discovery of his descent. His sense of his own dignity prevents him from getting a job, and he comes to see everything that happens in terms of his "high family".

(3) _____ is simple and hardworking, and has a practical outlook on life. She wants her daughter to rise in the world by making a successful marriage.

(4) _____ considers himself a freethinker, but his notions of morality turn out to be fairly conventional. He works at the Talbothay's dairy to gain practical experience because he hopes to buy a farm of his own.

(5) _____ is rapacious, possessive and manipulative. He is pursuing Tess unrelentingly and taking advantage of her in her weakest moments.

(6) _____ accompanies his sister when she must deliver the beehives in place of their father who becomes too drunk to take them.

(7) _____ nearly fights Tess when Tess laughs at her with others as she stains her dress with treacle. Tess decides to go with Alec the night he seduces her, partially because Tess is afraid of what this person might do to her.

(8) _____ is one of the dairymaids at Talbothays with whom Tess stays. She is also in love with Angel Clare and becomes an alcoholic later. Her friendship with Tess is strong, and when she finds out that Tess is separated from her husband, she invites Tess to come to Flintcomb-Ash where she works.

❷ Plot Review

Tess's father, John Durbeyfield, is greatly impressed with the news that he is the last (1)_____ of the once noble d'Urbervilles. He immediately orders a carriage to take him home and proceeds to (2) _____ for the rest of the evening. He gets too (3) _____ to make a delivery to the market that night. Tess, accompanied by her younger brother, has to go instead, but she falls asleep on the way, and the family's horse, unguided, is (4) _____ in an accident. Tess feels so guilty that she unwillingly follows her mother's wish to (5)"_____" with the rich d'Urberville. Meeting the manipulative Alec, the son of wealthy employer, proves to be her downfall. Cunningly (6)_____ by him, she has an illegitimate child, and although she knows that she will be ostracized, she (7)_____ to ask

Unit 4

Thomas Hardy and *Tess of the d'Urbervilles*

her seducer for aid. The death of her unfortunate child is devastating, but she bravely goes on. Working as a dairymaid at Talbothays she meets Angel Clare, who has denied a university education as he does not share the Christian faith of his family, and plans to learn about (8)_____ through practical experience. Gradually he (9)_____ _____ _____ with Tess, and she with him. As this love develops further towards an apparently inevitable (10)_____, Tess struggles with her (11)_____, ashamed of deceiving Angel by (12)_____ telling him what had happened to her, but fearful of the consequences if he knew. Shortly before the wedding day arrives, Tess makes a final failed effort to (13)_____ her "stain" to him. So it is not until their (14)_____ night, after Angel has himself confessed youthful misbehaviour, that her secret emerges. Angel leaves his wife, (15)_____ to bring himself to live with the real woman who has replaced the (16)_____ picture he had of her in his mind. Then begins a new period of suffering for Tess. Misfortunes and bitter hardships come upon her and her family, and accident throws her once more in the path of Alec. He has become an itinerant preacher, but his temporary religious conversion does not prevent him from persistently (17)_____ Tess. When her pathetic appeals to her husband, now in Brazil, remain (18)_____, she is driven for the sake of her family to become the mistress of Alec. Angel Clare, returning from Brazil and repenting of his harshness, searches and finds her living with Alec in Sandbourne, and then prepares to leave once again. Tess, maddened by this second wrong that has been done by Alec, stabs and kills him to liberate herself. After a brief happy period of concealment with the husband she truly loves in the New Forest, Tess, who has been (19)_____ for her punishment, is (20)_____ at Stonehenge, tried, and hanged.

❸ General Questions

(1) Why does Tess's father have a horse and carriage fetched for him to go home?

(2) What are Tess's parents like? What are their expectations of Tess? What had Tess hoped to be?

(3) Why does Tess finally agree to go to the d'Urbervilles as her

mother proposes?

(4) How does Tess resist Alec's advances? Is she free at this point to make her decision?

(5) What causes Tess to refuse Angel again and again although she is in love with him?

(6) Why does Angel say Tess is another woman after hearing her story?

(7) Why does Tess hit Alec in the face with a leather glove at Flintcomb-Ash?

(8) Why does Tess's family have to move from Marlott when her father dies?

(9) What force Tess finally to return to Alec although she dislikes him and refuses him time and time again?

(10) Why does Angel say: "It's my fault" after Tess tells him "It's too late"?

❹ Questions for essay or discussion

(1) Why does Hardy call Tess "a pure woman"? In what respects does Tess remain pure? Why does Hardy highlight this quality in the novel's subtitle?

(2) It may be tempting to think of Alec as a "bad" character and Angel as a "good" one. What are the real differences between Alec and Angel? How does Hardy use the two characters to complicate the categories of good and evil?

(3) Identify some key moments in the novel or film where Tess passively submits? What are the consequences of her passivity?

(4) How much is Tess to blame for what happens to her? Does Tess deserve her final punishment? Why or why not?

(5) Tess has been described as the victim of social changes in nineteenth-century England, or of her own personality, or of her inherited nature, or of Alec and Angel as different embodiment of man's inhumanity to woman. To what extent is she a helpless victim?

Volume Two

American Novels and Films

Unit 5

Nathaniel Hawthorne and *The Scarlet Letter*

5.1 Nathaniel Hawthorne: Life and Works

5.1.1 About the Author

Nathaniel Hawthorne has long been recognized as one of the greatest of American writers. He is the finest literary embodiment of the New England traditions in which he is so deeply imbued. He inherits characteristic Puritan preoccupations with sin, guilt and secrecy and becomes at once their chronicler and their critic. His best work is carefully and tightly organized, blending elements of realism, allegory and symbolism into a form that he himself likes to call "romance".

Hawthorne was born on July 4, 1804 in Salem, Massachusetts, the descendant of determined Puritans. One of his ancestors, William Hathorne, came to Salem in 1630 and gained notoriety for persecuting Quakers; another, John Hathorne, was a judge in the Salem witchcraft trials in 1692. A keen sense of these two ancestors brought Hawthorne (the author himself added the "w" to his surname) to envision them in "The Custom-House" (1850) as stern men resolute in their intolerance. When Hawthorne was four years old, his sea-captain father died of yellow fever on a voyage to the tropics. His

Unit 5

Nathaniel Hawthorne and *The Scarlet Letter*

mother brought him and his two sisters to her own family in Maine. In that rural setting he passed the years of his youth, reading widely in the English classics and nursing the hope of becoming a writer.

In 1821 Hawthorne attended Bowdoin College, which gave him a good education in Classical and Biblical literature, English composition and rhetoric, as well as natural sciences and philosophy, and there he made a number of important and lasting friends, including the future poet Henry Wadsworth Longfellow and the future president Franklin Pierce. After graduating in 1825 Hawthorne returned to Salem and began to write historical sketches and allegorical tales. In 1828, anonymously and at his own expense, he published *Fanshawe*, a novel based on his college life. While the book itself received only slight critical attention and the ashamed author burned the unsold copies, it did initiate a long, productive friendship between Hawthorne and the publisher Samuel Goodrich, who then published many of his stories, which were later reprinted as *Twice-Told Tales* in 1837 and enlarged in 1842. These tales, dealing with the themes of guilt and secrecy, and intellectual and moral pride, show Hawthorne's constant preoccupation with the effects of Puritanism in New England. Throughout the 1830s he published more than seventy tales and sketches. In 1839 he became engaged to Sophia Peabody, one of the three famous sisters of a distinguished New England family. To save money for marriage, Hawthorne worked as salt and coal measurer in the Boston Custom House during 1839 and 1840, then the next year invested in the utopian community Brook Farm. He married in 1842 and moved to The Manse in Concord, the geographic center of literary transcendentalism. For a brief part of this time he was a member of the transcendentalist community at Brook Farm. His marriage to Sophia had a great effect on his life. Sophia encouraged his writing and opened his imagination to the beauty and strength of womanhood. In 1846 he published *Mosses from an Old Manse*, which includes the famous story "Young Goodman Brown." Through long service to the local Democrats, Hawthorne was named Surveyor of the Port of Salem in 1846, but he was turned out of office by the new Whig administration in June 1849. Shocked and disillusioned, Hawthorne channeled his energy into his first significant long work of fiction, *The Scarlet Letter* (1850), which won almost immediate acclaim. It was rapidly followed by *The House of the Seven Gables* (1851), a study in ancestral guilt and expiation, also deeply rooted in New England and his own family history, and *The Blithedale Romance* (1852), which was based on his Brook Farm experience. He also published *The Snow Image and Other Tales* (1851), which includes stories such as "Ethan Brand" and "My Kinsman Major Molineux." The publication of *A Wonder Book* (1852), which retells Greek myths for children, and *Tanglewood Tales* (1853) marked the end of his most prolific period.

In 1853 Franklin Pierce became President and Hawthorne, who had written his campaign biography, was appointed US consul at Liverpool. He lived in England for four years and in Italy for two. On his return to the USA he published his final novel, *The Marble Faun* (1860), and *Our Old Home* (1863), a book of essays on England.

Hawthorne died on May 19, 1864 in Plymouth, New Hampshire after a long period of illness, and was buried in the Sleepy Hollow Cemetery at Concord. Hawthorne's life with his wife and children left them vivid, happy memories of him. His wife edited his notebooks as *Passages from the American Notebooks* (1868), *Passages from the English Notebooks* (1870) and *Passages from the French and Italian Notebooks* (1871), and his children made many contributions to the study of their father's works.

5.1.2 Nathaniel Hawthorne's Major Works

The Scarlet Letter (1850) 《红字》
The House of the Seven Gables (1851) 《有七个尖角阁的房子》
The Blithedale Romance (1852) 《福谷传奇》
The Marble Faun (1860) 《玉石雕像》
Twice-Told Tales (1837, 1851) 《重讲一遍的故事》(短篇小说集)
Mosses from an Old Manse (1846, 1854)《古屋青苔》(短篇小说集)

Unit 5
Nathaniel Hawthorne and *The Scarlet Letter*

5.2 *The Scarlet Letter*

5.2.1 About the Novel

The Scarlet Letter was declared a classic almost immediately after its publication in 1850. It is regarded not only as Hawthorne's greatest accomplishment, but frequently as the greatest novel in American literary history.

The book is made up of twenty-four chapters with an introductory autobiographical essay, "The Custom House," in which Hawthorne describes the author's experiences as an official of the Salem Custom House and his supposed discovery of a scarlet cloth letter and documents relating the story of Hester Prynne. The story is set in the mid-seventeenth century in a Puritan colony on the edge of an untamed forest still inhabited by Native Americans. The landscape is wholly American. It is a poignant, fiery tale about a Puritan woman who committed adultery and bore an illegitimate child, and then four people's lives are terribly affected by a community's punishment for adultery. The illicit love affair of Hester with the Reverend Arthur Dimmesdale and the birth of their child Pearl take place before the book opens. It begins at the close of Hester's imprisonment many months after her affair and proceeds through many years to her final acceptance of her place in the community as the wearer of the scarlet letter, excluding the representation of the passionate moment which enables the entire novel. In the book, Hawthorne gives us a way of thinking about crime and punishment. He manages to show several thematic elements that came to define the American national identity: the effects of strict religious morality, the long struggle against a vast frontier, the troubled relationship between white settlers and Native Americans. These issues were just as relevant in Hawthorne's day as they were in Puritan times, and the way Americans and the United States government addressed these issues shaped the development of the nation.

5.2.2 Characters

- **Hester Prynne** Mother of Pearl, and the wife of Roger Prynne.
- **Arthur Dimmesdale** An eminent minister in Boston.
- **Roger Prynne (Chillingworth)** Hester's husband. He arrives in Boston the day that Hester is publicly shamed and forced to wear the scarlet letter.
- **Pearl** Hester's daughter. She is characterized as a living version of the scarlet letter.
- **Governor Bellingham** The elderly governor of Massachusetts.
- **John Wilson** The eldest clergyman in Boston, he is a friend of Arthur Dimmesdale.
- **Mistress Hibbins** Governor Bellingham's widowed sister. She is commonly known to be a witch who ventures into the forest at night to ride with the "Black Man." A few years after the events of the novel, she is executed as a witch.

5.2.3 Selected Readings from the Novel

5.2.3.1 Important Quotations

(1) I happened to place it (scarlet letter A) on my breast... It seemed to me, then, that I experienced a sensation not altogether physical, yet almost so, as of a burning heat; and as if the letter were not of red cloth, but red-hot iron. I shuddered, and involuntarily let it fall upon the floor. **(The Custom House)**

(2) In our nature, however, there is a provision, alike marvellous and merciful, that the sufferer should never know the intensity of what he endures by its present torture, but chiefly by the pang that rankles after it. **(Chapter 2 The Market-Place)**

(3) It is too deeply branded. Ye cannot take it off. And would that I might endure his agony, as well as mine! **(Chapter 3 The Recognition)**

(4) But she named the infant "Pearl," as being of great price, –purchased with all she had, –her mother's only treasure! **(Chapter 6 Pearl)**

(5) A bodily disease, which we look upon as whole and entire within itself, may,

Unit 5

Nathaniel Hawthorne and *The Scarlet Letter*

after all, be but a symptom of some ailment in the spiritual part. (Chapter 10 The Leech and His Patient)

(6) A pure hand needs no glove to cover it. (Chapter 12 The Minister's Vigil)

(7) It is to the credit of human nature, that, except where its selfishness is brought into play, it loves more readily than it hates. (Chapter 13 Another View of Hester)

(8) But this had been a sin of passion, not of principle, nor even purpose. (Chapter 18 A Flood of Sunshine)

(9) No man, for any considerable period, can wear one face to himself, and another to the multitude, without finally getting bewildered as to which may be the true. (Chapter 20 The Minister in a Maze)

(10) Among many morals which press upon us from the poor minister's miserable experience, we put only this into a sentence:"Be true! Be true! Be true! Show freely to the world, if not your worst, yet some trait whereby the worst may be inferred!" (Chapter 24 Conclusion)

5.2.3.2 Excerpts Related to Some Scenes in the Film

✣ Excerpt 1 (from Chapter 4)

After the ordeal of the public humiliation, Hester is found to be in a state of great nervous excitement. When at last medical aid is called, the misshapen man from the marketplace visits Hester. He also asks Hester to name the father of her child. When she refuses, he vows to discover the man who has dishonored him and takes revenge.

"I have thought of death," said she,—"have wished for it,—would even have prayed for it, were it fit that such as I should pray for anything. Yet, if death be in this cup, I bid thee think again, ere thou beholdest me quaff it. See! It is even now at my lips."

"Drink, then," replied he, still with the same cold composure. "Dost thou know me so little, Hester Prynne? Are my purposes wont to be so shallow? Even if I imagine a scheme of vengeance, what could I do better for my object than to let thee live,—than to give thee medicines against all harm and peril of life,—so that this burning shame may still blaze upon thy bosom?" As he spoke, he laid his long forefinger on the scarlet letter, which forthwith seemed to scorch into Hester's breast, as if it had been red-hot. He noticed her involuntary gesture, and smiled. "Live, therefore, and bear about thy doom with thee, in the eyes of men and women,—in the eyes of him whom thou didst call thy husband,—in the eyes of yonder child! And, that thou mayest live, take off this draught."

… "Hester," said he, "I ask not wherefore, nor how, thou hast fallen into the pit, or say, rather, thou hast ascended to the pedestal of infamy, on which I found thee. The reason is not far to seek. It was my folly, and thy weakness. I,—a man of thought,—the bookworm of great libraries,—a man already in decay, having given my best years to feed the hungry dream of knowledge,—what had I to do with youth and beauty like thine own! Misshapen from my birth-hour, how could I delude myself with the idea that intellectual gifts might veil physical deformity in a young girl's fantasy! Men call me wise. If sages were ever wise in their own behoof, I might have foreseen all this. I might have known that, as I came out of the vast and dismal forest, and entered this settlement of Christian men, the very first object to meet my eyes would be thyself, Hester Prynne, standing up, a statue of ignominy, before the people. Nay, from the moment when we came down the old church steps together, a married pair, I might have beheld the bale-fire of that scarlet letter blazing at the end of our path!"

"Thou knowest," said Hester,—for, depressed as she was, she could not endure this last quiet stab at the token of her shame,—"thou knowest that I was frank with thee. I felt no love, nor feigned any."

"True!" replied he. "It was my folly! I have said it. But, up to that epoch of my life, I had lived in vain. The world had been so cheerless! My heart was

Unit 5

Nathaniel Hawthorne and *The Scarlet Letter*

a habitation large enough for many guests, but lonely and chill, and without a household fire. I longed to kindle one! It seemed not so wild a dream,–old as I was, and sombre as I was, and misshapen as I was,–that the simple bliss, which is scattered far and wide for all mankind to gather up, might yet be mine. And so, Hester, I drew thee into my heart, into its innermost chamber, and sought to warm thee by the warmth which thy presence made there!"

"I have greatly wronged thee," murmured Hester.

"We have wronged each other," answered he. "Mine was the first wrong, when I betrayed thy budding youth into a false and unnatural relation with my decay. Therefore, as a man who has not thought and philosophized in vain, I seek no vengeance, plot no evil against thee. Between thee and me, the scale hangs fairly balanced. But, Hester, the man lives who has wronged us both! Who is he?"

"Ask me not!" replied Hester Prynne, looking firmly into his face. "That thou shalt never know!"

"Never, sayest thou?" rejoined he, with a smile of dark and self–relying intelligence. "Never know him! Believe me, Hester, there are few things,–whether in the outward world, or, to a certain depth, in the invisible sphere of thought,–few things hidden from the man who devotes himself earnestly and unreservedly to the solution of a mystery. Thou mayest cover up thy secret from the prying multitude. Thou mayest conceal it, too, from the ministers and magistrates, even as thou didst this day, when they sought to wrench the name out of thy heart, and give thee a partner on thy pedestal. But, as for me, I come to the inquest with other senses than they possess. I shall seek this man as I have sought truth in books; as I have sought gold in alchemy. There is a sympathy that will make me conscious of him. I shall see him tremble. I shall feel myself shudder, suddenly and unawares. Sooner or later, he must needs be mine!"

The eyes of the wrinkled scholar glowed so intensely upon her, that Hester Prynne clasped her hands over her heart, dreading lest he should read the secret there at once.

"Thou wilt not reveal his name? Not the less he is mine," resumed he, with a look of confidence, as if destiny were at one with him. "He bears no letter of infamy wrought into his garment, as thou dost; but I shall read it on his heart. Yet fear not for him! Think not that I shall interfere with Heaven's own method of retribution, or, to my own loss, betray him to the gripe of human law. Neither do thou imagine that I shall contrive aught against his life; no, nor against his fame, if, as I judge, he be a man of fair repute. Let him live! Let him hide himself in outward honor, if he may! Not the less he shall be mine!"

"Thy acts are like mercy," said Hester, bewildered and appalled. "But thy words interpret thee as a terror!"

"One thing, thou that wast my wife, I would enjoin upon thee," continued the scholar. "Thou hast kept the secret of thy paramour. Keep, likewise, mine! There are none in this land that know me. Breathe not, to any human soul, that thou didst ever call me husband! Here, on this wild outskirt of the earth, I shall pitch my tent; for, elsewhere a wanderer, and isolated from human interests, I find here a woman, a man, a child, amongst whom and myself there exist the closest ligaments. No matter whether of love or hate; no matter whether of right or wrong! Thou and thine, Hester Prynne, belong to me. My home is where thou art, and where he is. But betray me not!"

"Wherefore dost thou desire it?" inquired Hester, shrinking, she hardly knew why, from this secret bond. "Why not announce thyself openly, and cast me off at once?"

"It may be," he replied, "because I will not encounter the dishonor that besmirches the husband of a faithless woman. It may be for other reasons. Enough, it is my purpose to live and die unknown. Let, therefore, thy husband be to the world as one already dead, and of whom no tidings shall ever come. Recognize me not, by word, by sign, by look! Breathe not the secret, above all, to the man thou wottest of. Shouldst thou fail me in this, beware! His fame, his position, his life, will be in my hands. Beware!"

"I will keep thy secret, as I have his," said Hester.

"Swear it!" rejoined he.

And she took the oath.

✣ Excerpt 2 (from Chapter 8)

When Pearl is three, Hester discovers that certain "good people" of the town, including Governor Bellingham, seek to "deprive her of her child". So she visits the Governor's Hall to plead with the magistrates not to take Pearl from her care.

Unit 5

Nathaniel Hawthorne and *The Scarlet Letter*

Governor Bellingham stepped through the window into the hall, followed by his three guests.

"Hester Prynne," said he, fixing his naturally stern regard on the wearer of the scarlet letter, "there hath been much question concerning thee, of late. The point hath been weightily discussed, whether we, that are of authority and influence, do well discharge our consciences by trusting an immortal soul, such as there is in yonder child, to the guidance of one who hath stumbled and fallen, amid the pitfalls of this world. Speak thou, the child's own mother! Were it not, thinkest thou, for thy little one's temporal and eternal welfare that she be taken out of thy charge, and clad soberly, and disciplined strictly, and instructed in the truths of heaven and earth? What canst thou do for the child, in this kind?"

"I can teach my little Pearl what I have learned from this!" answered Hester Prynne, laying her finger on the red token.

"Woman, it is thy badge of shame!" replied the stern magistrate. "It is because of the stain which that letter indicates, that we would transfer thy child to other hands."

"Nevertheless," said the mother, calmly, though growing more pale, "this badge hath taught me–it daily teaches me–it is teaching me at this moment–lessons whereof my child may be the wiser and better, albeit they can profit nothing to myself."

"We will judge warily," said Bellingham, "and look well what we are about to do. Good Master Wilson, I pray you, examine this Pearl–since that is her name,–and see whether she hath had such Christian nurture as befits a child of her age." ...

"Pearl," said he, with great solemnity, "thou must take heed to instruction, that so, in due season, thou mayest wear in thy bosom the pearl of great price. Canst thou tell me, my child, who made thee?"

Now Pearl knew well enough who made her; for Hester Prynne, the daughter of a pious home, very soon after her talk with the child about her Heavenly Father, had begun to inform her of those truths which the human spirit, at whatever stage of immaturity, imbibes with such eager interest. Pearl, therefore, so large were the attainments of her three years' lifetime, could have borne a fair examination in the New England Primer, or the first column of the Westminster Catechism although unacquainted with the outward form of either of those celebrated works. But that perversity which all children have more or less of, and of which little Pearl had a tenfold portion, now, at the most inopportune moment, took thorough possession of her, and closed her lips, or impelled her to speak words amiss. After putting her finger in her mouth, with many ungracious refusals to answer good Mr. Wilson's question, the child finally announced that she had not been made at all, but had been plucked by her mother off the bush of wild roses that grew by the prison-door.

This fantasy was probably suggested by the near proximity of the Governor's red roses, as Pearl stood outside of the window; together with her recollection of the prison rose-bush, which she had passed in coming hither...

"This is awful!" cried the Governor, slowly recovering from the astonishment into which Pearl's response had thrown him. "Here is a child of three years old, and she cannot tell who made her! Without question, she is equally in the dark as to her soul, its present depravity, and future destiny! Methinks, gentlemen, we need inquire no further."

Hester caught hold of Pearl, and drew her forcibly into her arms, confronting the old Puritan magistrate with almost a fierce expression. Alone in the world, cast off by it, and with this sole treasure to keep her heart alive, she felt that she possessed indefeasible rights against the world, and was ready to defend them to the death.

"God gave me the child!" cried she. "He gave her in requital of all things else, which ye had taken from me. She is my happiness!–she is my torture, none the less! Pearl keeps me here in life! Pearl punishes me too! See ye not, she is the scarlet letter, only capable of being loved, and so endowed with a million-fold the power of retribution for my sin? Ye shall not take her! I will die first!"

"My poor woman," said the not unkind old minister, "the child shall be well cared for!–far better than thou canst do it."

"God gave her into my keeping," repeated Hester Prynne, raising her voice almost to a shriek. "I will not give her up!"–And here, by a sudden impulse, she turned to the young clergyman, Mr. Dimmesdale, at whom, up to this moment, she had seemed hardly so much as once to direct her eyes.–"Speak thou for me!" cried she. "Thou wast my pastor, and hadst charge

Unit 5
Nathaniel Hawthorne and *The Scarlet Letter*

of my soul, and knowest me better than these men can. I will not lose the child! Speak for me! Thou knowest,–for thou hast sympathies which these men lack!–thou knowest what is in my heart, and what are a mother's rights, and how much the stronger they are when that mother has but her child and the scarlet letter! Look thou to it! I will not lose the child! Look to it!"

At this wild and singular appeal, which indicated that Hester Prynne's situation had provoked her to little less than madness, the young minister at once came forward, pale, and holding his hand over his heart, as was his custom whenever his peculiarly nervous temperament was thrown into agitation. He looked now more careworn and emaciated than as we described him at the scene of Hester's public ignominy; and whether it were his failing health, or whatever the cause might be, his large dark eyes had a world of pain in their troubled and melancholy depth.

"There is truth in what she says," began the minister, with a voice sweet, tremulous, but powerful, insomuch that the hall reechoed, and the hollow armor rang with it,–"truth in what Hester says, and in the feeling which inspires her! God gave her the child, and gave her, too, an instinctive knowledge of its nature and requirements,–both seemingly so peculiar,–which no other mortal being can possess. And, moreover, is there not a quality of awful sacredness in the relation between this mother and this child?"

"Ay!–how is that, good Master Dimmesdale?" interrupted the Governor. "Make that plain, I pray you!"

"It must be even so," resumed the minister. "For, if we deem it otherwise, do we not thereby say that the Heavenly Father, the Creator of all flesh, hath lightly recognized a deed of sin, and made of no account the distinction between unhallowed lust and holy love? This child of its father's guilt and its mother's shame has come from the hand of God, to work in many ways upon her heart, who pleads so earnestly, and with such bitterness of spirit, the right to keep her. It was meant for a blessing; for the one blessing of her life! It was meant, doubtless, as the mother herself hath told us, for a retribution too; a torture to be felt at many an unthought-of moment; a pang, a sting, an ever-recurring agony, in the midst of a troubled joy! Hath she not expressed this thought in the garb of the poor child, so forcibly reminding us of that red symbol which sears her bosom?

"Well said, again!" cried good Mr. Wilson. "I feared the woman had no better thought than to make a mountebank of her child!"

"Oh, not so!–not so!" continued Mr. Dimmesdale. "She recognizes, believe me, the solemn miracle which God hath wrought, in the existence of that child. And may she feel, too,–what, methinks, is the very truth,–that this boon was meant, above all things else, to keep the mother's soul alive, and to preserve her from blacker depths of sin into which Satan might else have sought to plunge her! Therefore it is good for this poor, sinful woman that she hath an infant immortality, a being capable of eternal joy or sorrow, confided to her care,–to be trained up by her to righteousness,–to remind her, at every moment, of her fall,–but yet to teach her, as it were by the Creator's sacred pledge, that, if she bring the child to heaven, the child also will bring its parent thither! Herein is the sinful mother happier than the sinful father. For Hester Prynne's sake, then, and no less for the poor child's sake, let us leave them as Providence hath seen fit to place them!"

"You speak, my friend, with a strange earnestness," said old Roger Chillingworth, smiling at him.

"And there is weighty import in what my young brother hath spoken," added the Reverend Mr. Wilson. "What say you, worshipful Master Bellingham? Hath he not pleaded well for the poor woman?"

"Indeed hath he," answered the magistrate, "and hath adduced such arguments that we will even leave the matter as it now stands; so long, at least, as there shall be no further scandal in the woman. Care must be had, nevertheless, to put the child to due and stated examination in the catechism, at thy hands or Master Dimmesdale's. Moreover, at a proper season, the tithing-men must take heed that she go both to school and to meeting."

❦ Excerpt 3 (from Chapter 14)

Hester Prynne is so shocked at Dimmesdale's feeble and unhealthy condition that she determines to meet Chillingworth and do what might be in her power for the rescue of the victim on whom he had so evidently set his grip.

"I would speak a word with you," said she,– "a word that concerns us much."

Unit 5

Nathaniel Hawthorne and *The Scarlet Letter*

"Aha! And is it Mistress Hester that has a word for old Roger Chillingworth?" answered he, raising himself from his stooping posture. "With all my heart! Why, Mistress, I hear good tidings of you on all hands! No longer ago than yester-eve, a magistrate, a wise and godly man, was discoursing of your affairs, Mistress Hester, and whispered me that there had been question concerning you in the council. It was debated whether or no, with safety to the common weal, yonder scarlet letter might be taken off your bosom. On my life, Hester, I made my entreaty to the worshipful magistrate that it might be done forthwith!"

"It lies not in the pleasure of the magistrates to take off this badge," calmly replied Hester. "Were I worthy to be quit of it, it would fall away of its own nature, or be transformed into something that should speak a different purport."

"Nay, then, wear it, if it suit you better," rejoined he. "A woman must needs follow her own fancy, touching the adornment of her person. The letter is gayly embroidered, and shows right bravely on your bosom!"

*   *   *   *   *   *   *   *

"When we last spake together," said Hester, "now seven years ago, it was your pleasure to extort a promise of secrecy, as touching the former relation betwixt yourself and me. As the life and good fame of yonder man were in your hands, there seemed no choice to me, save to be silent, in accordance with your behest. Yet it was not without heavy misgivings that I thus bound myself; for, having cast off all duty towards other human beings, there remained a duty towards him; and something whispered me that I was betraying it, in pledging myself to keep your counsel. Since that day, no man is so near to him as you. You tread behind his every footstep. You are beside him, sleeping and waking. You search his thoughts. You burrow and rankle in his heart! Your clutch is on his life, and you cause him to die daily a living death; and still he knows you not. In permitting this, I have surely acted a false part by the only man to whom the power was left me to be true!"

"What choice had you?" asked Roger Chillingworth. "My finger, pointed at this man, would have hurled him from his pulpit into a dungeon,–thence, peradventure, to the gallows!"

"It had been better so!" said Hester Prynne.

"What evil have I done the man?" asked Roger Chillingworth again.

"I tell thee, Hester Prynne, the richest fee that ever physician earned from monarch could not have bought such care as I have wasted on this miserable priest! But for my aid, his life would have burned away in torments within the first two years after the perpetration of his crime and thine. For, Hester, his spirit lacked the strength that could have borne up, as thine has, beneath a burden like thy scarlet letter. Oh, I could reveal a goodly secret! But enough! What art can do, I have exhausted on him. That he now breathes, and creeps about on earth, is owing all to me!"

"Better he had died at once!" said Hester Prynne.

"Yea, woman, thou sayest truly!" cried old Roger Chillingworth, letting the lurid fire of his heart blaze out before her eyes. "Better had he died at once! Never did mortal suffer what this man has suffered. And all, all, in the sight of his worst enemy! He has been conscious of me. He has felt an influence dwelling always upon him like a curse. He knew, by some spiritual sense,–for the Creator never made another being so sensitive as this,–he knew that no friendly hand was pulling at his heart-strings, and that an eye was looking curiously into him, which sought only evil, and found it. But he knew not that the eye and hand were mine! With the superstition common to his brotherhood, he fancied himself given over to a fiend, to be tortured with frightful dreams, and desperate thoughts, the sting of remorse, and despair of pardon; as a foretaste of what awaits him beyond the grave. But it was the constant shadow of my presence!–the closest propinquity of the man whom he had most vilely wronged!–and who had grown to exist only by this perpetual poison of the direst revenge! Yea, indeed!–he did not err!–there was a fiend at his elbow! A mortal man, with once a human heart, has become a fiend for his especial torment!"

The unfortunate physician, while uttering these words, lifted his hands with a look of horror, as if he had beheld some frightful shape, which he could not recognize, usurping the place of his own image in a glass. It was one of those moments–which sometimes occur only at the interval of years when a man's moral aspect is faithfully revealed to his mind's eye. Not improbably, he had never before viewed himself as he did now.

"Hast thou not tortured him enough?" said Hester, noticing the old man's look. "Has he not paid thee all?"

"No!–no! He has but increased the debt!" answered the physician; and

Unit 5
Nathaniel Hawthorne and *The Scarlet Letter*

as he proceeded, his manner lost its fiercer characteristics, and subsided into gloom. "Dost thou remember me, Hester, as I was nine years agone? Even then, I was in the autumn of my days, nor was it the early autumn. But all my life had been made up of earnest, studious, thoughtful, quiet years, bestowed faithfully for the increase of mine own knowledge, and faithfully, too, though this latter object was but casual to the other,–faithfully for the advancement of human welfare. No life had been more peaceful and innocent than mine; few lives so rich with benefits conferred. Dost thou remember me? Was I not, though you might deem me cold, nevertheless a man thoughtful for others, craving little for himself,–kind, true, just, and of constant, if not warm affections? Was I not all this?"

"All this, and more," said Hester.

"And what am I now?" demanded he, looking into her face, and permitting the whole evil within him to be written on his features. "I have already told thee what I am! A fiend! Who made me so?"

"It was myself!" cried Hester, shuddering. "It was I, not less than he. Why hast thou not avenged thyself on me?"

"I have left thee to the scarlet letter," replied Roger Chillingworth. "If that have not avenged me, I can do no more!"

He laid his finger on it, with a smile.

"It has avenged thee!" answered Hester Prynne.

"I judged no less," said the physician. "And now, what wouldst thou with me touching this man?"

"I must reveal the secret," answered Hester, firmly. "He must discern thee in thy true character. What may be the result, I know not. But this long debt of confidence, due from me to him, whose bane and ruin I have been, shall at length be paid. So far as concerns the overthrow or preservation of his fair fame and his earthly state, and perchance his life, he is in thy hands. Nor do I,–whom the scarlet letter has disciplined to truth, though it be the truth of red-hot iron, entering into the soul,–nor do I perceive such advantage in his living any longer a life of ghastly emptiness, that I shall stoop to implore thy mercy. Do with him as thou wilt! There is no good for him,–no good for me,–no good for thee! There is no good for little Pearl! There is no path to guide us out of this dismal maze!"

"Woman, I could well nigh pity thee!" said Roger Chillingworth, unable

175

to restrain a thrill of admiration too; for there was a quality almost majestic in the despair which she expressed. "Thou hadst great elements. Peradventure, hadst thou met earlier with a better love than mine, this evil had not been. I pity thee, for the good that has been wasted in thy nature!"

"And I thee," answered Hester Prynne, "for the hatred that has transformed a wise and just man to a fiend! Wilt thou yet purge it out of thee, and be once more human? If not for his sake, then doubly for thine own! Forgive, and leave his further retribution to the Power that claims it! I said, but now, that there could be no good event for him, or thee, or me, who are here wandering together in this gloomy maze of evil, and stumbling, at every step, over the guilt wherewith we have strewn our path. It is not so! There might be good for thee, and thee alone, since thou hast been deeply wronged, and hast it at thy will to pardon. Wilt thou give up that only privilege? Wilt thou reject that priceless benefit?"

"Peace, Hester, peace!" replied the old man, with gloomy sternness. "It is not granted me to pardon. I have no such power as thou tellest me of. My old faith, long forgotten, comes back to me, and explains all that we do, and all we suffer. By thy first step awry, thou didst plant the germ of evil; but since that moment, it has all been a dark necessity. Ye that have wronged me are not sinful, save in a kind of typical illusion; neither am I fiend-like, who have snatched a fiend's office from his hands. It is our fate. Let the black flower blossom as it may! Now go thy ways, and deal as thou wilt with yonder man."

✣ Excerpt 4 (from Chapter 17)

Hester decides to tell Dimmesdale the truth and warns him against his physician. Now Hester is waiting with Pearl in the woods for Dimmesdale as he is returning from a missionary journey to the Indians.

After a while, the minister fixed his eyes on Hester Prynne's.

"Hester," said he, "hast thou found peace?"

She smiled drearily, looking down upon her bosom.

"Hast thou?" she asked.

"None!–nothing but despair!" he answered. "What else could I look

Unit 5

Nathaniel Hawthorne and *The Scarlet Letter*

for, being what I am, and leading such a life as mine? Were I an atheist,–a man devoid of conscience,–a wretch with coarse and brutal instincts,–I might have found peace, long ere now. Nay, I never should have lost it! But, as matters stand with my soul, whatever of good capacity there originally was in me, all of God's gifts that were the choicest have become the ministers of spiritual torment. Hester, I am most miserable!"

"The people reverence thee," said Hester. "And surely thou workest good among them! Doth this bring thee no comfort?"

"More misery, Hester!–only the more misery!" answered the clergyman, with a bitter smile. "As concerns the good which I may appear to do, I have no faith in it. It must needs be a delusion. What can a ruined soul, like mine, effect towards the redemption of other souls?–or a polluted soul towards their purification? And as for the people's reverence, would that it were turned to scorn and hatred! Canst thou deem it, Hester, a consolation, that I must stand up in my pulpit, and meet so many eyes turned upward to my face, as if the light of heaven were beaming from it!–must see my flock hungry for the truth, and listening to my words as if a tongue of Pentecost were speaking!–and then look inward, and discern the black reality of what they idolize? I have laughed, in bitterness and agony of heart, at the contrast between what I seem and what I am! And Satan laughs at it!"

"You wrong yourself in this," said Hester gently. "You have deeply and sorely repented. Your sin is left behind you, in the days long past. Your present life is not less holy, in very truth, than it seems in people's eyes. Is there no reality in the penitence thus sealed and witnessed by good works? And wherefore should it not bring you peace?"

"No, Hester, no!" replied the clergyman. "There is no substance in it! It is cold and dead, and can do nothing for me! Of penance, I have had enough! Of penitence, there has been none! Else, I should long ago have thrown off these garments of mock holiness, and have shown myself to mankind as they will see me at the judgment-seat. Happy are you, Hester, that wear the scarlet letter openly upon your bosom! Mine burns in secret! Thou little knowest what a relief it is, after the torment of a seven years' cheat, to look into an eye that recognizes me for what I am! Had I one friend–or were it my worst enemy!–to whom, when sickened with the praises of all other men, I could daily betake myself and be known as the vilest of all sinners, methinks my soul might keep itself alive thereby. Even thus much of truth would save me! But, now, it is all falsehood!–all emptiness!–all death!"

Hester Prynne looked into his face, but hesitated to speak. Yet, uttering his long-restrained emotions so vehemently as he did, his words here offered her the very point of circumstances in which to interpose what she came to say. She conquered her fears, and spoke.

"Such a friend as thou hast even now wished for," said she, "with whom to weep over thy sin, thou hast in me, the partner of it!" –Again she hesitated, but brought out the words with an effort.– "Thou hast long had such an enemy, and dwellest with him, under the same roof!"

The minister started to his feet, gasping for breath, and clutching at his heart, as if he would have torn it out of his bosom.

"Ha! What sayest thou!" cried he. "An enemy! And under mine own roof! What mean you?"

Hester Prynne was now fully sensible of the deep injury for which she was responsible to this unhappy man, in permitting him to lie for so many years, or, indeed, for a single moment, at the mercy of one whose purposes could not be other than malevolent. The very contiguity of his enemy, beneath whatever mask the latter might conceal himself, was enough to disturb the magnetic sphere of a being so sensitive as Arthur Dimmesdale. There had been a period when Hester was less alive to this consideration; or, perhaps, in the misanthropy of her own trouble, she left the minister to bear what she might picture to herself as a more tolerable doom. But of late, since the night of his vigil, all her sympathies towards him had been both softened and invigorated. She now read his heart more accurately. She doubted not, that the continual presence of Roger Chillingworth,–the secret poison of his malignity, infecting all the air about him,–and his authorized interference, as a physician, with the minister's physical and spiritual infirmities,–that these bad opportunities had been turned to a cruel purpose. By means of them, the sufferer's conscience had been kept in an irritated state, the tendency of which was, not to cure by wholesome pain, but to disorganize and corrupt his spiritual being. Its result, on earth, could hardly fail to be insanity, and, hereafter, that eternal alienation from the Good and True, of which madness is perhaps the earthly type.

Such was the ruin to which she had brought the man, once,–nay, why

Unit 5

Nathaniel Hawthorne and *The Scarlet Letter*

should we not speak it?–still so passionately loved! Hester felt that the sacrifice of the clergyman's good name, and death itself, as she had already told Roger Chillingworth, would have been infinitely preferable to the alternative which she had taken upon herself to choose. And now, rather than have had this grievous wrong to confess, she would gladly have laid down on the forest leaves and died there, at Arthur Dimmesdale's feet.

"O Arthur," cried she, "forgive me! In all things else, I have striven to be true! Truth was the one virtue which I might have held fast, and did hold fast, through all extremity; save when thy good,–thy life,–thy fame,–were put in question! Then I consented to a deception. But a lie is never good, even though death threaten on the other side! Dost thou not see what I would say? That old man!–the physician!–he whom they call Roger Chillingworth!–he was my husband!"

The minister looked at her for an instant, with all that violence of passion, which–intermixed, in more shapes than one, with his higher, purer, softer qualities–was, in fact, the portion of him which the Devil claimed, and through which he sought to win the rest. Never was there a blacker or a fiercer frown than Hester now encountered. For the brief space that it lasted, it was a dark transfiguration. But his character had been so much enfeebled by suffering, that even its lower energies were incapable of more than a temporary struggle. He sank down on the ground, and buried his face in his hands.

"I might have known it!" murmured he. "I did know it! Was not the secret told me, in the natural recoil of my heart, at the first sight of him, and as often as I have seen him since? Why did I not understand? O Hester Prynne, thou little, little knowest all the horror of this thing! And the shame! –the indelicacy! –the horrible ugliness of this exposure of a sick and guilty heart to the very eye that would gloat over it! Woman, woman, thou art accountable for this! I cannot forgive thee!"

"Thou shalt forgive me!" cried Hester, flinging herself on the fallen leaves beside him. "Let God punish! Thou shalt forgive!"

With sudden and desperate tenderness, she threw her arms around him, and pressed his head against her bosom; little caring though his cheek rested on the scarlet letter. He would have released himself, but strove in vain to do so. Hester would not set him free, lest he should look her sternly in the face.

All the world had frowned on her,—for seven long years had it frowned upon this lonely woman,—and still she bore it all, nor ever once turned away her firm, sad eyes. Heaven, likewise, had frowned upon her, and she had not died. But the frown of this pale, weak, sinful, and sorrow-stricken man was what Hester could not bear and live!

"Wilt thou yet forgive me?" she repeated, over and over again. "Wilt thou not frown? Wilt thou forgive?"

"I do forgive you, Hester," replied the minister, at length, with a deep utterance, out of an abyss of sadness, but no anger. "I freely forgive you now. May God forgive us both! We are not, Hester, the worst sinners in the world. There is one worse than even the polluted priest! That old man's revenge has been blacker than my sin. He has violated, in cold blood, the sanctity of a human heart. Thou and I, Hester, never did so!"

"Never, never!" whispered she. "What we did had a consecration of its own. We felt it so! We said so to each other! Hast thou forgotten it?"

"Hush, Hester!" said Arthur Dimmesdale, rising from the ground. "No; I have not forgotten!"

Excerpt 5 (from Chapter 23)

On Election Day Dimmesdale delivers a powerful sermon. As the procession leaves the church, everyone has only words of praise for the minister's inspired address, but Dimmesdale's strength fails him. In front of the whole community he reaches for Hester and Pearl, and with them ascends the scaffold. Almost fainting, but with a voice terrible and majestic, Dimmesdale admitted his guilt to the watching people.

"Hester," said he, "come hither! Come, my little Pearl!"

It was a ghastly look with which he regarded them; but there was something at once tender and strangely triumphant in it. The child, with the bird-like motion which was one of her characteristics, flew to him, and clasped her arms about his knees. Hester Prynne—slowly, as if impelled by inevitable fate, and against her strongest will—likewise drew near, but paused before she reached him. At this instant, old Roger Chillingworth thrust himself through the crowd,—or, perhaps, so dark, disturbed, and evil, was his look, he rose up out of some nether region,—to snatch back his victim from what he sought to do! Be that as it might, the old man rushed forward, and caught the minister by the arm.

"Madman, hold! What is your purpose?" whispered he. "Wave back that woman! Cast off this child! All shall be well! Do not blacken your fame and perish in dishonor! I can yet save you! Would you bring infamy on your sacred profession?"

"Ha, tempter! Methinks thou art too late!" answered the minister, encountering his eye, fearfully, but firmly. "Thy power is not what it was! With God's help, I shall escape thee now!"

He again extended his hand to the woman of the scarlet letter.

"Hester Prynne," cried he, with a piercing earnestness, "in the name of Him, so terrible and so merciful, who gives me grace, at this last moment, to do what—for my own heavy sin and miserable agony—I withheld myself from doing seven years ago, come hither now, and twine thy strength about me! Thy strength, Hester; but let it be guided by the will which God hath granted me! This wretched and wronged old man is opposing it with all his might! with all his own might, and the fiend's! Come, Hester, come! Support me up yonder scaffold!"

The crowd was in a tumult. The men of rank and dignity, who stood more immediately around the clergyman, were so taken by surprise, and so perplexed as to the purport of what they saw,—unable to receive the explanation which most readily presented itself, or to imagine any other,—that they remained silent and inactive spectators of the judgment which Providence seemed about to work. They beheld the minister, leaning on Hester's shoulder and supported by her arm around him, approach the scaffold, and ascend its steps; while still the little hand of the sin-born child was clasped in his. Old Roger Chillingworth followed, as one intimately connected with the drama of guilt and sorrow in which they had all been actors, and well entitled, therefore, to be present at its closing scene."

"Hadst thou sought the whole earth over," said he, looking darkly at the clergyman, "there was no one place so secret,—no high place nor lowly place, where thou couldst have escaped me,—save on this very scaffold!"

"Thanks be to Him who hath led me hither!" answered the minister.

Yet he trembled, and turned to Hester with an expression of doubt and anxiety in his eyes, not the less evidently betrayed, that there was a feeble smile upon his lips.

"Is not this better," murmured he, "than what we dreamed of in the forest?"

"I know not! I know not!" she hurriedly replied. "Better? Yea; so we may both die, and little Pearl die with us!"

"For thee and Pearl, be it as God shall order," said the minister; "and God is merciful! Let me now do the will which He hath made plain before my sight. For, Hester, I am a dying man. So let me make haste to take my shame upon me!"

Partly supported by Hester Prynne, and holding one hand of little Pearl's, the Reverend Mr. Dimmesdale turned to the dignified and venerable rulers; to the holy ministers, who were his brethren; to the people, whose great heart was thoroughly appalled, yet overflowing with tearful sympathy, as knowing that some deep life-matter–which, if full of sin, was full of anguish and repentance likewise–was now to be laid open to them. The sun, but little past its meridian, shone down upon the clergyman, and gave a distinctness to his figure, as he stood out from all the earth, to put in his plea of guilty at the bar of Eternal Justice.

"People of New England!" cried he, with a voice that rose over them, high, solemn, and majestic,–yet had always a tremor through it, and sometimes a shriek, struggling up out of a fathomless depth of remorse and woe,–"ye, that have loved me!–ye, that have deemed me holy!–behold me here, the one sinner of the world! At last!–at last!–I stand upon the spot where, seven years since, I should have stood; here, with this woman, whose arm, more than the little strength wherewith I have crept hitherward, sustains me, at this dreadful moment, from grovelling down upon my face. Lo, the scarlet letter which Hester wears! Ye have all shuddered at it! Wherever her walk hath been,–wherever, so miserably burdened, she may have hoped to find repose,–it hath cast a lurid gleam of awe and horrible repugnance round about her. But there stood one in the midst of you, at whose brand of sin and infamy ye have not shuddered!"

It seemed, at this point, as if the minister must leave the remainder of his secret undisclosed. But he fought back the bodily weakness,–and, still more, the faintness of heart,–that was striving for the mastery with him. He threw off all assistance, and stepped passionately forward a pace before the woman and the child.

Unit 5
Nathaniel Hawthorne and *The Scarlet Letter*

"It was on him!" he continued, with a kind of fierceness, so determined was he to speak out the whole. "God's eye beheld it! The angels were forever pointing at it! The Devil knew it well, and fretted it continually with the touch of his burning finger! But he hid it cunningly from men, and walked among you with the mien of a spirit, mournful, because so pure in a sinful world!–and sad, because he missed his heavenly kindred! Now, at the death-hour, he stands up before you! He bids you look again at Hester's scarlet letter! He tells you, that, with all its mysterious horror, it is but the shadow of what he bears on his own breast, and that even this, his own red stigma, is no more than the type of what has seared his inmost heart! Stand any here that question God's judgment on a sinner? Behold! Behold a dreadful witness of it!"

With a convulsive motion, he tore away the ministerial band from before his breast. It was revealed! But it were irreverent to describe that revelation. For an instant, the gaze of the horror-stricken multitude was concentrated on the ghastly miracle; while the minister stood, with a flush of triumph in his face, as one who, in the crisis of acutest pain, had won a victory. Then, down he sank upon the scaffold! Hester partly raised him, and supported his head against her bosom. Old Roger Chillingworth knelt down beside him, with a blank, dull countenance, out of which the life seemed to have departed.

"Thou hast escaped me!" he repeated more than once. "Thou hast escaped me!"

"May God forgive thee!" said the minister. "Thou, too, hast deeply sinned!"

He withdrew his dying eyes from the old man, and fixed them on the woman and the child.

"My little Pearl," said he, feebly, –and there was a sweet and gentle smile over his face, as of a spirit sinking into deep repose; nay, now that the burden was removed, it seemed almost as if he would be sportive with the child, –"dear little Pearl, wilt thou kiss me now? Thou wouldst not, yonder, in the forest! But now thou wilt?"

Pearl kissed his lips. A spell was broken. The great scene of grief, in which the wild infant bore a part, had developed all her sympathies; and as her tears fell upon her father's cheek, they were the pledge that she would grow up amid human joy and sorrow, nor forever do battle with the world, but be a woman in it. Towards her mother, too, Pearl's errand as a messenger of anguish was all fulfilled.

"Hester," said the clergyman, "farewell!"

"Shall we not meet again?" whispered she, bending her face down close to his. "Shall we not spend our immortal life together? Surely, surely, we have ransomed one another, with all this woe! Thou lookest far into eternity, with those bright dying eyes! Then tell me what thou seest?"

"Hush, Hester, hush!" said he, with tremulous solemnity. "The law we broke!–the sin here so awfully revealed!–let these alone be in thy thoughts! I fear! I fear! It may be that, when we forgot our God,–when we violated our reverence each for the other's soul,–it was thenceforth vain to hope that we could meet hereafter, in an everlasting and pure reunion. God knows; and He is merciful! He hath proved his mercy, most of all, in my afflictions. By giving me this burning torture to bear upon my breast! By sending yonder dark and terrible old man to keep the torture always at red-heat! By bringing me hither, to die this death of triumphant ignominy before the people! Had either of these agonies been wanting, I had been lost forever! Praised be His name! His will be done! Farewell!"

5.2.3.3 Passages for Understanding the Film

(1) ...the Reverend Mr. Dimmesdale; a young clergyman, who had come from one of the great English universities, bringing all the learning of the age into our wild forest-land. His eloquence and religious fervor had already given the earnest of high eminence in his profession. He was a person of very striking aspect, with a white, lofty, and impending brow, large, brown, melancholy eyes, and a mouth which, unless when he forcibly compressed it, was apt to be tremulous, expressing both nervous sensibility and a vast power of self-restraint. Notwithstanding his high native gifts and scholar-like attainments, there was an air about this young minister, –an apprehensive, a startled, a half-frightened look, –as of a being who felt himself quite astray and at a loss in the pathway of human existence, and could only be at ease in some seclusion of his own. Therefore, so far as his duties would permit, he trode in the shadowy by-paths, and thus kept himself simple and childlike; coming forth, when occasion was, with a freshness, and fragrance, and dewy purity of thought, which, as many people said, affected

Unit 5

Nathaniel Hawthorne and *The Scarlet Letter*

them like the speech of an angel. **(Chapter 3)**

(2) It was not an age of delicacy, and her position, although she understood it well, and was in little danger of forgetting it, was often brought before her vivid self-perception, like a new anguish, by the rudest touch upon the tenderest spot. The poor, as we have already said, whom she sought out to be the objects of her bounty, often reviled the hand that was stretched forth to succor them. Dames of elevated rank, likewise, whose doors she entered in the way of her occupation, were accustomed to distil drops of bitterness into her heart; sometimes through that alchemy of quiet malice, by which women can concoct a subtile poison from ordinary trifles; and sometimes, also, by a coarser expression, that fell upon the sufferer's defenceless breast like a rough blow upon an ulcerated wound. Hester had schooled herself long and well; she never responded to these attacks, save by a flush of crimson that rose irrepressibly over her pale cheek, and again subsided into the depths of her bosom. She was patient, –a martyr, indeed, –but she forebore to pray for enemies, lest, in spite of her forgiving aspirations, the words of the blessing should stubbornly twist themselves into a curse. **(Chapter 5)**

(3) OLD ROGER CHILLINGWORTH, throughout life, had been calm in temperament, kindly, though not of warm affections, but ever, and in all his relations with the world, a pure and upright man. He had begun an investigation, as he imagined, with the severe and equal integrity of a judge, desirous only of truth, even as if the question involved no more than the air-drawn lines and figures of a geometrical problem, instead of human passions, and wrongs inflicted on himself. But, as he proceeded, a terrible fascination, a kind of fierce, though still calm, necessity seized the old man within its gripe and never set him free again until he had done all its bidding. He now dug into the poor clergyman's heart, like a miner searching for gold; or, rather, like a sexton delving into a grave, possibly in quest of a jewel that had been buried on the dead man's bosom, but likely to find nothing save mortality and corruption. Alas for his own soul, if these were what he sought! **(Chapter 10)**

(4) … by the constitution of his nature, he (Dimmesdale) loved the truth and loathed the lie, as few men ever did. Therefore, above all things else, he loathed his miserable self!

… In Mr. Dimmesdale's secret closet, under lock and key, there was a bloody scourge. Oftentimes, this Protestant and Puritan divine had plied it on his own shoulders; laughing bitterly at himself the while, and smiting so much the more pitilessly because of that bitter laugh. It was his custom, too, as it has been that of many other pious Puritans, to fast,—not, however, like them, in order to purify the body and render it the fitter medium of celestial illumination, but rigorously, and until his knees trembled beneath him, as an act of penance. **(Chapter 11)**

(5) Hester Prynne did not now occupy precisely the same position in which we beheld her during the earlier periods of her ignominy. Years had come, and gone. Pearl was now seven years old. Her mother, with the scarlet letter on her breast, glittering in its fantastic embroidery, had long been a familiar object to the townspeople.... the blameless purity of her life during all these years in which she had been set apart to infamy, was reckoned largely in her favor ... It was perceived, too, that while Hester never put forward even the humblest title to share in the world's privileges,—farther than to breathe the common air, and earn daily bread for little Pearl and herself by the faithful labor of her hands,—she was quick to acknowledge her sisterhood with the race of man, whenever benefits were to be conferred. None so ready as she to give of her little substance to every demand of poverty; even though the bitter-hearted pauper threw back a gibe in requital of the food brought regularly to his door, or the garments wrought for him by the fingers that could have embroidered a monarch's robe. None so self-devoted as Hester, when pestilence stalked through the town. In all seasons of calamity, indeed, whether general or of individuals, the outcast of society at once found her place... Such helpfulness was found in her,—so much power to do, and power to sympathize,—that many people refused to interpret the scarlet A by its original signification. They said that it meant Able; so strong was Hester Prynne, with a woman's strength. **(Chapter 13)**

(6) AFTER MANY DAYS, when time sufficed for the people to arrange their thoughts in reference to the foregoing scene, there was more than one account of what had been witnessed on the scaffold.

Most of the spectators testified to having seen, on the breast of the unhappy minister, a SCARLET LETTER—the very semblance of that worn by Hester Prynne—imprinted in the flesh. As regarded its origin, there were various explanations, all of which must necessarily have been conjectural. Some affirmed that the Reverend Mr. Dimmesdale, on the very day when

Unit 5
Nathaniel Hawthorne and *The Scarlet Letter*

Hester Prynne first wore her ignominious badge, had begun a course of penance,–which he afterwards, in so many futile methods, followed out,–by inflicting a hideous torture on himself. Others contended that the stigma had not been produced until a long time subsequent, when old Roger Chillingworth, being a potent necromancer, had caused it to appear, through the agency of magic and poisonous drugs. Others, again,–and those best able to appreciate the minister's peculiar sensibility, and the wonderful operation of his spirit upon the body,–whispered their belief, that the awful symbol was the effect of the ever-active tooth of remorse, gnawing from the inmost heart outwardly, and at last manifesting Heaven's dreadful judgment by the visible presence of the letter. The reader may choose among these theories.

    *   *   *   *   *   *   *   *

Nothing was more remarkable than the change which took place, almost immediately after Mr. Dimmesdale's death, in the appearance and demeanor of the old man known as Roger Chillingworth. All his strength and energy–all his vital and intellectual force–seemed at once to desert him; … At old Roger Chillingworth's decease (which took place within the year), and by his last will and testament, of which Governor Bellingham and the Reverend Mr. Wilson were executors, he bequeathed a very considerable amount of property, both here and in England, to little Pearl, the daughter of Hester Prynne.

So Pearl–the elf-child, –the demon offspring, as some people, up to that epoch, persisted in considering her, –became the richest heiress of her day, in the New World…in no long time after the physician's death, the wearer of the scarlet letter disappeared, and Pearl along with her…(many years later) Hester Prynne had returned, and taken up her long-forsaken shame! But where was little Pearl? **(Chapter 24)**

5.2.3.4 Chapter Reading

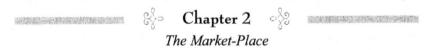

Chapter 2
The Market-Place

THE GRASS-PLOT BEFORE THE JAIL, in Prison Lane, on a certain summer morning, not less than two centuries ago, was occupied by a pretty large number of the inhabitants (居民) of Boston, all with their eyes intently fastened on the iron-clamped oaken (橡木的) door. Amongst any other population, or at a later period in the history of New England, the grim rigidity that petrified the bearded physiognomies of these good people would have augured (预言) some awful business in hand. It could have betokened (预示) nothing short of the anticipated execution of some noted culprit, on whom the sentence of a legal tribunal (法庭) had but confirmed the verdict (裁决) of public sentiment. But, in that early severity of the Puritan character, an inference of this kind could not so indubitably (无疑地) be drawn. It might be that a sluggish (懒散的) bond-servant, or an undutiful child, whom his parents had given over to the civil authority, was to be corrected at the whipping-post. It might be that an Antinomian, a Quaker, or other heterodox (异端的) religionist was to be scourged (鞭笞) out of the town, or an idle and vagrant (漂泊的) Indian, whom the white man's fire-water (烈酒) had made riotous (喧闹的) about the streets, was to be driven with stripes into the shadow of the forest. It might be, too, that a witch, like old Mistress Hibbins, the bitter-tempered widow of the magistrate, was to die upon the gallows (绞架). In either case, there was very much the same solemnity of demeanor (举止) on the part of the spectators; as befitted a people amongst whom religion and law were almost identical, and in whose character both were so thoroughly interfused (融合), that the mildest and severest acts of public discipline were alike made venerable (神圣庄严的) and awful. Meagre, indeed, and cold was the sympathy that a transgressor (违背者) might look for from such by-standers at the scaffold (刑台). On the other hand, a penalty (处罚), which, in our days, would infer a degree of mocking infamy (丑行，恶行) and ridicule, might then be invested with almost as stern a dignity as the punishment of death itself.

It was a circumstance to be noted, on the summer morning when our story begins its course, that the women, of whom there were several in the crowd, appeared to take a peculiar interest in whatever penal infliction might be expected to ensue (相继发生). The age had not so much refinement, that any sense of impropriety restrained the wearers of petticoat (衬裙) and farthingale (撑裙) from stepping forth into the public ways, and wedging (挤入) their not unsubstantial persons, if occasion were, into the throng (人群) nearest to the scaffold at an execution. Morally, as well as materially, there was a coarser fibre in those wives and maidens of old English birth and breeding, than

Unit 5

Nathaniel Hawthorne and *The Scarlet Letter*

in their fair descendants, separated from them by a series of six or seven generations; for, throughout that chain of ancestry, every successive mother has transmitted (遗传) to her child a fainter bloom, a more delicate and briefer beauty, and a slighter physical frame, if not a character of less force and solidity, than her own. The women who were now standing about the prison-door stood within less than half a century of the period when the man-like Elizabeth had been the not altogether unsuitable representative of the sex. They were her countrywomen; and the beef and ale of their native land, with a moral diet not a whit more refined, entered largely into their composition. The bright morning sun, therefore, shone on broad shoulders and well-developed busts (胸部) and on round and ruddy (红润的) cheeks, that had ripened in the far-off island, and had hardly yet grown paler or thinner in the atmosphere of New England. There was, moreover, a boldness and rotundity (声音洪亮) of speech among these matrons (已婚妇女), as most of them seemed to be, that would startle us at the present day, whether in respect to its purport (含义) or its volume of tone.

"Goodwives," said a hard-featured dame of fifty, "I'll tell ye a piece of my mind. It would be greatly for the public behoof (好处), if we women, being of mature age and church-members in good repute (名声), should have the handling of such malefactresses (坏女人) as this Hester Prynne. What think ye, gossips? If the hussy (荡妇) stood up for judgment before us five, that are now here in a knot together, would she come off with such a sentence as the worshipful magistrates have awarded? Marry, I trow (相信) not!"

"People say," said another, "that the Reverend Master Dimmesdale, her godly pastor, takes it very grievously to heart that such a scandal should have come upon his congregation (会众)."

"The magistrates are God-fearing gentlemen, but merciful overmuch,– that is a truth," added a third autumnal (已过中年的) matron. "At the very least, they should have put the brand of a hot iron on Hester Prynne's forehead. Madam Hester would have winced (畏缩) at that, I warrant me. But she,–the naughty baggage (婊子),–little will she care what they put upon the bodice (女衣上部) of her gown! Why, look you, she may cover it with a brooch (胸针), or such like heathenish (异教的) adornment (饰物), and so walk the streets as brave as ever!"

"Ah, but," interposed, more softly, a young wife, holding a child by the hand, "let her cover the mark as she will, the pang of it will be always in her heart."

"What do we talk of marks and brands, whether on the bodice of her gown, or the flesh of her forehead?" cried another female, the ugliest as well as the most pitiless of these self-constituted（自命的）judges. "This woman has brought shame upon us all, and ought to die. Is there no law for it? Truly, there is, both in the Scripture（圣经）and the statute-book（法令全书）. Then let the magistrates, who have made it of no effect, thank themselves if their own wives and daughters go astray!"

"Mercy on us, goodwife," exclaimed a man in the crowd, "is there no virtue in woman, save what springs from a wholesome fear of the gallows? That is the hardest word yet! Hush, now, gossips! for the lock is turning in the prison-door, and here comes Mistress Prynne herself."

The door of the jail being flung open from within, there appeared, in the first place, like a black shadow emerging into sunshine, the grim and grisly（令人毛骨悚然的）presence of the town-beadle, with a sword by his side, and his staff of office in his hand. This personage（角色）prefigured and represented in his aspect the whole dismal severity of the Puritanic code of law（清教徒法典）, which it was his business to administer in its final and closest application to the offender. Stretching forth the official staff in his left hand, he laid his right upon the shoulder of a young woman, whom he thus drew forward; until, on the threshold of the prison-door, she repelled（抵制）him, by an action marked with natural dignity and force of character, and stepped into the open air, as if by her own free will. She bore in her arms a child, a baby of some three months old, who winked and turned aside its little face from the too vivid light of day; because its existence, heretofore（此时以前）, had brought it acquainted only with the gray twilight of a dungeon（地牢）, or other darksome apartment of the prison.

When the young woman–the mother of this child–stood fully revealed before the crowd, it seemed to be her first impulse to clasp the infant closely to her bosom; not so much by an impulse of motherly affection, as that she might thereby（因此）conceal a certain token, which was wrought or fastened into her dress. In a moment, however, wisely judging that one token of her shame would but poorly serve to hide another, she took the baby on her arm, and, with a burning blush, and yet a haughty smile, and a glance that would

Unit 5

Nathaniel Hawthorne and *The Scarlet Letter*

not be abashed（局促不安的）, looked around at her townspeople and neighbors. On the breast of her gown, in fine red cloth, surrounded with an elaborate embroidery（刺绣）and fantastic flourishes（华饰）of gold-thread, appeared the letter A. It was so artistically done, and with so much fertility and gorgeous luxuriance of fancy, that it had all the effect of a last and fitting decoration to the apparel（衣服）which she wore; and which was of a splendor in accordance with the taste of the age, but greatly beyond what was allowed by the sumptuary regulations of the colony.

  The young woman was tall, with a figure of perfect elegance on a large scale. She had dark and abundant hair, so glossy（有光泽的）that it threw off the sunshine with a gleam, and a face which, besides being beautiful from regularity of feature and richness of complexion, had the impressiveness belonging to a marked brow and deep black eyes. She was lady-like, too, after the manner of the feminine gentility of those days; characterized by a certain state and dignity, rather than by the delicate, evanescent（易消散的）, and indescribable（难以形容的）grace, which is now recognized as its indication. And never had Hester Prynne appeared more lady-like, in the antique interpretation of the term, than as she issued from the prison. Those who had before known her, and had expected to behold her dimmed and obscured by a disastrous cloud, were astonished, and even startled, to perceive how her beauty shone out, and made a halo（光环）of the misfortune and ignominy（耻辱）in which she was enveloped. It may be true, that, to a sensitive observer, there was something exquisitely painful in it. Her attire, which, indeed, she had wrought for the occasion, in prison, and had modelled much after her own fancy, seemed to express the attitude of her spirit, the desperate recklessness of her mood, by its wild and picturesque peculiarity. But the point which drew all eyes, and, as it were, transfigured the wearer,—so that both men and women, who had been familiarly acquainted with Hester Prynne, were now impressed as if they beheld her for the first time,—was that SCARLET LETTER, so fantastically embroidered and illuminated upon her bosom. It had the effect of a spell, taking her out of the ordinary relations with humanity, and enclosing her in a sphere by herself.

  "She hath good skill at her needle, that's certain," remarked one of the female spectators; "but did ever a woman, before this brazen（厚颜无耻的）hussy, contrive such a way of showing it! Why, gossips, what is it but to laugh in the faces of our godly magistrates, and make a pride out of what they, worthy gentlemen, meant for a punishment?"

"It were well," muttered the most iron-visaged of the old dames, "if we stripped Madam Hester's rich gown off her dainty (迷人的) shoulders; and as for the red letter, which she hath stitched so curiously, I'll bestow a rag of mine own rheumatic flannel (风湿病用的法兰绒), to make a fitter one!"

"O, peace, neighbors, peace!" whispered their youngest companion; "do not let her hear you! Not a stitch in that embroidered letter, but she has felt it in her heart."

The grim beadle now made a gesture with his staff.

"Make way, good people, make way, in the King's name!" cried he. "Open a passage; and, I promise ye, Mistress Prynne shall be set where man, woman, and child may have a fair sight of her brave apparel, from this time till an hour past meridian (正午). A blessing on the righteous Colony of the Massachusetts, where iniquity (罪行) is dragged out into the sunshine! Come along, Madam Hester, and show your scarlet letter in the market-place!"

A lane was forthwith (立刻) opened through the crowd of spectators. Preceded by the beadle, and attended by an irregular procession of stern-browed men and unkindly visaged women, Hester Prynne set forth towards the place appointed for her punishment. A crowd of eager and curious school-boys, understanding little of the matter in hand, except that it gave them a half-holiday, ran before her progress, turning their heads continually to stare into her face, and at the winking baby in her arms, and at the ignominious (耻辱的) letter on her breast. It was no great distance, in those days, from the prison-door to the market-place. Measured by the prisoner's experience, however, it might be reckoned a journey of some length; for, haughty as her demeanor was, she perchance (或许) underwent an agony from every footstep of those that thronged to see her, as if her heart had been flung into the street for them all to spurn and trample upon. In our nature, however, there is a provision (准备), alike marvellous and merciful, that the sufferer should never know the intensity of what he endures by its present torture, but chiefly by the pang that rankles (引起) after it. With almost a serene deportment (举止), therefore, Hester Prynne passed through this portion of her ordeal, and came to a sort of scaffold, at the western extremity of the market-place. It stood nearly beneath the eaves of Boston's earliest church, and appeared to be a

Unit 5

Nathaniel Hawthorne and *The Scarlet Letter*

fixture(固定装置) there.

In fact, this scaffold constituted a portion of a penal(刑罚的) machine, which now, for two or three generations past, has been merely historical and traditionary among us, but was held, in the old time, to be as effectual(有效的) an agent, in the promotion of good citizenship, as ever was the guillotine(断头台) among the terrorists of France. It was, in short, the platform of the pillory(示众); and above it rose the framework of that instrument of discipline, so fashioned as to confine the human head in its tight grasp, and thus hold it up to the public gaze. The very ideal of ignominy was embodied and made manifest in this contrivance of wood and iron. There can be no outrage, methinks, against our common nature,—whatever be the delinquencies(过失) of the individual,—no outrage more flagrant(恶名昭著的) than to forbid the culprit to hide his face for shame; as it was the essence of this punishment to do. In Hester Prynne's instance, however, as not unfrequently in other cases, her sentence bore, that she should stand a certain time upon the platform, but without undergoing that gripe about the neck and confinement of the head, the proneness to which was the most devilish characteristic of this ugly engine. Knowing well her part, she ascended a flight of wooden steps, and was thus displayed to the surrounding multitude, at about the height of a man's shoulders above the street.

Had there been a Papist among the crowd of Puritans, he might have seen in this beautiful woman, so picturesque in her attire and mien, and with the infant at her bosom, an object to remind him of the image of Divine Maternity(圣母), which so many illustrious painters have vied(竞争) with one another to represent; something which should remind him, indeed, but only by contrast, of that sacred image of sinless motherhood, whose infant was to redeem(救赎) the world. Here, there was the taint of deepest sin in the most sacred quality of human life, working such effect, that the world was only the darker for this woman's beauty, and the more lost for the infant that she had borne.

The scene was not without a mixture of awe, such as must always invest the spectacle of guilt and shame in a fellow-creature, before society shall have grown corrupt enough to smile, instead of shuddering, at it. The witnesses of Hester Prynne's disgrace had not yet passed beyond their simplicity. They were stern enough to look upon her death, had that been the sentence, without a murmur at its severity, but had none of the heartlessness of another social state, which would find only a theme for jest in an exhibition like the present. Even had there been a disposition to turn the matter into ridicule, it must have been repressed and overpowered by the solemn presence of men no less dignified than the Governor, and several of his counsellors, a judge, a general, and the ministers of the town; all of whom sat or stood in a balcony of the meeting-house, looking down upon the platform. When such personages（要人） could constitute a part of the spectacle, without risking the majesty or reverence of rank and office, it was safely to be inferred that the infliction of a legal sentence would have an earnest and effectual meaning. Accordingly, the crowd was sombre（阴郁的） and grave. The unhappy culprit sustained herself as best a woman might, under the heavy weight of a thousand unrelenting（冷酷的） eyes, all fastened upon her, and concentrated at her bosom. It was almost intolerable to be borne. Of an impulsive and passionate nature, she had fortified herself to encounter the stings and venomous（狠毒的） stabs of public contumely（侮辱）, wreaking（发泄） itself in every variety of insult; but there was a quality so much more terrible in the solemn mood of the popular mind, that she longed rather to behold all those rigid countenances contorted（扭曲） with scornful merriment, and herself the object. Had a roar of laughter burst from the multitude,–each man, each woman, each little shrill-voiced child, contributing their individual parts,–Hester Prynne might have repaid them all with a bitter and disdainful smile. But, under the leaden（沉重的） infliction which it was her doom to endure, she felt, at moments, as if she must needs shriek out with the full power of her lungs, and cast herself from the scaffold down upon the ground, or else go mad at once.

Yet there were intervals when the whole scene, in which she was the most conspicuous object, seemed to vanish from her eyes, or, at least, glimmered indistinctly before them, like a mass of imperfectly shaped and spectral images. Her mind, and especially her memory, was preternaturally（异乎寻常地） active, and kept bringing up other scenes than this roughly hewn（劈出） street of a little town, on the edge of the Western wilderness; other faces than were lowering upon her from beneath the brims of those steeple-crowned（顶端高而尖的） hats. Reminiscences（回忆） the most trifling and immaterial（无关紧要的）, passages of infancy and schooldays, sports, childish quarrels, and the little domestic traits of her maiden years, came swarming

Unit 5
Nathaniel Hawthorne and *The Scarlet Letter*

back upon her, intermingled with recollections of whatever was gravest in her subsequent life; one picture precisely as vivid as another; as if all were of similar importance, or all alike a play. Possibly it was an instinctive device of her spirit, to relieve itself, by the exhibition of these phantasmagoric（幻影似的）forms, from the cruel weight and hardness of the reality.

  Be that as it might, the scaffold of the pillory was a point of view that revealed to Hester Prynne the entire track along which she had been treading since her happy infancy. Standing on that miserable eminence, she saw again her native village, in Old England, and her paternal home; a decayed house of gray stone, with a poverty-stricken aspect, but retaining a half-obliterated shield of arms over the portal（入口）, in token of antique gentility. She saw her father's face, with its bald brow, and reverend white beard, that flowed over the old-fashioned Elizabethan ruff（轮状皱领）; her mother's, too, with the look of heedful（深切注意的）and anxious love which it always wore in her remembrance, and which, even since her death, had so often laid the impediment（阻碍）of a gentle remonstrance in her daughter's pathway. She saw her own face, glowing with girlish beauty, and illuminating all the interior of the dusky mirror in which she had been wont（惯于）to gaze at it. There she beheld another countenance, of a man well stricken in years, a pale, thin, scholar-like visage, with eyes dim and bleared（模糊）by the lamplight that had served them to pore（钻研）over many ponderous（冗长的）books. Yet those same bleared optics had a strange, penetrating power, when it was their owner's purpose to read the human soul. This figure of the study and the cloister（隐居生活）, as Hester Prynne's womanly fancy failed not to recall, was slightly deformed（畸形的）, with the left shoulder a trifle higher than the right. Next rose before her, in memory's picture-gallery, the intricate and narrow thoroughfares（主道）, the tall, gray houses, the huge cathedrals, and the public edifices（建筑物）, ancient in date and quaint in architecture, of a Continental（欧洲大陆的）city; where a new life had awaited her, still in connection with the misshapen（畸形的）scholar; a new life, but feeding itself on time-worn materials, like a tuft（一簇）of green moss on a crumbling wall. Lastly, in lieu of these shifting scenes, came back the rude market-place of the Puritan settlement, with all the townspeople assembled and levelling their stern regards at Hester Prynne,–yes, at herself,–who stood on the scaffold of the pillory, an infant on her arm, and the letter A, in scarlet, fantastically embroidered with gold-thread, upon her bosom!

Could it be true? She clutched the child so fiercely to her breast that it sent forth a cry; she turned her eyes downward at the scarlet letter, and even touched it with her finger, to assure herself that the infant and the shame were real. Yes!–these were her realities,–all else had vanished!

Notes and Glossary for Chapter Reading

(1) physiognomies /ˌfizi'ɔgnəmiz/ n. faces, as revealing of characters 面相，相貌

(2) bond-servant: one bound to service without wages 无工资奴仆，奴隶

(3) Antinomian: A person who believed in Antinomianism（唯信仰论）, heretical thinking that challenged the seventeenth-century orthodox Puritan thinking of the Massachusetts Bay Colony. According to progressive Antinomian beliefs, one needed only have faith in God to be saved : Grace was more important than good works. 唯信仰论者

(4) Quakers: A member of the Religious Society of Friends, another heterodox sect, according to the Puritans. This religious group was founded in seventeenth-century England by George Fox. 教友派信徒，贵格会会员

(5) town-beadle: a minor parish official, one of whose duties was to lead processions

(6) The man-like Elizabeth: Queen Elizabeth I of England, 1558-1603.

(7) prefigure /priː'figə/ vt. to suggest, indicate, or represent by an antecedent form or model; foreshadow 预示，预见

(8) sumptuary /'sʌmptjuəri/ relating to or regulating expenditure; regulating personal behavior on moral or religious grounds 限制费用的，禁止奢侈的；规范的，约束的

(9) transfigure /trænsˈfigə/ vt. to alter the outward appearance of; to exalt or glorify 使…变形；美化：使变得崇高或更美

(10) spurn /spəːn/ vi. to kick at or tread on disdainfully 轻视地踏或踢

(11) Papist: a Roman Catholic, considered as a partisan of the Pope 教皇制信奉者，天主教徒

Unit 5
Nathaniel Hawthorne and *The Scarlet Letter*

5.2.4 Exercises

❶ Identify the following characters

(1) _____ suffers under the burden of her symbol of shame, but eventually becomes an accepted and even a highly valued member of the community.

(2) _____ shows no outward evidence of his sin, but he lives with the great anguish of his secret guilt until he confesses publicly and dies on the scaffold.

(3) _____ is willful and wild, considered by some townspeople to be a demon's child. She is also the truth-sayer in the novel. She sees what the adults try to hide, and she reacts to it.

(4) _____ is a scholar and uses his knowledge to disguise himself as a doctor, intent on discovering and tormenting his wife's anonymous lover rather than forgiving those that have trespassed against him.

(5) _____ makes several provoking appearances in the novel. She tempts both Hester and Dimmesdale to enter in the League of the "Blank Man", who, as a representative of the devil, haunts the wild forest.

(6) _____ is a great scholar, like most of his contemporaries in the profession. He is a grandfatherly sort of personage, and usually a vast favorite with children.

(7) _____ is described as a "stern magistrate". He is convinced that Pearl should be taken from her mother in order to receive a proper moral upbringing until Dimmesdale persuades him that the union of Pearl and her mother is a part of God's design.

❷ Plot Review

The Scarlet Letter, a novel by (1)_____, was published in (2)_____. The scene of the story is the Puritan New England of the (3)_____ century. An aged English scholar sends his young wife, Hester Prynne, to establish their home in Boston, intending to follow her, but is captured by the Indians upon his arrival in New England. While living alone in Boston and believing her husband (4) _____,

Hester commits (5) _____ and becomes pregnant. When he arrives two years later, he finds Hester in the pillory with her illegitimate child in her arms. She has resisted all attempts of the Boston clergy to make her (6) _____ the name of her child's father, and has been sentenced to this ordeal and to wear a letter A, signifying (7) _____, as a token of her sin. Seeing her shame, the husband keeps his (8) _____ secret, assumes the name Roger Chillingworth, and makes Hester swear that she will (9) _____ his identity. After her release Hester takes a cottage on the outskirts of the town and supports her child Pearl and herself with her (10) _____. By brave submission to her fate, she devotes herself to work of mercy, and gradually wins the (11) _____ of the townsfolk. Indeed some people say that the A on her dress stands for (12) _____. Arthur Dimmesdale has struggled for years with his burden of hidden (13) _____, but, though he does secret penance, pride prevents him from confessing (14) _____, and he continues to be tortured by his conscience. Chillingworth's life is (15) _____ by his preoccupation with his cruel search, and he becomes a morally degraded monomaniac. Hester, emancipated by her experience, proposes to Dimmesdale that they shall flee to Europe, and he would like to do so, but he sees flight as yielding to further (16) _____ from the Evil One. Soon Hester learns that Chillingworth has blocked her plan of escape by booking a passage on the same ship. After delivering a powerful sermon on Election Day the young minister makes a public (17) _____ on the pillory in which Hester had once been placed. As Dimmesdale dies in his lover's arms, (18) _____ by Pearl, Chillingworth cries out in agony at having lost the sole object of his perverse life. Hester and Pearl, now free from restraints of the mortified community, (19) _____ Boston. The book ends with Hester's (20) _____ to Boston and her voluntary decision to resume wearing the scarlet letter. While Pearl settles in Europe, Hester continues her life of penance, a model of endurance, goodness and victory over sin.

❸ General Questions

(1) Why is Hester taken to the scaffold in the market-place? What symbol does Hester Prynne have to wear?

Unit 5

Nathaniel Hawthorne and *The Scarlet Letter*

(2) What is Hester thinking as she stands with her baby on the scaffold?
(3) Why does Chillingworth not reveal that he is Hester's husband?
(4) Why does Hester not leave the village after she leaves prison?
(5) What happens to Dimmesdale and Chillingworth in their relationship with each other?
(6) What does Hester's letter "A" eventually come to represent to the townspeople?
(7) What does Hester resolve to do to escape their suffering? Who destroys Hester's plan to leave Boston? And how?
(8) How do the four stand on the scaffold the last time? What does Dimmesdale reveal?
(9) How do the townspeople interpret this final revelation? What happens to Chillingworth?
(10) Why does Hester return to Boston many years later?

❹ Questions for essay or discussion

(1) Why does Chillingworth choose to torture Dimmesdale and Hester when he could simply reveal that he is Hester's husband?
(2) Why did Chillingworth leave his property to Pearl?
(3) Discuss the relationship between the scarlet letter and Hester's identity. What is the difference between the identity she creates for herself and the identity society assigns to her?
(4) Does Hester show heroic qualities in the novel or in the film? If so, what are those heroic qualities?
(5) With which characters did you sympathize most while you read? With which did you sympathize the least? Explain.

Unit 6

Mark Twain and *Adventures of Huckleberry Finn*

6.1 Mark Twain: Life and Works

6.1.1 About the Author

Mark Twain is an American humorist, journalist, lecturer, and novelist. He is at the same time revered as a classic American writer and one of the most popular–in his own lifetime and at present in the United States and abroad. H. L. Mencken called him "the true father of our national literature."

Mark Twain was born Samuel Langhorne Clemens on November 30, 1835 in the village of Florida, Missouri, and grew up in the Mississippi River town of Hannibal that he later fictionalized as St. Petersburg in *The Adventures of Tom Sawyer* and *Adventures of Huckleberry Finn*. His father John Marshall Clemens was an ambitious and respected but unsuccessful country lawyer and storekeeper; his mother Jane Lampton, warm, witty, outspoken, lively and good at story-telling, was a key influence in his life.

Clemens' formal education ended soon after his father's death in 1847. He quit school and took several odd jobs before becoming apprenticed to a local printer. In 1851, when his brother Orion became a publisher

Unit 6
Mark Twain and *Adventures of Huckleberry Finn*

in Hannibal, Clemens went to work for him. From 1853, he traveled widely, as a journeyman printer, in the Eastern States and in the West. As a result of a steamboat journey down the Mississippi, he met Horace Bixby, the captain of the boat, and turned to a career on the river. After an apprenticeship of one and a half years, he became a licensed pilot in 1859. He left the Mississippi at the outbreak of the Civil War, and became, in swift succession, an army volunteer, a gold prospector in Nevada, a timber speculator and a journalist. While writing for the *Territorial Enterprise* in Virginia City in 1863, he began signing his articles "Mark Twain" –an expression used by riverboat crewmen to refer to a safe navigating depth of two fathoms. Under this name he published his first successful story "Jim Smiley and his Jumping Frog" in 1865 in the New York Saturday Press. This comic version of an old folk tale became the title story of *The Celebrated Jumping Frog of Calaveras County, and Other Sketches* (1867), which established him as a leading humorist, a reputation consolidated by *The Innocents Abroad* (1869), an account of a voyage through the Mediterranean. His popularity continued to grow through a series of works: *Roughing It* (1872), a humorous narrative of his adventures as miner and journalist in Nevada; *The Gilded Age* (1873), a satirical novel of the post-Civil War era which he co-wrote with Charles Dudley Warner; and *A Tramp Abroad* (1880), another travel narrative. The last works of what might be called Twain's optimistic period were *The Prince and the Pauper* (1882) and *Life on the Mississippi* (1883). Twain's nostalgic recollections of his early boyhood in Hannibal stirred him to write his "boys' book," *The Adventures of Tom Sawyer* (1876) and *Adventures of Huckleberry Finn* (1884). He followed up with the publication of several more books, including *A Connecticut Yankee in King Arthur's Court* (1889) and *Pudd'nhead Wilson* (1894).

The 1890s proved tragic for Twain. He had made a number of questionable investments, and the nationwide financial panic of 1893 left him bankrupt. He had to resort to lecture tours to pay his debts. His 1895–96 round-the-world lecture tour cemented his professional reputation and he earned the admiration of many of the leading artists and writers of Europe. Though his fame grew, personal tragedy followed him. His eldest and best-loved daughter Susy–who had remained in America during this period–unexpectedly died of meningitis in 1896. This was a devastating blow for her parents, from which neither would fully recover. His wife began her decline into permanent invalidism, and died in 1904. In 1909, his youngest daughter Jean died. Twain was left bitter and lonely. In 1898, the year that he cleared his debts, he wrote three works expressing his acute pessimism, *The Man that Corrupted Hadleyburg* (1900), the philosophizing treatise *What is Man?* (1906) and *The Mysterious Stranger* (1916). In 1906 he started preparing material for his Autobiography, and in 1907 received an honorary doctorate of Oxford University. He died at Redding, Connecticut, on 21 April 1910. Although only his daughter Clara outlived him, thousands of mourners filed past his casket to pay their respects at his funeral.

6.1.2 Mark Twain's Major Works

The Celebrated Jumping Frog of Calaveras County (1865)
《卡拉韦拉斯县驰名的跳蛙》（短篇）
Innocents Abroad (1869) 《傻子出国记》
Roughing It (1872) 《含辛茹苦》
The Gilded Age (1873) 《镀金时代》
The Adventures of Tom Sawyer (1876) 《汤姆·索亚历险记》
Life on the Mississippi (1883) 《密西西比河上的生活》
Adventures of Huckleberry Finn (1884, 1885)
《哈克贝利·费恩历险记》

6.2 *Adventures of Huckleberry Finn*

6.2.1 About the Novel

Adventures of Huckleberry Finn, as a sequel to *The Adventures of Tom Sawyer*, is generally accepted as Mark Twain's masterpiece and one of the great works of American fiction. It marked the climax of Mark Twain's literary creativity. Nobel Prize-winning author Ernest Hemingway claimed that "all modern American literature comes from one book by Mark Twain called Huck Finn...There was nothing before. There has been nothing as good since."

Adventures of Huckleberry Finn was first published in England in December 1884, and the corrected version of the first American edition was in February 1885. The novel took Twain eight years to write. He began it in 1876 and completed it, after several stops and starts, in 1883. To create this novel Mark Twain first overcame the difficulty of writing in the first person from a young boy's perspective. The novel is also a testament to the various dialects of the southern regions and embodies many of the characteristics of those regions. Set in the Mississippi Valley of the 1840s, the story is told by the 13-year-old Huck and involves his escape from the abusive control of his alcoholic father, the growth of his friendship with the runaway slave Jim and their adventures on the Mississippi as they journey south. Huck's moral development is the novel's major theme, and this development is evident in his decision to assist Jim in his quest for freedom. The novel has enjoyed extraordinary popularity since its publication more than one hundred years ago although the overall American critical reaction to the publishing of *Adventures of Huck Finn* in 1885 was summed up in one word: "trash". Its unpretentious, colloquial, yet poetic style, its wide-ranging humor, its embodiment of the enduring and universally shared dream of perfect innocence and freedom, its recording of a vanished way of life in the pre-Civil War Mississippi Valley have moved millions of people of all ages and conditions, and all over the world.

6.2.2 Characters

- **Huckleberry Finn**   The protagonist and narrator of the novel.
- **Widow Douglas**   She takes Huck into her home and tries to civilize him.
- **Miss Watson**   The sister of the Widow Douglas. She tries to teach Huck how to read and write properly.
- **Jim**   Miss Watson's household slave.
- **Pap**   Huck's father, an irredeemable drunk.

- **The duke and the king** A pair of impostors with whom Huck is forced to travel.
- **The Shepherdsons and the Grangerfords** Two feuding families.
- **Mary Jane Wilks** The eldest daughter of the deceased Peter Wilks in this version of film, but in the novel Mary Jane is the eldest daughter of George Wilks, Peter Wilks' brother.
- **Joanna Wilks** The youngest sister of Mary Jane in the novel.
- **William Wilks and Harvey Wilks** The British brothers of Peter Wilks whom the king and the duke impersonate until the real William and Harvey arrive.
- **Silas and Sally Phelps** Tom Sawyer's aunt and uncle, whom Huck coincidentally encounters in his search for Jim after Jim has been sold by the impostor.
- **Aunt Polly** Tom Sawyer's aunt and guardian and Sally Phelps's sister. Aunt Polly appears at the end of the novel and properly identifies Huck, who has pretended to be Tom, and Tom, who has pretended to be his own younger brother, Sid. Aunt Polly is not present in this version of film.

6.2.3 Selected Readings from the Novel

6.2.3.1 Important Quotations

(1) That is just the way with some people. They get down on a thing when they don't know nothing about it. **(Chapter 1)**

(2) ... she (the widow) said the thing a body could get by praying for it was "spiritual gifts." This was too many for me, but she told me what she meant —I must help other people, and do everything I could for other people, and look out for them all the time, and never think about myself. **(Chapter 3)**

(3) Pap always said it warn't no harm to borrow things if you was meaning to pay them back some time; but the widow said it warn't anything but a soft name for stealing, and no decent body would do it. **(Chapter 12)**

(4) Well, he was right; he was most always right; he had an uncommon level head for a nigger. **(Chapter 14)**

Unit 6

Mark Twain and *Adventures of Huckleberry Finn*

(5) The average man don't like trouble and danger. (Chapter 22)

(6) The pitifulest thing out is a mob; that's what an army is-a mob; they don't fight with courage that's born in them, but with courage that's borrowed from their mass, and from their officers. But a mob without any *man* at the head of it is *beneath* pitifulness. (Chapter 22)

(7) All I say is, kings is kings, and you got to make allowances. Take them all around, they're a mighty ornery lot. It's the way they're raised. (Chapter 23)

(8) I says to myself, I reckon a body that ups and tells the truth when he is in a tight place is taking considerable many resks, though I ain't had no experience, and can't say for certain; but it looks so to me, anyway; and yet here's a case where I'm blest if it don't look to me like the truth is better and actuly *safer* than a lie. (Chapter 28)

(9) That's just the way: a person does a low-down thing, and then he don't want to take no consequences of it. Thinks as long as he can hide, it ain't no disgrace. That was my fix exactly. (Chapter 31)

(10) Human beings *can* be awful cruel to one another. (Chapter 33)

6.2.3.2 Excerpts Related to Some Scenes in the Film

> **⚜ Excerpt 1 (from Chapter 1)**
>
> Huck is adopted by the Widow Douglas and Miss Watson, both of whom take pains to raise him properly. Widow Douglas is somewhat gentler in her beliefs and has more patience with the mischievous Huck. When Huck acts in a manner contrary to societal expectations, it is Widow Douglas that he fears disappointing.

YOU don't know about me without you have read a book by the name of *The Adventures of Tom Sawyer*; but that ain't no matter. That book was made by Mr. Mark Twain, and he told the truth, mainly. There was things which he stretched, but mainly he told the truth. That is nothing. I never seen anybody but lied one time or another, without it was Aunt Polly, or the widow, or maybe Mary. Aunt Polly–Tom's Aunt Polly, she is–and Mary, and the Widow Douglas is all told about in that book, which is mostly a true book, with some stretchers, as I said before.

Now the way that the book winds up is this: Tom and me found the money that the robbers hid in the cave, and it made us rich. We got six thousand dollars apiece–all gold. It was an awful sight of money when it was piled up. Well, Judge Thatcher he took it and put it out at interest, and it fetched us a dollar a day apiece all the year round–more than a body could tell what to do with. The Widow Douglas she took me for her son, and allowed she would sivilize me; but it was rough living in the house all the time, considering how dismal regular and decent the widow was in all her ways; and so when I couldn't stand it no longer I lit out. I got into my old rags and my sugar hogshead again, and was free and satisfied. But Tom Sawyer he hunted me up and said he was going to start a band of robbers, and I might join if I would go back to the widow and be respectable. So I went back.

The widow she cried over me, and called me a poor lost lamb, and she called me a lot of other names, too, but she never meant no harm by it. She put me in them new clothes again, and I couldn't do nothing but sweat and sweat, and feel all cramped up. Well, then, the old thing commenced again. The widow rung a bell for supper, and you had to come to time. When you got to the table you couldn't go right to eating, but you had to wait for the widow to tuck down her head and grumble a little over the victuals, though there warn't really anything the matter with them–that is, nothing only everything was cooked by itself. In a barrel of odds and ends it is different; things get mixed up, and the juice kind of swaps around, and the things go better.

After supper she got out her book and learned me about Moses and the Bulrushers, and I was in a sweat to find out all about him; but by and by she let it out that Moses had been dead a considerable long time; so then I didn't care no more about him, because I don't take no stock in dead people.

Unit 6
Mark Twain and *Adventures of Huckleberry Finn*

Pretty soon I wanted to smoke, and asked the widow to let me. But she wouldn't. She said it was a mean practice and wasn't clean, and I must try to not do it any more. That is just the way with some people. They get down on a thing when they don't know nothing about it. Here she was a-bothering about Moses, which was no kin to her, and no use to anybody, being gone, you see, yet finding a power of fault with me for doing a thing that had some good in it. And she took snuff, too; of course that was all right, because she done it herself.

Her sister, Miss Watson, a tolerable slim old maid, with goggles on, had just come to live with her, and took a set at me now with a spelling book. She worked me middling hard for about an hour, and then the widow made her ease up. I couldn't stood it much longer. Then for an hour it was deadly dull, and I was fidgety. Miss Watson would say, "Don't put your feet up there, Huckleberry"; and "Don't scrunch up like that, Huckleberry–set up straight"; and pretty soon she would say, "Don't gap and stretch like that, Huckleberry–why don't you try to behave?" Then she told me all about the bad place, and I said I wished I was there. She got mad then, but I didn't mean no harm. All I wanted was to go somewheres; all I wanted was a change, I warn't particular. She said it was wicked to say what I said; said she wouldn't say it for the whole world; *she* was going to live so as to go to the good place. Well, I couldn't see no advantage in going where she was going, so I made up my mind I wouldn't try for it. But I never said so, because it would only make trouble, and wouldn't do no good.

Now she had got a start, and she went on and told me all about the good place. She said all a body would have to do there was to go around all day long with a harp and sing, forever and ever. So I didn't think much of it. But I never said so. I asked her if she reckoned Tom Sawyer would go there, and she said not by a considerable sight. I was glad about that, because I wanted him and me to be together.

Miss Watson she kept pecking at me, and it got tiresome and lonesome. By and by they fetched the niggers in and had prayers, and then everybody was off to bed. I went up to my room with a piece of candle, and put it on the table. Then I set down in a chair by the window and tried to think of something cheerful, but it warn't no use. I felt so lonesome I most wished I was dead.

Excerpt 2 (from Chapter 5)

Huck's father hasn't been seen in these parts for a year or more. When he hears Huck become rich he returns, scheming to get Huck's fortune away from him. When he finds Huck living at the Widow Douglas's and going to school, he accuses Huck of trying to be better than his father.

I stood a-looking at him; he set there a-looking at me, with his chair tilted back a little. I set the candle down. I noticed the window was up; so he had clumb in by the shed. He kept a-looking me all over. By and by he says:

"Starchy clothes–very. You think you're a good deal of a big-bug, *don't* you?"

"Maybe I am, maybe I ain't," I says.

"Don't you give me none o' your lip," says he. "You've put on considerable many frills since I been away. I'll take you down a peg before I get done with you. You're educated, too, they say–can read and write. You think you're better'n your father, now, don't you, because he can't? *I'll* take it out of you. Who told you you might meddle with such hifalut'n foolishness, hey? –who told you you could?"

"The widow. She told me."

"The widow, hey? –and who told the widow she could put in her shovel about a thing that ain't none of her business?"

"Nobody never told her."

"Well, I'll learn her how to meddle. And looky here–you drop that school, you hear? I'll learn people to bring up a boy to put on airs over his own father and let on to be better'n what *he* is. You lemme catch you fooling around that school again, you hear? Your mother couldn't read, and she couldn't write, nuther, before she died. None of the family couldn't before *they* died. *I* can't; and here you're a-swelling yourself up like this. I ain't the man to stand it–you hear? Say, lemme hear you read."

I took up a book and begun something about General Washington and the wars. When I'd read about a half a minute, he fetched the book a whack with his hand and knocked it across the house. He says:

"It's so. You can do it. I had my doubts when you told me. Now looky

Unit 6
Mark Twain and *Adventures of Huckleberry Finn*

here; you stop that putting on frills. I won't have it. I'll lay for you, my smarty; and if I catch you about that school I'll tan you good. First you know you'll get religion, too. I never see such a son."

He took up a little blue and yaller picture of some cows and a boy, and says:

"What's this?"

"It's something they give me for learning my lessons good."

He tore it up, and says:

"I'll give you something better—I'll give you a cowhide."

He sat there a-mumbling and a-growling a minute, and then he says:

"*Ain't* you a sweet-scented dandy, though? A bed; and bedclothes; and a look'n' glass; and a piece of carpet on the floor—and your own father got to sleep with the hogs in the tanyard. I never see such a son. I bet I'll take some o' these frills out o' you before I'm done with you. Why, there ain't no end to your airs—they say you're rich. Hey? —how's that?"

"They lie—that's how."

"Looky here—mind how you talk to me; I'm a-standing about all I can stand now—so don't gimme no sass. I've been in town two days, and I hain't heard nothing but about you bein' rich. I heard about it away down the river, too. That's why I come. You git me that money tomorrow—I want it."

"I hain't got no money."

"It's a lie. Judge Thatcher's got it. You git it. I want it."

"I hain't got no money, I tell you. You ask Judge Thatcher; he'll tell you the same."

"All right. I'll ask him; and I'll make him pungle, too, or I'll know the reason why. Say, how much you got in your pocket? I want it."

"I hain't got only a dollar, and I want that to—"

"It don't make no difference what you want it for—you just shell it out."

He took it and bit it to see if it was good, and then he said he was going downtown to get some whisky; said he hadn't had a drink all day. When he had got out on the shed he put his head in again, and cussed me for putting on frills and trying to be better than him; and when I reckoned he was gone he came back and put his head in again, and told me to mind about that school, because he was going to lay for me and lick me if I didn't drop that.

Excerpt 3 (from Chapter 8)

Pap kidnaps Huck and brings him to a cabin in the woods where he confines his son to their shack and beats his son when he's drunk. Huck decides to escape. He kills a wild pig and leaves a bloody trail from the pig so that his father will think that he has been murdered. Then he climbs into a boat and goes to Jackson's Island to hide. After three days of freedom, Huck wandered to another part of the island and there he is surprised to discover Jim, Miss Watson's Negro slave.

"Hello, Jim!" and skipped out.

He bounced up and stared at me wild. Then he drops down on his knees, and puts his hands together

and says:

"Doan' hurt me–don't! I hain't ever done no harm to a ghos'. I alwuz liked dead people, en done all I could for 'em. You go en git in de river ag'in, whah you b'longs, en doan' do nuffn to Ole Jim, 'at 'uz awluz yo' fren'."

Well, I warn't long making him understand I warn't dead. I was ever so glad to see Jim. I warn't lonesome now. I told him I warn't afraid of *him* telling the people where I was. I talked along, but he only set there and looked at me; never said nothing. Then I says:

"It's good daylight. Le's get breakfast. Make up your campfire good."

"What's de use er makin' up de campfire to cook strawbries en sich truck? But you got a gun, hain't you? Den we kin git sumfn better den strawbries."

"Strawberries and such truck," I says. "Is that what you live on?"

"I couldn't git nuffn else," he says.

"Why, how long you been on the island, Jim?"

"I come heah de night arter you's killed."

* * * * * * * *

By and by Jim says:

"But looky here, Huck, who wuz it dat 'uz killed in dat shanty ef it warn't you?"

Then I told him the whole thing, and he said it was smart. He said Tom Sawyer couldn't get up no better plan than what I had. Then I says:

"How do you come to be here, Jim, and how'd you get here?"

Unit 6

Mark Twain and *Adventures of Huckleberry Finn*

He looked pretty uneasy, and didn't say nothing for a minute. Then he says:

"Maybe I better not tell."

"Why, Jim?"

"Well, dey's reasons. But you wouldn't tell on me ef I 'uz to tell you, would you, Huck?"

"Blamed if I would, Jim."

"Well, I blieve you, Huck. I–I *run off*."

"Jim!"

"But mind, you said you wouldn' tell–you know you said you wouldn' tell, Huck."

"Well, I did. I said I wouldn't, and I'll stick to it. Honest *injun*, I will. People would call me a low-down Abolitionist and despise me for keeping mum–but that don't make no difference. I ain't a-going to tell, and I ain't a-going back there, anyways. So, now, le's know all about it."

"Well, you see, it 'uz dis way. Ole missus–dat's Miss Watson–she pecks on me all de time, en treats me pooty rough, but she awluz said she wouldn' sell me down to Orleans. But I noticed dey wuz a nigger trader roun' de place considable lately, en I begin to git oneasy. Well, one night I creeps to de do' pooty late, en de do' warn't quite shet, en I hear old missus tell de widder she gwyne to sell me down to Orleans, but she didn' want to, but she could git eight hund'd dollars for me, en it 'uz sich a big stack o' money she couldn' resis'. De widder she try to git her to say she wouldn't do it, but I never waited to hear de res'. I lit out mighty quick, I tell you.

> ### ⚜ Excerpt 4 (from Chapter 16)
>
> Jim tells Huck of his plans to work hard in the North in order to buy his wife and children from their masters and Huck is troubled about helping a slave escape. But when two slave hunters come on the scene, Huck hasn't got the courage to give Jim up. He tells them that his family are ill on the raft with smallpox. On hearing this the men give Huck two twenty-dollar gold pieces but refuse to approach the raft for fear of infection.

Right then along comes a skiff with two men in it with guns, and they stopped and I stopped. One of them says:

"What's that yonder?"

"A piece of a raft," I says.

"Do you belong on it?"

"Yes, sir."

"Any men on it?"

"Only one, sir."

"Well, there's five niggers run off tonight up yonder, above the head of the bend. Is your man white or black?"

I didn't answer up promptly. I tried to, but the words wouldn't come. I tried for a second or two to brace up and out with it, but I warn't man enough – hadn't the spunk of a rabbit. I see I was weakening; so I just give up trying, and up and says:

"He's white."

"I reckon we'll go and see for ourselves."

"I wish you would," says I, "because it's pap that's there, and maybe you'd help me tow the raft ashore where the light is. He's sick – and so is mam and Mary Ann."

"Oh, the devil! We're in a hurry, boy. But I s'pose we've got to. Come, buckle to your paddle, and let's got along."

I buckled to my paddle and they laid to their oars. When we had made a stroke or two, I says:

"Pap'll be mighty much obliged to you, I can tell you. Everybody goes away when I want them to help me tow the raft ashore, and I can't do it by myself."

"Well, that's infernal mean. Odd, too. Say, boy, what's the matter with your father?"

"It's the–a–the–well, it ain't anything much."

They stopped pulling. It warn't but a mighty little ways to the raft now. One says:

"Boy, that's a lie. What *is* the matter with your pap? Answer up square now, and it'll be the better for you."

"I will, sir, I will, honest–but don't leave us, please. It's the–the–Gentlemen, if you'll only pull ahead, and let me heave you the headline, you won't have to come a-near the raft–please do."

"Set her back, John, set her back!" says one. They backed water. "Keep

Unit 6

Mark Twain and *Adventures of Huckleberry Finn*

away, boy–keep to looard. Confound it, I just expect the wind has blowed it to us. Your pap's got the smallpox, and you know it precious well. Why didn't you come out and say so? Do you want to spread it all over?"

"Well," says I, a–blubbering, "I've told everybody before, and they just went away and left us."

"Poor devil, there's something in that. We are right down sorry for you, but we–well, hang it, we don't want the smallpox, you see. Look here, I'll tell you what to do. Don't you try to land by yourself, or you'll smash everything to pieces. You float along down about twenty miles, and you'll come to a town on the left-hand side of the river. It will be long after sunup then, and when you ask for help you tell them your folks are all down with chills and fever. Don't be a fool again, and let people guess what is the matter. Now we're trying to do you a kindness; so you just put twenty miles between us, that's a good boy. It wouldn't do any good to land yonder where the light is –it's only a woodyard. Say, I reckon your father's poor, and I'm bound to say he's in pretty hard luck. Here, I'll put a twenty-dollar gold piece on this board, and you get it when it floats by. I feel mighty mean to leave you; but my kingdom! it won't do to fool with smallpox, don't you see?"

"Hold on, Parker," says the other man, "here's a twenty to put on the board for me. Good-bye, boy; you do as Mr. Parker told you, and you'll be all right."

"That's so, my boy–good-by, good-by. If you see any runaway niggers you get help and nab them, and you can make some money by it."

"Good-by, sir," says I; "I won't let no runaway niggers get by me if I can help it."

☙ Excerpt 5 (from Chapter 26)

On their journey down the Mississippi, Huck and Jim rescue two men pursued by some villagers. The two men claim to be royalty and immediately take control of the raft. Huck quickly realizes the men are frauds, but he and Jim remain at their mercy. When the two impostors chance to learn about a large inheritance meant for three recently orphaned girls, they scheme to impersonate the girls' British uncles, whom no one in the town have ever seen, and tempt Huck to go with them. Seeing that the Wilks girls are so innocent, trusting and good-hearted, Huck vows to protect these victims.

And when it was all done me and the harelip had supper in the kitchen off of the leavings, whilst the others was helping the niggers clean up the things. The harelip she got to pumping me about England, and blest if I didn't think the ice was getting mighty thin sometimes. She says:

"Did you ever see the king?"

"Who? William Fourth? Well, I bet I have–he goes to our church. I knowed he was dead years ago, but I never let on. So when I says he goes to our church, she says:

"What–regular?"

"Yes–regular. His pew's right over opposite ourn–on t'other side the pulpit."

"I thought he lived in London?"

"Well, he does. Where *would* he live?"

"But I thought *you* lived in Sheffield?"

I see I was up a stump. I had to let on to get choked with a chicken bone, so as to get time to think how to get down again.

* * * * * * *

Next, she says:

"Do you go to church, too?"

"Yes–regular."

"Where do you set?"

"Why, in our pew."

"*Whose* pew?"

"Why, *ourn*–your Uncle Harvey's."

"His'n? What does *he* want with a pew?"

"Wants it to set in. What did you *reckon* he wanted with it"

"Why, I thought he'd be in the pulpit."

Rot him, I forgot he was a preacher. I see I was up a stump again, so I played another chicken bone and got another think.

* * * * * * *

She says:

"Honest injun, now, hain't you been telling me a lot of lies?"

"Honest injun," says I.

"None of it at all?"

"None of it at all. Not a lie in it," says I.

Unit 6
Mark Twain and *Adventures of Huckleberry Finn*

"Lay your hand on this book and say it."

I see it warn't nothing but a dictionary, so I laid my hand on it and said it. So then she looked a little better satisfied, and says:

"Well, then, I'll believe some of it; but I hope to gracious if I'll believe the rest."

"What is it you won't believe, Jo?" says Mary Jane, stepping in with Susan behind her. "It ain't right nor kind for you to talk so to him, and him a stranger and so far from his people. How would you like to be treated so?"

"That's always your way, Maim–always sailing in to help somebody before they're hurt. I hain't done nothing to him. He's told some stretchers, I reckon, and I said I wouldn't swallow it all; and that's every bit and grain I *did* say. I reckon he can stand a little thing like that, can't he?"

"I don't care whether 'twas little or whether 'twas big; he's here in our house and a stranger, and it wasn't good of you to say it. If you was in his place it would make you feel ashamed; and so you oughtn't to say a thing to another person that will make *them* feel ashamed."

"Why, Maim, he said–"

"It don't make no difference what he *said*–that ain't the thing. The thing is for you to treat him *kind*, and not be saying things to make him remember he ain't in his own country and amongst his own folks."

I says to myself, *this* is a girl that I'm letting that old reptile rob her of her money!

Then Susan *she* waltzed in; and if you'll believe me, she did give Harelip hark from the tomb!

Says I to myself, and this is *another* one that I'm letting him rob her of her money!

Then Mary Jane she took another inning, and went in sweet and lovely again–which was her way; but when she got done there warn't hardly anything left o' poor Harelip. So she hollered.

"All right, then," says the other girls; "you just ask his pardon."

She done it, too; and she done it beautiful. She done it so beautiful it was good to hear; and I wished I could tell her a thousand lies, so she could do it again.

I says to myself, this is *another* one that I'm letting him rob her of her money. And when she got through they all jest laid theirselves out to make me feel at home and know I was amongst friends. I felt so ornery and low down and mean that I says to myself, my mind's made up; I'll hive that money for them or bust.

6.2.4.3 Passages for Understanding the Film

(1) WE judged that three nights more would fetch us to Cairo, at the bottom of Illinois, where the Ohio River comes in, and that was what we was after. We would sell the raft and get on a steamboat and go way up the Ohio amongst the free states, and then be out of trouble. **(Chapter 15)**

(2) They went off and I got aboard the raft, feeling bad and low, because I knowed very well I had done wrong, and I see it warn't no use for me to try to learn to do right; a body that don't get **started** right when he's little ain't got no show—when the pinch comes there ain't nothing to back him up and keep him to his work, and so he gets beat. Then I thought a minute, and says to myself, hold on; s'pose you'd 'a' done right and give Jim up, would you felt better than what you do now? No, says I, I'd feel bad—I'd feel just the same way I do now. Well, then, says I, what's the use you learning to do right when it's troublesome to do right and ain't no trouble to do wrong, and the wages is just the same? I was stuck. I couldn't answer that. So I reckoned I wouldn't bother no more about it, but after this always do whichever come handiest at the time. **(Chapter 16)**

(3) It's lovely to live on a raft. We had the sky up there, all speckled with stars, and we used to lay on our backs and look up at them, and discuss about whether they was made or only just happened.

* * * * * * *

One morning about daybreak I found a canoe and crossed over a chute to the main shore—it was only two hundred yards—and paddled about a mile up a crick amongst the cypress woods, to see if I couldn't get some berries. Just as I was passing a place where a kind of a cowpath crossed the crick, here comes a couple of men tearing up the path as tight as they could foot it. I thought I was a goner, for whenever anybody was after anybody I judged it was **me**—or maybe Jim. I was about to dig out from there in a hurry, but

Unit 6

Mark Twain and *Adventures of Huckleberry Finn*

they was pretty close to me then, and sung out and begged me to save their lives–said they hadn't been doing nothing, and was being chased for it–said there was men and dogs a-coming.

"What got you into trouble?" says the baldhead to t'other chap.

"Well, I'd been selling an article to take the tartar off the teeth–and it does take it off, too, and generly the enamel along with it–but I stayed about one night longer than I ought to, and was just in the act of sliding out when I ran across you on the trail this side of town, and you told me they were coming, and begged me to help you to get off. So I told you I was expecting trouble myself, and would scatter out *with* you. That's the whole yarn–what's youm?"

"Well, I'd ben a-runnin' a little temperance revival thar 'bout a week, and was the pet of the women folks, big and little, for I was makin' it mighty warm for the rummies, I *tell* you, and takin' as much as five or six dollars a night–ten cents a head, children and niggers free–and business a-growin' all the time, when somehow or another a little report got around last night that I had a way of puttin' in my time with a private jug on the sly. A nigger rousted me out this mornin', and told me the people was getherin' on the quiet with their dogs and horses, and they'd be along pretty soon and give me 'bout half an hour's start, and then run me down if they could; and if they got me they'd tar and feather me and ride me on a rail, sure. I didn't wait for no breakfast–I warn't hungry."

* * * * * * * *

It didn't take me long to make up my mind that these liars warn't no kings nor dukes at all, but just low-down humbugs and frauds. But I never said nothing, never let on; kept it to myself; it's the best way; then you don't have no quarrels, and don't get into no trouble. If they wanted us to call them kings and dukes, I hadn't no objections, 'long as it would keep peace in the family; and it warn't no use to tell Jim, so I didn't tell him. If I never learnt nothing else out of pap, I learnt that the best way to get along with his kind of people is to let them have their own way. **(Chapter 19)**

(4) I went to sleep, and Jim didn't call me when it was my turn. He often done that. When I waked up just at daybreak he was sitting there with his head down betwixt his knees, moaning and mourning to himself. I didn't take notice nor let on. I knowed what it was about. He was thinking about his wife

and his children, away up yonder, and he was low and homesick; because he hadn't ever been away from home before in his life; and I do believe he cared just as much for his people as white folks does for their'n. It don't seem natural, but I reckon it's so. He was often moaning and mourning that way nights, when he judged I was asleep, and saying, "Po' little 'Liza-beth! po' little Johnny! it's mighty hard; I spec' I ain't ever gwyne to see you no mo', no mo'!" He was a mighty good nigger, Jim was. (Chapter 23)

(5) Old Miss Watson died two months ago, and she was ashamed she ever was going to sell him down the river, and *said* so; and she set him free in her will. (Chapter 42)

6.2.4.4 Chapter Reading

Chapter 31

WE dasn't stop again at any town for days and days; kept right along down the river. We was down south in the warm weather now, and a mighty long ways from home. We begun to come to trees with Spanish moss on them, hanging down from the limbs like long, gray beards. It was the first I ever see it growing, and it made the woods look solemn and dismal. So now the frauds (骗子) reckoned they was out of danger, and they begun to work the villages again.

First they done a lecture on temperance (戒酒); but they didn't make enough for them both to get drunk on. Then in another village they started a dancing-school; but they didn't know no more how to dance than a kangaroo (袋鼠) does; so the first prance (蹦跳) they made the general public jumped in and pranced them out of town. Another time they tried to go at yellocution; but they didn't yellocute long till the audience got up and give them a solid good cussing (乱骂), and made them skip out. They tackled missionarying (传教), and mesmerizing (催眠), and doctoring (治病), and telling fortunes, and a little of everything; but they couldn't seem to have no luck. So at last they got just about dead broke, and laid around the raft as she floated along, thinking and thinking, and never saying nothing, by the half a day at a time, and dreadful blue (沮丧的) and desperate.

Unit 6
Mark Twain and *Adventures of Huckleberry Finn*

And at last they took a change and begun to lay their heads together in the wigwam (棚屋) and talk low and confidential two or three hours at a time. Jim and me got uneasy. We didn't like the look of it. We judged they was studying up some kind of worse deviltry (恶行) than ever. We turned it over and over, and at last we made up our minds they was going to break into somebody's house or store, or was going into the counterfeit (伪造) – money business, or something. So then we was pretty scared, and made up an agreement that we wouldn't have nothing in the world to do with such actions, and if we ever got the least show (机会) we would give them the cold shake (甩掉他们) and clear out and leave them behind. Well, early one morning we hid the raft in a good, safe place about two mile below a little bit of a shabby village named Pikesville, and the king he went ashore and told us all to stay hid whilst he went up to town and smelt around to see if anybody had got any wind (风声) of the "Royal Nonesuch" there yet. ("House to rob, you *mean*," says I to myself; "and when you get through robbing it you'll come back here and wonder what has become of me and Jim and the raft–and you'll have to take it out in wondering.") And he said if he warn't back by midday the duke and me would know it was all right, and we was to come along.

So we stayed where we was. The duke he fretted (焦躁) and sweated around, and was in a mighty sour way. He scolded us for everything, and we couldn't seem to do nothing right; he found fault with every little thing. Something was a-brewing (酝酿中), sure. I was good and glad when midday come and no king; we could have a change, anyway–and maybe a chance for *the* change, on top of it. So me and the duke went up to the village, and hunted around there for the king, and by and by we found him in the back room of a little low doggery (酒馆), very tight, and a lot of loafers bullyragging (恐吓) him for sport, and he a-cussing and a-threatening with all his might, and so tight he couldn't walk, and couldn't do nothing to them. The duke he begun to abuse him for an old fool, and the king begun to sass (出言不逊) back, and the minute they was fairly at it I lit out (赶快离开) and shook the reefs out of my hind legs, and spun down the river road like a deer, for I see our chance; and I made up my mind that it would be a long day before they ever see me and Jim again. I got down there all out of breath but loaded up with joy, and sung out:

"Set her loose, Jim; we're all right now!"

But there warn't no answer, and nobody come out of the wigwam. Jim was gone! I set up a shout–and then another–and then another one; and run this way and that in the woods, whooping (高叫) and screeching (尖声喊叫); but it warn't no use–old Jim was gone. Then I set down and cried; I couldn't help it. But I couldn't set still long. Pretty soon I went out on the road, trying to think what I better do, and I run across a boy walking, and asked him if he'd seen a strange nigger dressed so and so, and he says:

"Yes."

"Whereabouts?" says I.

"Down to Silas Phelps' place, two mile below here. He's a runaway nigger, and they've got him. Was you looking for him?"

"You bet I ain't! I run across him in the woods about an hour or two ago, and he said if I hollered (叫喊) he'd cut my livers out–and told me to lay down and stay where I was; and I done it. Been there ever since; afeard to come out."

"Well," he says, "you needn't be afeard no more, becuz they've got him. He run off f'm down South, som'ers."

"It's a good job they got him."

"Well, I *reckon*! There's two hundred dollars' reward on him. It's like picking up money out'n the road."

"Yes, it is–and *I* could 'a' had it if I'd been big enough; I see him *first*. Who nailed him?"

"It was an old fellow–a stranger–and he sold out his chance in him for forty dollars, becuz he's got to go up the river and can't wait. Think o' that, now! You bet I'*d* wait, if it was seven year."

"That's me, every time," says I. "But maybe his chance ain't worth no more than that, if he'll sell it so cheap. Maybe there's something ain't straight about it."

"But it *is*, though–straight as a string. I see the handbill (传单) myself. It tells all about him, to a dot–paints him like a picture, and tells the plantation he's frum, below New*r*leans. No-sirree-*bob*, they ain't no trouble 'bout *that* speculation, you bet you. Say, gimme a chaw tobacker, won't ye?"

I didn't have none, so he left. I went to the raft, and set down in the wigwam to think. But I couldn't come to nothing. I thought till I wore my

Unit 6

Mark Twain and *Adventures of Huckleberry Finn*

head sore, but I couldn't see no way out of the trouble. After all this long journey, and after all we'd done for them scoundrels, here it was all come to nothing, everything all busted up (破灭) and ruined, because they could have the heart to serve Jim such a trick as that, and make him a slave again all his life, and amongst strangers, too, for forty dirty dollars.

Once I said to myself it would be a thousand times better for Jim to be a slave at home where his family was, as long as he'd *got* to be a slave, and so I'd better write a letter to Tom Sawyer and tell him to tell Miss Watson where he was. But I soon give up that notion for two things: she'd be mad and disgusted at his rascality (恶行) and ungratefulness for leaving her, and so she'd sell him straight down the river again; and if she didn't, everybody naturally despises an ungrateful nigger, and they'd make Jim feel it all the time, and so he'd feel ornery (卑劣的) and disgraced. And then think of *me*! It would get all around that Huck Finn helped a nigger to get his freedom; and if I was ever to see anybody from that town again I'd be ready to get down and lick his boots for shame. That's just the way: a person does a low-down thing, and then he don't want to take no consequences of it. Thinks as long as he can hide, it ain't no disgrace. That was my fix exactly. The more I studied about this the more my conscience went to grinding me, and the more wicked and low-down and ornery I got to feeling. And at last, when it hit me all of a sudden that here was the plain hand of Providence (上帝) slapping me in the face and letting me know my wickedness was being watched all the time from up there in heaven, whilst I was stealing a poor old woman's nigger that hadn't ever done me no harm, and now was showing me there's One that's always on the lookout, and ain't a–going to allow no such miserable doings to go only just so fur and no further, I most dropped in my tracks I was so scared. Well, I tried the best I could to kinder soften it up somehow for myself by saying I was brung up wicked, and so I warn't so much to blame; but something inside of me kept saying, "There was the Sunday-school, you could 'a' gone to it; and if you'd 'a' done it they'd 'a' learnt you there that people that acts as I'd been acting about that nigger goes to everlasting fire."

It made me shiver. And I about made up my mind to pray, and see if I couldn't try to quit being the kind of a boy I was and be better. So I kneeled down. But the words wouldn't come. Why wouldn't they? It warn't no use to try and hide it from Him. Nor from *me*, neither. I knowed very well why they wouldn't come. It was because my heart warn't right; it was because I warn't square (诚实的); it was because I was playing double (耍两面派). I was letting *on* to give up sin, but away inside of me I was holding on to the biggest one of all. I was trying to make my mouth *say* I would do the right thing and the clean thing, and go and write to that nigger's owner and tell where he was; but deep down in me I knowed it was a lie, and He knowed it. You can't pray a lie–I found that out.

So I was full of trouble, full as I could be; and didn't know what to do. At last I had an idea; and I says, I'll go and write the letter–and *then* see if I can pray. Why, it was astonishing, the way I felt as light as a feather right straight off (立刻), and my troubles all gone. So I got a piece of paper and a pencil, all glad and excited, and set down and wrote:

Miss Watson, your runaway nigger Jim is down here two mile below Pikesville, and Mr. Phelps has got him and he will give him up for the reward if you send.

HUCK FINN.

I felt good and all washed clean of sin for the first time I had ever felt so in my life, and I knowed I could pray now. But I didn't do it straight off, but laid the paper down and set there thinking–thinking how good it was all this happened so, and how near I come to being lost and going to hell. And went on thinking. And got to thinking over our trip down the river; and I see Jim before me all the time: in the day and in the nighttime, sometimes moonlight, sometimes storms, and we a–floating along, talking and singing and laughing. But somehow I couldn't seem to strike no places to harden me against him, but only the other kind. I'd see him standing my watch on top of his'n, 'stead of calling me, so I could go on sleeping; and see him how glad he was when I come back out of the fog; and when I come to him again in the swamp, up there where the feud was; and such-like times; and would always call me honey, and pet me, and do everything he could think of for me, and how good he always was; and at last I struck the time I saved him by telling the men we had smallpox aboard, and he was so grateful, and said I was the best friend old Jim ever had in the world, and the *only* one he's got now; and then I happened to look around and see that paper.

It was a close place. I took it up, and held it in my hand. I was

Unit 6

Mark Twain and *Adventures of Huckleberry Finn*

a-trembling, because I'd got to decide, forever, betwixt two things, and I knowed it. I studied a minute, sort of holding my breath, and then says to myself:

"All right, then, I'll *go* to hell"–and tore it up.

It was awful thoughts and awful words, but they was said. And I let them stay said; and never thought no more about reforming. I shoved the whole thing out of my head, and said I would take up wickedness again, which was in my line, being brung up to it, and the other warn't. And for a starter I would go to work and steal Jim out of slavery again; and if I could think up anything worse, I would do that, too; because as long as I was in, and in for good, I might as well go the whole hog.

Then I set to thinking over how to get at it, and turned over some considerable many ways in my mind; and at last fixed up a plan that suited me. So then I took the bearings (方位) of a woody island that was down the river a piece, and as soon as it was fairly dark I crept out with my raft and went for it, and hid it there, and then turned in. I slept the night through, and got up before it was light, and had my breakfast, and put on my store clothes, and tied up some others and one thing or another in a bundle, and took the canoe and cleared for shore. I landed below where I judged was Phelps's place, and hid my bundle in the woods, and then filled up the canoe with water, and loaded rocks into her and sunk her where I could find her again when I wanted her, about a quarter of a mile below a little steam sawmill (锯木厂) that was on the bank.

Then I struck up the road, and when I passed the mill I see a sign on it, "Phelps's Sawmill," and when I come to the farmhouses, two or three hundred yards further along, I kept my eyes peeled, but didn't see nobody around, though it was good daylight now. But I didn't mind, because I didn't want to see nobody just yet–I only wanted to get the lay (位置) of the land. According to my plan, I was going to turn up there from the village, not from below. So I just took a look, and shoved along, straight for town. Well, the very first man I see when I got there was the duke. He was sticking up (粘贴) a bill for the "Royal Nonesuch"–three night performance–like that other time. *They* had the cheek, them frauds! I was right on him before I could shirk. He looked astonished, and says:

"Hel-*lo*! Where'd *you* come from?" Then he says, kind of glad and eager, "Where's the raft?–got her in a good place?"

I says:

"Why, that's just what I was going to ask your grace."

Then he didn't look so joyful, and says:

"What was your idea for asking *me*?" he says.

"Well," I says, "when I see the king in that doggery yesterday I says to myself, we can't get him home for hours, till he's soberer; so I went a-loafing around town to put in the time and wait. A man up and offered me ten cents to help him pull a skiff (小船) over the river and back to fetch a sheep, and so I went along; but when we was dragging him to the boat, and the man left me a-holt of the rope and went behind him to shove him along, he was too strong for me and jerked loose and run, and we after him. We didn't have no dog, and so we had to chase him all over the country till we tired him out. We never got him till dark; then we fetched him over, and I started down for the raft. When I got there and see it was gone, I says to myself, 'They've got into trouble and had to leave; and they've took my nigger, which is the only nigger I've got in the world, and now I'm in a strange country, and ain't got no property no more, nor nothing, and no way to make my living;' so I set down and cried. I slept in the woods all night. But what *did* become of the raft, then? –and Jim–poor Jim!"

"Blamed if *I* know–that is, what's become of the raft. That old fool had made a trade and got forty dollars, and when we found him in the doggery the loafers had matched half dollars with him and got every cent but what he'd spent for whisky; and when I got him home late last night and found the raft gone, we said, 'That little rascal has stole our raft and shook us, and run off down the river.'"

"I wouldn't shake (甩掉) my *nigger*, would I? –the only nigger I had in the world, and the only property."

"We never thought of that. Fact is, I reckon we'd come to consider him *our* nigger; yes, we did consider him so–goodness knows we had trouble enough for him. So when we see the raft was gone and we flat broke (身无分文), there warn't anything for it but to try the 'Royal Nonesuch' another shake. And I've pegged along (苦干) ever since, dry as a powder-horn (火药筒). Where's that ten cents? Give it here."

I had considerable money, so I give him ten cents, but begged him to

Unit 6

Mark Twain and *Adventures of Huckleberry Finn*

spend it for something to eat, and give me some, because it was all the money I had, and I hadn't had nothing to eat since yesterday. He never said nothing. The next minute he <u>whirls</u> (突然转向) on me and says:

"Do you reckon that nigger would blow on us? We'd skin him if he done that!"

"How can he blow? Hain't he run off?"

"No! That old fool sold him, and never divided with me, and the money's gone."

"*Sold* him?" I says, and begun to cry; "why, he was *my* nigger, and that was my money. Where is he? –I want my nigger."

"Well, you can't *get* your nigger, that's all–so dry up your blubbering. Looky here–do you think y*ou'd* venture to blow on us? Blamed if I think I'd trust you. Why, if you *was* to blow on us–"

He stopped, but I never see the duke look so ugly out of his eyes before. I went on a-whimpering, and says:

"I don't want to blow on nobody; and I ain't got no time to blow, nohow; I got to turn out and find my nigger."

He looked kinder bothered, and stood there with his bills fluttering on his arm, thinking, and wrinkling up his forehead. At last he says:

"I'll tell you something. We got to be here three days. If you'll promise you won't blow, and won't let the nigger blow, I'll tell you where to find him."

So I promised, and he says:

"A farmer by the name of Silas Ph–" and then he stopped. You see, he started to tell me the truth; but when he stopped that way, and begun to study and think again, I reckoned he was changing his mind. And so he was. He wouldn't trust me; he wanted to make sure of having me out of the way the whole three days. So pretty soon he says:

"The man that bought him is named Abram Foster–Abram G. Foster–and he lives forty mile back here in the country, on the road to Lafayette."

"All right," I says, "I can walk it in three days. And I'll start this very afternoon."

"No you won't, you'll start *now*; and don't you lose any time about it, neither, nor do any gabbling by the way. Just keep a tight tongue in your head and move right along, and then you won't get into trouble with *us*, d'ye hear?"

That was the order I wanted, and that was the one I played for. I wanted to be left free to work my plans.

"So clear out," he says; "and you can tell Mr. Foster whatever you want to. Maybe you can get him to believe that Jim *is* your nigger–some idiots don't require <u>documents</u>–<u>leastways</u>（至少）I've heard there's such down South here. And when you tell him the handbill and the reward's <u>bogus</u>（伪造的）, maybe he'll believe you when you explain to him what the idea was for getting 'em out. Go 'long now, and tell him anything you want to; but mind you don't work your jaw any *between* here and there."

So I left, and struck for the back country. I didn't look around, but I kinder felt like he was watching me. But I knowed I could tire him out at that. I went straight out in the country as much as a mile before I stopped; then I doubled back through the woods towards Phelps's. I reckoned I better start in on my plan straight off without fooling around, because I wanted to stop Jim's mouth till these fellows could get away. I didn't want no trouble with their kind. I'd seen all I wanted to of them, and wanted to get entirely shut of them.

Notes and Glossary for Chapter Reading

(1) dasn't: dare not
(2) 语法上不规范的有很多，例如：We <u>was</u> (=were) down south...：
We <u>begun</u> (=began) to come to trees...
they <u>was</u> (=were) out of danger...
First they <u>done</u> (=did) a lecture ...
用双重否定来表示否定：they <u>didn't</u> know <u>no</u> more how to dance...
they <u>couldn't</u> seem to have <u>no</u> luck...
we <u>couldn't</u> seem to do <u>nothing</u> right.
(3) mighty /ˈmaitiː/ *ad.* [infml, esp. AmE] very 很；极其
(4) Spanish moss: fungus 菌类，蘑菇
(5) yellocution: elocution 演说法
(6) dead broke: completely penniless 一文不名

Unit 6

Mark Twain and *Adventures of Huckleberry Finn*

(7) sour way: bad humor

(8) maybe a chance for *the* change, on top of it 除此之外，也许还会有那种变化的机会呢。on top of: in addition to 除……之外（还）.

(9) shook the reefs out of my hind legs: began to run very quickly

(10) becuz: because

(11) nailed: captured

(12) Newrleans: New Orleans 新奥尔良

(13) lick his boots: to obey someone like a slave through fear, or desire for favor; be servile 巴结，对……卑躬屈膝

(14) fix *n.* [*infml*] an awkward or difficult position 窘境，困境

(15) most dropped in my tracks: almost fell down on the ground 差点儿当场倒地; in one's track: [*infml*] where one is at that moment 就地，当场

(16) soften it up: make it easier

(17) Sunday school: religious instruction classes for young people, held on Sundays.

(18) It was a close place. 这叫我左右为难。

(19) go the whole hog: [*infml*]to do something thoroughly 干到底

(20) put in the time: 消磨时间

(21) left me a-holt of: let me hold

(22) documents: legal documents (relating to ownership)

6.2.4 Exercises

❶ Identify the following characters

(1) _____ adopts Huck and attempts to provide a stable home for him. She sends him to school and reads the Bible to him. Although at first Huck finds life with her restrictive, eventually he gets "sort of used to her ways. Later, when Huck refers to her, she represents all that is good and decent to him.

(2) _____ is Huck's companion as they travel on a raft down the Mississippi river. He is superstitious and believes that the hidden forces governing the world manifest themselves in signs and omens. He serves the function of making Huck confront his conscience and overcome society's influence.

(3) _____ likes to be free and finds life with the respectable old lady very difficult at first. When he makes some progress

with reading and arithmetic, and is just getting used to the "civilized" life, he is kidnapped and taken to a shack on the river. He escapes by faking his own death, and lives a life of freedom on the raft. On his trip he learns to decide for himself in various situations the right thing to do.

(4) _____ represents a view of Christianity that is severe and unforgiving. It is her attempts to "sivilize" Huck that he finds most annoying: "she kept pecking at me, and it got tiresome and lonesome."

(5) _____ is a dirty, illiterate, and disreputable drunkard and he is completely lacking in affection for his son. He disapproves of his son's education and beats him frequently. He represents both the general debasement of white society and the failure of family structures in the novel.

(6) _____ "was most awful beautiful, and her face and her eyes was all lit up like glory". Her trusting and good-hearted nature in the face of the King and Duke's fraud finally drives Huck to take a stand against the two scoundrels.

❷ Plot Review

Adventures of Huckleberry Finn is a story about the (1)_____ that develops between two fugitives–Huck and Jim–trying to (2) _____ from oppression, their adventures on the Mississippi as they journey south, and the peaceful times they spend together on the raft, safely separated from the "civilization" on the shore.

Huck often becomes impatient under the "civilizing" influence of Miss Watson and her sister, then suffers under the abusive control of his alcoholic (3) _____ Huck wants to escape the figurative bonds of his life, so he (4) _____ his death and takes to the Mississippi River. Jim, Miss Watson's (5) _____ overhears her talking about (6) _____ him to New Orleans. Rather than face harsher treatment from a master in the Deep South, Jim runs away. He and Huck meet up with each other while they are both hiding out on (7) _____ When it becomes clear that Jim is suspected of Huck's (8)_____ and is being (9) _____ they take to a raft and head downriver with the idea of helping Jim (10) _____

Unit 6

Mark Twain and *Adventures of Huckleberry Finn*

Huck and Jim have to put into shore from time to time for news, directions, and supplies. And each time they do, they (11) _____. Huck sees a wide variety of adults onshore: fine country gentlemen, con men, a lynch mob, and more. Through Huck's (12) _____, we see the corruption at the core of society. Huck is saddened and disgusted by almost everything he sees (13) _____ and finds solace and happiness only in rejoining Jim on the (14) _____, which has become their (15) _____ from society. On their trip, Huck confronts the ethics he has learned from society that tells him Jim is only (16)_____ and not a human being. By this moral code, his act of helping Jim to escape is a (17)_____. But Jim's frequent acts of selflessness, his longing for his family, and his friendship with Huck and Tom demonstrate to Huck that humanity has nothing to do with (18) _____. Rather than (19) _____ Jim, Huck decides, "All right, then. I'll go to hell." Ultimately, Jim and Huck find (20) _____. Jim is set free and Huck plans to head west for further adventure.

❸ General Questions

(1) Widow Douglas and her sister Miss Watson are both trying to civilize Huck. Compare and contrast their attitudes toward Huck. What method does each one use in her efforts to turn him into a "respectable" citizen?
(2) How does Huck like the life with the two women?
(3) Is Huck's father a responsible parent? How does he treat Huck?
(4) Why does Jim run away from Miss Watson? What is his dream?
(5) What symbol does the river best serve as to Huck and Jim?
(6) What does Jim tell Huck about his daughter Elizabeth? Why does Mark Twain put in such a scene?
(7) Which town are Jim and Huck trying to reach during their trip downriver? Why do they fail to reach the town as they expected?
(8) How does Huck thwart the scheme of the two impostors who try to steal the inheritance of the Wilks?
(9) Why does Huck tear up the letter that he has written to Miss Watson, saying to himself: "All right, then. I'll Go to hell"?
(10) What does Huck pretend to be when he is caught pretending to be a girl? How does he help Jim to get freedom in the film?

❹ Questions for essay or discussion

(1) Lying occurs frequently in *Adventures of Huckleberry Finn*. What is the difference of Huck's lies and the two impostors' lies? Are both "wrong"? Why does so much lying go on in the text?

(2) One critic has said that Jim is Huck's "true father." Defend or refute this statement.

(3) Discuss how Huck exhibits his good nature and ingenuity. Give at least two specific examples from the novel or the film.

(4) Discuss the role of women in the film or the novel.

(5) Why was it so hard for Huck to see that slavery was wrong and to decide to help Jim escape to freedom?

Unit 7

Edith Wharton and *The Age of Innocence*

7.1 Edith Wharton: Life and Works

7.1.1 About the Author

Edith Wharton was one of the most esteemed American novelists of the twentieth century, dominating the best-seller lists from the 1905 publication of *The House of Mirth* through her autobiography *A Backward Glance* (1934). She published some fifty varied volumes in her lifetime, and left a number of unpublished manuscripts and a voluminous correspondence at her death.

Edith was born Edith Newbold Jones into a patriarchal, rich, cultivated, and rather rigid family in New York City on January 24, 1862. She was the youngest child and the only daughter of George Frederic Jones and Lucretia Stevens Rhinelander who already had two much older sons. Like other girls of her time and class, her life was sheltered and was tutored at home rather than sent out to school. She surprised and perhaps alarmed her parents by her intellectual interests and her devotion to reading, and in 1878, when a volume of her poems was privately published, she achieved something like eccentricity. Her familiarity with the world of the American aristocracy was increased by her marriage in

1885 to Edward Wharton, a social equal thirteen years her senior. At first their life together appeared to be one of gratifying ease and riches. They traveled frequently between Europe and America, purchased homes in New York City and in fashionable Newport, Rhode Island, visited relatives and friends in city mansions and country estates, and entertained on a considerable scale, and with a good deal of elegance and flair. But the marriage soon came to be described as "unfortunate." Their relationship was passionless. They had little in common beyond their upper-class backgrounds. Edith Wharton's interests were intellectual and artistic, none of which her husband shared. She became distant. He became more and more erratic, disruptive, irascible. Their separations grew more and more extended. Faced with a disintegrating marriage and hoping to escape what she saw as a stultifying life as a society matron, Edith Wharton returned to writing. Drawing first on her interest in the decorative arts, she collaborated on a popular guide to interior decorating *The Decoration of Houses* (1897), and began writing short fiction for the genteel magazines of the day. In 1899 came her first volume of short stories *The Greater Inclination*. It was a surprising success, and, as she later wrote, it "broke the chains that had held me so long in a kind of torpor." In 1902, she published her first novel *The Valley of Decision*. It was not until the publication of the bestselling *The House of Mirth* in 1905 that she was recognized as one of the most important novelists of her time for her keen social insight and subtle sense of satire. In 1906 Edith Wharton visited Paris, which inspired *Madame de Treymes* (1907), and made her home there in 1907, finally divorcing her husband of twenty-eight years in 1913. The years before the outbreak of World War I represented the core of her artistic achievement with the publication of *Ethan Frome* in 1911, *The Reef* in 1912, and *The Custom of the Country* in 1913. During the war she remained in France organizing relief for Belgian refugees, for which she was later awarded the Legion of Honor. She also wrote two novels about the war, *The Marne* (1918) and *A Son at the Front* (1923). Although living in France she continued to write about New England and the Newport society she knew so well and described in *Summer*, the companion to *Ethan Frome*, and *The Age of Innocence*. Her other works include the four nouvelles known collectively as *Old New York* (1924), *The Mother's Recompense* (1925), *The Children* (1928), *Hudson River Bracketed* (1929), and her autobiographical *A*

Unit 7
Edith Wharton and *The Age of Innocence*

Backward Glance (1934).

Her work is distinguished by her brilliance as a stylist, the clarity and urbane intelligence with which she manipulated the English language, and her acuity as a social observer and critic, particularly of the leisure class. Subjects repeatedly drawing her attention are the rapaciousness and vulgarity of the nouveaux riches, the timidity and repression of the established upper class, the contrast between European and American customs and values, and the inequality and repression of women, which often manifest itself in patriarchal culture–by design, in hostility and rivalry among women. Perceived in her own time as an extraordinary writer, she received the Pulitzer Prize in 1921 for *The Age of Innocence* and in 1923 she was the first woman to be honored by Yale University with the degree of Doctor of Letters. In 1930 she was awarded the gold medal of the National Institute of Arts and Letters, the first woman to be so honored; and in 1934 she was selected for membership in the American Academy of Arts and Letters. She died of a stroke in August 1937 and was buried in France, the country she chose to make her home for the last twenty-five years of her life.

7.1.2 Edith Wharton's Major Works

The Valley of Decision (1902)	《决断之谷》
The House of Mirth (1905)	《快乐之家》
Ethan Frome (1911)	《伊森·弗洛姆》
The Reef (1912)	《暗礁》
The Custom of the Country (1913)	《乡村习俗》
Summer (1917)	《夏天》
Age of Innocence (1920)	《纯真年代》《天真时代》
Twilight Sleep (1927)	《朦胧入睡》
Hudson River Bracketed (1929)	《夹在中间的哈德孙河》
The Gods Arrive (1932)	《诸神降临》
A Backward Glance (1934)	《回顾》

7.2 The Age of Innocence

7.2.1 About the Novel

The Age of Innocence was published in 1920 and awarded a Pulitzer Prize the following year. It has remained Edith Wharton's most popular novel and is in many ways her most characteristic work. The novel is both nostalgic and satirical in its depiction of old New York, with its often-stifling conventions and manners and its insistence on propriety. It is regarded as a skilled portrayal of the struggle between the individual and the community. It is also a work that explores the dangers and liberties of change as a society moves from a familiar, traditional culture to one that is less formal and affords its members greater freedom. The novel's staying power is generally attributed to its presentation of such universal concerns as women's changing roles, the importance of family in a civilized society, and the universal conflict between passion and duty.

The novel is divided into two books, made up of a total of thirty-four chapters. It presents a picture of upper-class New York society in the 1870s. The action of the novel revolves upon Newland Archer's attempt to challenge the entrenched social order of wealthy New York. He ultimately fails, and the representatives of social order succeed in bringing him back into line: he is separated from Ellen Olenska, the woman he loves, and married to May Welland. Although reabsorbed into society, Archer never quite loses the edge of dissatisfaction; far from being actively unhappy, he nevertheless feels that he has somehow been deprived of "the flower of life" and continues to cherish the image of Ellen as "the composite vision of all that he had missed." The important scene between Newland and his son, Dallas, at the very end of the novel clearly reveals that Archer has sadly failed to appreciate the quality of May's life-long love and silent devotion, failed even to suspect that she, too, might be living a "buried life." It is in this final scene that Edith Wharton firmly places the whole story in its full moral and temporal perspective. Dallas, as the brash representative of a younger, more forthright generation, regards with humorous incredulity the scrupulosity, the reserve, the acceptance of social standards, which had been responsible for the "buried lives" of his father and his father's contemporaries. Here, as throughout the novel, our sympathies are kept nicely in balance.

7.2.2 Characters

- **Newland Archer** The main protagonist of the novel, he has a position as a lawyer.
- **May Welland** The conventional fiancée, then wife of Newland Archer.
- **Ellen Olenska** May's cousin, a non-conformist.
- **Mrs. Archer** Newland Archer's conventional widowed mother.
- **Miss Janey Archer** Newland Archer's unmarried sister.
- **Dallas Archer** Newland's eldest son; he marries Fanny Beaufort.
- **Catherine Mingott** (Catherine Spicer) May and Ellen's grandmother, the Mingott-Welland family matriarch.
- **Mrs. Welland** May's extremely conventional mother.
- **Julius Beaufort** A scandalous womanizer. He represents new money and new standards.
- **Regina Beaufort** The wife of Julius Beaufort. She marries Julius for the unconventional reason that he has recently become a millionaire. She is a relative of Catherine Mingott.
- **Fanny Beaufort** The daughter of Julius Beaufort from his second marriage.
- **Lawrence Lefferts** The foremost authority on "form" in New York.
- **Sillerton Jackson** New York society's central gossip; a good friend of the Archer family.
- **Louisa van der Luyden** Louisa and her husband are the last of the true aristocrats living in New York.
- **Mr. Letterblair** Newland's boss at the law firm.
- **Monsieur Rivière** Newland and May meet him on their honeymoon. Later, he meets Archer in New York and he describes himself as Count Olenski's secretary.

7.2.3 Selected Readings from the Novel

7.2.3.1 Important Quotations

(1) I'm sick of the hypocrisy that would bury alive a woman of her age if her husband prefers to live with harlots… Women ought to be free–as free as we are. (Chapter V, Newland Archer)

(2) The real loneliness is living among all these kind people who only ask one to pretend! (Chapter IX, Ellen Olenska)

(3) If one had habitually breathed the New York air there were times when anything less crystalline seemed stifling. (Chapter XI)

(4) Our ideas about marriage and divorce are particularly old-fashioned. Our legislation favours divorce–our social customs don't. (Chapter XII, Newland Archer)

(5) The individual, in such cases, is nearly always sacrificed to what is supposed to be the collective interest: people cling to any convention that keeps the family together– (Chapter XII)

(6) Though it was supposed to be proper for them to have an occupation, the crude fact of money-making was still regarded as derogatory, and the law, being a profession, was accounted a more gentlemanly pursuit than business. (Chapter XIV)

(7) I couldn't have my happiness made out of a wrong–an unfairness–to somebody else. … What sort of a life could we build on such foundations? (Chapter XVI, May Welland)

(8) I can't love you unless I give you up. (Chapter XVIII, Ellen Olenska)

(9) It was less trouble to conform with the tradition… (Chapter XX)

(10) The air of ideas is the only air worth breathing. (Chapter XX, M. Rivière)

Unit 7

Edith Wharton and *The Age of Innocence*

7.2.3.2 Excerpts Related to Some Scenes in the Film

❈ Excerpt 1 (from Chapter 5)

Sillerton Jackson enjoys his frequent visits to the Archer home more than the actual dining. Newland Archer's mother and his sister Janey are both shy women and shrink from society, but they like to be well informed as to its doings. Therefore, whenever anything happens that Mrs. Archer wants to know about, she asks their bachelor friend Mr. Jackson to dine.

"It was, at any rate, in better taste not to go to the ball," Mrs. Archer continued.

A spirit of perversity moved her son to rejoin: "I don't think it was a question of taste with her. May said she meant to go, and then decided that the dress in question wasn't smart enough."

Mrs. Archer smiled at this confirmation of her inference. "Poor Ellen," she simply remarked; adding compassionately: "We must always bear in mind what an eccentric bringing-up Medora Manson gave her. What can you expect of a girl who was allowed to wear black satin at her coming-out ball?"

"Ah–don't I remember her in it!" said Mr. Jackson; adding: "Poor girl!" in the tone of one who, while enjoying the memory, had fully understood at the time what the sight portended.

"It's odd," Janey remarked, "that she should have kept such an ugly name as Ellen. I should have changed it to Elaine." She glanced about the table to see the effect of this.

Her brother laughed. "Why Elaine?"

"I don't know; it sounds more–more Polish," said Janey, blushing.

"It sounds more conspicuous; and that can hardly be what she wishes," said Mrs. Archer distantly.

"Why not?" broke in her son, growing suddenly argumentative. "Why shouldn't she be conspicuous if she chooses? Why should she slink about as if it were she who had disgraced herself? She's 'poor Ellen' certainly, because she had the bad luck to make a wretched marriage; but I don't see that that's a reason for hiding her head as if she were the culprit."

"That, I suppose," said Mr. Jackson, speculatively, "is the line the Mingotts mean to take."

The young man reddened. "I didn't have to wait for their cue, if that's what you mean, sir. Madame Olenska has had an unhappy life: that doesn't make her an outcast."

"There are rumours," began Mr. Jackson, glancing at Janey.

"Oh, I know: the secretary," the young man took him up. "Nonsense, mother; Janey's grown-up. They say, don't they," he went on, "that the secretary helped her to get away from her brute of a husband, who kept her practically a prisoner? Well, what if he did? I hope there isn't a man among us who wouldn't have done the same in such a case."

Mr. Jackson glanced over his shoulder to say to the sad butler: "Perhaps ... that sauce ... just a little, after all–"; then, having helped himself, he remarked: "I'm told she's looking for a house. She means to live here."

"I hear she means to get a divorce," said Janey boldly.

"I hope she will!" Archer exclaimed.

The word had fallen like a bombshell in the pure and tranquil atmosphere of the Archer dining-room. Mrs. Archer raised her delicate eyebrows in the particular curve that signified: "The butler–" and the young man, himself mindful of the bad taste of discussing such intimate matters in public, hastily branched off into an account of his visit to old Mrs. Mingott.

After dinner, according to immemorial custom, Mrs. Archer and Janey trailed their long silk draperies up to the drawing-room, where, while the gentlemen smoked below stairs, they sat beside a Carcel lamp with an engraved globe, facing each other across a rosewood work-table with a green silk bag under it, and stitched at the two ends of a tapestry band of fieldflowers destined to adorn an "occasional" chair in the drawing-room of young

Mrs. Newland Archer.

While this rite was in progress in the drawing-room, Archer settled Mr. Jackson in an armchair near the fire in the Gothic library and handed him a cigar. Mr. Jackson sank into the armchair with satisfaction, lit his cigar with perfect confidence (it was Newland who bought them), and stretching his thin old ankles to the coals, said: "You say the secretary merely helped her to get away, my dear fellow? Well, he was still helping her a year later, then; for somebody met 'em living at Lausanne together."

Newland reddened. "Living together? Well, why not? Who had the right to make her life over if she hadn't? I'm sick of the hypocrisy that would bury alive a woman of her age if her husband prefers to live with harlots."

He stopped and turned away angrily to light his cigar. "Women ought to be free–as free as we are," he declared, making a discovery of which he was too irritated to measure the terrific consequences.

Mr. Sillerton Jackson stretched his ankles nearer the coals and emitted a sardonic whistle.

"Well," he said after a pause, "apparently Count Olenski takes your view; for I never heard of his having lifted a finger to get his wife back."

Excerpt 2 (from Chapter 12)

As a lawyer, Newland Archer is sent to talk Ellen out of pursuing the divorce. Despite his opinion that she should be free to do as she wishes, Newland explains to Ellen that New York society will not support her divorce. He warns her about the unpleasant accusations contained in the letter from her husband. Ellen dismisses these, but when he cautions her that New York is a very old-fashioned city, and any hint of scandal could affect her entire family Ellen agrees reluctantly to do as he sees best, which apparently makes him feel great pity for her.

"I want to cast off all my old life, to become just like everybody else here."

Archer reddened. "You'll never be like everybody else," he said.

She raised her straight eyebrows a little. "Ah, don't say that. If you knew how I hate to be different!"

Her face had grown as sombre as a tragic mask. She leaned forward, clasping her knee in her thin hands, and looking away from him into remote dark distances.

"I want to get away from it all," she insisted.

He waited a moment and cleared his throat. "I know. Mr. Letterblair has told me."

"Ah?"

"That's the reason I've come. He asked me to–you see I'm in the firm."

She looked slightly surprised, and then her eyes brightened. "You mean you can manage it for me? I can talk to you instead of Mr. Letterblair? Oh, that will be so much easier!"

Her tone touched him, and his confidence grew with his self-satisfaction. He perceived that she had spoken of business to Beaufort simply to get rid of him; and to have routed Beaufort was something of a triumph.

"I am here to talk about it," he repeated.

She sat silent, her head still propped by the arm that rested on the back of the sofa. Her face looked pale and extinguished, as if dimmed by the rich red of her dress. She struck Archer, of a sudden, as a pathetic and even pitiful figure.

"Now we're coming to hard facts," he thought, conscious in himself of the same instinctive recoil that he had so often criticised in his mother and her contemporaries. How little practice he had had in dealing with unusual situations! Their very vocabulary was unfamiliar to him, and seemed to belong to fiction and the stage. In face of what was coming he felt as awkward and embarrassed as a boy.

After a pause Madame Olenska broke out with unexpected vehemence: "I want to be free; I want to wipe out all the past."

"I understand that."

Her face warmed. "Then you'll help me?"

"First–" he hesitated– "perhaps I ought to know a little more."

She seemed surprised. "You know about my husband–my life with him?"

He made a sign of assent.

"Well–then–what more is there? In this country are such things tolerated? I'm a Protestant–our church does not forbid divorce in such cases."

"Certainly not."

They were both silent again, and Archer felt the spectre of Count Olenski's letter grimacing hideously between them. The letter filled only half

Unit 7

Edith Wharton and *The Age of Innocence*

a page, and was just what he had described it to be in speaking of it to Mr. Letterblair: the vague charge of an angry blackguard. But how much truth was behind it? Only Count Olenski's wife could tell.

"I've looked through the papers you gave to Mr. Letterblair," he said at length.

"Well–can there be anything more abominable?"

"No."

She changed her position slightly, screening her eyes with her lifted hand.

"Of course you know," Archer continued, "that if your husband chooses to fight the case–as he threatens to–"

"Yes–?"

"He can say things–things that might be unpl–might be disagreeable to you: say them publicly, so that they would get about, and harm you even if–"

"If–?"

"I mean: no matter how unfounded they were."

She paused for a long interval; so long that, not wishing to keep his eyes on her shaded face, he had time to imprint on his mind the exact shape of her other hand, the one on her knee, and every detail of the three rings on her fourth and fifth fingers; among which, he noticed, a wedding ring did not appear.

"What harm could such accusations, even if he made them publicly, do me here?"

It was on his lips to exclaim: "My poor child–far more harm than anywhere else!" Instead, he answered, in a voice that sounded in his ears like Mr. Letterblair's: "New York society is a very small world compared with the one you've lived in. And it's ruled, in spite of appearances, by a few people with–well, rather old-fashioned ideas."

She said nothing, and he continued: "Our ideas about marriage and divorce are particularly old-fashioned. Our legislation favours divorce–our social customs don't."

"Never?"

"Well–not if the woman, however injured, however irreproachable, has appearances in the least degree against her, has exposed herself by any unconventional action to–to offensive insinuations–"

She drooped her head a little lower, and he waited again, intensely hoping for a flash of indignation, or at least a brief cry of denial. None came.

A little travelling clock ticked purringly at her elbow, and a log broke in two and sent up a shower of sparks. The whole hushed and brooding room seemed to be waiting silently with Archer.

"Yes," she murmured at length, "that's what my family tell me."

He winced a little. "It's not unnatural–"

"*Our* family," she corrected herself; and Archer coloured. "For you'll be my cousin soon," she continued gently.

"I hope so."

"And you take their view?"

He stood up at this, wandered across the room, stared with void eyes at one of the pictures against the old red damask, and came back irresolutely to her side. How could he say: "Yes, if what your husband hints is true, or if you've no way of disproving it"?

"Sincerely–" she interjected, as he was about to speak.

He looked down into the fire. "Sincerely, then–what should you gain that would compensate for the possibility–the certainty–of a lot of beastly talk?"

"But my freedom–is that nothing?"

It flashed across him at that instant that the charge in the letter was true, and that she hoped to marry the partner of her guilt. How was he to tell her that, if she really cherished such a plan, the laws of the State were inexorably opposed to it? The mere suspicion that the thought was in her mind made him feel harshly and impatiently toward her. "But aren't you as free as air as it is?" he returned. "Who can touch you? Mr. Letterblair tells me the financial question has been settled–"

"Oh, yes," she said indifferently.

"Well, then: is it worth while to risk what may be infinitely disagreeable and painful? Think of the newspapers–their vileness! It's all stupid and narrow and unjust–but one can't make over society."

"No," she acquiesced; and her tone was so faint and desolate that he felt a sudden remorse for his own hard thoughts.

"The individual, in such cases, is nearly always sacrificed to what is supposed to be the collective interest: people cling to any convention that keeps the family together–protects the children, if there are any," he rambled

Unit 7
Edith Wharton and *The Age of Innocence*

on, pouring out all the stock phrases that rose to his lips in his intense desire to cover over the ugly reality which her silence seemed to have laid bare. Since she would not or could not say the one word that would have cleared the air, his wish was not to let her feel that he was trying to probe into her secret. Better keep on the surface, in the prudent old New York way, than risk uncovering a wound he could not heal.

"It's my business, you know," he went on, "to help you to see these things as the people who are fondest of you see them. The Mingotts, the Wellands, the van der Luydens, all your friends and relations: if I didn't show you honestly how they judge such questions, it wouldn't be fair of me, would it?" He spoke insistently, almost pleading with her in his eagerness to cover up that yawning silence.

She said slowly: "No; it wouldn't be fair."

The fire had crumbled down to greyness, and one of the lamps made a gurgling appeal for attention. Madame Olenska rose, wound it up and returned to the fire, but without resuming her seat.

Her remaining on her feet seemed to signify that there was nothing more for either of them to say, and Archer stood up also.

"Very well; I will do what you wish," she said abruptly. The blood rushed to his forehead; and, taken aback by the suddenness of her surrender, he caught her two hands awkwardly in his.

"I–I do want to help you," he said.

"You do help me. Good-night, my cousin."

He bent and laid his lips on her hands, which were cold and lifeless. She drew them away, and he turned to the door, found his coat and hat under the faint gas-light of the hall, and plunged out into the winter night bursting with the belated eloquence of the inarticulate.

❧ Excerpt 3 (From Chapter 16)

Newland's speaking in private with Ellen is interrupted by the arrival of Julius Beaufort. A few days later, Ellen sends Newland a note asking to see him. Instead of responding to the invitation, Newland packs his bags and leaves for St. Augustine, Florida, where May has been vacationing with her parents for the winter. There he pleads with May to advance the date of their wedding.

Her first exclamation was: "Newland–has anything happened?" and it occurred to him that it would have been more "feminine" if she had instantly read in his eyes why he had come. ...

"What is it?" he asked, smiling; and she looked at him with surprise, and answered: "Nothing." ...

"Tell me what you do all day," he said, crossing his arms under his tilted-back head, and pushing his hat forward to screen the sun-dazzle. To let her talk about familiar and simple things was the easiest way of carrying on his own independent train of thought; ...

"Why should we dream away another year? Look at me, dear! Don't you understand how I want you for my wife?"

For a moment she remained motionless; then she raised on him eyes of such despairing clearness that he half-released her waist from his hold. But suddenly her look changed and deepened inscrutably. "I'm not sure if I *do* understand," she said. "Is it–is it because you're not certain of continuing to care for me?"

Archer sprang up from his seat. "My God–perhaps–I don't know," he broke out angrily.

May Welland rose also; as they faced each other she seemed to grow in womanly stature and dignity. Both were silent for a moment, as if dismayed by the unforeseen trend of their words: then she said in a low voice: "If that is it – is there some one else?"

"Some one else between you and me?" He echoed her words slowly, as though they were only half-intelligible and he wanted time to repeat the question to himself. She seemed to catch the uncertainty of his voice, for she went on in a deepening tone: "Let us talk frankly, Newland. Sometimes I've felt a difference in you; especially since our engagement has been announced."

"Dear–what madness!" he recovered himself to exclaim.

She met his protest with a faint smile. "If it is, it won't hurt us to talk about it." She paused, and added, lifting her head with one of her noble movements: "Or even if it's true: why shouldn't we speak of it? You might so easily have made a mistake."

He lowered his head, staring at the black leaf-pattern on the sunny path at their feet. "Mistakes are always easy to make; but if I had made one of

Unit 7

Edith Wharton and *The Age of Innocence*

the kind you suggest, is it likely that I should be imploring you to hasten our marriage?"

She looked downward too, disturbing the pattern with the point of her sunshade while she struggled for expression. "Yes," she said at length. "You might want–once for all–to settle the question: it's one way."

Her quiet lucidity startled him, but did not mislead him into thinking her insensible. Under her hat-brim he saw the pallor of her profile, and a slight tremor of the nostril above her resolutely steadied lips.

"Well–?" he questioned, sitting down on the bench, and looking up at her with a frown that he tried to make playful.

She dropped back into her seat and went on: "You mustn't think that a girl knows as little as her parents imagine. One hears and one notices–one has one's feelings and ideas. And of course, long before you told me that you cared for me, I'd known that there was some one else you were interested in; every one was talking about it two years ago at Newport. And once I saw you sitting together on the verandah at a dance–and when she came back into the house her face was sad, and I felt sorry for her; I remembered it afterward, when we were engaged."

Her voice had sunk almost to a whisper, and she sat clasping and unclasping her hands about the handle of her sunshade. The young man laid his upon them with a gentle pressure; his heart dilated with an inexpressible relief.

"My dear child–was *that* it? If you only knew the truth!"

She raised her head quickly. "Then there is a truth I don't know?"

He kept his hand over hers. "I meant, the truth about the old story you speak of."

"But that's what I want to know, Newland–what I ought to know. I couldn't have my happiness made out of a wrong–an unfairness–to somebody else. And I want to believe that it would be the same with you. What sort of a life could we build on such foundations?"

Her face had taken on a look of such tragic courage that he felt like bowing himself down at her feet. "I've wanted to say this for a long time," she went on. "I've wanted to tell you that, when two people really love each other, I understand that there may be situations which make it right that they should–should go against public opinion. And if you feel yourself in any way pledged ... pledged to the person we've spoken of ... and if there is any way ... any way in which you can fulfill your pledge ... even by her getting a divorce ... Newland, don't give her up because of me!"

His surprise at discovering that her fears had fastened upon an episode so remote and so completely of the past as his love affair with Mrs. Thorley Rushworth gave way to wonder at the generosity of her view. There was something superhuman in an attitude so recklessly unorthodox, and if other problems had not pressed on him he would have been lost in wonder at the prodigy of the Wellands' daughter urging him to marry his former mistress. But he was still dizzy with the glimpse of the precipice they had skirted, and full of a new awe at the mystery of young-girlhood.

For a moment he could not speak; then he said: "There is no pledge–no obligation whatever–of the kind you think. Such cases don't always–present themselves quite as simply as ... But that's no matter ... I love your generosity, because I feel as you do about those things ... I feel that each case must be judged individually, on its own merits ... irrespective of stupid conventionalities ... I mean, each woman's right to her liberty –" He pulled himself up, startled by the turn his thoughts had taken, and went on, looking at her with a smile: "Since you understand so many things, dearest, can't you go a little farther, and understand the uselessness of our submitting to another form of the same foolish conventionalities? If there's no one and nothing between us, isn't that an argument for marrying quickly, rather than for more delay?"

She flushed with joy and lifted her face to his; as he bent to it he saw that her eyes were full of happy tears. But in another moment she seemed to have descended from her womanly eminence to helpless and timorous girlhood; and he understood that her courage and initiative were all for others, and that she had none for herself. It was evident that the effort of speaking had been much greater than her studied composure betrayed, and that at his first word of reassurance she had dropped back into the usual, as a too adventurous child takes refuge in its mother's arms.

Archer had no heart to go on pleading with her; he was too much disappointed at the vanishing of the new being who had cast that one deep look at him from her transparent eyes. May seemed to be aware of his disappointment, but without knowing how to alleviate it; and they stood up and walked silently home.

> ### Excerpt 4 (from Chapter 18)
> *Returning to New York, Newland visits Ellen the next day. He tells her his talk with May and May's fears. Newland confesses that May's intuition is accurate.*

Archer reddened, and hurried on with a rush. "We had a frank talk–almost the first. She thinks my impatience a bad sign."

"Merciful heavens–a bad sign?"

"She thinks it means that I can't trust myself to go on caring for her. She thinks, in short, I want to marry her at once to get away from some one that I–care for more."

Madame Olenska examined this curiously. "But if she thinks that–why isn't she in a hurry too?"

"Because she's not like that: she's so much nobler. She insists all the more on the long engagement, to give me time–"

"Time to give her up for the other woman?"

"If I want to."

Madame Olenska leaned toward the fire and gazed into it with fixed eyes. Down the quiet street Archer heard the approaching trot of her horses.

"That *is* noble," she said, with a slight break in her voice.

"Yes. But it's ridiculous."

"Ridiculous? Because you don't care for any one else?"

"Because I don't mean to marry anyone else."

"Ah." There was another long interval. At length she looked up at him and asked: "This other woman–does she love you?"

"Oh, there's no other woman; I mean, the person that May was thinking of is–was never–"

"Then, why, after all, are you in such haste?"

"There's your carriage," said Archer.

She half-rose and looked about her with absent eyes. Her fan and gloves lay on the sofa beside her and she picked them up mechanically.

"Yes; I suppose I must be going."

"You're going to Mrs. Struthers's?"

"Yes." She smiled and added: "I must go where I am invited, or I should be too lonely. Why not come with me?"

Archer felt that at any cost he must keep her beside him, must make her give him the rest of her evening. Ignoring her question, he continued to lean against the chimney-piece, his eyes fixed on the hand in which she held her gloves and fan, as if watching to see if he had the power to make her drop them.

"May guessed the truth," he said. "There is another woman–but not the one she thinks."

Ellen Olenska made no answer, and did not move. After a moment he sat down beside her, and, taking her hand, softly unclasped it, so that the gloves and fan fell on the sofa between them.

She started up, and freeing herself from him moved away to the other side of the hearth. "Ah, don't make love to me! Too many people have done that," she said, frowning.

Archer, changing colour, stood up also: it was the bitterest rebuke she could have given him. "I have never made love to you," he said, "and I never shall. But you are the woman I would have married if it had been possible for either of us."

"Possible for either of us?" She looked at him with unfeigned astonishment. "And you say that–when it's you who've made it impossible?"

He stared at her, groping in a blackness through which a single arrow of light tore its blinding way.

"*I've* made it impossible–?"

"You, you, *you*!" she cried, her lip trembling like a child's on the verge of tears. "Isn't it you who made me give up divorcing–give it up because you showed me how selfish and wicked it was, how one must sacrifice ones self to preserve the dignity of marriage ... and to spare one's family the publicity, the scandal? And because my family was going to be your family–for May's sake and for yours–I did what you told me, what you proved to me that I ought to do. Ah," she broke out with a sudden laugh, "I've made no secret of having done it for you!"

Unit 7
Edith Wharton and *The Age of Innocence*

❧ Excerpt 5 (from Chapter 32)
Newland tries to talk to May about his feelings for Ellen, but May cleverly guides the conversation and lets him know whatever he wants to say makes no difference, since Ellen has decided to leave for Paris. Newland is obviously shaken by the news.

"May–" he began, standing a few feet from her chair, and looking over at her as if the slight distance between them were an unbridgeable abyss. The sound of his voice echoed uncannily through the homelike hush, and he repeated: "There is something I've got to tell you ... about myself ..."

She sat silent, without a movement or a tremor of her lashes. She was still extremely pale, but her face had a curious tranquillity of expression that seemed drawn from some secret inner source.

Archer checked the conventional phrases of self-accusal that were crowding to his lips. He was determined to put the case baldly, without vain recrimination or excuse.

"Madame Olenska–" he said; but at the name his wife raised her hand as if to silence him. As she did so the gas-light struck on the gold of her wedding-ring.

"Oh, why should we talk about Ellen tonight?" she asked, with a slight pout of impatience.

"Because I ought to have spoken before."

Her face remained calm. "Is it really worth while, dear? I know I've been unfair to her at times–perhaps we all have. You've understood her, no doubt, better than we did: you've always been kind to her. But what does it matter, now it's all over?"

Archer looked at her blankly. Could it be possible that the sense of unreality in which he felt himself imprisoned had communicated itself to his wife?

"All over–what do you mean?" he asked in an indistinct stammer.

May still looked at him with transparent eyes. "Why–since she's going back to Europe so soon; since Granny approves and understands, and has arranged to make her independent of her husband–"

She broke off, and Archer, grasping the corner of the mantelpiece in one convulsed hand, and steadying himself against it, made a vain effort to extend the same control to his reeling thoughts.

"I supposed," he heard his wife's even voice go on, "that you had been kept at the office this evening about the business arrangements. It was settled this morning, I believe." She lowered her eyes under his unseeing stare, and another fugitive flush passed over her face.

He understood that his own eyes must be unbearable, and turning away, rested his elbows on the mantel–shelf and covered his face. Something drummed and clanged furiously in his ears; he could not tell if it were the blood in his veins, or the tick of the clock on the mantel.

May sat without moving or speaking while the clock slowly measured out five minutes. A lump of coal fell forward in the grate, and hearing her rise to push it back, Archer at length turned and faced her.

"It's impossible," he exclaimed.

"Impossible?"

"How do you know–what you've just told me?"

"I saw Ellen yesterday–I told you I'd seen her at Granny's."

"It wasn't then that she told you?"

"No; I had a note from her this afternoon. –Do you want to see it?"

He could not find his voice, and she went out of the room, and came back almost immediately.

"I thought you knew," she said simply.

She laid a sheet of paper on the table, and Archer put out his hand and took it up. The letter contained only a few lines.

"May dear, I have at last made Granny understand that my visit to her could be no more than a visit; and she has been as kind and generous as ever. She sees now that if I return to Europe I must live by myself, or rather with poor Aunt Medora, who is coming with me. I am hurrying back to Washington to pack up, and we sail next week. You must be very good to Granny when I'm gone–as good as you've always been to me. Ellen.

"If any of my friends wish to urge me to change my mind, please tell them it would be utterly useless."

Archer read the letter over two or three times; then he flung it down and burst out laughing.

The sound of his laugh startled him. It recalled Janey's midnight fright when she had caught him rocking with incomprehensible mirth over May's

Unit 7

Edith Wharton and *The Age of Innocence*

telegram announcing that the date of their marriage had been advanced.

"Why did she write this?" he asked, checking his laugh with a supreme effort.

May met the question with her unshaken candour. "I suppose because we talked things over yesterday–"

"What things?"

"I told her I was afraid I hadn't been fair to her–hadn't always understood how hard it must have been for her here, alone among so many people who were relations and yet strangers; who felt the right to criticise, and yet didn't always know the circumstances." She paused. "I knew you'd been the one friend she could always count on; and I wanted her to know that you and I were the same–in all our feelings."

She hesitated, as if waiting for him to speak, and then added slowly: "She understood my wishing to tell her this. I think she understands everything."

She went up to Archer, and taking one of his cold hands pressed it quickly against her cheek.

"My head aches too; good-night, dear," she said, and turned to the door, her torn and muddy wedding-dress dragging after her across the room.

❦ Excerpt 6 (from Chapter 33)

Without having any opportunity to talk to Ellen privately in the elaborate going-away dinner before she is driven home, Newland resolves to go through with his plan. But when he tells May that he has decided to travel, May responds by revealing to him the news that she had told Ellen in their long conversation two weeks earlier.

"It *did* go off beautifully, didn't it?" May questioned from the threshold of the library.

Archer roused himself with a start. As soon as the last carriage had driven away, he had come up to the library and shut himself in, with the hope that his wife, who still lingered below, would go straight to her room. But there she stood, pale and drawn, yet radiating the factitious energy of one who has passed beyond fatigue.

"May I come and talk it over?" she asked.

"Of course, if you like. But you must be awfully sleepy–"

"No, I'm not sleepy. I should like to sit with you a little."

"Very well," he said, pushing her chair near the fire.

She sat down and he resumed his seat; but neither spoke for a long time. At length Archer began abruptly: "Since you're not tired, and want to talk, there's something I must tell you. I tried to the other night–"

She looked at him quickly. "Yes, dear. Something about yourself?"

"About myself. You say you're not tired: well, I am. Horribly tired ..."

In an instant she was all tender anxiety. "Oh, I've seen it coming on, Newland! You've been so wickedly overworked–"

"Perhaps it's that. Anyhow, I want to make a break–"

"A break? To give up the law?"

"To go away, at any rate–at once. On a long trip, ever so far off–away from everything–"

He paused, conscious that he had failed in his attempt to speak with the indifference of a man who longs for a change, and is yet too weary to welcome it. Do what he would, the chord of eagerness vibrated. "Away from everything–" he repeated.

"Ever so far? Where, for instance?" she asked.

"Oh, I don't know. India–or Japan."

She stood up, and as he sat with bent head, his chin propped on his hands, he felt her warmly and fragrantly hovering over him.

"As far as that? But I'm afraid you can't, dear ..." she said in an unsteady voice. "Not unless you'll take me with you." And then, as he was silent, she went on, in tones so clear and evenly pitched that each separate syllable tapped like a little hammer on his brain: "That is, if the doctors will let me go ... but I'm afraid they won't. For you see, Newland, I've been sure since this morning of something I've been so longing and hoping for–"

He looked up at her with a sick stare, and she sank down, all dew and roses, and hid her face against his knee.

"Oh, my dear," he said, holding her to him while his cold hand stroked her hair.

There was a long pause, which the inner devils filled with strident laughter; then May freed herself from his arms and stood up.

"You didn't guess–?"

Unit 7
Edith Wharton and *The Age of Innocence*

"Yes–I; no. That is, of course I hoped–"

They looked at each other for an instant and again fell silent; then, turning his eyes from hers, he asked abruptly: "Have you told any one else?"

"Only Mamma and your mother." She paused, and then added hurriedly, the blood flushing up to her forehead: "That is–and Ellen. You know I told you we'd had a long talk one afternoon–and how dear she was to me."

"Ah–" said Archer, his heart stopping.

He felt that his wife was watching him intently. "Did you *mind* my telling her first, Newland?"

"Mind? Why should I?" He made a last effort to collect himself. "But that was a fortnight ago, wasn't it? I thought you said you weren't sure till today."

Her colour burned deeper, but she held his gaze. "No; I wasn't sure then –but I told her I was. And you see I was right!" she exclaimed, her blue eyes wet with victory.

7.2.3.3 Passages for Understanding the Film

(1) Few things seemed to Newland Archer more awful than an offence against "Taste," that far-off divinity of whom "Form" was the mere visible representative and vicegerent. Madame Olenska's pale and serious face appealed to his fancy as suited to the occasion and to her unhappy situation; but the way her dress (which had no tucker) sloped away from her thin shoulders shocked and troubled him. He hated to think of May Wellands being exposed to the influence of a young woman so careless of the dictates of Taste.

The act was ending, and there was a general stir in the box. Suddenly Newland Archer felt himself impelled to decisive action. The desire to be the first man to enter Mrs. Mingott's box, to proclaim to the waiting world his engagement to May Welland, and to see her through whatever difficulties her cousin's anomalous situation might involve her in; this impulse had abruptly overruled all scruples and hesitations, and sent him hurrying through the red corridors to the farther side of the house… The persons of their world lived in an atmosphere of faint implications and pale delicacies, and the fact that he and she understood each other without a word seemed to the young man to bring them nearer than any explanation would have done. **(Chapter II)**

(2) The Beauforts' house was one of the few in New York that possessed a ball-room (it antedated even Mrs. Manson Mingott's and the Headly Chiverses'); and at a time when it was beginning to be thought "provincial" to put a "crash" over the drawing-room floor and move the furniture upstairs, the possession of a ball-room that was used for no other purpose, and left for three-hundred-and-sixty-four days of the year to shuttered darkness, with its gilt chairs stacked in a corner and its chandelier in a bag; this undoubted superiority was felt to compensate for whatever was regrettable in the Beaufort past...The question was: who *was* Beaufort? He passed for an Englishman, was agreeable, handsome, ill-tempered, hospitable and witty. He had come to America with letters of recommendation from old Mrs. Manson Mingott's English son-in-law, the banker, and had speedily made himself an important position in the world of affairs; but his habits were dissipated, his tongue was bitter, his antecedents were mysterious; **(Chapter III)**

(3) That terrifying product of the social system he belonged to and believed in, the young girl who knew nothing and expected everything, looked back at him like a stranger through May Welland's familiar features; and once more it was borne in on him that marriage was not the safe anchorage he had been taught to think, but a voyage on uncharted seas...

In reality they all lived in a kind of hieroglyphic world, where the real thing was never said or done or even thought, but only represented by a set of arbitrary signs; as when Mrs. Welland, who knew exactly why Archer had pressed her to announced her daughter's engagement at the Beaufort ball (and had indeed expected him to do no less), yet felt obliged to simulate reluctance, and the air of having her hand forced, quite as, in the books on Primitive Man that people of advanced culture were beginning to read, the savage bride is dragged with shrieks from her parents' tent. **(Chapter VI)**

(4) ... he must see Madame Olenska himself rather than let her secrets be bared to other eyes. A great wave of compassion had swept away his indifference and impatience: she stood before him as an exposed and pitiful figure, to be saved at all costs from farther wounding herself in her mad plunges against fate.

Unit 7
Edith Wharton and *The Age of Innocence*

He remembered what she had told him of Mrs. Welland's request to be spared whatever was "unpleasant" in her history, and winced at the thought that it was perhaps this attitude of mind which kept the New York air so pure. "Are we only Pharisees after all?" he wondered, puzzled by the effort to reconcile his instinctive disgust at human vileness with his equally instinctive pity for human frailty. **(Chapter XI)**

(5) It was not usual, in New York society, for a lady to address her parlor-maid as "my dear one," and send her out on an errand wrapped in her own opera-cloak; and Archer, through all his deeper feelings, tasted the pleasurable excitement of being in a world where action followed on emotion with such Olympian speed. **(Chapter XVIII)**

(6) He perceived with a flash of chilling insight that in future many problems would be thus negatively solved for him; but as he paid the hansom and followed his wife's long train into the house he took refuge in the comforting platitude that the first six months were always the most difficult in marriage. "After that I suppose we shall have pretty nearly finished rubbing off each other's angles," he reflected; but the worst of it was that May's pressure was already bearing on the very angles whose sharpness he most wanted to keep. **(Chapter XX)**

(7) It was the perfect balance she [Ellen] had held between their loyalty to others and their honesty to themselves that had so stirred and yet tranquillized him; ... It was clear to him, and it grew more clear under closer scrutiny, that if she should finally decide on returning to Europe - returning to her husband—it would not be because her old life tempted her, even on the new terms offered. No: she would go only if she felt herself becoming a temptation to Archer, a temptation to fall away from the standard they had both set up. Her choice would be to stay near him as long as he did not ask her to come nearer; and it depended on himself to keep her just there, safe but secluded. **(Chapter XXV)**

(8) He guessed himself to have been, for months, the centre of countless silently observing eyes and patiently listening ears, he understood that, by means as yet unknown to him, the separation between himself and the partner of his guilt had been achieved, and that now the whole tribe had rallied about his wife on the tacit assumption that nobody knew anything, or had ever imagined anything, and that the occasion of the entertainment was simply

May Archer's natural desire to take an affectionate leave of her friend and cousin.

It was the old New York way of taking life "without effusion of blood;" the way of people who dreaded scandal more than disease, who placed decency above courage, and who considered that nothing was more ill-bred than "scenes," except the behavior of those who gave rise to them.

As these thoughts succeeded each other in his mind Archer felt like a prisoner in the centre of an armed camp. **(Chapter XXXIII)**

7.2.3.4 Chapter Reading

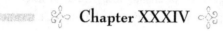
Chapter XXXIV

NEWLAND ARCHER sat at the writing-table in his library in East Thirty-ninth Street.

He had just got back from a big official reception for the inauguration (落成典礼) of the new galleries at the Metropolitan (都市的) Museum, and the spectacle of those great spaces crowded with the spoils of the ages, where the throng of fashion circulated through a series of scientifically catalogued treasures, had suddenly pressed on a rusted spring (弹簧) of memory.

"Why, this used to be one of the old Cesnola rooms," he heard some one say; and instantly everything about him vanished, and he was sitting alone on a hard leather divan (长沙发) against a radiator, while a slight figure in a long sealskin (海豹皮) cloak moved away down the meagrely-fitted vista (狭长通道) of the old Museum.

The vision had roused a host of other associations, and he sat looking with new eyes at the library which, for over thirty years, had been the scene of his solitary musings (沉思) and of all the family confabulations (闲谈) .

It was the room in which most of the real things of his life had happened. There his wife, nearly twenty-six years ago, had broken to him, with a blushing circumlocution that would have caused the young women of the new generation to smile, the news that she was to have a child; and there their eldest boy, Dallas, too delicate to be taken to church in midwinter, had been christened by their old friend the Bishop of New York, the ample magnificent

Unit 7
Edith Wharton and *The Age of Innocence*

irreplaceable (不能替代的) Bishop, so long the pride and ornament of his diocese (主教区). There Dallas had first staggered across the floor shouting "Dad," while May and the nurse laughed behind the door; there their second child, Mary (who was so like her mother), had announced her engagement to the dullest and most reliable of Reggie Chivers's many sons; and there Archer had kissed her through her wedding veil before they went down to the motor which was to carry them to Grace Church–for in a world where all else had reeled (旋转) on its foundations the "Grace Church wedding" remained an unchanged institution.

It was in the library that he and May had always discussed the future of the children: the studies of Dallas and his young brother Bill, Mary's incurable indifference to "accomplishments," and passion for sport and philanthropy (慈善事业), and the vague leanings toward "art" which had finally landed the restless and curious Dallas in the office of a rising New York architect.

The young men nowadays were emancipating themselves from the law and business and taking up all sorts of new things. If they were not absorbed in state politics or municipal (市政的) reform, the chances were that they were going in for Central American archaeology, for architecture or landscape-engineering; taking a keen and learned interest in the prerevolutionary buildings of their own country, studying and adapting Georgian types, and protesting at the meaningless use of the word "Colonial." Nobody nowadays had "Colonial" houses except the millionaire grocers of the suburbs.

But above all–sometimes Archer put it above all–it was in that library that the Governor of New York, coming down from Albany one evening to dine and spend the night, had turned to his host, and said, banging his clenched fist on the table and gnashing (咬) his eye-glasses: "Hang the professional politician! You're the kind of man the country wants, Archer. If the stable's ever to be cleaned out, men like you have got to lend a hand in the cleaning."

"Men like you–" how Archer had glowed at the phrase! How eagerly he had risen up at the call! It was an echo of Ned Winsett's old appeal to roll his sleeves up and get down into the muck (泥潭); but spoken by a man who set the example of the gesture, and whose summons to follow him was irresistible.

Archer, as he looked back, was not sure that men like himself *were* what his country needed, at least in the active service to which Theodore Roosevelt had pointed; in fact, there was reason to think it did not, for after a year in the State Assembly he had not been re-elected, and had dropped back thankfully into obscure if useful municipal work, and from that again to the writing of occasional articles in one of the reforming weeklies that were trying to shake the country out of its apathy (冷漠). It was little enough to look back on; but when he remembered to what the young men of his generation and his set had looked forward–the narrow groove of money-making, sport and society to which their vision had been limited–even his small contribution to the new state of things seemed to count, as each brick counts in a well-built wall. He had done little in public life; he would always be by nature a contemplative and a dilettante; but he had had high things to contemplate, great things to delight in; and one great man's friendship to be his strength and pride.

He had been, in short, what people were beginning to call "a good citizen." In New York, for many years past, every new movement, philanthropic, municipal or artistic, had taken account of his opinion and wanted his name. People said: "Ask Archer" when there was a question of starting the first school for crippled children, reorganising the Museum of Art, founding the Grolier Club, inaugurating the new Library, or getting up a new society of chamber music. His days were full, and they were filled decently. He supposed it was all a man ought to ask.

Something he knew he had missed: the flower of life. But he thought of it now as a thing so unattainable and improbable that to have repined (苦恼) would have been like despairing because one had not drawn the first prize in a lottery. There were a hundred million tickets in *his* lottery, and there was only one prize; the chances had been too decidedly against him. When he thought of Ellen Olenska it was abstractly, serenely, as one might think of some imaginary beloved in a book or a picture: she had become the composite vision of all that he had missed. That vision, faint and tenuous (稀薄) as it was, had kept him from thinking of other women. He had been what was called a faithful husband; and when May had suddenly died–carried off by the infectious pneumonia through which she had nursed their youngest child–he had honestly mourned her. Their long years together had shown him that it did not so much matter if marriage was a dull duty, as long as it kept the dignity of a duty: lapsing from that, it became a mere battle of ugly

Unit 7
Edith Wharton and *The Age of Innocence*

appetites. Looking about him, he honoured his own past, and mourned for it. After all, there was good in the old ways.

His eyes, making the round of the room–done over by Dallas with English mezzotints（金属版印刷品）, Chippendale cabinets, bits of chosen blue-and-white and pleasantly shaded electric lamps–came back to the old Eastlake writing-table that he had never been willing to banish, and to his first photograph of May, which still kept its place beside his inkstand.

There she was, tall, round-bosomed and willowy, in her starched muslin and flapping（垂边）Leghorn（意大利草帽）, as he had seen her under the orange-trees in the Mission garden. And as he had seen her that day, so she had remained; never quite at the same height, yet never far below it: generous, faithful, unwearied; but so lacking in imagination, so incapable of growth, that the world of her youth had fallen into pieces and rebuilt itself without her ever being conscious of the change. This hard bright blindness had kept her immediate horizon apparently unaltered. Her incapacity to recognise change made her children conceal their views from her as Archer concealed his; there had been, from the first, a joint pretence of sameness, a kind of innocent family hypocrisy, in which father and children had unconsciously collaborated. And she had died thinking the world a good place, full of loving and harmonious households like her own, and resigned to leave it because she was convinced that, whatever happened, Newland would continue to inculcate in Dallas the same principles and prejudices which had shaped his parents' lives, and that Dallas in turn (when Newland followed her) would transmit the sacred trust to little Bill. And of Mary she was sure as of her own self. So, having snatched little Bill from the grave, and given her life in the effort, she went contentedly to her place in the Archer vault in St Mark's, where Mrs. Archer already lay safe from the terrifying "trend" which her daughter-in-law had never even become aware of.

Opposite May's portrait stood one of her daughter. Mary Chivers was as tall and fair as her mother, but large-waisted, flat-chested and slightly slouching（没精打采的）, as the altered fashion required. Mary Chivers's mighty feats of athleticism could not have been performed with the twenty-inch waist that May Archer's azure（天蓝色）sash（腰带）so easily spanned. And the difference seemed symbolic; the mother's life had been as closely girt（束住）as her figure. Mary, who was no less conventional, and no more intelligent, yet led a larger life and held more tolerant views. There was good in the new order too.

The telephone clicked, and Archer, turning from the photographs, unhooked the transmitter at his elbow. How far they were from the days when the legs of the brass-buttoned messenger boy had been New York's only means of quick communication!

"Chicago wants you."

Ah–it must be a long-distance from Dallas, who had been sent to Chicago by his firm to talk over the plan of the Lakeside palace they were to build for a young millionaire with ideas. The firm always sent Dallas on such errands.

"Hello, Dad–Yes: Dallas. I say–how do you feel about sailing on Wednesday? Mauretania. Yes, next Wednesday as ever is. Our client wants me to look at some Italian gardens before we settle anything, and has asked me to nip over on the next boat. I've got to be back on the first of June –" the voice broke into a joyful conscious laugh– "so we must look alive. I say, Dad, I want your help: do come."

Dallas seemed to be speaking in the room: the voice was as near by and natural as if he had been lounging in his favourite armchair by the fire. The fact would not ordinarily have surprised Archer, for long-distance telephoning had become as much a matter of course as electric lighting and five-day Atlantic voyages. But the laugh did startle him; it still seemed wonderful that across all those miles and miles of country–forest, river, mountain, prairie, roaring cities and busy indifferent millions–Dallas's laugh should be able to say: "Of course, whatever happens, I must get back on the first, because Fanny Beaufort and I are to be married on the fifth."

The voice began again: "Think it over? No, sir: not a minute. You've got to say yes now. Why not, I'd like to know? If you can allege a single reason–No; I knew it. Then it's a go, eh? Because I count on you to ring up the Cunard office first thing tomorrow; and you'd better book a return on a boat from Marseilles. I say, Dad; it'll be our last time together, in this kind of way–. Oh, good! I knew you would."

Chicago rang off, and Archer rose and began to pace up and down the room.

It would be their last time together in this kind of way: the boy was right.

Unit 7
Edith Wharton and *The Age of Innocence*

They would have lots of other "times" after Dallas's marriage, his father was sure; for the two were born comrades, and Fanny Beaufort, whatever one might think of her, did not seem likely to interfere with their intimacy. On the contrary, from what he had seen of her, he thought she would be naturally included in it. Still, change was change, and differences were differences, and much as he felt himself drawn toward his future daughter-in-law, it was tempting to seize this last chance of being alone with his boy.

There was no reason why he should not seize it, except the profound one that he had lost the habit of travel. May had disliked to move except for valid reasons, such as taking the children to the sea or in the mountains: she could imagine no other motive for leaving the house in Thirty-ninth Street or their comfortable quarters at the Wellands' in Newport. After Dallas had taken his degree she had thought it her duty to travel for six months; and the whole family had made the old-fashioned tour through England, Switzerland and Italy. Their time being limited (no one knew why) they had omitted France. Archer remembered Dallas's wrath (愤怒) at being asked to contemplate Mont Blanc instead of Rheims and Chartres. But Mary and Bill wanted mountain-climbing, and had already yawned (打呵欠) their way in Dallas's wake (跟在达拉斯后面) through the English cathedrals; and May, always fair to her children, had insisted on holding the balance evenly between their athletic and artistic proclivities. She had indeed proposed that her husband should go to Paris for a fortnight, and join them on the Italian lakes after they had "done" Switzerland; but Archer had declined. "We'll stick together," he said; and May's face had brightened at his setting such a good example to Dallas.

Since her death, nearly two years before, there had been no reason for his continuing in the same routine. His children had urged him to travel: Mary Chivers had felt sure it would do him good to go abroad and "see the galleries." The very mysteriousness of such a cure made her the more confident of its efficacy (功效). But Archer had found himself held fast by habit, by memories, by a sudden startled shrinking from new things.

Now, as he reviewed his past, he saw into what a deep rut he had sunk. The worst of doing one's duty was that it apparently unfitted one for doing anything else. At least that was the view that the men of his generation had taken. The trenchant (鲜明的) divisions between right and wrong, honest and dishonest, respectable and the reverse, had left so little scope for the unforeseen. There are moments when a man's imagination, so easily subdued to what it lives in, suddenly rises above its daily level, and surveys the long windings of destiny. Archer hung there and wondered…

What was left of the little world he had grown up in, and whose standards had bent and bound him? He remembered a sneering prophecy of poor Lawrence Lefferts's, uttered years ago in that very room: "If things go on at this rate, our children will be marrying Beaufort's bastards."

It was just what Archer's eldest son, the pride of his life, was doing; and nobody wondered or reproved. Even the boy's Aunt Janey, who still looked so exactly as she used to in her elderly youth, had taken her mother's emeralds (绿宝石) and seed-pearls (小粒珍珠) out of their pink cotton-wool, and carried them with her own twitching hands to the future bride; and Fanny Beaufort, instead of looking disappointed at not receiving a "set" from a Paris jeweller, had exclaimed at their old-fashioned beauty, and declared that when she wore them she should feel like an Isabey miniature.

Fanny Beaufort, who had appeared in New York at eighteen, after the death of her parents, had won its heart much as Madame Olenska had won it thirty years earlier; only instead of being distrustful and afraid of her, society took her joyfully for granted. She was pretty, amusing and accomplished: what more did any one want? Nobody was narrow-minded enough to rake up (重提，翻出) against her the half-forgotten facts of her father's past and her own origin. Only the older people remembered so obscure an incident in the business life of New York as Beaufort's failure, or the fact that after his wife's death he had been quietly married to the notorious Fanny Ring, and had left the country with his new wife, and a little girl who inherited her beauty. He was subsequently heard of in Constantinople, then in Russia; and a dozen years later American travellers were handsomely entertained by him in Buenos Ayres, where he represented a large insurance agency. He and his wife died there in the odour of prosperity; and one day their orphaned daughter had appeared in New York in the charge of May Archer's sister-in-law, Mrs. Jack Welland, whose husband had been appointed the girl's guardian. The fact threw her into almost cousinly relationship with Newland Archer's children, and nobody was surprised when Dallas's engagement was announced.

Nothing could more clearly give the measure of the distance that the

Unit 7
Edith Wharton and *The Age of Innocence*

world had travelled. People nowadays were too busy–busy with reforms and "movements," with fads and fetishes and frivolities–to bother much about their neighbours. And of what account was anybody's past, in the huge kaleidoscope（万花筒）where all the social atoms spun around on the same plane（平面）?

Newland Archer, looking out of his hotel window at the stately gaiety of the Paris streets, felt his heart beating with the confusion and eagerness of youth.

It was long since it had thus plunged and reared under his widening waistcoat, leaving him, the next minute, with an empty breast and hot temples. He wondered if it was thus that his son's conducted itself in the presence of Miss Fanny Beaufort–and decided that it was not. "It functions as actively, no doubt, but the rhythm is different," he reflected, recalling the cool composure with which the young man had announced his engagement, and taken for granted that his family would approve.

"The difference is that these young people take it for granted that they're going to get whatever they want, and that we almost always took it for granted that we shouldn't. Only, I wonder–the thing one's so certain of in advance: can it ever make one's heart beat as wildly?"

It was the day after their arrival in Paris, and the spring sunshine held Archer in his open window, above the wide silvery prospect of the Place Vendôme. One of the things he had stipulated（订明）–almost the only one–when he had agreed to come abroad with Dallas, was that, in Paris, he shouldn't be made to go to one of the new-fangled "palaces."

"Oh, all right–of course," Dallas good-naturedly agreed. "I'll take you to some jolly old-fashioned place–the Bristol, say–" leaving his father speechless at hearing that the century–long home of kings and emperors was now spoken of as an old-fashioned inn, where one went for its quaint inconveniences and lingering local colour.

Archer had pictured often enough, in the first impatient years, the scene of his return to Paris; then the personal vision had faded, and he had simply tried to see the city as the setting of Madame Olenska's life. Sitting alone at night in his library, after the household had gone to bed, he had evoked the radiant outbreak of spring down the avenues of horse-chestnuts（七叶树）, the flowers and statues in the public gardens, the whiff (一阵香气) of lilacs from the flower-carts, the majestic roll of the river under the great bridges, and the life of art and study and pleasure that filled each mighty artery to bursting. Now the spectacle was before him in its glory, and as he looked out on it he felt shy, old-fashioned, inadequate: a mere grey speck of a man compared with the ruthless magnificent fellow he had dreamed of being...

Dallas's hand came down cheerily on his shoulder. "Hullo, father: this is something like, isn't it?" They stood for a while looking out in silence, and then the young man continued: "By the way, I've got a message for you: the Countess Olenska expects us both at half-past five."

He said it lightly, carelessly, as he might have imparted any casual item of information, such as the hour at which their train was to leave for Florence the next evening. Archer looked at him, and thought he saw in his gay young eyes a gleam of his great grandmother Mingott's malice.

"Oh, didn't I tell you?" Dallas pursued. "Fanny made me swear to do three things while I was in Paris: get her the score of the last Debussy songs, go to the Grand-Guignol and see Madame Olenska. You know she was awfully good to Fanny when Mr. Beaufort sent her over from Buenos Ayres to the Assomption. Fanny hadn't any friends in Paris, and Madame Olenska used to be kind to her and trot her about on holidays. I believe she was a great friend of the first Mrs. Beaufort's. And she's our cousin, of course. So I rang her up this morning, before I went out, and told her you and I were here for two days and wanted to see her."

Archer continued to stare at him. "You told her I was here?"

"Of course–why not?" Dallas's eye brows went up whimsically. Then, getting no answer, he slipped his arm through his father's with a confidential pressure.

"I say, father: what was she like?"

Archer felt his colour rise under his son's unabashed gaze. "Come, own up: you and she were great pals, weren't you? Wasn't she most awfully lovely?"

"Lovely? I don't know. She was different."

"Ah–there you have it! That's what it always comes to, doesn't it? When she comes, *she's different*–and one doesn't know why. It's exactly what I feel about Fanny."

Unit 7
Edith Wharton and *The Age of Innocence*

His father drew back a step, releasing his arm. "About Fanny? But, my dear fellow–I should hope so! Only I don't see–"

"Dash it, Dad, don't be prehistoric! Wasn't she–once–your Fanny?"

Dallas belonged body and soul to the new generation. He was the first-born of Newland and May Archer, yet it had never been possible to inculcate in him even the rudiments (入门) of reserve. "What's the use of making mysteries? It only makes people want to nose 'em out," he always objected when enjoined to discretion. But Archer, meeting his eyes, saw the filial light under their banter.

"My Fanny?"

"Well, the woman you'd have chucked (抛弃) everything for: only you didn't," continued his surprising son.

"I didn't," echoed Archer with a kind of solemnity.

"No: you date, you see, dear old boy. But mother said–"

"Your mother?"

"Yes: the day before she died. It was when she sent for me alone – you remember?" She said she knew we were safe with you, and always would be, because once, when she asked you to, you'd given up the thing you most wanted."

Archer received this strange communication in silence. His eyes remained unseeingly fixed on the thronged sunlit square below the window. At length he said in a low voice: "She never asked me."

"No. I forgot. You never did ask each other anything, did you? And you never told each other anything. You just sat and watched each other, and guessed at what was going on underneath. A deaf-and-dumb (聋哑的) asylum, in fact! Well, I back (打赌) your generation for knowing more about each other's private thoughts than we ever have time to find out about our own. I say, Dad," Dallas broke off, "you're not angry with me? If you are, let's make it up and go and lunch at Henri's. I've got to rush out to Versailles (凡尔赛宫) afterward."

Archer did not accompany his son to Versailles. He preferred to spend the afternoon in solitary roamings through Paris. He had to deal all at once with the packed regrets and stifled memories of an inarticulate lifetime.

After a little while he did not regret Dallas's indiscretion. It seemed to take an iron band from his heart to know that, after all, someone had guessed and pitied ... And that it should have been his wife moved him indescribably. Dallas, for all his affectionate insight, would not have understood that. To the boy, no doubt, the episode was only a pathetic instance of vain frustration, of wasted forces. But was it really no more? For a long time Archer sat on a bench in the Champs Elysées and wondered, while the stream of life rolled by...

A few streets away, a few hours away, Ellen Olenska waited. She had never gone back to her husband, and when he had died, some years before, she had made no change in her way of living. There was nothing now to keep her and Archer apart–and that afternoon he was to see her.

He got up and walked across the Place de la Concorde and the Tuileries gardens to the Louvre. She had once told him that she often went there, and he had a fancy to spend the intervening time in a place where he could think of her as perhaps having lately been. For an hour or more he wandered from gallery to gallery through the dazzle of afternoon light, and one by one the pictures burst on him in their half-forgotten splendour, filling his soul with the long echoes of beauty. After all, his life had been too starved...

Suddenly, before an <u>effulgent</u> (光彩夺目的) <u>Titian</u>, he found himself saying: "But I'm only fifty-seven–" and then he turned away. For such summer dreams it was too late; but surely not for a quiet harvest of friendship, of comradeship, in the blessed hush of her nearness.

He went back to the hotel, where he and Dallas were to meet; and together they walked again across the Place de la Concorde and over the bridge that leads to the Chamber of Deputies.

Dallas, unconscious of what was going on in his father's mind, was talking excitedly and abundantly of Versailles. He had had but one previous glimpse of it, during a holiday trip in which he had tried to pack all the sights he had been deprived of when he had had to go with the family to Switzerland; and <u>tumultuous</u> (极其激动的) enthusiasm and <u>cock-sure</u> (过于自信的) criticism tripped each other up on his lips.

As Archer listened, his sense of inadequacy and inexpressiveness increased. The boy was not insensitive, he knew; but he had the facility and self-confidence that came of looking at fate not as a master but as an equal. "That's it: they feel equal to things–they know their way about," he mused,

Unit 7
Edith Wharton and *The Age of Innocence*

thinking of his son as the spokesman of the new generation which had swept away all the old landmarks, and with them the signposts and the danger signal.

Suddenly Dallas stopped short, grasping his father's arm. "Oh, by Jove!" he exclaimed.

They had come out into the great tree-planted space before the Invalides. The dome of Mansart floated ethereally above the budding trees and the long grey front of the building: drawing up into itself all the rays of afternoon light, it hung there like the visible symbol of the race's glory.

Archer knew that Madame Olenska lived in a square near one of the avenues radiating from the Invalides; and he had pictured the quarter as quiet and almost obscure, forgetting the central splendour that lit it up. Now, by some queer process of association, that golden light became for him the pervading illumination in which she lived. For nearly thirty years, her life–of which he knew so strangely little–had been spent in this rich atmosphere that he already felt to be too dense and yet too stimulating for his lungs. He thought of the theatres she must have been to, the pictures she must have looked at, the sober and splendid old houses she must have frequented, the people she must have talked with, the incessant stir of ideas, curiosities, images and associations thrown out by an intensely social race in a setting of immemorial manners; and suddenly he remembered the young Frenchman who had once said to him: "Ah, good conversation–there is nothing like it, is there?"

Archer had not seen M. Rivière, or heard of him, for nearly thirty years; and that fact gave the measure of his ignorance of Madame Olenska's existence. More than half a lifetime divided them, and she had spent the long interval among people he did not know, in a society he but faintly guessed at, in conditions he would never wholly understand. During that time he had been living with his youthful memory of her; but she had doubtless had other and more tangible (切实的) companionship. Perhaps she too had kept her memory of him as something apart; but if she had, it must have been like a relic (遗物) in a small dim chapel, where there was not time to pray every day …

They had crossed the Place des Invalides, and were walking down one of the thoroughfares (大道) flanking the building. It was a quiet quarter, after all, in spite of its splendour and its history; and the fact gave one an idea of the riches Paris had to draw on, since such scenes as this were left to the few and the indifferent.

The day was fading into a soft sun-shot haze, pricked here and there by a yellow electric light, and passers were rare in the little square into which they had turned. Dallas stopped again, and looked up.

"It must be here," he said, slipping his arm through his father's with a movement from which Archer's shyness did not shrink; and they stood together looking up at the house.

It was a modern building, without distinctive character, but many-windowed, and pleasantly balconied up its wide cream-coloured front. On one of the upper balconies, which hung well above the rounded tops of the horse-chestnuts in the square, the awnings (遮篷) were still lowered, as though the sun had just left it.

"I wonder which floor?" Dallas conjectured; and moving toward the *porte-cochère* (门廊) he put his head into the porter's lodge (门房), and came back to say: "The fifth. It must be the one with the awnings."

Archer remained motionless, gazing at the upper windows as if the end of their pilgrimage had been attained.

"I say, you know, it's nearly six," his son at length reminded him.

The father glanced away at an empty bench under the trees.

"I believe I'll sit there a moment," he said.

"Why–aren't you well?" his son exclaimed.

"Oh, perfectly. But I should like you, please, to go up without me."

Dallas paused before him, visibly bewildered. "But, I say, Dad: do you mean you won't come up at all?"

"I don't know," said Archer slowly.

"If you don't she won't understand."

"Go, my boy; perhaps I shall follow you."

Dallas gave him a long look through the twilight.

"But what on earth shall I say?"

"My dear fellow, don't you always know what to say?" his father rejoined with a smile.

"Very well. I shall say you're old-fashioned, and prefer walking up the five flights because you don't like lifts."

His father smiled again. "Say I'm old-fashioned: that's enough."

Dallas looked at him again, and then, with an incredulous gesture, passed out of sight under the vaulted doorway.

Unit 7
Edith Wharton and *The Age of Innocence*

Archer sat down on the bench and continued to gaze at the awninged balcony. He calculated the time it would take his son to be carried up in the lift to the fifth floor, to ring the bell, and be admitted to the hall, and then ushered into the drawing-room. He pictured Dallas entering that room with his quick assured step and his delightful smile, and wondered if the people were right who said that his boy "took after him."

Then he tried to see the persons already in the room—for probably at that sociable hour there would be more than one—and among them a dark lady, pale and dark, who would look up quickly, half rise, and hold out a long thin hand with three rings on it... He thought she would be sitting in a sofa-corner near the fire, with azaleas（杜鹃花）banked behind her on a table.

"It's more real to me here than if I went up," he suddenly heard himself say; and the fear lest that last shadow of reality should lose its edge kept him rooted to his seat as the minutes succeeded each other.

He sat for a long time on the bench in the thickening dusk, his eyes never turning from the balcony. At length a light shone through the windows, and a moment later a man-servant came out on the balcony, drew up the awnings, and closed the shutters.

At that, as if it had been the signal he waited for, Newland Archer got up slowly and walked back alone to his hotel.

Notes and Glossary for Chapter Reading

(1) spoils /spɔilz/ *n.* goods or property seized from a victim after a conflict, especially after a military victory 战利品，掠夺物

(2) circumlocution /ˌsɜːkəmləˈkjuːʃən/ *n.* a roundabout expression; evasive talk 迂回的说法，赘词，拐弯抹角

(3) emancipate /iˈmænsipeit/ *vt.* free or relieve sb. esp. from conventional restrictions 使摆脱束缚，解放

(4) stable /ˈsteibl/ *n.* persons having a common affiliation 有共同目标（或利益）的人群

(5) dilettante /ˈdilitɑːnt/ *n.* a lover of the fine arts; a dabbler in a subject or field of knowledge superficially 爱好艺术者；浅尝者

(6) Chippendale /ˈtʃipəndeil/ of or relating to an 18th-century English style of furniture characterized by flowing lines and often rococo ornamentation. 奇彭代尔式的：一种 18 世纪英国特征为优美的外廓并常有华丽的装饰家具样式的

(7) inculcate /inˈkʌlkeit/ vt. to teach moral principles, social conventions, etc. by frequent instruction or repetition 反复灌输

(8) nip /nip/ vi. go quickly and for only a short time 快速走；急忙，赶紧

(9) look alive: to act or respond quickly; be quick 快点

(10) proclivity /prəuˈklivəti/ n. natural or habitual tendencies or inclinations 倾向，喜好

(11) newfangled /ˈnjuːˌfæŋgld/ a. new and often needlessly novel 新奇的，新型的

(12) Titian /ˈtiʃən/ Italian painter who introduced vigorous colors and the compositional use of backgrounds to the Venetian school 提香（意大利画家，他把鲜明的色彩和背景的混合使用带入了威尼斯画派。）

7.2.4 Exercises

❶ Identify the following characters

(1) _____ is a genteel New Yorker by birth and training. Quiet and self-controlled, conformity to the discipline of a small society had become almost his second nature. Because he reads a variety of books, he fancies himself erudite and well-educated, not realizing how much his own thoughts and experiences are limited by his immediate environment.

(2) _____, described as beautiful, proper, and innocent, is the sum of her New York society upbringing. She seems childlike and carefree, but the reader soon realizes that she is more knowledgeable about the complexities of relationships than her fiancé / husband is.

(3) _____ arrives in New York and creates a stir merely by attending the opera. After marrying a Polish count and living in Europe for a number of years, she returns to New York to seek a divorce. She bravely follows her conscience without regard for personal or material outcome.

(4) _____ often lectures on the virtues of marital fidelity, even though everyone knows about his affairs. He prefers to focus

Unit 7

Edith Wharton and *The Age of Innocence*

on negative gossip than on the positive aspects of their social culture.

(5) _____ is a bachelor who lives with his sister, Sophy. He was an authority on "family". He has an incredible memory for old gossip and New York families.

(6) _____ was not born into New York society, but is accepted because he has married into a respectable family. When his unscrupulous business dealings become public knowledge, he and his wife are quickly shunned by society.

(7) _____ widowed at the age of twenty-eight, lives in a slightly unconventional house, which she never leaves because her obesity will not allow it. She insists on family solidarity and remains confident in Ellen, supporting her financially when she returns to Europe.

(8) _____ and her husband agree to come to Ellen's rescue when Ellen has been disgraced by the society. Their influence is great, despite their lack of socializing. "When they chose, they knew how to give a lesson."

(9) _____, once a French tutor, shows up in New York, telling Newland that he was sent by Ellen's husband to try to convince her to return to Poland.

(10) _____ is beautiful but indecisive, and ignorant of her husband's financial decision. When her husband's business dealings cause their ruin, she visits Catherine to ask for help, but she is refused.

❷ Plot Review

The Age of Innocence, set in late (1)_____ -century New York society, became a best-seller and won the (2) _____ prize in 1921. Edith Wharton was the (3)_____ woman to receive this high literary honor. *The Age of Innocence* opens with Newland Archer about to announce his (4) _____ to May, a gracious, beautiful, entirely conventional, and seemingly (5)_____ young girl of his set. Ellen Olenska, May's (6)_____, having escaped an abusive husband, returns to New York and expects her old family to help her obtain a (7) _____. Instead, the family, through Newland, advised her to (8) _____ the attempt lest she blemish the reputation of the family. Reluctantly, Ellen (9) _____ their advice. Newland, attracted by Ellen's foreign exoticism and (10) _____ spirit, gradually (11)_____ with her. Learning of the efforts that Newland has made for her, and seeing in him the gentility and integrity so (12) _____ in her European marriage, Ellen is also entranced, but insists that they should behave (13)_____. So Newland goes through with his marriage to May, but soon feels (14) _____ with the monotonous married life. May's cool beauty and correct but unexciting personality begins to suffer in his estimation. He continues to see Ellen who nevertheless refuses happiness at the (15)_____of others, particularly of May. After a failed attempt of an illicit meet with Ellen, Newland decides to follow her to Europe. But May's abrupt announcement of her (16) _____ shatters his plan. After an elaborate farewell banquet in her honor, Ellen (17)_____ to Europe, while Newland remains a (18) _____ husband in a placid household. Life continues in a (19)_____ way for about 30 years until one day, an unexpected chance brings Newland to the place where Ellen lives, but the last minute before they meet, Newland decides to walk away from their (20) _____ meeting.

❸ General Questions

(1) Why does Newland have a sudden urge to announce their engagement?
(2) How is Ellen Olenska different from May Welland? And how does Newland view May and Ellen from his selection of the flowers?
(3) Why does Ellen Olenska's family wish for her to return to her husband?
(4) What make Newland Archer and Ellen Olenska fall in love?
(5) Why does Newland want to rush his marriage?
(6) Why does May Welland question Archer's eagerness to marry her?
(7) Why does Ellen suddenly decide to leave for Europe?
(8) Why does May tell Ellen what she has not been sure of in their long conversation? And how does May respond to Newland's question about it later?

Unit 7
Edith Wharton and *The Age of Innocence*

(9) What is Newland informed when he tells May that he has decided to travel? Why does he choose to stay with May?

(10) Why does Newland decide not to see Ellen in Paris?

❹ Questions for writing or discussion

(1) What are some of the instances of a double standard as it applies to men and women's roles and liberties?

(2) In what ways is May different from what Newland thinks she is? How does Edith Wharton reveal strengths and individuality in her that Newland doesn't perceive?

(3) Is Newland Archer consistent in his actions? Is he a fully developed character? How and Why?

(4) Why does Newland Archer conclude that there was good in the old ways, and there was good in the new order too?

(5) Write a comparison of the old New York society and the society of Dallas Archer's present time.

Unit 8

F. Scott Fitzgerald and *The Great Gatsby*

8.1 F. Scott Fitzgerald: Life and Works

8.1.1 About the Author

Francis Scott Fitzgerald is a most representative figure of the 1920s, and is often acclaimed literary spokesman of the Jazz Age. He was born in St. Paul, Minnesota on September 24, 1896, descended on his mother's side from southern colonial landowners and legislators, on his father's from Irish immigrants. St. Paul played its part in Scott Fitzgerald's own life and career. It was here that he completed his first novel *This Side of Paradise* (1920). After his marriage to Zelda Sayre (1900–1948), he settled for some time in St. Paul and it was here that their only daughter was born in 1921. In his novels, especially *The Great Gatsby*, St. Paul, or the Mid-West at least, was to contribute a considerable influence on the shaping of the characters' moral outlook.

From 1913 Fitzgerald attended Princeton University, where he enjoyed social success and popularity, although he left without graduating in 1917 and joined the army. While stationed near Montgomery, Alabama, Fitzgerald met and became engaged to Zelda. Fitzgerald's prospects, however, were

Unit 8
F. Scott Fitzgerald and *The Great Gatsby*

still not very bright. Zelda therefore broke the engagement and Fitzgerald returned to St. Paul. His first novel *This Side of Paradise* was published in 1920 and became a best-seller. He returned to Zelda and this time married her. Fitzgerald managed to keep writing, producing the short-story collections *Flappers and Philosophers* (1920) and *Tales of the Jazz Age* (1922) and the novel *The Beautiful and Damned* (1922). With a considerable income, the Fitzgeralds became celebrity figures in New York and seemed to personify the new age. In 1924 they moved to France, dividing their time between America and fashionable resorts in Europe. There Fitzgerald finished his most brilliant achievement *The Great Gatsby* (1925). It was also at this time that Fitzgerald wrote many of his short stories which helped to pay for his extravagant lifestyle. The following years saw a gradual deterioration in Fitzgerald's life. He began to struggle with alcoholism, while Zelda underwent a series of mental breakdown that resulted in long periods in sanatorium. The troubles of these years are reflected in his next novel *Tender is the Night* (1934), and in the autobiographical essay *The Crack-Up*, posthumously published in 1945.

By 1937 Fitzgerald was sick, alcoholic, unable to write, and no longer earning royalties. He turned to Hollywood screenwriting; the money he made enabled him to pay for his wife's medical care and the education of his daughter (although he had long since surrendered her upbringing to others). Toward the end of the decade things were looking up for him and he planned to revive his career as a fiction writer. But he died of a heart attack in Hollywood on December 21, 1940, leaving an unfinished novel, *The Last Tycoon*, which was brought out by Edmund Wilson in 1941. At the time of his death Fitzgerald was considered a failed literary hope, a writer victimized by his own indulgences. But since the 1940s his literary reputation has steadily risen. Today he is judged to be one of the major American prose writers of his century. In a number of his short stories, and in his finest novels, *The Great Gatsby* and *Tender is the Night*, Fitzgerald had revealed, as no other American writer had, the stridency of an age of glittering innocence. In vivid and graceful prose he had, at the same time, portrayed the hollowness of the American worship of riches and the American dreams of love and splendor and gratified desire.

8.1.2　Scott Fitzgerald's Major Works

This Side of Paradise (1920)　　《人间天堂》
Flappers and Philosophers (1920)　《姑娘们与哲学家们》
The Beautiful and the Damned (1922)《美丽与毁灭》
Tales of the Jazz Age (1922)　　《爵士乐年代故事集》
The Great Gatsby (1925)　　　　《了不起的盖茨比》
Tender is the Night (1934)　　　《夜色温柔》

8.2　The Great Gatsby

8.2.1　About the Novel

The Great Gatsby is considered a vastly more mature and artistically masterful treatment of Fitzgerald's themes than his earlier works that examine the results of the Jazz Age generation's adherence to false material values. *The Great Gatsby* is a short novel of only nine chapters. The entire story takes place in the summer of 1922. Set in New York and narrated by Nick Carraway, the novel explores the self-transformation of Jimmy Gatz from modest Mid-Western origins to the wealthy and mysterious Jay Gatsby of Long Island whose ambition is to regain his former lover Daisy Fay, now the wife of Tom Buchanan. The novel ends with Gatsby, having been exposed as a bootlegger, killed by a garage owner, George Wilson, who mistakenly believes that Gatsby has had an affair with his now-dead wife, Myrtle. The story is not told in a straightforwardly chronological manner, but unfolds as Carraway learns more about Gatsby. One striking fact about the novel's design is the way in which the chapter divisions neatly provide the structural framework for the narrative. From Chapters I to IV the juxtaposition of the two sets of characters is effectively achieved so that the contrasts and similarities between them are consistently maintained. And from Chapters V to IX the action advances steadily and with mounting momentum towards a climax and resolution. Each chapter, containing one or two significant

Unit 8
F. Scott Fitzgerald and *The Great Gatsby*

episodes, urges the plot forward another step towards the ultimate tragedy.

The novel's primary concern is with the duplicitous nature of American Dream, as Fitzgerald explores Gatsby's inability to enter the world of the Buchanans, which depends on inherited rather than on earned wealth. In this respect the novel explores the failure of the American Dream. However, Gatsby becomes heroic precisely because of his belief in dreams: in this respect, it is important to acknowledge that Carraway creatively shapes his representation of Gatsby to make him into a necessary heroic figure embodying a deeply-held American romantic belief in the ability to transform dreams into realities. Thus the novel is finely balanced between the will to believe in the promises of America and recognition that they are corruptible and worthless illusions. Fitzgerald's narrative device ensures that this balance is maintained. In a fundamental way Fitzgerald examines the need for belief in order to animate life and give it direction and meaning, even if the object of that belief turns out to be unattainable or illusory. As he wrote, the novel's theme is "the loss of those illusions that give such color to the world so that you don't care whether things are true or false as long as they partake of the magical glory."

8.2.2 Characters

- **Nick Carraway**   The novel's narrator, he comes from a well-to-do Minnesota family.
- **Jay Gatsby**   The novel's protagonist, his real name is James Gatz.
- **Tom Buchanan**   A brutal, hulking man, he is a former Yale football player who comes from an immensely wealthy Midwestern family.
- **Daisy Fay Buchanan**   Born Daisy Fay, she is Nick's cousin, Tom's wife, and the woman Gatsby loves.
- **Jordan Baker**   Daisy's longtime friend, she is a professional golfer who cheated in order to win her first tournament.
- **George B. Wilson**   A listless, impoverished man who runs a shabby garage in the valley of ashes.
- **Myrtle Wilson**   Wife of George Wilson, she has a long-term affair with Tom Buchanan.

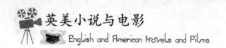

- **Meyer Wolfsheim** A notorious underworld figure, and a business associate of Gatsby.
- **Henry Gatz** Gatsby's father.
- **Catherine** Myrtle Wilson's sister.
- **Owl Eyes** A bespectacled man whom Nick meets at one of Gatsby's parties.

8.2.3 Selected Readings from the Novel

8.2.3.1 Important Quotations

(1) In my younger and more vulnerable years my father gave me some advice that I've been turning over in my mind ever since. "Whenever you feel like criticizing anyone," he told me, "just remember that all the people in this world haven't had the advantages that you've had." **(Chapter I, Nick Carraway)**

(2) I'm glad it's a girl. And I hope she'll be a fool–that's the best thing a girl can be in this world, a beautiful little fool. **(Chapter I, Daisy on her newborn girl)**

(3) He's so dumb he doesn't know he's alive. **(Chapter II, Tom on Wilson)**

(4) I married him because I thought he was a gentleman… I thought he knew something about breeding, but he wasn't fit to lick my shoe. **(Chapter II, Myrtle on Wilson)**

(5) You can't live forever; you can't live forever. **(Chapter II Myrtle Wilson)**

(6) Everyone suspects himself of at least one of the cardinal virtues, and this is mine: I am one of the few honest people that I have ever known. **(Chapter III, Nick)**

(7) It's a great advantage not to drink among hard–drinking people. You can hold your tongue, and, moreover, you can time any little irregularity of your own so that everybody else is so blind that they don't see or care. **(Chapter IV, Jordan Baker)**

(8) It makes me sad because I've never seen such–such beautiful shirts before. **(Chapter V, Daisy)**

Unit 8
F. Scott Fitzgerald and *The Great Gatsby*

(9) I'm one of these trusting fellas and I don't think any harm to *no*body, but when I get to know a thing I know it... God knows what you've been doing, everything you've been doing. You may fool me, but you can't fool God! (Chapter VIII, George Wilson)

(10) When a man gets killed I never like to get mixed up in it in any way. I keep out. When I was a young man it was different–if a friend of mine died, no matter how, I stuck with them to the end... Let us learn to show our friendship for a man when he is alive and not after he is dead... After that my own rule is to let everything alone. (Chapter IX, Meyer Wolfsheim)

8.2.3.2 Excerpts Related to Some Scenes in the Film

✣ Excerpt 1 (from Chapter 1)
Nick Carraway, a man from the Mid-West, comes to New York to work as a bondsman. He is invited to dine with his cousin Daisy and her husband Tom Buchanan. Almost at once he learns that Daisy and Tom are not happily married. As he leaves the Buchanans, Nick feels confused and disgusted.

"In two weeks it'll be the longest day in the year." She looked at us all radiantly. "Do you always watch for the longest day of the year and then miss it? I always watch for the longest day in the year and then miss it."

"We ought to plan something," yawned Miss Baker, sitting down at the table as if she were getting into bed.

"All right," said Daisy. "What'll we plan?" She turned to me helplessly: "What do people plan?"

Before I could answer her eyes fastened with an awed expression on her little finger.

"Look!" she complained; "I hurt it."

We all looked–the knuckle was black and blue.

"You did it, Tom," she said accusingly. "I know you didn't mean to, but you *did* do it. That's what I get for marrying a brute of a man, a great, big, hulking physical specimen of a–"

"I hate that word hulking," objected Tom crossly, "even in kidding."

"Hulking," insisted Daisy.

* * * * * * *

"Can't you talk about crops or something?"

I meant nothing in particular by this remark, but it was taken up in an unexpected way.

"Civilisation's going to pieces," broke out Tom violently. "I've gotten to be a terrible pessimist about things. Have you read *The Rise of the Colored Empires* by this man Goddard?"

"Why, no," I answered, rather surprised by his tone.

"Well, it's a fine book, and everybody ought to read it. The idea is if we don't look out the white race will be–will be utterly submerged. It's all scientific stuff; it's been proved."

"Tom's getting very profound," said Daisy, with an expression of unthoughtful sadness. "He reads deep books with long words in them. What was that word we–"

"Well, these books are all scientific," insisted Tom, glancing at her impatiently. "This fellow has worked out the whole thing. It's up to us, who are the dominant race, to watch out or these other races will have control of things."

"We've got to beat them down," whispered Daisy, winking ferociously towards the fervent sun.

"You ought to live in California–" began Miss Baker, but Tom interrupted her by shifting heavily in his chair.

"This idea is that we're Nordics. I am, and you are, and you are, and–" After an infinitesimal hesitation he included Daisy with a slight nod, and she

Unit 8
F. Scott Fitzgerald and *The Great Gatsby*

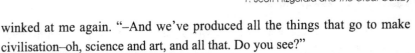

winked at me again. "–And we've produced all the things that go to make civilisation–oh, science and art, and all that. Do you see?"

There was something pathetic in his concentration, as if his complacency, more acute than of old, was not enough to him any more.

* * * * * * * *

"We don't know each other very well, Nick," she said suddenly. "Even if we are cousins. You didn't come to my wedding."

"I wasn't back from the war."

"That's true." She hesitated. "Well, I've had a very bad time, Nick, and I'm pretty cynical about everything."

Evidently she had reason to be. I waited but she didn't say any more, and after a moment I returned rather feebly to the subject of her daughter.

"I suppose she talks, and–eats, and everything."

"Oh, yes." She looked at me absently. "Listen, Nick; let me tell you what I said when she was born. Would you like to hear?"

"Very much."

"It'll show you how I've gotten to feel about–things. Well, she was less than an hour old and Tom was God knows where. I woke up out of the ether with an utterly abandoned feeling, and asked the nurse right away if it was a boy or a girl. She told me it was a girl, and so I turned my head away and wept. "All right," I said, "I'm glad it's a girl. And I hope she'll be a fool– that's the best thing a girl can be in this world, a beautiful little fool."

"You see I think everything's terrible anyhow," she went on in a convinced way. "Everybody thinks so–the most advanced people. And I *know*. I've been everywhere and seen everything and done everything." Her eyes flashed around her in a defiant way, rather like Tom's, and she laughed with thrilling scorn. "Sophisticated–God, I'm sophisticated!"

> ### Excerpt 2 (from Chapter 4)
> *Gatsby invites Nick to lunch with him in New York and introduces him to a man named Wolfsheim, who seems to be Gatsby's business partner. Wolfsheim hints at some dubious business deals that gives Nick the impression that Gatsby's fortune may not have been obtained honestly and that Gatsby may even have ties to the sort of organized crime with which Wolfsheim is associated.*

"He has to telephone," said Mr. Wolfsheim, following him with his eyes. "Fine fellow, isn't he? Handsome to look at and a perfect gentleman."

"Yes."

"He's an Oggsford man."

"Oh!"

"He went to Oggsford College in England. You know Oggsford College?"

"I've heard of it."

"It's one of the most famous colleges in the world."

"Have you known Gatsby for a long time?" I enquired.

"Several years," he answered in a gratified way. "I made the pleasure of his acquaintance just after the war. But I knew I had discovered a man of fine breeding after I talked with him an hour. I said to myself: 'There's the kind of man you'd like to take home and introduce to your mother and sister.'" He paused. "I see you're looking at my cuff buttons."

I hadn't been looking at them, but I did now. They were composed of oddly familiar pieces of ivory.

"Finest specimens of human molars," he informed me.

"Well!" I inspected them. "That's a very interesting idea."

"Yeah." He flipped his sleeves up under his coat. "Yeah, Gatsby's very careful about women. He would never so much as look at a friend's wife."

When the subject of this instinctive trust returned to the table and sat down, Mr. Wolfsheim drank his coffee with a jerk and got to his feet.

"I have enjoyed my lunch," he said, "and I'm going to run off from you two young men before I outstay my welcome."

"Don't hurry, Meyer," said Gatsby, without enthusiasm. Mr. Wolfsheim raised his hand in a sort of benediction.

"You're very polite, but I belong to another generation," he announced solemnly. "You sit here and discuss your sports and your young ladies and your–" He supplied an imaginary noun with another wave of his hand. "As for me, I am fifty years old, and I won't impose myself on you any longer."

As he shook hands and turned away his tragic nose was trembling. I wondered if I had said anything to offend him.

"He becomes very sentimental sometimes," explained Gatsby. "This is one of his sentimental days. He's quite a character around New York–a denizen of Broadway."

"Who is he, anyhow, an actor?"

"No."

"A dentist?"

"Meyer Wolfsheim? No, he's a gambler." Gatsby hesitated, then added coolly: "He's the man who fixed the World's Series back in 1919."

"Fixed the World's Series?" I repeated.

The idea staggered me. I remembered, of course, that the World's Series had been fixed in 1919, but if I had thought of it at all I would have thought of it as a thing that merely *happened*, the end of some inevitable chain. It never occurred to me that one man could start to play with the faith of fifty million people–with the single-mindedness of a burglar blowing a safe.

"How did he happen to do that?" I asked after a minute.

"He just saw the opportunity."

"Why isn't he in jail?"

"They can't get him, old sport. He's a smart man."

✍ Excerpt 3 (from Chapter 4)

Jordan Baker tells Nick the strange story of Daisy's wedding, Gatsby's love affair with Daisy five years ago, his intentions of buying his house in West Egg to be opposite Daisy, and holding large parties. After this account, Jordan tells Nick that Gatsby wants Nick to do him a favor.

"It was a strange coincidence," I said.

"But it wasn't a coincidence at all."

"Why not?"

"Gatsby bought that house so that Daisy would be just across the bay."

Then it had not been merely the stars to which he had aspired on that June night. He came alive to me, delivered suddenly from the womb of his purposeless splendor.

"He wants to know," continued Jordan, "if you'll invite Daisy to your house some afternoon and then let him come over."

The modesty of the demand shook me. He had waited five years and bought a mansion where he dispensed starlight to casual moths–so that he could "come over" some afternoon to a stranger's garden.

"Did I have to know all this before he could ask such a little thing?"

"He's afraid, he's waited so long. He thought you might be offended. You see, he's a regular tough underneath it all."

Something worried me.

"Why didn't he ask you to arrange a meeting?"

"He wants her to see his house," she explained. "And your house is right next door."

"Oh!"

"I think he half expected her to wander into one of his parties, some night," went on Jordan, "but she never did. Then he began asking people casually if they knew her, and I was the first one he found. It was that night he sent for me at his dance, and you should have heard the elaborate way he worked up to it. Of course, I immediately suggested a luncheon in New York–and I thought he'd go mad:

"'I don't want to do anything out of the way!' he kept saying. 'I want to see her right next door.'

"When I said you were a particular friend of Tom's, he started to abandon the whole idea. He doesn't know very much about Tom, though he says he's read a Chicago paper for years just on the chance of catching a glimpse of Daisy's name."

Excerpt 4 (from Chapter 6)

After the party Gatsby tells Nick of his anxieties. He feels that Daisy has not enjoyed his party. He insists that she doesn't understand him and his desire. Gatsby obviously expects to resume where they left off five years ago.

I stayed late that night, Gatsby asked me to wait until he was free, and I lingered in the garden until the inevitable swimming party had run up, chilled and exalted, from the black beach, until the lights were extinguished in the guest-rooms overhead. When he came down the steps at last the tanned skin was drawn unusually tight on his face, and his eyes were bright and tired.

"She didn't like it," he said immediately.

"Of course she did."

"She didn't like it," he insisted. "She didn't have a good time."

Unit 8

F. Scott Fitzgerald and *The Great Gatsby*

He was silent, and I guessed at his unutterable depression.

"I feel far away from her," he said. "It's hard to make her understand."

"You mean about the dance?"

"The dance?" He dismissed all the dances he had given with a snap of his fingers. "Old sport, the dance is unimportant."

He wanted nothing less of Daisy than that she should go to Tom and say: "I never loved you." After she had obliterated four years with that sentence they could decide upon the more practical measures to be taken. One of them was that, after she was free, they were to go back to Louisville and be married from her house–just as if it were five years ago.

"And she doesn't understand," he said. "She used to be able to understand. We'd sit for hours–"

He broke off and began to walk up and down a desolate path of fruit rinds and discarded favors and crushed flowers.

"I wouldn't ask too much of her," I ventured. "You can't repeat the past."

"Can't repeat the past?" he cried incredulously. "Why of course you can!"

He looked around him wildly, as if the past were lurking here in the shadow of his house, just out of reach of his hand.

"I'm going to fix everything just the way it was before," he said, nodding determinedly. "She'll see."

He talked a lot about the past, and I gathered that he wanted to recover something, some idea of himself perhaps, that had gone into loving Daisy. His life had been confused and disordered since then, but if he could once return to a certain starting place and go over it all slowly, he could find out what that thing was...

⚜ Excerpt 5 (from Chapter 7)

At the hotel Tom quickly shows his hostility to Gatsby by questioning his background, accusing Gatsby of trying to steal his wife. During the argument, Daisy sides with both men by turns. Tom, with no moral qualms about his own extramarital affairs, grows in confidence and defeats Gatsby's last efforts to win Daisy over by exposing some of his rival's illegal activities.

"Wait a minute," snapped Tom, "I want to ask Mr. Gatsby one more question."

"Go on," Gatsby said politely.

"What kind of a row are you trying to cause in my house anyhow?"

They were out in the open at last and Gatsby was content.

"He isn't causing a row," Daisy looked desperately from one to the other. "You're causing a row. Please have a little self-control."

"Self-control!" Repeated Tom incredulously. "I suppose the latest thing is to sit back and let Mr. Nobody from Nowhere make love to your wife. Well, if that's the idea you can count me out... Nowadays people begin by sneering at family life and family institutions, and next they'll throw everything overboard and have intermarriage between black and white."

Flushed with his impassioned gibberish, he saw himself standing alone on the last barrier of civilization.

"We're all white here," murmured Jordan.

"I know I'm not very popular. I don't give big parties. I suppose you've got to make your house into a pigsty in order to have any friends–in the modern world."

Angry as I was, as we all were, I was tempted to laugh whenever he opened his mouth. The transition from libertine to prig was so complete.

"I've got something to tell *you*, old sport–"began Gatsby. But Daisy guessed at his intention.

"Please don't!" she interrupted helplessly. "Please let's all go home. Why don't we all go home?"

"That's a good idea." I got up. "Come on, Tom. Nobody wants a drink."

"I want to know what Mr. Gatsby has to tell me."

"Your wife doesn't love you," said Gatsby. "She's never loved you. She loves me."

"You must be crazy!" exclaimed Tom automatically.

Gatsby sprang to his feet, vivid with excitement.

"She never loved you, do you hear?" he cried. "She only married you because I was poor and she was tired of waiting for me. It was a terrible mistake, but in her heart she never loved any one except me!"

At this point Jordan and I tried to go, but Tom and Gatsby insisted with competitive firmness that we remain–as though neither of them had

anything to conceal and it would be a privilege to partake vicariously of their emotions.

"Sit down, Daisy," Tom's voice groped unsuccessfully for the paternal note. "What's been going on? I want to hear all about it."

"I told you what's been going on," said Gatsby. "Going on for five years–and you didn't know."

Tom turned to Daisy sharply.

"You've been seeing this fellow for five years?"

"Not seeing," said Gatsby. "No, we couldn't meet. But both of us loved each other all that time, old sport, and you didn't know. I used to laugh sometimes"–but there was no laughter in his eyes– "to think that you didn't know."

"Oh–that's all." Tom tapped his thick fingers together like a clergyman and leaned back in his chair.

"You're crazy!" he exploded. "I can't speak about what happened five years ago, because I didn't know Daisy then–and I'll be damned if I see how you got within a mile of her unless you brought the groceries to the back door. But all the rest of that's a God damned lie. Daisy loved me when she married me and she loves me now."

"No," said Gatsby, shaking his head.

"She does, though. The trouble is that sometimes she gets foolish ideas in her head and doesn't know what she's doing." He nodded sagely. "And what's more I love Daisy too. Once in a while I go off on a spree and make a fool of myself, but I always come back, and in my heart I love her all the time."

"You're revolting," said Daisy. She turned to me, and her voice, dropping an octave lower, filled the room with thrilling scorn: "Do you know why we left Chicago? I'm surprised that they didn't treat you to the story of that little spree."

Gatsby walked over and stood beside her.

"Daisy, that's all over now," he said earnestly. "It doesn't matter any more. Just tell him the truth–that you never loved him–and it's all wiped out forever."

She looked at him blindly. "Why–how could I love him–possibly?"

"You never loved him."

She hesitated. Her eyes fell on Jordan and me with a sort of appeal, as though she realized at last what she was doing–and as though she had never, all along, intended doing anything at all. But it was done now. It was too late.

"I never loved him," she said, with perceptible reluctance.

"Not at Kapiolani?" demanded Tom suddenly.

"No."

From the ballroom beneath, muffled and suffocating chords were drifting up on hot waves of air.

"Not that day I carried you down from the Punch Bowl to keep your shoes dry?" There was a husky tenderness in his tone... "Daisy?"

"Please don't." Her voice was cold, but the rancor was gone from it. She looked at Gatsby. "There, Jay," she said–but her hand as she tried to light a cigarette was trembling. Suddenly she threw the cigarette and the burning match on the carpet.

"Oh, you want too much!" she cried to Gatsby. "I love you now–isn't that enough? I can't help what's past." She began to sob helplessly. "I did love him once–but I loved you too."

Gatsby's eyes opened and closed.

"You loved me *too*?" he repeated.

"Even that's a lie," said Tom savagely. "She didn't know you were alive. Why–there're things between Daisy and me that you'll never know, things that neither of us can ever forget."

The words seemed to bite physically into Gatsby.

"I want to speak to Daisy alone," he insisted. "She's all excited now–"

"Even alone I can't say I never loved Tom," she admitted in a pitiful voice. "It wouldn't be true."

"Of course it wouldn't," agreed Tom.

She turned to her husband.

"As if it mattered to you," she said.

"Of course it matters. I'm going to take better care of you from now on."

"You don't understand," said Gatsby, with a touch of panic. "You're not going to take care of her any more."

"I'm not?" Tom opened his eyes wide and laughed. He could afford to control himself now. "Why's that?"

"Daisy's leaving you."

Unit 8

F. Scott Fitzgerald and *The Great Gatsby*

"Nonsense."

"I am, though," she said with a visible effort.

"She's not leaving me!" Tom's words suddenly leaned down over Gatsby. "Certainly not for a common swindler who'd have to steal the ring he put on her finger."

"I won't stand this!" cried Daisy. "Oh, please let's get out."

"Who are you, anyhow?" broke out Tom. "You're one of that bunch that hangs around with Meyer Wolfsheim–that much I happen to know. I've made a little investigation into your affairs–and I'll carry it further tomorrow."

"You can suit yourself about that, old sport," said Gatsby steadily.

"I found out what your drug-stores were." He turned to us and spoke rapidly. "He and this Wolfsheim bought up a lot of side-street drug-stores here and in Chicago and sold grain alcohol over the counter. That's one of his little stunts. I picked him for a bootlegger the first time I saw him, and I wasn't far wrong."

"What about it?" said Gatsby politely. "I guess your friend Walter Chase wasn't too proud to come in on it."

"And you left him in the lurch, didn't you? You let him go to jail for a month over in New Jersey. God! You ought to hear Walter on the subject of *you*."

"He came to us dead broke. He was very glad to pick up some money, old sport."

"Don't you call me 'old sport'!" cried Tom. Gatsby said nothing. "Walter could have you up on the betting laws too, but Wolfsheim scared him into shutting his mouth."

That unfamiliar yet recognizable look was back again in Gatsby's face.

"That drug-store business was just small change," continued Tom slowly, "but you've got something on now that Walter's afraid to tell me about."

I glanced at Daisy, who was staring terrified between Gatsby and her husband, and at Jordan, who had begun to balance an invisible but absorbing object on the tip of her chin. Then I turned back to Gatsby–and was startled at his expression. He looked–and this is said in all contempt for the babbled slander of his garden–as if he had "killed a man". For a moment the set of his face could be described in just that fantastic way.

It passed, and he began to talk excitedly to Daisy, denying everything, defending his name against accusations that had not been made. But with every word she was drawing further and further into herself, so he gave that up, and only the dead dream fought on as the afternoon slipped away, trying to touch what was no longer tangible, struggling unhappily, undespairingly, towards that lost voice across the room.

The voice begged again to go.

"*Please*, Tom! I can't stand this any more."

Her frightened eyes told that whatever intentions, whatever courage she had had, were definitely gone.

"You two start on home, Daisy," said Tom. "In Mr. Gatsby's car."

She looked at Tom, alarmed now, but he insisted with magnanimous scorn.

"Go on. He won't annoy you. I think he realizes that his presumptuous little flirtation is over."

Excerpt 6 (from Chapter 8)

Nick learns from Gatsby, who has been waiting outside Tom's house, that Daisy was driving the car when it hit Myrtle, but Gatsby intends to take the blame. Gatsby insists that he will stay and watch all night over the Buchanans' house to make sure that Daisy is not bullied by her husband. That night Nick hardly sleeps at all. When it is nearly dawn, he goes quickly to Gatsby's house.

"You ought to go away," I said. "It's pretty certain they'll trace your car."

"Go away *now*, old sport?"

"Go to Atlantic City for a week, or up to Montreal."

He wouldn't consider it. He couldn't possibly leave Daisy until he knew what she was going to do. He was clutching at some last hope and I couldn't bear to shake him free.

It was this night that he told me the strange story of his youth with Dan Cody–told it to me because "Jay Gatsby" had broken up like glass against Tom's hard malice, and the long secret extravaganza was played out. I think that he would have acknowledged anything now, without reserve, but he wanted to talk about Daisy.

Unit 8

F. Scott Fitzgerald and *The Great Gatsby*

* * * * * * * *

"I can't describe to you how surprised I was to find out I loved her, old sport. I even hoped for a while that she'd throw me over, but she didn't, because she was in love with me too. She thought I knew a lot because I knew different things from her ... Well, there I was, 'way off my ambitions, getting deeper in love every minute, and all of a sudden I didn't care. What was the use of doing great things if I could have a better time telling her what I was going to do?

* * * * * * * *

I looked at my watch and stood up.

"Twelve minutes to my train."

I didn't want to go to the city. I wasn't worth a decent stroke of work, but it was more than that–I didn't want to leave Gatsby. I missed that train, and then another, before I could get myself away.

"I'll call you up," I said finally.

"Do, old sport."

"I'll call you about noon."

We walked slowly down the steps.

"I suppose Daisy'll call too. He looked at me anxiously, as if he hoped I'd corroborate this."

"I suppose so."

"Well, good-by."

We shook hands and I started away. Just before I reached the hedge I remembered something and turned around.

"They're a rotten crowd," I shouted across the lawn. "You're worth the whole damn bunch put together."

I've always been glad I said that. It was the only compliment I ever gave him, because I disapproved of him from beginning to end.

8.2.3.3 Passages for Understanding the Film

(1) Only Gatsby, the man who gives his name to this book, was exempt from my reaction–Gatsby, who represented everything for which I have an unaffected

scorn. If personality is an unbroken series of successful gestures, then there was something gorgeous about him, some heightened sensitivity to the promises of life, as if he were related to one of those intricate machines that register earthquakes ten thousand miles away. This responsiveness had nothing to do with that flabby impressionability which is dignified under the name of the "creative temperament" –it was an extraordinary gift for hope, a romantic readiness such as I have never found in any other person and which it is not likely I shall ever find again. No–Gatsby turned out all right at the end; it is what preyed on Gatsby, what foul dust floated in the wake of his dreams that temporarily closed out my interest in the abortive sorrows and short-winded elations of men. **(Chapter I, Nick)**

(2) James Gatz–that was really, or at least legally, his name. He had changed it at the age of seventeen and at the specific moment that witnessed the beginning of his career–when he saw Dan Cody's yacht drop anchor over the most insidious flat on Lake Superior. It was James Gatz who had been loafing along the beach that afternoon in a torn green jersey and a pair of canvas pants, but it was already Jay Gatsby who borrowed a rowboat, pulled out to the *Tuolomee*, and informed Cody that a wind might catch him and break him up in half an hour.

I suppose he'd had the name ready for a long time, even then. His parents were shiftless and unsuccessful farm people–his imagination had never really accepted them as his parents at all. The truth was that Jay Gatsby of West Egg, Long Island, sprang from his Platonic conception of himself. He was a son of God–a phrase which, if it means anything, means just that–and he must be about His Father's business, the service of a vast, vulgar and meretricious beauty. So he invented just the sort of Jay Gatsby that a seventeen-year-old boy would be likely to invent, and to this conception he was faithful to the end...

Cody was fifty years old then, a product of the Nevada silver fields, of the Yukon, of every rush for metal since seventy-five. The transactions in Montana copper that made him many times a millionaire found him physically robust but on the verge of soft-mindedness, and, suspecting this, an infinite number of women tried to separate him from his money... He (Gatsby) was employed in a vague personal capacity–while he remained with Cody he was in turn steward, mate, skipper, secretary and even jailor, for Dan

Unit 8
F. Scott Fitzgerald and *The Great Gatsby*

Cody sober knew what lavish doings Dan Cody drunk might soon be about, and he provided for such contingencies by reposing more and more trust in Gatsby. The arrangement lasted five years, during which the boat went three times around the Continent. It might have lasted indefinitely except for the fact that Ella Kaye came on board one night in Boston and a week later Dan Cody inhospitably died... And it was from Cody that he inherited money-a legacy of twenty-five thousand dollars. He didn't get it. He never understood the legal device that was used against him, but what remained of the millions went intact to Ella Kaye. He was left with his singularly appropriate education; the vague contour of Jay Gatsby had filled out to the substantiality of a man. **(Chapter VI)**

(3) Daisy and Tom were sitting opposite each other at the kitchen table, with a plate of cold fried chicken between them, and two bottles of ale. He was talking intently across the table at her, and in his earnestness his hand had fallen upon and covered her own. Once in a while she looked up at him and nodded in agreement.

They weren't happy, and neither of them had touched the chicken or the ale-and yet they weren't unhappy either. There was an unmistakable air of natural intimacy about the picture, and anybody would have said that they were conspiring together. **(Chapter VII)**

(4) She was the first "nice girl" he had ever known. In various unrevealed capacities he had come in contact with such people, but always with indiscernible barbed wire between. He found her excitingly desirable. He went to her house, at first with other officers from Camp Taylor, then alone. It amazed him-he had never been in such a beautiful house before. But what gave it an air of breathless intensity was that Daisy lived there ... It excited him, too, that many men had already loved Daisy-it increased her value in his eyes...

He might have despised himself, for he had certainly taken her under false pretenses. I don't mean that he had traded on his phantom millions, but he had deliberately given Daisy a sense of security; he let her believe that he was a person from much the same stratum as herself-that he was fully able to take care of her. As a matter of fact, he had no such facilities-he had no comfortable family standing behind him, and he was liable at the whim of an impersonal government to be blown anywhere about the world.

But he didn't despise himself and it didn't turn out as he had imagined. He had intended, probably, to take what he could and go-but now he found that he had committed himself to the following of a grail...

Gatsby was overwhelmingly aware of the youth and mystery that wealth imprisons and preserves, of the freshness of many clothes, and of Daisy, gleaming like silver, safe and proud above the hot struggles of the poor. **(Chapter VIII)**

(5) I couldn't forgive him or like him, but I saw that what he had done was, to him, entirely justified. It was all very careless and confused. They were careless people, Tom and Daisy-they smashed up things and creatures and then retreated back into their money or their vast carelessness, or whatever it was that kept them together, and let other people clean up the mess they had made...

I shook hands with him; it seemed silly not to, for I felt suddenly as though I were talking to a child. **(Chapter IX)**

8.2.3.4 Chapter Reading

Chapter III

THERE WAS MUSIC from my neighbor's house through the summer nights. In his blue gardens men and girls came and went like moths among the whisperings and the champagne and the stars. At high tide (涨 潮) in the afternoon I watched his guests diving from the tower of his raft, or taking the sun on the hot sand of his beach while his two motor-boats (摩托艇) slit (划破) the waters of the Sound, drawing aquaplanes (滑水板) over cataracts of foam. On week-ends his Rolls-Royce became an omnibus (公共汽车), bearing parties to and from the city between nine in the morning and long past midnight, while his station-wagon (旅行车) scampered (奔跑) like a brisk yellow bug to meet all trains. And on Mondays eight servants, including an extra gardener, toiled all day with mops and scrubbing-brushes and hammers and garden-shears, repairing the ravages (残迹) of the night before.

Every Friday five crates (板条箱) of oranges and lemons arrived from a fruiterer (水果商) in New York-every Monday these same oranges and

Unit 8
F. Scott Fitzgerald and *The Great Gatsby*

lemons left his back door in a pyramid of pulpless halves. There was a machine in the kitchen which could extract the juice of two hundred oranges in half an hour if a little button was pressed two hundred times by a butler's thumb.

At least once a fortnight a corps of caterers (酒席承办人) came down with several hundred feet of canvas and enough colored lights to make a Christmas tree of Gatsby's enormous garden. On buffet (自助餐) tables, garnished (装饰) with glistening hors d'oeuvre (开胃小吃，冷盘), spiced baked hams crowded against salads of harlequin (五颜六色的) designs and pastry pigs and turkeys bewitched to a dark gold. In the main hall a bar with a real brass rail was set up, and stocked with gins and liquors and with cordials (露 酒) so long forgotten that most of his female guests were too young to know one from another.

By seven o'clock the orchestra has arrived, no thin five-piece affair, but a whole pitful of oboes (双簧管) and trombones (长号) and saxophones (萨克斯管) and viols (古提琴) and cornets (短号) and piccolos (短笛), and low and high drums. The last swimmers have come in from the beach now and are dressing up-stairs; the cars from New York are parked five deep in the drive (车道), and already the halls and salons (客厅) and verandas (走廊) are gaudy (炫丽的) with primary colors, and hair shorn in strange new ways, and shawls beyond the dreams of Castile. The bar is in full swing, and floating rounds of cocktails permeate (弥漫) the garden outside, until the air is alive with chatter and laughter, and casual innuendo (暗 讽) and introductions forgotten on the spot (立刻), and enthusiastic meetings between women who never knew each other's names.

The lights grow brighter as the earth lurches (倾斜) away from the sun, and now the orchestra is playing yellow cocktail music, and the opera of voices pitches a key higher. Laughter is easier minute by minute, spilled with prodigality, tipped out at a cheerful word. The groups change more swiftly, swell with new arrivals, dissolve and form in the same breath; already there are wanderers, confident girls who weave here and there among the stouter and more stable, become for a sharp, joyous moment the centre of a group, and then, excited with triumph, glide on through the sea-change of faces and voices and color under the constantly changing light.

Suddenly one of the gypsies (像吉卜赛人的人), in trembling opal, seizes a cocktail out of the air, dumps it down for courage and, moving her hands like Frisco, dances out alone on the canvas platform. A momentary hush; the orchestra leader varies his rhythm obligingly for her, and there is a burst of chatter as the erroneous news goes around that she is Gilda Gray's understudy (替角) from the *Follies*. The party has begun.

  I believe that on the first night I went to Gatsby's house I was one of the few guests who had actually been invited. People were not invited–they went there. They got into automobiles which bore them out to Long Island, and somehow they ended up at Gatsby's door. Once there they were introduced by somebody who knew Gatsby, and after that they conducted themselves according to the rules of behavior associated with amusement park. Sometimes they came and went without having met Gatsby at all, came for the party with a simplicity of heart that was its own ticket of admission.

  I had been actually invited. A chauffeur in a uniform of robin's-egg blue crossed my lawn early that Saturday morning with a surprisingly formal note from his employer: the honor would be entirely Gatsby's, it said, if I would attend his "little party" that night. He had seen me several times, and had intended to call on me long before, but a peculiar combination of circumstances had prevented it–signed Jay Gatsby, in a majestic hand.

  Dressed up in white flannels I went over to his lawn a little after seven, and wandered around rather ill at ease among swirls (旋转) and eddies (漩涡) of people I didn't know–though here and there was a face I had noticed on the commuting train. I was immediately struck by the number of young Englishmen dotted about, all well dressed, all looking a little hungry, and all talking in low, earnest voices to solid and prosperous Americans. I was sure that they were selling something: bonds or insurance or automobiles. They were at least agonizingly aware of the easy money in the vicinity and convinced that it was theirs for a few words in the right key.

  As soon as I arrived I made an attempt to find my host, but the two or three people of whom I asked his whereabouts stared at me in such an amazed way, and denied so vehemently (激烈地) any knowledge of his movements, that I slunk off in the direction of the cocktail table–the only place in the garden where a single man could linger without looking purposeless and alone.

  I was on my way to get roaring drunk from sheer embarrassment when

Unit 8

F. Scott Fitzgerald and *The Great Gatsby*

Jordan Baker came out of the house and stood at the head of the marble steps, leaning a little backward and looking with contemptuous interest down into the garden.

Welcome or not, I found it necessary to attach myself to someone before I should begin to address <u>cordial</u> (热忱的) remarks to the passers-by.

"Hello!" I roared, advancing towards her. My voice seemed unnaturally loud across the garden.

"I thought you might be here," she responded absently as I came up. "I remembered you lived next door to—"

She held my hand <u>impersonally</u> (不带感情地), as a promise that she'd take care of me in a minute, and gave ear to two girls in twin yellow dresses, who stopped at the foot of the steps.

"Hello!" they cried together. "Sorry you didn't win."

That was for the golf tournament. She had lost in the finals the week before.

"You don't know who we are," said one of the girls in yellow, "but we met you here about a month ago."

"You've dyed your hair since then," remarked Jordan, and I started, but the girls had moved casually on and her remark was addressed to the premature moon, produced like the supper, no doubt, out of a caterer's basket. With Jordan's slender golden arm resting in mine, we descended the steps and <u>sauntered</u> (闲逛) about the garden. A tray of cocktails floated at us through the twilight, and we sat down at a table with the two girls in yellow and three men, each one introduced to us as Mr Mumble.

"Do you come to these parties often?" inquired Jordan of the girl beside her.

"The last one was the one I met you at," answered the girl, in an alert confident voice. She turned to her companion: "Wasn't it for you, Lucille?"

It was for Lucille, too.

"I like to come," Lucille said. "I never care what I do, so I always have a good time. When I was here last I tore my gown on a chair, and he asked me my name and address—inside of a week I got a package from Croirier's with a new evening gown in it."

"Did you keep it?" asked Jordan.

"Sure I did. I was going to wear it tonight, but it was too big in the bust and had to be altered. It was gas blue with lavender (淡紫色) beads. Two hundred and sixty-five dollars."

"There's something funny about a fellow that'll do a thing like that," said the other girl eagerly. "He doesn't want any trouble with *any*body."

"Who doesn't?" I enquired.

"Gatsby. Somebody told me—"

The two girls and Jordan leaned together confidentially.

"Somebody told me they thought he killed a man once."

A thrill passed over all of us. The three Mr Mumbles bent forward and listened eagerly.

"I don't think it's so much *that*," argued Lucille sceptically; "it's more that he was a German spy during the war."

One of the men nodded in confirmation.

"I heard that from a man who knew all about him, grew up with him in Germany," he assured us positively.

"Oh, no," said the first girl, "it couldn't be that, because he was in the American army during the war." As our credulity switched back to her she leaned forward with enthusiasm. "You look at him sometimes when he thinks nobody's looking at him. I'll bet he killed a man."

She narrowed her eyes and shivered. Lucille shivered. We all turned and looked around for Gatsby. It was testimony to the romantic speculation he inspired that there were whispers about him from those who found little that it was necessary to whisper about in this world.

The first supper—there would be another one after midnight—was now being served, and Jordan invited me to join her own party, who were spread around a table on the other side of the garden. There were three married couples and Jordan's escort, a persistent undergraduate given to violent innuendo, and obviously under the impression that sooner or later Jordan was going to yield him up her person to a greater or lesser degree. Instead of rambling, this party had preserved a dignified homogeneity (同质), and assumed to itself the function of representing the staid nobility of the countryside—East Egg condescending to West Egg, and carefully on guard against its spectroscopic (分光镜的) gaiety.

"Let's get out," whispered Jordan, after a somehow wasteful and inappropriate half-hour; "this is much too polite for me."

Unit 8
F. Scott Fitzgerald and *The Great Gatsby*

We got up, and she explained that we were going to find the host: I had never met him, she said, and it was making me uneasy. The undergraduate nodded in a cynical, melancholy way.

The bar, where we glanced first, was crowded, but Gatsby was not there. She couldn't find him from the top of the steps, and he wasn't on the veranda. On a chance we tried an important-looking door, and walked into a high Gothic library, panelled (嵌镶) with carved English oak, and probably transported complete from some ruin overseas.

A stout, middle-aged man, with enormous owl-eyed spectacles, was sitting somewhat drunk on the edge of a great table, staring with unsteady concentration at the shelves of books. As we entered he wheeled excitedly around and examined Jordan from head to foot.

"What do you think?" he demanded impetuously (性急地).

"About what?"

He waved his hand towards the book-shelves.

"About that. As a matter of fact you needn't bother to ascertain (查明). I ascertained. They're real."

"The books?"

He nodded.

"Absolutely real—have pages and everything. I thought they'd be a nice durable cardboard. Matter of fact, they're absolutely real. Pages and—Here! Lemme show you."

Taking our scepticism (怀疑主义) for granted, he rushed to the bookcases and returned with Volume One of the "Stoddard Lectures".

"See!" he cried triumphantly. "It's a bona-fide (真实的) piece of printed matter. It fooled me. This fella's a regular Belasco. It's a triumph. What thoroughness! What realism! Knew when to stop, too—didn't cut the pages. But what do you want? What do you expect?"

He snatched the book from me and replaced it hastily on its shelf, muttering that if one brick was removed the whole library was liable to collapse.

"Who brought you?" he demanded. "Or did you just come? I was brought. Most people were brought."

Jordan looked at him alertly, cheerfully, without answering.

"I was brought by a woman named Roosevelt," he continued. "Mrs.

Claud Roosevelt. Do you know her? I met her somewhere last night. I've been drunk for about a week now, and I thought it might sober me up to sit in a library."

"Has it?"

"A little bit, I think. I can't tell yet. I've only been here an hour. Did I tell you about the books? They're real. They're–"

"You told us."

We shook hands with him gravely and went back outdoors.

There was dancing now on the canvas in the garden; old men pushing young girls backwards in eternal graceless circles, superior couples holding each other tortuously (扭曲地), fashionably, and keeping in the corners–and a great number of single girls dancing individualistically or relieving the orchestra for a moment of the burden of the banjo (班卓琴) or the traps (打击乐器). By midnight the hilarity (欢闹) had increased. A celebrated tenor (男高音) had sung in Italian, and a notorious contralto (女低音) had sung in jazz, and between the numbers people were doing "stunts" (绝技) all over the garden, while happy, vacuous (空洞的) bursts of laughter rose towards the summer sky. A pair of stage twins, who turned out to be the girls in yellow, did a baby act in costume, and champagne was served in glasses bigger than finger-bowls (洗指碗). The moon had risen higher, and floating in the Sound was a triangle of silver scales, trembling a little to the stiff, tinny drip of the banjoes on the lawn.

I was still with Jordan Baker. We were sitting at a table with a man of about my age and a rowdy (吵闹的) little girl, who gave way upon the slightest provocation to uncontrollable laughter. I was enjoying myself now. I had taken two finger-bowls of champagne, and the scene had changed before my eyes into something significant, elemental and profound.

At a lull (间歇) in the entertainment the man looked at me and smiled.

"Your face is familiar," he said, politely. "Weren't you in the Third Division (师) during the war?"

"Why, yes. I was in the Ninth Machine-Gun Battalion (营)."

"I was in the Seventh Infantry (步兵团) until June nineteen-eighteen. I knew I'd seen you somewhere before."

We talked for a moment about some wet, gray little villages in France. Evidently he lived in this vicinity, for he told me that he had just bought a

Unit 8
F. Scott Fitzgerald and *The Great Gatsby*

hydroplane (水上滑艇), and was going to try it out in the morning.

"Want to go with me, <u>old sport</u>? Just near the shore along the Sound."

"What time?"

"Any time that suits you best."

It was on the tip of my tongue to ask his name when Jordan looked around and smiled.

"Having a gay time now?" she enquired.

"Much better." I turned again to my new acquaintance. "This is an unusual party for me. I haven't even seen the host. I live over there–" I waved my hand at the invisible hedge in the distance, "and this man Gatsby sent over his chauffeur with an invitation."

For a moment he looked at me as if he failed to understand.

"I'm Gatsby," he said suddenly.

"What!" I exclaimed. "Oh, I beg your pardon."

"I thought you knew, old sport. I'm afraid I'm not a very good host."

He smiled understandingly–much more than understandingly. It was one of those rare smiles with a quality of eternal reassurance in it, that you may come across four or five times in life. It faced–or seemed to face–the whole eternal world for an instant, and then concentrated on *you* with an irresistible prejudice in your favor. It understood you just so far as you wanted to be understood, believed in you as you would like to believe in yourself, and assured you that it had precisely the impression of you that, at your best, you hoped to convey. Precisely at that point it vanished–and I was looking at an elegant young <u>roughneck</u>, a year or two over thirty, whose elaborate formality of speech just missed being absurd. Some time before he introduced himself I'd got a strong impression that he was picking his words with care.

Almost at the moment when Mr. Gatsby identified himself, a butler hurried towards him with the information that Chicago was calling him on the wire. He excused himself with a small bow that included each of us in turn.

"If you want anything just ask for it, old sport," he urged me. "Excuse me. I will rejoin you later."

When he was gone I turned immediately to Jordan–constrained to assure her of my surprise. I had expected that Mr. Gatsby would be a <u>florid</u> (脸色红润的) and <u>corpulent</u> (肥胖的) person in his middle years.

"Who is he?" I demanded. "Do you know?"

"He's just a man named Gatsby."

"Where is he from, I mean? And what does he do?"

"Now *you're* started on the subject," she answered with a wan (面带倦容的) smile. "Well, he told me once he was an Oxford man."

A dim background started to take shape behind him, but at her next remark it faded away.

"However, I don't believe it."

"Why not?"

"I don't know," she insisted, "I just don't think he went there."

Something in her tone reminded me of the other girl's "I think he killed a man", and had the effect of stimulating my curiosity. I would have accepted without question the information that Gatsby sprang from the swamps of Louisiana or from the lower East Side of New York. That was comprehensible. But young men didn't–at least in my provincial inexperience I believed they didn't–drift coolly out of nowhere and buy a palace on Long Island Sound.

"Anyhow, he gives large parties," said Jordan, changing the subject with an urbane distaste for the concrete. "And I like large parties. They're so intimate. At small parties there isn't any privacy."

There was the boom of a bass drum, and the voice of the orchestra leader rang out suddenly above the echolalia (嘈杂的声音) of the garden.

"Ladies and gentlemen," he cried. "At the request of Mr.Gatsby we are going to play for you Mr.Vladimir Tostoff's latest work, which attracted so much attention at Carnegie Hall last May. If you read the papers, you know there was a big sensation." He smiled with jovial condescension, and added: "Some sensation!" Whereupon everybody laughed.

"The piece is known," he concluded lustily, "as Vladimir Tostoff's Jazz History of the World."

The nature of Mr. Tostoff's composition eluded me, because just as it began my eyes fell on Gatsby, standing alone on the marble steps and looking from one group to another with approving eyes. His tanned skin was drawn attractively tight on his face and his short hair looked as though it were trimmed every day. I could see nothing sinister about him. I wondered if the fact that he was not drinking helped to set him off from his guests, for

Unit 8
F. Scott Fitzgerald and *The Great Gatsby*

it seemed to me that he grew more correct as the fraternal（兄弟般的）hilarity increased. When the *Jazz History of the World* was over, girls were putting their heads on men's shoulders in a puppyish（像小狗的）, convivial（欢乐的）way, girls were swooning（昏晕）backward playfully into men's arms, even into groups, knowing that someone would arrest their falls–but no one swooned backward on Gatsby, and no French bob（短发）touched Gatsby's shoulder, and no singing quartets were formed with Gatsby's head for one link.

"I beg your pardon."

Gatsby's butler was suddenly standing beside us.

"Miss Baker?" he inquired. "I beg your pardon, but Mr. Gatsby would like to speak to you alone."

"With me?" she exclaimed in surprise.

"Yes, madame."

She got up slowly, raising her eyebrows at me in astonishment, and followed the butler toward the house. I noticed that she wore her evening-dress, all her dresses, like sports clothes–there was a jauntiness（轻松活泼）about her movements as if she had first learned to walk upon golf courses on clean, crisp mornings.

I was alone and it was almost two. For some time confused and intriguing sounds had issued from a long, many-windowed room which overhung the terrace. Eluding Jordan's undergraduate, who was now engaged in an obstetrical（助产的）conversation with two chorus（合唱队）girls, and who implored me to join him, I went inside.

The large room was full of people. One of the girls in yellow was playing the piano, and beside her stood a tall, red-haired young lady from a famous chorus, engaged in song. She had drunk a quantity of champagne, and during the course of her song she had decided, ineptly（不适当地）, that everything was very, very sad–she was not only singing, she was weeping too. Whenever there was a pause in the song she filled it with gasping, broken sobs, and then took up the lyric again in a quavering soprano（女高音）. The tears coursed down her cheeks–not freely, however, for when they came into contact with her heavily beaded eyelashes they assumed an inky color, and pursued the rest of their way in slow black rivulets. A humorous suggestion was made that she sing the notes on her face, whereupon she threw up her

303

hands, sank into a chair, and went off into a deep vinous (醉醺醺的) sleep.

"She had a fight with a man who says he's her husband," explained a girl at my elbow.

I looked around. Most of the remaining women were now having fights with men said to be their husbands. Even Jordan's party, the quartet (四人) from East Egg, were rent asunder (碎片) by dissension (意见分歧). One of the men was talking with curious intensity to a young actress, and his wife, after attempting to laugh at the situation in a dignified and indifferent way, broke down entirely and resorted to flank (侧面) attacks—at intervals she appeared suddenly at his side like an angry diamond, and hissed: "You promised!" into his ear.

The reluctance to go home was not confined to wayward (任性的) men. The hall was at present occupied by two deplorably sober men and their highly indignant wives. The wives were sympathizing with each other in slightly raised voices.

"Whenever he sees I'm having a good time he wants to go home."

"Never heard anything so selfish in my life."

"We're always the first ones to leave."

"So are we."

"Well, we're almost the last tonight," said one of the men sheepishly (怯懦地). "The orchestra left half an hour ago."

In spite of the wives' agreement that such malevolence (恶意) was beyond credibility, the dispute ended in a short struggle, and both wives were lifted, kicking, into the night.

As I waited for my hat in the hall the door of the library opened and Jordan Baker and Gatsby came out together. He was saying some last word to her, but the eagerness in his manner tightened abruptly into formality as several people approached him to say good-by.

Jordan's party were calling impatiently to her from the porch, but she lingered for a moment to shake hands.

"I've just heard the most amazing thing," she whispered. "How long were we in there?"

"Why, about an hour."

"It was… simply amazing," she repeated abstractedly. "But I swore I wouldn't tell it and here I am tantalizing (逗弄) you." She yawned gracefully

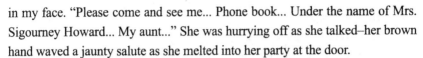

Unit 8
F. Scott Fitzgerald and *The Great Gatsby*

in my face. "Please come and see me... Phone book... Under the name of Mrs. Sigourney Howard... My aunt..." She was hurrying off as she talked–her brown hand waved a jaunty salute as she melted into her party at the door.

Rather ashamed that on my first appearance I had stayed so late, I joined the last of Gatsby's guests, who were clustered around him. I wanted to explain that I'd hunted for him early in the evening and to apologize for not having known him in the garden.

"Don't mention it," he enjoined (吩咐) me eagerly. "Don't give it another thought, old sport." The familiar expression held no more familiarity than the hand which reassuringly brushed my shoulder. "And don't forget we're going up in the hydroplane tomorrow morning, at nine o'clock."

Then the butler, behind his shoulder:

"Philadelphia wants you on the 'phone, sir."

"All right, in a minute. Tell them I'll be right there...Good night."

"Good night."

"Good night." He smiled–and suddenly there seemed to be a pleasant significance in having been among the last to go, as if he had desired it all the time. "Good-night, old sport. ... Good night."

But as I walked down the steps I saw that the evening was not quite over. Fifty feet from the door a dozen headlights illuminated (照亮) a bizarre and tumultuous (喧 器 的) scene. In the ditch beside the road, right side up, but violently shorn of one wheel, rested a new coupé (小客车) which had left Gatsby's drive not two minutes before. The sharp jut (伸出部分) of a wall accounted for the detachment of the wheel, which was now getting considerable attention from half a dozen curious chauffeurs. However, as they had left their cars blocking the road, a harsh, discordant (不和谐的) din (喧闹) from those in the rear had been audible for some time, and added to the already violent confusion of the scene.

A man in a long duster (长风衣) had dismounted (下车) from the wreck and now stood in the middle of the road, looking from the car to the tire and from the tire to the observers in a pleasant, puzzled way.

"See!" he explained. "It went in the ditch."

The fact was infinitely astonishing to him, and I recognized first the unusual quality of wonder, and then the man–it was the late patron of Gatsby's library.

305

"How'd it happen?"

He shrugged his shoulders.

"I know nothing whatever about mechanics," he said decisively.

"But how did it happen? Did you run into the wall?"

"Don't ask me," said Owl Eyes, washing his hands of the whole matter. "I know very little about driving–next to nothing. It happened, and that's all I know."

"Well, if you're a poor driver you oughtn't to try driving at night."

"But I wasn't even trying," he explained indignantly, "I wasn't even trying."

An awed hush fell upon the bystanders.

"Do you want to commit suicide?"

"You're lucky it was just a wheel! A bad driver and not even *try*ing!"

"You don't understand," explained the criminal. "I wasn't driving. There's another man in the car."

The shock that followed this declaration found voice in a sustained "Ah-h-h!" as the door of the coupé swung slowly open. The crowd–it was now a crowd–stepped back involuntarily, and when the door had opened wide there was a ghostly pause. Then, very gradually, part by part, a pale, dangling individual stepped out of the wreck, pawing tentatively at the ground with a large uncertain dancing shoe.

Blinded by the glare of the headlights and confused by the incessant （连续不断的）groaning of the horns, the apparition（幽灵）stood swaying for a moment before he perceived the man in the duster.

"Wha's matter?" he inquired calmly. "Did we run outa gas?"

"Look!"

Half a dozen fingers pointed at the amputated（截掉）wheel–he stared at it for a moment, and then looked upward as though he suspected that it had dropped from the sky.

"It came off," some one explained.

He nodded.

"At first I din' notice we'd stopped."

A pause. Then, taking a long breath and straightening his shoulders, he remarked in a determined voice:

"Wonder'ff tell me where there's a gas'line station?"

Unit 8
F. Scott Fitzgerald and *The Great Gatsby*

At least a dozen men, some of them little better off than he was, explained to him that wheel and car were no longer joined by any physical bond.

"Back out," he suggested after a moment. "Put her in reverse."

"But the *wheel's* off!"

He hesitated.

"No harm in trying," he said.

"The caterwauling（叫春似的）horns had reached a crescendo（高潮）and I turned away and cut across the lawn toward home. I glanced back once. A wafer of a moon was shining over Gatsby's house, making the night fine as before, and surviving the laughter and the sound of his still glowing garden. A sudden emptiness seemed to flow now from the windows and the great doors, endowing with complete isolation the figure of the host, who stood on the porch, his hand up in a formal gesture of farewell.

Reading over what I have written so far, I see I have given the impression that the events of three nights several weeks apart were all that absorbed me. On the contrary, they were merely casual events in a crowded summer, and, until much later, they absorbed me infinitely less than my personal affairs.

Most of the time I worked. In the early morning the sun threw my shadow westward as I hurried down the white chasms of lower New York to the Probity Trust. I knew the other clerks and young bond-salesmen by their first names, and lunched with them in dark, crowded restaurants on little pig sausages and mashed potatoes and coffee. I even had a short affair with a girl who lived in Jersey City and worked in the accounting department, but her brother began throwing mean looks in my direction, so when she went on her vacation in July I let it blow quietly away.

I took dinner usually at the Yale Club—for some reason it was the gloomiest event of my day—and then I went upstairs to the library and studied investments and securities for a conscientious hour. There were generally a few rioters around, but they never came into the library, so it was a good place to work. After that, if the night was mellow, I strolled down Madison Avenue past the old Murray Hill Hotel, and over 33rd Street to the Pennsylvania Station.

I began to like New York, the racy, adventurous feel of it at night, and the satisfaction that the constant flicker of men and women and machines gives to the restless eye. I liked to walk up Fifth Avenue and pick out romantic women from the crowd and imagine that in a few minutes I was going to enter into their lives, and no one would ever know or disapprove. Sometimes, in my mind, I followed them to their apartments on the corners of hidden streets, and they turned and smiled back at me before they faded through a door into warm darkness. At the enchanted（使心醉）metropolitan twilight I felt a haunting loneliness sometimes, and felt it in others—poor young clerks who loitered in front of windows waiting until it was time for a solitary restaurant dinner—young clerks in the dusk, wasting the most poignant moments of night and life.

Again at eight o'clock, when the dark lanes of the Forties were lined five deep with throbbing taxicabs bound for the theatre district, I felt a sinking in my heart. Forms leaned together in the taxis as they waited, and voices sang, and there was laughter from unheard jokes, and lighted cigarettes outlined unintelligible gestures inside. Imagining that I, too, was hurrying toward gayety and sharing their intimate excitement, I wished them well.

For a while I lost sight of Jordan Baker, and then in midsummer I found her again. At first I was flattered to go places with her, because she was a golf champion, and everyone knew her name. Then it was something more. I wasn't actually in love, but I felt a sort of tender curiosity. The bored haughty face that she turned to the world concealed something—most affectations conceal something eventually, even though they don't in the beginning—and one day I found what it was. When we were on a house-party together up in Warwick, she left a borrowed car out in the rain with the top down, and then lied about it—and suddenly I remembered the story about her that had eluded me that night at Daisy's. At her first big golf tournament there was a row that nearly reached the newspapers—a suggestion that she had moved her ball from a bad lie（位置）in the semi-final round. The thing approached the proportions of a scandal—then died away. A caddy（球童）retracted（收回）his statement, and the only other witness admitted that he might have been mistaken. The incident and the name had remained together in my mind.

Jordan Baker instinctively avoided clever, shrewd men, and now I saw that this was because she felt safer on a plane where any divergence from a

Unit 8

F. Scott Fitzgerald and *The Great Gatsby*

code would be thought impossible. She was incurably dishonest. She wasn't able to endure being at a disadvantage and, given this unwillingness, I suppose she had begun dealing in subterfuges (花招) when she was very young in order to keep that cool, insolent smile turned to the world and yet satisfy the demands of her hard, jaunty body.

  It made no difference to me. Dishonesty in a woman is a thing you never blame deeply–I was casually sorry, and then I forgot. It was on that same house-party that we had a curious conversation about driving a car. It started because she passed so close to some workmen that our fender (挡泥板) flicked a button on one man's coat.

  "You're a rotten driver," I protested. "Either you ought to be more careful, or you oughtn't to drive at all."

  "I am careful."

  "No, you're not."

  "Well, other people are," she said lightly.

  "What's that got to do with it?"

  "They'll keep out of my way," she insisted. "It takes two to make an accident."

  "Suppose you met somebody just as careless as yourself."

  "I hope I never will," she answered. "I hate careless people. That's why I like you."

  Her grey, sun-strained eyes stared straight ahead, but she had deliberately shifted our relations, and for a moment I thought I loved her. But I am slow-thinking and full of interior rules that act as brakes on my desires, and I knew that first I had to get myself definitely out of that tangle back home. I'd been writing letters once a week and signing them: "Love, Nick", and all I could think of was how, when that certain girl played tennis, a faint mustache of perspiration appeared on her upper lip. Nevertheless there was a vague understanding that had to be tactfully broken off before I was free.

  Every one suspects himself of at least one of the cardinal (主要的) virtues, and this is mine: I am one of the few honest people that I have ever known.

英美小说与电影
English and American Novels and Films

Notes and Glossary for Chapter Reading

(1) the Sound: Long Island Sound, a narrow finger of the Atlantic Ocean between Long Island and the state of Connecticut on the mainland, just east of New York City

(2) Rolls-Royce: a very expensive and luxurious British automobile

(3) Castile: a region of Spain, once an independent kingdom, renowned for its lace and embroidered shawls 西班牙一地区，以生产花边和绣花披肩而闻名。

(4) prodigality /ˌprɔdiˈgæləti/ n. extravagant wastefulness; extreme abundance; lavishness

(5) in the same breath: at or almost at the same time 在或几乎在同时

(6) Frisco: short for San Francisco; here, a slang term meaning rapidly, vigorously. San Francisco 的简称，这里指"像旧金山人似的"

(7) the Follies: the Ziegfeld Follies, a musical theatrical revue produced by Florenz Ziegfeld, very popular in the 1920s. Gilda Gray was one of its famous stars.

(8) white flannels: casual men's trousers of the 1920s made of wool flannel 白法兰绒

(9) slunk /slʌŋk/ [slink 的过去式及过去分词] to move somewhere quietly and secretly, especially because you are afraid or ashamed 鬼鬼祟祟地走，偷偷溜走

(10) Gothic: a style of architecture which originated in France in the 12th century, characterized by great height in the buildings, pointed arches, rib vaulting and large window spaces. 哥特式的，哥特风格的

(11) Belasco: David Belasco (1853—1931), a famous American actor, theatrical producer, manager and writer, known for his minutely detailed and spectacular stage settings.

(12) old sport: Gatsby's favorite phrase is English origin. It is probably one he picked up during his Oxford days.

(13) rough neck: a man who usually behaves in a rough, rude or angry way

(14) Carnegie Hall: 卡内基音乐厅，美国最有名的音乐厅之一。

(15) rent /rent/ v. [rend 的过去式及过去分词] to pull, split, or divide as if by tearing 分裂

Unit 8

F. Scott Fitzgerald and *The Great Gatsby*

8.2.4 Exercises

❶ Identify the following characters

(1) _____ travels to New York to learn the bond business; there, he becomes involved with both Gatsby and the Buchanans. To escape the world where reality is grotesque and where even nature is not nurturing but threatening, he decides to go home.

(2) _____ is sensitive and idealistic, almost divine in his dedication to his love and faith. But he is also sinister, because of his criminal activities. "He paid a high price for living too long with a single dream."

(3) _____ is rich, ruthless and cunning. His social attitudes are laced with racism and sexism. He is indirectly responsible for Gatsby's death.

(4) _____ was brought up in Louisville society. Her physical appeal creates an image of beauty, wealth and innocence. Whatever her physical image, her character contains a darker, less attractive side. She is not only flighty and trivial, but also selfish and irresponsible.

(5) _____ is extremely cynical, with a masculine, icy demeanor that Nick initially finds compelling. She belongs to the thoughtless, uncaring crowd which takes advantage of other people's vulnerability.

(6) _____ shares a loveless marriage with her husband, desperate to improve her life. After a fight with her husband, she runs out into the street and is accidentally hit and killed by Gatsby's car.

(7) _____ "was his wife's man and not his own." When he wasn't working, he sat on a chair in the doorway and stared at the people and the cars that passed along the road. When anyone spoke to him he invariably laughed in an agreeable, colorless way. His wife's sudden death drives him to murder Gatsby before committing suicide.

(8) _____ is Gatsby's friend and business contact, deeply

involved in organized crime, and claims credit for fixing the 1919 World Series. He is so selfish and insecure that he refuses to attend Gatsby's funeral.

(9) _____ tells Nick about Gatsby's schedule and dreams of self-improvement, as well as Gatsby's generosity since he made a success. He believes that Gatsby was bound to get ahead.

(10) _____ is an eccentric, bespectacled man who is wrongly accused of driving the car that lands in a ditch after the Gatsby's party. He is one of the few people to attend Gatsby's funeral.

❷ Plot Review

The Great Gatsby was published in (1)_____. Most literary critics think the novel to be the quintessential representation of the American Dream. In the novel Fitzgerald presents the rise and (2) _____ of Jay Gatsby, as related in a (3) _____ narrative by Nick Carraway, a quiet young Midwesterner who has a habit of (4) judgment on others. But on the subject of Gatsby Nick is (5) to withhold his admiration and awe. He abhors the things that happened to Gatsby. Nick rents a modest house in West Egg, Long Island, next door to Gatsby's mansion which is the scene of (6) _____ nightly parties, attended by many people who are (7) _____ and do not know their host. Nick, both cynical and curious about Gatsby, soon becomes his confidant. Nick learns from Jordan that five years ago in Louisville Gatsby met Daisy while he was in the (8) _____ during World War I, and that they fell in love and planned to marry. But when Gatsby was called to serve overseas, Daisy grew (9) _____ for him to return and married Tom, a rich though boring man from Yale. Now Gatsby has found Daisy and (10) _____ bought his house to be opposite her, hoping that she would appear at a party. As she (11) _____, Gatsby asks Nick to invite Daisy to tea so that he can meet her again. After the reunion, Gatsby takes Daisy and Nick to his mansion and shows them around. Daisy is greatly impressed by her former lover's generous attentions and his newly acquired (12) _____. Tom, who himself has had a longstanding affair with Myrtle Wilson, the wife of a

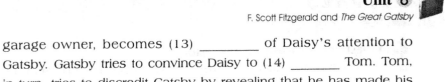

Unit 8
F. Scott Fitzgerald and *The Great Gatsby*

garage owner, becomes (13) _____ of Daisy's attention to Gatsby. Gatsby tries to convince Daisy to (14) _____ Tom. Tom, in turn, tries to discredit Gatsby by revealing that he has made his money from bootlegging. After the tension, Gatsby and Daisy leave in Gatsby's car with (15) _____ driving. Myrtle Wilson, recognizing the car as it passes her husband's garage, runs out into the street and is accidently hit and killed. Gatsby, attempting to (16) _____ Daisy, lets the blame fall on himself. When he is still waiting for Daisy to (17) _____ him to tell him her plans, the Buchanans have left town. Wilson murders Gatsby and then commits suicide. Nick alone arranges Gatsby's funeral, for all of Gatsby's acquaintances (18) _____ him: his business associates claim to be too busy, the party guests vanish, Tom and Daisy retreat "back into their money, or their vast (19) _____, or whatever it was that kept them together". Months later Nick meets Tom and realizes that it was he who told Wilson where to find Gatsby in order to (20) _____ himself.

❸ General Questions

(1) What are the signs of wealth at Gatsby's parties? What rumors have been told about Gatsby?

(2) What is the owl-eyed man in the library most surprised about? What is the significance of the scene in the library?

(3) What does Nick Carraway think of Jordan Baker when he meets her again after the Gatsby's party?

(4) Why does Gatsby throw extravagant parties? And why does he stop throwing parties later?

(5) Why does Gatsby offer Nick work? How does Nick feel about this?

(6) Why does Gatsby want Daisy to see his house and his clothes? What is Daisy's reaction during and after the visit?

(7) Why does Nick think that Gatsby may be disappointed with Daisy?

(8) Who is Dan Cody and what is his significance in Gatsby's life?

(9) Why does Gatsby allow Daisy to drive his car? Why is Gatsby waiting outside the Buchanans' house after the accident?

(10) What does Nick say about people like Daisy and Tom? Why does Nick say to Gatsby, "You're worth the whole damn bunch put together?"

❹ Questions for essay or discussion

(1) What is the American Dream? How does Gatsby represent this dream?

(2) What is Nick Carraway's role in the novel? Why does Nick think he is one of the few honest people that he has ever known?

(3) Why does Gatsby wait so long to arrange a meeting with Daisy and use Jordan and Nick to bring it about?

(4) Discuss Fitzgerald's use of symbols, such as the eyes of Dr. T. J. Eckleburg, the green light on Daisy's dock, and the valley of ashes.

(5) Discuss the implicit separation of love and money in *The Great Gatsby*.

主要参考书目

Abrams, M. H. and Stephen Greenblatt, eds. *The Norton Anthology of English Literature*. New York: Norton, 2001.

Alsen, Eberhard, ed. *The New Romanticism: A Collection of Critical Essays*. New York: Garland Pub, 2000.

Austen, Jane. *Pride and Prejudice*. New York: Barres & Noble, 1993.

Baym, Nina et al, eds. *The Norton Anthology of American Literature*. New York: Norton, 2003.

Beja, Morris. *Film and Literature: An Introduction*. New York: Longman, 1979.

Bell, Millicent, ed. *The Cambridge Companion to Edith Wharton*. Cambridge: Cambridge UP, 1995.

Brontë, Charlotte. *Jane Eyre*. Oxford: Oxford UP, 1980.

Bruccoli, Matthew J. ed. *New Essays on The Great Gatsby*. Cambridge: Cambridge UP, 1987.

Budd, Louis J. *Critical Essays on Mark Twain*. Boston: G.K. Hall, 1983.

Colacurcio, Michael J., ed. *New essays on The Scarlet Letter*. Cambridge: Cambridge UP, 1985.

Curnutt, Kirk. *The Cambridge Introduction to F. Scott Fitzgerald*. Cambridge University Press, 2007.

Dickens, Charles. *Oliver Twist*. London: Penguin, 1985.

Drabble, Margaret, ed. *The Oxford Companion to English Literature*, Oxford University Press, 2000.

Dunn, Richard J. *Jane Eyre: An Authoritative Text*. New York: Norton, 1993.

Elliott, Emory et al, eds. *American Literature A Prentice Hall Anthology*. New Jerssey: Prentice-Hall, 1991.

Fitzgerald, F. Scott. *The Great Gatsby*. New York, Charles Scribner's Sons, 1925.

Glen, Heathen, ed. *The Cambridge Companion to the Brontës*. Cambridge: Cambridge UP, 2002.

Glen, Heathen, ed. *The Cambridge Companion to Thomas Hardy*. Cambridge: Cambridge UP, 1999.

Hardy, Thomas. *Tess of the D'Urbervilles*. London: Macmillan & Co Ltd, 1965.

Hart, Janes D., ed. *The Oxford Companion to American Literature*, Oxford

University Press, 1995.

Hawthorne, Nathaniel. *The Scarlet Letter.* New York, Washington Square Press, 1972.

Kennedy-Andrews, Elmer, ed. *Nathanial Hawthorne, The Scarlet Letter.* New York: Columbia UP, 2000.

Lauter, Paul et al, eds. *Heath Anthology of American Literature.* Lexington: D. C. Heath and Company, 1990.

McMichael, George et al, eds. *Anthology of American Literature.* New Jersey: Prentice-Hall, 2000.

Messent, Peter. *The Cambridge Introduction to Mark Twain,* Cambridge University Press, 2007.

Person, Leland S. *The Cambridge Introduction to Nathanial Hawthorne,* Cambridge University Press, 2007.

Prigozy, Ruth, ed. *The Cambridge Companion to F. Scott Fitzgerald.* Cambridge: Cambridge UP, 2002.

Sanders, Andrew. *The Short Oxford History of English Literature,* Oxford University Press, 1994.

Seger, Linda. *The Art of Adaptation: Turning Fact and Fiction into Film.* New York: Henry Holt and Company, 1992.

Showalter, Elaine. *A Literature of Their Own: British Women Novelists from Bronte to lessing.* Princeton University Press,1999.

Singley, Carol J. *Edith Wharton: Matters of Mind and Spirit,* Cambridge University Press, 1995.

Southam, B. C. ed. *Critical Essays on Jane Austen.* London: Routledge & K. Paul, 1968.

Suchoff, David Bruth. *Critical theory and the novel: mass society and cultural criticism in Dickens, Melville, and Kafka.* Madison: U of Wisconsin P, 1994.

Todd, Janet. *The Cambridge Introduction to Jane Austen,* Cambridge University Press, 2006.

Twain, Mark. *Adventures of Huckleberry Finn.* New American Library, 1959.

Wharton, Edith. *The Age of Innocence.* New York: Scribner, 1979.

Williams, Merryn. *A Preface to Hardy,* Peking University Press, 2005.

Wilson, Raymond. *Macmillan Master Guides Pride and Prejudice by Jane Austen,* Macmillan Education Ltd., 1985.